ALSO BY SCOTT SMITH

A Simple Plan

The Ruins

The Ruins

A NOVEL

SCOTT SMITH

ALFRED A. KNOPF NEW YORK 2006

This Is a Borzoi Book Published by Alfred A. Knopf

Copyright © 2006 by Scott B. Smith, Inc.
All rights reserved. Published in the United States by Alfred A. Knopf,
a division of Random House, Inc., New York, and
in Canada by Random House of Canada, Limited, Toronto.
www.aaknopf.com

Grateful acknowledgment is made to Alfred Publishing Co. for permission to reprint an excerpt from
"One," words and music by Harry Nilsson, © 1968 (Renewed) Unichappell Music, Inc. Copyright
assigned in the U.S. to Golden Syrup Music. All rights on behalf of Golden Syrup Music administered
by Warner-Tamerlane Publishing Corp. All rights reserved. Used by permission.

Knopf, Borzoi Books, and the colophon are registered trademarks
of Random House, Inc.

Library of Congress Cataloging-in-Publication Data
Smith, Scott, {date}
The ruins : a novel / Scott Smith. — 1st ed.
p.   cm.
ISBN: 1-4000-4387-5 (alk. paper)
1. Cancún (Mexico)—Fiction.   2. Mayas—Fiction.   I. Title.
PS3569.M5379759R85 2006
813'.54—dc22   2005057782

Manufactured in the United States of America
First Edition

For Elizabeth, who's known horror

I want to thank my wife, Elizabeth Hill, my editor, Victoria Wilson, and my agents, Gail Hochman and Lynn Pleshette, for their very generous assistance in the completion of this book. The following people also read the manuscript in a still-unfinished state and offered criticism and comments that were invariably helpful: Michael Cendejas, Stuart Cornfeld, Carlyn Coviello, Carol Edwards, Marianne Merola, John Pleshette, Doug and Linda Smith, and Ben Stiller. I thank them all.

The Ruins

They met Mathias on a day trip to Cozumel. They'd hired a guide
to take them snorkeling over a local wreck, but the buoy marking its location had broken off in a storm, and the guide was
having difficulty finding it. So they were just swimming about, looking
at nothing in particular. Then Mathias rose toward them from the
depths, like a merman, a scuba tank on his back. He smiled when they
told him their situation, and led them to the wreck. He was German,
dark from the sun, and very tall, with a blond crew cut and pale blue
eyes. He had a tattoo of an eagle on his right forearm, black with red
wings. He let them take turns borrowing his tank so they could drop
down thirty feet and see the wreck up close. He was friendly in a quiet
way, and his English was only slightly accented, and when they pulled
themselves into their guide's boat to head back to shore, he climbed
in, too.

They met the Greeks two nights later, back in Cancún, on the beach
near their hotel. Stacy got drunk and made out with one of them. Nothing happened beyond that, but the Greeks always seemed to be turning
up afterward, no matter where they went or what they were doing. None
of them spoke Greek, of course, and the Greeks didn't speak English, so
it was mostly smiling and nodding and the occasional sharing of food
or drinks. There were three Greeks—in their early twenties, like Mathias and the rest of them—and they seemed friendly enough, even if
they did appear to be following them about.

The Greeks not only didn't know English; they couldn't speak Spanish, either. They'd adopted Spanish names, though, which they seemed to find very amusing. Pablo and Juan and Don Quixote was how they introduced themselves, saying the names in their odd accents and gesturing at their chests. Don Quixote was the one Stacy made out with. All three looked enough alike, however—wide-shouldered and slightly padded, with their dark hair grown long and tied back in ponytails— that even Stacy had a hard time keeping track of who was who. It also seemed possible that they were trading the names around, that this was part of the joke, so the one who answered to Pablo on Tuesday would smilingly insist on Wednesday that he was Juan.

They were visiting Mexico for three weeks. It was August, a foolish time to travel to the Yucatán. The weather was too hot, too humid. There were sudden rainstorms nearly every afternoon, downpours that could flood a street in a matter of seconds. And with darkness, the mosquitoes arrived, vast humming clouds of them. In the beginning, Amy complained about all these things, wishing they'd gone to San Francisco, which had been her idea. But then Jeff lost his temper, telling her she was ruining it for everyone else, and she stopped talking about California—the bright, brisk days, the trolley cars, the fog rolling in at dusk. It wasn't really that bad anyway. It was cheap and uncrowded, and she decided to make the best of it.

There were four of them in all: Amy and Stacy and Jeff and Eric. Amy and Stacy were best friends. They'd cut their hair boyishly short for the trip, and they wore matching Panama hats, posing for photos arm in arm. They looked like sisters—Amy the fair one, Stacy the dark—both of them tiny, barely five feet tall, birdlike in their thinness. They were sisterly in their behavior, too, full of whispered secrets, wordless intimacies, knowing looks.

Jeff was Amy's boyfriend; Eric was Stacy's. The boys were friendly with each other, but not exactly friends. It had been Jeff's idea to travel to Mexico, a last fling before he and Amy started medical school in the fall. He'd found a good deal on the Internet: cheap, impossible to pass up. It would be three lazy weeks on the beach, lying in the sun, doing nothing. He'd convinced Amy to come with him, then Amy had convinced Stacy, and Stacy had convinced Eric.

Mathias told them that he'd come to Mexico with his younger brother, Henrich, but Henrich had gone missing. It was a confusing story, and none of them understood all the details. Whenever they asked him about it, Mathias became vague and upset. He slipped into German and waved his hands, and his eyes grew cloudy with the threat of tears. After awhile, they didn't ask anymore; it felt impolite to press. Eric believed that drugs were somehow involved, that Mathias's brother was on the run from the authorities, but whether these authorities were German, American, or Mexican, he couldn't say for certain. There'd been a fight, though; they all agreed upon this. Mathias had argued with his brother, perhaps even struck him, and then Henrich had disappeared. Mathias was worried, of course. He was waiting for him to return so that they could fly back to Germany. Sometimes he seemed confident that Henrich would eventually reappear and that all would be fine in the end, but other times he didn't. Mathias was reserved by nature, a listener rather than a talker, and prone in his present situation to sudden bouts of gloom. The four of them worked hard to cheer him up. Eric told funny stories. Stacy did her imitations. Jeff pointed out interesting sights. And Amy took countless photographs, ordering everyone to smile.

In the day, they sunned on the beach, sweating beside one another on their brightly colored towels. They swam and snorkeled; they got burned and began to peel. They rode horses, paddled around in kayaks, played miniature golf. One afternoon, Eric convinced them all to rent a sailboat, but it turned out he wasn't as adept at sailing as he'd claimed, and they had to be towed back to the dock. It was embarrassing, and expensive. At night, they ate seafood and drank too much beer.

Eric didn't know about Stacy and the Greek. He'd gone to sleep after dinner, leaving the other three to wander the beach with Mathias. There'd been a bonfire burning behind one of the neighboring hotels, a band playing in a gazebo. That was where they met the Greeks. The Greeks were drinking tequila and clapping in rhythm with the music. They offered to share the bottle. Stacy sat next to Don Quixote, and there was much talking, in their mutually exclusive languages, and much laughter, and the bottle passed back and forth, everyone wincing at the burning taste of the liquor, and then Amy turned and found Stacy embracing the Greek. It didn't last very long. Five minutes of kissing, a shy touch of her left breast, and the band was finished for the night. Don Quixote wanted her to go back to his room, but she smiled and shook her head, and it was over as easily as that.

In the morning, the Greeks laid out their towels alongside Mathias and the four of them on the beach, and in the afternoon they all went jet skiing together. You wouldn't have known about the kissing if you hadn't seen it; the Greeks were very gentlemanly, very respectful. Eric seemed to like them, too. He was trying to get them to teach him dirty words in Greek. He was frustrated, though, because it was hard to tell if the words they were teaching him were the ones he wanted to learn.

It turned out that Henrich had left a note. Mathias showed it to Amy and Jeff early one morning, during the second week of their vacation. It was handwritten, in German, with a shakily drawn map at the bottom. They couldn't read the note, of course; Mathias had to translate it for them. There wasn't anything about drugs or the police—that was just Eric being Eric, jumping to conclusions, the more dramatic the better. Henrich had met a girl on the beach. She'd flown in that morning, was on her way to the interior, where she'd been hired to work on an archaeological dig. It was at an old mining camp, maybe a silver mine, maybe emeralds—Mathias wasn't certain. Henrich and the girl had spent the day together. He'd bought her lunch and they'd gone swimming. Then he took her back to his room, where they showered and had sex. Afterward, she left on a bus. In the restaurant, over lunch, she'd drawn a map for him on a napkin, showing him where the dig was. She told him he should come, too, that they'd be glad for his help. Once she left, Henrich couldn't stop talking about her. He didn't eat dinner and he couldn't fall asleep. In the middle of the night, he sat up in bed and announced to Mathias that he was going to join the dig.

Mathias called him a fool. He'd only just met this girl, they were in the midst of their vacation, and he didn't know the first thing about archaeology. Henrich assured him that it was really none of his business. He wasn't asking for Mathias's permission; he was merely informing him of his decision. He climbed out of bed and started to pack. They called each other names, and Henrich threw an electric razor at Mathias, hitting him on the shoulder. Mathias rushed him, knocking him over. They rolled around on the hotel room floor, grappling, grunting obscenities, until Mathias accidentally head-butted Henrich in the mouth, cutting his lip. Henrich made much of this, rushing to the bathroom so that he could spit blood into the sink. Mathias pulled on some clothes and went out to get him ice, but then ended up going downstairs to the all-night bar by the pool. It was three in the morning. Mathias felt he needed to calm down. He drank two beers, one quickly, the other slowly. When he got back to their room, the note was sitting on his pillow. And Henrich was gone.

The note was three-quarters of a page long, though it seemed shorter when Mathias read it out loud in English. It occurred to Amy that Mathias might be skipping some of the passages, preferring to keep them private, but it didn't matter—she and Jeff got the gist of it. Henrich said that Mathias often seemed to mistake being a brother with being a parent. He forgave him for this, yet he still couldn't accept it. Mathias might call him a fool, but he believed it was possible he'd met the love of his life that morning, and he'd never be able to forgive himself—or Mathias, for that matter—if he let this opportunity slip past without pursuing it. He'd try to be back by their departure date, though he couldn't guarantee this. He hoped Mathias would manage to have fun on his own while he was gone. If Mathias grew lonely, he could always come and join them at the dig; it was only a half day's drive to the west. The map at the bottom of the note—a hand-drawn copy of the one the girl had sketched on the napkin for Henrich—showed him how to get there.

As Amy listened to Mathias tell his story and then struggle to translate his brother's note, she gradually began to realize that he was asking for their advice. They were sitting on the veranda of their hotel. A breakfast buffet was offered here every morning: eggs and pancakes and French toast, juice and coffee and tea, an immense pile of fresh fruit. A short flight of stairs led to the beach. Seagulls hovered overhead, begging for scraps of food, shitting on the umbrellas above the tables. Amy could hear the steady sighing of the surf, could see the occasional jogger shuffling past, an elderly couple searching for shells, a trio of hotel employees raking the sand. It was very early, just after seven. Mathias had awakened them, calling from the house phone downstairs. Stacy and Eric were still asleep.

Jeff leaned forward to study the map. It was clear to Amy, without anything explicit having been said, that it was his advice Mathias was soliciting. Amy didn't take offense; she was used to this sort of thing. Jeff had something about him that made people trust him, an air of competence and self-confidence. Amy sat back in her seat and watched him smooth the wrinkles from the map with the palm of his hand. Jeff had curly, dark hair, and eyes that changed color with the light. They could be hazel or green or the palest of brown. He wasn't as tall as Mathias, or as broad in the shoulders, but despite this, he somehow seemed to be the larger of the two. He had a gravity to him: he was calm, always calm. Someday, if all went according to plan, Amy imagined that this would be what would make him a good doctor. Or, at the very least, what would make people think of him as a good doctor.

Mathias's leg was jiggling, his knee jumping up and down. It was Wednesday morning. He and his brother were scheduled to fly home on Friday afternoon. "I go," he said. "I get him. I take him home. Right?"

Jeff glanced up from the map. "You'd be back this evening?" he asked.

Mathias shrugged, waved at the note. He only knew what his brother had written.

Amy recognized some of the towns on the map—Tizimín, Valladolid, Cobá—names she'd seen in their guidebook. She hadn't really read the book; she'd only looked at the pictures. She remembered a ruined hacienda on the Tizimín page, a street lined with whitewashed buildings for Valladolid, a gigantic stone face buried in vines for Cobá. Mathias's map had an X drawn somewhere vaguely west of Cobá. This was where the dig was. You rode a bus from Cancún to Cobá, where you hired a taxi, which took you eleven miles farther west. Then there was a path leading away from the road, two miles long, that you had to hike. If you came to the Mayan village, you'd gone too far.

Watching Jeff examine the map, she could guess what he was thinking. It had nothing to do with Mathias or his brother. He was thinking of the jungle, of the ruins there, and what it might be like to explore them. They'd talked vaguely of doing this when they'd first arrived: how they could hire a car, a local guide, and see whatever there was to be seen. But it was so hot; the idea of trudging through the jungle to take pictures of giant flowers or lizards or crumbling stone walls seemed less and less attractive the more they discussed it. So they stayed on the beach. But now? The morning was deceptively cool, with a breeze coming in off the water; she knew that it must be hard for Jeff to remember how humid the day would ultimately become. Yes, it was easy enough for her to guess what he was thinking: *why shouldn't it be fun?* They were slipping into a torpor, with all the sun and the food and the drinking. A little adventure like this might be just the thing to wake them up.

Jeff slid the map back across the table to Mathias. "We'll go with you," he said.

Amy didn't speak. She sat there, reclining in her chair. Inside, she was thinking, *No, I don't want to go,* but she knew she couldn't say this. She complained too much; everyone said so. She was a gloomy person. She didn't have the gift of happiness; somewhere along the way, someone had neglected to give it to her, and now she made everyone else suffer for her lack of it. The jungle would be hot and dirty, its shadowed spaces aswarm with mosquitoes, but she tried not to think of this; she tried to rise above it. Mathias was their friend, wasn't he? He'd loaned them his scuba tank, showed them where to dive. And now he was in need. Amy let this thought gather strength in her mind, a hand pulling shut doors, slamming them in rapid succession, until only one was left open. When Mathias turned toward her, grinning, pleased with Jeff's words, looking for her to echo them, she couldn't help herself: she smiled back at him, nodded.

"Of course," she said.

Eric was dreaming that he couldn't fall asleep. It was a dream he often had, a dream of frustration and weariness. In it, he was trying to meditate, to count sheep, to think calming thoughts. There was the taste of vomit in his mouth, and he wanted to get up and brush his teeth. He needed to empty his bladder, too, but he sensed that if he moved, even slightly, whatever little chance he had of falling back asleep would be forever lost to him. So he didn't move; he lay there, wishing he could sleep, willing sleep to come, but not sleeping. The taste of vomit and the sensation of a full bladder were not regular details of this dream. They were only present now because they were real. He'd drunk too much the night before, had roused himself to throw up into the toilet sometime just before dawn, and now he needed to pee. Even his dreaming self sensed this, that there was an unusual heft to these two sensations, as if his psyche were trying to warn him of something, the threat of choking on another wave of puke, or of soaking the bed in urine.

It was the Greeks who'd pushed and prodded him to the point of vomiting. They'd tried to teach him a drinking game. This involved dice, shaken in a cup. The rules were explained to him in Greek, which certainly must've contributed to how complicated they seemed. Eric bravely rolled the dice and passed the cup, but he never managed to understand why he won on some tosses and lost on others. At first, it seemed as if high numbers were best, but then, erratically, low numbers began also to triumph. He rolled the dice and sometimes the Greeks gestured for him to drink, but other times they didn't. After awhile, it began not to matter so much. They taught him some new words and laughed at how quickly he forgot them. Everyone became very drunk, and then Eric somehow managed to stumble back to his room and go to sleep.

Unlike the others, who were heading off to graduate schools of one sort or another in the fall, Eric was preparing to start a job. He'd been hired to teach English at a prep school outside of Boston. He'd live in a dorm with the boys, help run the student paper, coach soccer in the fall, baseball in the spring. He was going to be good at it, he believed. He had an easy, confident way with people. He was funny; he could get kids laughing, make them want him to like them. He was tall and lean, with dark hair, dark eyes; he believed himself to be handsome. And smart: a winner. Stacy was going to be in Boston, studying to become a social worker. They'd see each other every weekend; in another year or two, he'd ask her to marry him. They'd live somewhere in New England and she'd get some sort of job helping people and maybe he'd keep teaching, or maybe he wouldn't. It didn't matter. He was happy; he was going to keep being happy; they'd be happy together.

Eric was an optimist by nature, still innocent of the blows even the most blessed lives can suffer. His psyche was too sanguinary to allow him an outright nightmare, and it offered him a safety net now, a voice in his head that said, *It's okay, you're just dreaming.* A moment later, someone started to knock at the door. Then Stacy was rolling off the bed, and Eric was opening his eyes, staring blearily about the room. The curtains were drawn; his and Stacy's clothes were strewn across the floor. Stacy had dragged the bedspread with her. She was standing at the door with it wrapped around her shoulders, naked underneath, talking to someone. Eric gradually realized it was Jeff. He wanted to go pee and brush his teeth and find out what was happening, but he couldn't quite rouse himself into motion. He fell back asleep and the next thing he knew Stacy was standing over him, dressed in khakis and a T-shirt, rubbing dry her hair, telling him to hurry.

"Hurry?" he asked.

She glanced at the clock. "It leaves in forty minutes," she said.

"What leaves?"

"The bus."

"What bus?"

"To Cobá."

"Cobá . . ." He struggled to sit up, and for an instant thought he might vomit again. The bedspread was lying on the floor near the door, and he had to strain to grasp how it had gotten there. "What did Jeff want?"

"For us to get ready."

"Why are you wearing pants?"

"He said we ought to. Because of the bugs."

"Bugs?" Eric asked. He was having trouble understanding her. He was still a little drunk. "What bugs?"

"We're going to Cobá," she said. "To an old mine. To see the ruins." She started back toward the bathroom. He could hear her running water, and it reminded him of his bladder. He climbed out of bed, shuffled across the room to the open doorway. She had the light on over the sink, and it hurt his eyes. He stood on the threshold for a moment, blinking at her. She yanked on the shower, then nudged him into it. He wasn't wearing any clothes; all he had to do was step over the rim of the tub. Then he was soaping himself, reflexively, and urinating into the space between his feet, but still not quite awake. Stacy herded him along, and with her assistance he managed to finish his shower, to brush his teeth and comb his hair and pull on a pair of jeans and a T-shirt, but it wasn't until they'd made it downstairs and were hurriedly eating breakfast that he finally began to grasp where they were going.

They all met in the lobby to wait for the van that would take them to the bus station. Mathias passed Henrich's note around, and everyone took turns staring at the German words with their odd capitalizations, the crookedly drawn map at the bottom. Stacy and Eric had shown up empty-handed, and Jeff sent them back to their room, telling them to fill a pack with water, bug spray, sunscreen, food. Sometimes he felt he was the only one of them who knew how to move through the world. He could tell that Eric was still half-drunk. Stacy's nickname in college had been "Spacy," and it was well earned. She was a daydreamer; she liked to hum to herself, to sit staring at nothing. And then there was Amy, who had a tendency to pout when she was displeased. Jeff could tell that she didn't want to go find Mathias's brother. Everything seemed to be taking her a little longer than necessary. She'd vanished into the bathroom after breakfast, leaving him to fill their backpack on his own. Then she'd come out to change into pants, and ended up lying facedown on the bed in her underwear until he prodded her into action. She wasn't talking to him, was only answering his questions with shrugs or monosyllables. He told her she didn't have to go, that she could spend the day alone on the beach if she liked, and she just stared at him. They both knew who she was, how she'd rather be with the group, doing something she didn't like, than alone, doing something she enjoyed.

While they were waiting for Eric and Stacy to return with their backpack, one of the Greeks came walking into the lobby. It was the one who'd been calling himself Pablo lately. He hugged everyone in turn. All the Greeks liked to hug; they did it at every opportunity. After the hugs, he and Jeff had a brief discussion in their separate languages, both of them resorting to pantomime to fill in the gaps.

"Juan?" Jeff asked. "Don Quixote?" He lifted his hands, raised his eyebrows.

Pablo said something in Greek and made a casting motion with his arm. Then he pretended to reel in a large fish, straining against its weight. He pointed to his watch, at the six, then the twelve.

Jeff nodded, smiled, showing he understood: the other two had gone fishing. They'd left at six and would be back at noon. He took Henrich's note, showed it to the Greek. He gestured at Amy and Mathias, waved upward to indicate Stacy and Eric, then pointed at Cancún on the map. He slowly moved his finger to Cobá, then to the X, which marked the dig. He couldn't think how to explain the purpose of their trip, how to signal *brother* or *missing,* so he just kept tracing his finger across the map.

Pablo got very excited. He smiled and nodded and pointed at his own chest, then at the map, talking rapidly in Greek all the while. It appeared he wanted to go with them. Jeff nodded; the others nodded, too. The Greeks were staying in the neighboring hotel. Jeff pointed toward it, then down at Pablo's bare legs, then at his own jeans. Pablo just stared at him. Jeff pointed at the others, at their pants, and the Greek began nodding again. He started to leave, but then came back suddenly, reaching for Henrich's note. He took it to the concierge's desk; they saw him borrow a pen, a piece of paper, then bend to write. It took him a long time. In the middle of it, Eric and Stacy reappeared, with their backpack, and Pablo tossed down his pen, rushed over to hug them. He and Eric made shaking motions with their hands, casting imaginary dice. They pretended to drink, then laughed and shook their heads, and Pablo told a long story in Greek that no one could make any sense of. It seemed to have something to do with an airplane, or a bird, something with wings, and it took him several minutes to relate. It was obviously funny, or at least he found it to be so, because he kept having to stop and laugh. His laughter was infectious, and the others joined in, though they couldn't say why. Finally, he went back and resumed whatever he was doing with Henrich's note.

When he returned, they saw that he'd made his own copy of the hand-drawn map. He'd written a paragraph in Greek above it; Jeff assumed it was a note for Juan and Don Quixote, telling them to come join them at the dig. He tried to explain to Pablo that they were only intending to go for the day, that they'd be back late that evening, but he couldn't find a way to make this clear. He kept pointing at his watch, and so did Pablo, who seemed to think Jeff was asking when the other two Greeks would return from fishing. They were both pointing at the twelve, but Jeff meant midnight, and Pablo meant noon. Finally, Jeff gave up; they were going to miss their bus if this continued. He waved Pablo toward his hotel, gesturing at his bare legs again. Pablo smiled and nodded and hugged them all once more, then jogged out of the lobby, clutching the copy of Henrich's map in his hand.

Jeff waited by the front door, watching for their van. Mathias paced about behind him, folding and unfolding Henrich's note, sliding it into his pocket, only to pull it out again. Stacy, Eric, and Amy sat together on a couch in the center of the lobby, and when Jeff glanced toward them, he felt a sudden wavering. They shouldn't go, he realized; it was a terrible idea. Eric's head kept dipping; he was drunk and overtired and having great difficulty staying awake. Amy was pouting, arms folded across her chest, eyes fixed on the floor in front of her. Stacy was wearing sandals and no socks; in a few more hours, her feet were going to be covered in bug bites. Jeff couldn't imagine accompanying these three on a two-mile hike through the Yucatán heat. He knew he should just explain this to Mathias, apologize, ask for his forgiveness. All he had to do was think of a way to say it, to make Mathias understand, and they could spend another aimless day on the beach. It ought to have been easy enough, finding the right words, and Jeff was just starting to form them in his head when Pablo returned, dressed in jeans, carrying a pack. There were hugs again, all around, everyone talking at once. Then the van arrived, and they were piling into it, one after another, and suddenly it was too late to speak with Mathias, too late not to go. They were pulling out into traffic, away from the hotel, the beach, everything that had grown so familiar in the past two weeks. Yes, they were on their way, they were leaving, they were going, they were gone.

As Stacy was hurrying after the others into the bus station, a boy grabbed her breast. He reached in from behind and gave it a hard, painful squeeze. Stacy spun, scrambling to thrust his hand from her body. That was the whole point—the spin, the scrambling, the distraction inherent in these motions—it gave a second boy the opportunity to snatch her hat and sunglasses from her head. Then they were off, both of them, racing down the sidewalk, two dark-haired little boys—twelve years old, she would've guessed—vanishing now into the crowd.

The day was abruptly bright without her glasses. Stacy stood blinking, a little dazed, still feeling the boy's hand on her breast. The others were already pushing their way into the station. She'd yelped—she thought she'd yelped—but apparently no one had heard. She had to run to catch up with them, her hand reflexively rising to hold her hat to her head, the hat that was no longer there, that was beyond the plaza already, moving farther and farther into the distance with each passing second, traveling toward some new owner's hands, a stranger who'd have no idea of her, of course, no sense of this moment, of her running into the Cancún bus station, struggling suddenly against the urge to cry.

Inside, it felt more like an airport than a bus station, clean and heavily air-conditioned and very bright. Jeff had already found the right ticket counter; he was talking to the attendant, asking questions in his careful, precisely enunciated Spanish. The others were huddled behind him, pulling out their wallets, gathering the money for their fares. When Stacy reached them, she said, "A boy stole my hat."

Only Pablo turned; the others were all leaning toward Jeff, trying to hear what the attendant was telling him. Pablo smiled at her. He gestured around them at the bus station, in the way someone might indicate a particularly pleasing view from a balcony.

Stacy was beginning to calm down now. Her heart had been racing, adrenaline-fueled, her body trembling with it, and now that it was starting to ease, she felt more embarrassed than anything else, as if the whole incident were somehow her own fault. This was the sort of thing that always seemed to be happening to her. She dropped cameras off ferries; she left purses on airplanes. The others didn't lose things or break things or have them stolen, so why should she? She should've been paying attention. She should've seen the boys coming. She was calmer, but she still felt like crying.

"And my sunglasses," she said.

Pablo nodded, his smile deepening. He seemed very happy to be here. It was unsettling, having him respond with such oblivious contentment to what she believed must be her obvious distress; for a moment, Stacy wondered if he might be mocking her. She glanced past him to the others.

"Eric," she called.

Eric waved her away without looking at her. "I got it," he said. He was handing Jeff money for their tickets.

Mathias was the only one who turned. He stared for a moment, examining her face, then stepped toward her. He was so tall and she was so small; he ended up crouching in front of her, as if she were a child, looking at her with what appeared to be genuine concern. "What's wrong?" he asked.

On the night of the bonfire, when Stacy had kissed the Greek, it hadn't been only Amy she'd felt staring at her, but Mathias, too. Amy's expression had been one of pure surprise; Mathias's had been perfectly blank. In the days to follow, she'd caught him watching her in the exact same manner: not judgmental, exactly, but with a hidden, held-back quality that nonetheless made her feel as if she were being weighed in some balance, appraised and assessed, and found wanting. Stacy was a coward at heart—she had no illusions about this, knew that she'd sacrifice much to escape difficulty or conflict—and she'd avoided Mathias as best she could. Avoided not only his presence but his eyes, too, that watchful gaze. And now here he was, crouched in front of her, looking at her so sympathetically, while the others, all unknowing, busied themselves purchasing their tickets. It was too confusing; she lost her voice.

Mathias reached out, touched her forearm, just with his fingertips, resting them there, as if she were some small animal he was trying to calm. "What is it?" he asked.

"A boy stole my hat," Stacy managed to say. She gestured toward her head, her eyes. "And my sunglasses."

"Just now?"

Stacy nodded, pointed toward the doors. "Outside."

Mathias stood up; his fingertips left her arm. He seemed ready to stride off and find the boys. Stacy lifted her hand to stop him.

"They're gone," she said. "They ran away."

"Who ran away?" Amy asked. She was standing, suddenly, beside Mathias.

"The boys who stole my hat."

Eric was there, too, now, handing her a piece of paper. She took it, held it at her side, with no sense of what it was, or why Eric wanted her to have it. "Look at it," he said. "Look at your name."

Stacy peered down at the piece of paper. It was her ticket; her name was printed on it. "Spacy Hutchins," it said.

Eric was smiling, pleased with himself. "They asked for our names."

"Her hat was stolen," Mathias said.

Stacy nodded, feeling that embarrassment again. Everyone was staring at her. "And my sunglasses."

Now Jeff was there, too, not stopping, moving past them. "Hurry," he said. "We're gonna miss it." He was heading off toward their gate, and the others started after him: Pablo and Mathias and Amy, all in a line. Eric lingered beside her.

"How?" he asked.

"It wasn't my fault."

"I'm not saying that. I'm just—"

"They grabbed them. They grabbed them and ran." She could still feel the boy's grip on her breast. That, and the oddly cool touch of Mathias's fingertips on her arm. If Eric asked her another question, she was afraid it would be too much for her; she'd surrender, begin to cry.

Eric glanced toward the others. They were almost out of sight. "We better go," he said. He waited until she nodded, and then they started off together, his hand clasping hers, pulling her along through the crowd.

The bus wasn't at all what Amy had expected. She'd pictured something dirty and broken-down, with rattling windows and blown shocks and a smell coming from the bathroom. But it was nice. There was air conditioning; there were little TVs hanging from the ceiling. Amy's seat number was on her ticket. She and Stacy were together, toward the middle of the bus. Pablo and Eric were directly in front of them, with Jeff and Mathias across the aisle.

As soon as the bus pulled out of the station, the TVs turned on. They were playing a Mexican soap opera. Amy didn't know any Spanish, but she watched anyway, imagining a story line to fit the actors' startled expressions, their gestures of disgust. It wasn't that difficult—all soap operas are more or less the same—and it made her feel better, losing herself a little in her imagined narrative. It was immediately clear that the dark-haired man who was maybe some sort of lawyer was cheating on his wife with the bleached-blond woman, but that he didn't realize the blonde was taping their conversations. There was an elderly woman with lots of jewelry who was obviously manipulating everyone else with her money. There was a woman with long black hair whom the elderly woman trusted but who appeared to be plotting something against her. She was in league with the elderly woman's doctor, who seemed also to be the bleached blonde's husband.

After awhile, by the time they'd left the city behind and were heading south along the coast, Amy felt easy enough with herself that she reached out and took Stacy's hand. "It's all right," she said. "You can borrow my hat, if you want."

And Stacy's smile at this—so open, so immediate, so loving—changed everything, made the whole day seem possible, even exciting. They were best friends, and they were going on an adventure, a hike through the jungle to see the ruins. They held hands and watched the soap opera. Stacy couldn't speak Spanish, either, so they argued about what was happening, each of them struggling to propose the most outlandish scenario possible. Stacy imitated the elderly woman's expressions, which were like a silent movie actress's, expansive and exaggerated, full of greed and malice, and they hunched low in their seats, giggling together, each making the other feel better—safer, happier—as the bus pushed its way down the coast through the day's burgeoning heat.

Pablo had a bottle of tequila in his pack. No: Eric could hear a clinking sound, so there must've been two bottles, or more. Eric only saw one, though. Pablo pulled it out to show him, smiling, raising his eyebrows. Apparently, he wanted them to share it on their ride to Cobá. There was something with a coin, too—some sort of Greek coin. Pablo took it out, mimed flipping it, then drinking. Another game. As far as Eric could understand, it seemed like a pretty simple one. They'd flip the coin. If it came up heads, Eric had to drink; if it came up tails, the Greek did. Eric, displaying a wisdom unnatural to him, waved the idea aside. He tilted his seat back, shut his eyes, and fell asleep with the speed of a man on an anesthesia drip. *One hundred, ninety-nine, ninety-eight, ninety-seven* . . . and he was gone.

He woke briefly, blearily, sometime later, to find that they were parked in front of a long line of souvenir stalls. It wasn't their stop, but some of the other passengers were gathering their things and climbing off, while still others lined up outside the door, waiting to get on. Pablo was asleep beside him, openmouthed, snoring softly. Amy and Stacy were hunched low in their seats, whispering together. Jeff was reading their communal guidebook, bent close over it, intent, as if memorizing it. Mathias's eyes were shut, but he wasn't sleeping. Eric couldn't say how he knew this; he just did, and as he stared at him, wondering why this was so, Mathias rolled his head toward him, opened his eyes. It was an odd moment: they sat there, with only the aisle separating them, holding each other's gaze. Finally, one of the new passengers came shuffling toward the rear of the bus, momentarily blocking their view of each other. When she'd passed, Mathias had turned his head forward again and shut his eyes.

Beyond the window, the freshly disembarked passengers stood uncertainly beside the bus, staring about, as if questioning their wisdom in choosing this as their destination. The vendors in their stalls called to them, gesturing for them to approach. The passengers smiled, nodded, waved, or struggled to pretend that they couldn't hear the shouts of greeting. They stood, not moving. The stalls sold soft drinks, food, clothing, straw hats, jewelry, Mayan statues, leather belts and sandals. Most of the stalls had signs in both Spanish and English. There was a goat tied to a stake beside one of them, and some dogs loitered about, warily eyeing the bus and its former passengers. Beyond the stalls, the town began. Eric could glimpse the gray stone tower of a church, the whitewashed walls of houses. He imagined fountains hidden in courtyards, gently swaying hammocks, caged birds, and for an instant he thought of rousing himself, urging the others off the bus, shepherding them into this place that felt so much more "real" than Cancún. They could be travelers, for once, rather than tourists; they could explore and discover and . . . But he was hungover, and so tired, and it was hot out there; Eric could sense it even through the smoked glass of the window, see it in the way the dogs held themselves, heads low, their tongues hanging from their mouths. And then there was Mathias's brother, too—the reason they'd ventured forth on this expedition. Eric turned his head, half-expecting to find the German staring at him again, but Mathias was facing straight ahead, his eyes still shut.

Eric did the same: he turned back toward the front of the bus, closed his eyes. He was still conscious when they rolled into motion. They jolted and bumped in a wide circle, pulled out onto the road. Pablo shifted in his sleep, fell against him, and Eric had to push him away. The Greek muttered something in his own language but didn't wake. The words had an edge to them, though, as if they were an accusation, or a curse, and Eric thought of the smiles the Greeks sometimes exchanged, the sense of shared secrets they gave off. *Who are they?* he wondered. He was half-asleep already, his mind moving on its own; he wasn't even certain whom he meant. The Mexicans, maybe, the Mayans calling from their stalls. Or Pablo and the other Greeks with their constant chattering, their nods and hugs and winks. Or Mathias with his mysteriously missing brother, that ominous tattoo, that blank stare. Or—well, why not?—Jeff and Amy and Stacy. *Who are they?*

He slept and didn't dream, and when he opened his eyes again, they were pulling into Cobá. Everyone was standing up and stretching, and the question was no longer in his head, nor the memory of it. It was just before noon, and as he woke more fully to himself, Eric realized that he felt as good as he had all day. He was thirsty and hungry and he needed to urinate, but his head was clearer and his body stronger, and he felt he was ready now, finally, for whatever the day might bring.

Jeff found them a taxi. It was a bright yellow pickup truck. Jeff showed Mathias's map to the driver, a short, heavyset man with thick glasses, who studied it with great deliberation. The driver spoke a mix of English and Spanish. He was wearing a T-shirt that clung tightly to his padded frame. There were immense salt stains under his arms, and his face was shiny with perspiration. He kept wiping it with a bandanna as he examined the map; he seemed displeased by what he found there. He frowned at the six of them, one by one, then at his truck, then at the sun hanging in the sky above them.

"Twenty dollars," he said.

Jeff shook his head, waving this aside. He had no idea what a fair price would be, but he sensed that it was important to bargain. "Six," he said, picking a sum at random.

The driver looked appalled, as if Jeff had just leaned forward and spit onto his sandaled feet. He handed the map back to him, started to walk away.

"Eight!" Jeff called after him.

The driver turned to face him but didn't come back. "Fifteen."

"Twelve."

"Fifteen," the driver insisted.

The bus was leaving now, and the other passengers were drifting off into the town. The yellow pickup was the only cab in sight big enough to accommodate them all.

"Fifteen," Jeff agreed. He sensed that he was overpaying, and felt foolish for it. He could see that the driver was having difficulty hiding his pleasure, but no one else seemed to notice this. They were already moving toward the truck. It didn't matter; none of it mattered. This was only a stage in their journey, quickly finished. And Mathias was beside him suddenly, opening his wallet, paying the man. Jeff didn't object, didn't offer to contribute. Mathias was the reason they were here, after all. They'd be half-asleep on the beach right now if it weren't for him.

There was a small dog in the rear of the pickup, chained to a cinder block. When they approached the truck, the dog began to throw his body against the length of chain, growling and barking and drooling great strings of saliva. He was the size of a large cat—black, with white paws and a shaggy, greasy-looking coat—but he had the voice of a much larger dog. His anger, his desire to do them harm, seemed almost human. They stopped walking, stood staring.

The driver waved them on, laughing. "No problem," he said in his heavily accented English. "No problem." He lowered the tailgate, waved toward the dog, showed them how its chain only reached halfway down the truck bed. Two of them could sit up front. The other four could arrange themselves in such a way as to remain out of reach of the fierce little dog. Most of this was communicated in hand signals, punctuated with a steady recitation of those two words: "No problem, no problem, no problem . . ."

Stacy and Amy volunteered to sit in front. They hurried forward, yanked open the passenger-side door, and climbed inside before anyone could protest. The others warily pulled themselves up into the back. The dog's barking rose in volume. He threw himself with such force against his chain that it seemed possible he might break his neck. The driver tried to soothe the dog, murmuring to him in Mayan, but this had no apparent effect. Finally, the man just smiled, shrugging at them, and swung the tailgate closed.

The truck needed three attempts before it managed to start; then they were in motion. They swung out onto a paved road, heading away from town. After a mile or so, they turned left onto a gravel road. There were fields of some sort—Jeff couldn't tell what was growing in them, but one had a broken-down tractor in it, another a pair of horses. Then, abruptly, they were in the jungle: thick, damp-looking foliage growing right up against the road. The sun was in the center of the sky, directly above them, so it was hard to tell which direction they were heading, but he assumed it was west. The driver had kept the map. They just had to trust that he knew how to follow it.

The four of them sat with their backs flat against the tailgate, their feet drawn into their bodies, watching the dog, who continued to lunge toward them, growling and barking and slobbering without pause. It was hot, with the thick, slightly fetid humidity of a greenhouse. There was the false breeze of the truck's motion, but it wasn't enough, and soon they were sweating through their shirts. Now and then, Pablo would shout something in Greek at the dog, and they'd all laugh nervously, though they had no idea, of course, what he was saying. Even Mathias, who otherwise rarely seemed to laugh, joined them in this.

After awhile, the gravel road turned to dirt and became heavily rutted. The truck slowed, bouncing across the ruts, jostling them against one another. The larger bumps lifted the cinder block briefly into the air before slamming it back down against the truck bed. Each time this happened, the dog managed to drag it an inch or two closer to them. It seemed like they'd gone farther than the eleven miles the map had demanded. They drove more and more slowly as the road became worse and worse, the trees crowding in upon them, hanging over them, brushing against the side of the truck. A cloud of bugs gathered overhead, following their slow passage, biting their arms and necks, making them slap at themselves. Eric dug a can of mosquito repellent out of his backpack but then fumbled it, dropping it to the truck bed. It rolled toward the dog, clanged against the cinder block, coming to rest there. The dog sniffed at it briefly, then resumed his barking. Pablo was no longer shouting, and they'd stopped laughing. Time was stretching itself out—they'd gone too far—and Jeff was beginning to suspect that they'd made an immense mistake, that the man was taking them into the jungle to rob and kill them. He'd rape the girls; he'd shoot them or stab them or smash their skulls with a shovel. He'd feed them to his little dog; he'd bury their bones in the damp earth, and no one would ever hear of them again.

Then a turnaround appeared on the right-hand side of the road, and the truck pulled into it, stopped, idled. A path led off into the trees. They'd arrived. The four of them scrambled quickly over the tailgate, laughing again, abandoning the can of repellent, the dog still lunging at his length of chain, growling and barking his farewell.

Stacy was sitting by the window, which was shut tight against the day's growing heat. The truck's air conditioner was on high; she'd begun to shiver as the ride progressed, her sweat drying, goose bumps rising on her forearms. It hadn't seemed like an exceptionally long drive to her. She'd hardly noticed it, in fact, her mind floating elsewhere, fifteen years back and two thousand miles away. The color of the pickup truck: that was what triggered it. A legal-pad yellow. Her uncle had died in a car this color. Uncle Roger, her father's elder brother, caught in a Massachusetts spring downpour, trying to ease his way through a flooded patch of road. A creek had overflown its banks; it snatched the car, spun it downstream, flipped it over, then cast it aside on the edge of an apple orchard. That was where they'd found Uncle Roger, still with his seat belt on, hanging upside down, batlike, in his yellow car. Drowned.

Stacy and her parents and her two brothers were in Florida when they received the news. It was spring break, and her father had flown them to Disney World. They were staying in one room, all five of them together, her parents in one bed, the two boys in another, Stacy on a foldout cot between them. She was seven years old; her brothers were four and nine. She could remember her father on the phone, hushing them with his free hand, while he said, "What . . . What . . . What . . ." It was a bad connection, and he'd had to shout, repeating, in a questioning tone, everything that was said to him. "Roger . . . A rainstorm . . . Drowned . . ." Afterward, he'd started to cry, bent into himself, eyes clenched shut, fumbling to replace the receiver on its hook, thumping it against the night table, missing again and again, until finally Stacy's mother took it from him and hung it up herself. Stacy and her brothers were sitting on the other bed, staring in astonishment. They'd never seen their father weep, never would again. Their mother gathered them up, took them for an ice cream in the hotel restaurant, and by the time they returned, it was over. Their father was himself again, busily packing their bags. He'd already booked them seats on a plane home later that evening.

Uncle Roger had been a portly man, graying early, who'd always seemed uncomfortable around his brother's children, resorting to shadow animals and knock-knock jokes as a means of diverting their attention. He'd come to stay with them the Christmas before his death. The guest room was across from Stacy's bedroom, and she'd awakened one night to a tremendous thump. Curious, a little frightened, she'd crept to her door, peeked outside into the hall. Uncle Roger was lying there, very drunk, struggling to pull himself back to his feet. After a few attempts, he gave up. He rolled, shifted with a groan, and managed to arrange his body in something resembling a sitting position, his back against the guest room's door.

That was when he noticed Stacy. He winked at her, smiling, and she opened her door a little farther. Then she crouched there, watching him.

What he said next would remain so vivid to her, so unblurred by the limitations of her seven-year-old consciousness, that she was no longer certain if it had actually happened. Its lucidity seemed more dream than memory. "I'm going to tell you something important," he said. "Are you listening?" When she nodded, he wagged an admonishing finger at her. "If you're not careful, you can reach a point where you've made choices without thinking. Without planning. You can end up not living the life you'd meant to. Maybe one you deserve, but not one you intended." Here he wagged his finger again. "Make sure you think," he said. "Make sure you plan."

Then he fell silent. It wasn't the way one was supposed to talk to a seven-year-old, and he seemed, belatedly, to realize this. He forced a smile at her. He lifted his hands and attempted some shadow animals in the weak light coming from the stairway. He did his rabbit, his barking dog, his flying eagle. They weren't very impressive, and he seemed to realize this, too. He yawned, closed his eyes, fell almost immediately asleep. Stacy shut her door and crept back to bed.

She never told her parents about this conversation, yet she'd thought of it, off and on, throughout her childhood. She still thought of it now, as an adult, perhaps all the more so. It haunted her, because she sensed the truth in what he'd said, or what she'd dreamed he'd said, and she knew she wasn't a thinker, wasn't a planner, would never be one. It was easy enough to imagine herself trapped in some unanticipated way, through negligence or lassitude. Aging, say, and all alone, in a bathrobe spotted with stains, watching late-night TV with the sound on low while half a dozen cats slept beside her. Or in the suburbs, maybe, marooned in a big house full of echoing rooms, with sore nipples and an infant upstairs, screaming to be fed. This latter image was the one she had in her mind as she sat in the yellow pickup truck, bumping her way down the rutted dirt road, and it made her feel hollow, balloonlike, popable. She pushed it aside, an act of will. It wasn't her life, after all, not now, not yet. She was leaving for graduate school in a few weeks; anything could happen. She'd meet new people, friends she'd probably keep for the rest of her life. She spent a few moments picturing herself in Boston—at a coffee shop, maybe, with a stack of books on the table in front of her, late at night, the place almost empty, and a boy coming in, one of her classmates, his shy smile, how he'd ask if he could sit with her—when suddenly, inexplicably, she found herself thinking of Uncle Roger again, alone on that flooded road, of that magical instant when the creek first took hold of his car, lifting it, giving him that weightless feeling, not panic yet, just pure surprise, and maybe even a touch of giddy pleasure, the start of a little adventure, a funny story to tell his neighbors when he got home.

Never attempt to drive across moving water. There were so many rules to remember. No wonder people ended up in places they'd never chosen to be.

It was with this thought—in hindsight, such an appropriately ominous foreshadowing—that she glanced up through the windshield, to discover they'd arrived.

When the truck stopped, the man held the map toward Amy. She reached to take it, but he didn't let her. She pulled, and he held on: a brief tug-of-war. Stacy was fumbling with the door handle; she didn't notice what was happening. The truck rocked slightly as Jeff and the others jumped to the ground. The windows were up, the air conditioner on high, but Amy could hear them laughing. The dog was still barking. Stacy got the door open, finally, and rolled out into the heat, leaving it ajar, for Amy to follow. But the man wouldn't let go of the map.

"This place," he said, nodding toward the path. "Why you go?"

Amy could tell that the man's English was limited. She tried to think how she could describe the purpose of their mission in the simplest words possible. She leaned forward; the others were gathering beside the truck, slinging their packs, waiting for her. She pointed to Mathias. "His brother?" she said. "We have to find him."

The driver turned, stared at Mathias for a moment, then back at her. He frowned but didn't say anything. They were both still holding the map.

"*Hermano?*" Amy tried. She didn't know where the word arrived from, or if it was correct. Her Spanish was limited to movie titles, the names of restaurants. "*Perdido?*" she said, pointing at Mathias again. "*Hermano perdido.*" She wasn't certain what she was saying. The dog was still barking, and it was beginning to give her a headache, making it hard to think clearly. She wanted to get out of the truck, but when she tugged at the map again, the driver still wouldn't let her have it.

He shook his head. "This place," he said. "No good."

"No good?" she asked. She had no idea how he meant this.

He nodded. "No good you go this place."

Outside, the others had turned to stare at the truck. They were waiting for her. Beyond them, the path started. The trees grew over it, forming a shady tunnel, almost to the point of darkness. She couldn't see
very far along it. "I don't understand," Amy said.

"Fifteen dollars, I take you back."

"We're looking for his brother."

The driver shook his head, vehement. "I take you new place. Fifteen
dollars. Everyone happy." He smiled to demonstrate what he meant:
wide, showing his teeth. They were large, very thick-looking, and black
along the gums.

"This is the right place," Amy said. "It's on the map, isn't it?" She
pulled at the map, and he let her have it. She pointed down at the X,
then toward the path. "This is it, right?"

The driver's smile faded; he shook his head, as if in disgust, and waved
her toward the open door. "Go, then," he said. "I tell you no good, but
still you go."

Amy held out the map, pointing at the X again. "We're looking
for—"

"Go," the man said, cutting her off, his voice rising, as if he'd suddenly lost patience with this whole conversation, as if he were growing
angry. He kept waving toward the door, his face turned away from her,
from the proffered map. "Go, go, go."

So she did. She climbed out, pushed shut the door, and watched the
truck pull slowly away, back onto the road.

The heat was like a hand that reached forward and wrapped itself
around her. At first, it felt nice after the chill of the air conditioning,
but then, very quickly, the hand began to squeeze. She was sweating,
and there were mosquitoes—hovering, humming, biting. Jeff had
taken a can of insect repellent from his pack and was spraying everyone
with it. The dog kept lunging at them even as the pickup drove off,
lurching and swaying along the deep ruts in the road. They could still
hear its barking long after the truck was out of sight.

"What did he want?" Stacy asked. She'd already been sprayed. Her
skin was shiny with it, and she smelled like air freshener. The mosquitoes were still biting her, though; she kept slapping at her arms.

"He said we shouldn't go."

"Go where?"

Amy pointed down the path.

"Why not?" Stacy asked.

"He said it's no good."

"What's no good?"

"Where we're going."

"The ruins are no good?"

Amy shrugged; she didn't know. "He wanted fifteen dollars to drive us somewhere else."

Jeff came over with the can of repellent. He took the map from her and began to spray. Amy held out her arms, then lifted them above her head so he could get her torso. She turned in a slow circle, all the way around. When she was facing him again, he stopped spraying, crouched to put the repellent back in his pack. They all stood there, watching him.

A disquieting thought occurred to Amy. "How're we getting back?" she asked.

Jeff squinted up at her. "Back?"

She pointed down the road after the vanished pickup truck. "To Cobá."

He turned to stare at the road, thinking on this. "The guidebook said you can always flag down a passing bus." He shrugged; he seemed to realize how foolish this was. "So I assumed . . ."

"There aren't going to be any buses on that road," Amy said.

Jeff nodded. This was obvious enough.

"A bus couldn't even fit on that road."

"It also said you can hitch—"

"You see any cars pass, Jeff?"

Jeff sighed, cinching his pack shut. He stood up, slung it over his shoulder. "Amy—" he began.

"The whole time we were driving, did you see any—"

"They must have a way to get supplies in."

"Who?"

"The archaeologists. They must have a truck. Or access to a truck. When we find Mathias's brother, we can just ask them to, you know, take us all back to Cobá."

"Christ, Jeff. We're stranded out here, aren't we? That's, like, a twenty-mile walk we're gonna have to do. Through the fucking jungle."

"Eleven."

"What?"

"It's eleven miles."

"There's no way that was eleven miles." Amy turned to the others for support, but only Pablo met her eyes. He was smiling; he had no idea what they were talking about. Mathias was digging through his pack.

Stacy and Eric were staring at the ground. She could tell they thought this was just her complaining again, and it made her angry. "Nobody else is bothered by this?"

"Why is it my responsibility?" Jeff asked. "Why am I the one who was supposed to figure this whole thing out?"

Amy threw up her hands, as if the answer were obvious. "Because . . . ," she said, but then she fell silent. Why was it Jeff's responsibility? She felt certain it was, yet she couldn't think why.

Jeff turned to the others, gestured toward the path. "Ready?" he asked. Everyone but Amy nodded. He started forward, followed by Mathias, then Pablo, then Eric.

Stacy gave Amy a sympathetic look. "Just go with it, sweetie," she said. "Okay? You'll see. It'll all work out."

She hooked arms with her, pulled her into motion. Amy didn't resist; they started toward the path together, arm in arm, Jeff and Mathias already vanishing into the shadows ahead of them, birds crying out overhead to mark their passage into the jungle's depths.

The map said they had to go two miles along the path. Then they'd see another trail, branching off to their left. This one would lead them gradually uphill. At the top of the hill, they'd find the ruins.

They'd been walking for almost twenty minutes when Pablo stopped to pee. Eric stopped, too. He dropped his pack to the trail, sat on it, resting. The trees alongside the path blocked the sun, but it was still too hot to be walking this far. His shirt was soaked through with sweat; his hair clung damply to his forehead. There were mosquitoes and some other type of very small fly, which didn't sting but seemed to be drawn to Eric's perspiration. They swirled around him in a cloud, giving off a high-pitched hum. Either he'd sweated all the bug spray off or it was worthless.

Stacy and Amy caught up with them while Pablo was still peeing. Eric heard them talking as they approached, but they fell silent when they got close. Stacy gave Eric a smile, patted him on the head as she went by. They didn't stop, didn't even slow, and after they got a little ways down the trail, he heard them begin to speak again. He felt a little flicker of disquiet, the sense that they might be gossiping about him. Or maybe not. Maybe it was Jeff. They were secret keepers, though, whisperers; it was something Eric still hadn't grown accustomed to, their closeness. Sometimes he caught himself scowling at Amy for no good reason, not liking her: he was jealous. He wanted to be the one Stacy whispered to, not the one she whispered about, and it bothered him that this wasn't the case.

The Greek had an immense bladder. He was still peeing, a puddle forming at his feet. The tiny black flies appeared to find urine even more alluring than sweat; they hovered over the puddle, dropping into it and taking flight again, dimpling its surface. The Greek pissed and pissed and pissed.

When he finished, he pulled one of the tequila bottles from his pack, broke its seal. A quick swallow, then he passed it to Eric. Eric stood up to drink, the liquor bringing tears to his eyes. He coughed, handed the bottle back. Pablo took another swallow before returning it to his pack. He said something in Greek, shaking his head, wiping his face with his shirt. Eric assumed it was a comment on the heat; it had the proper air of complaint to it.

He nodded. "Hot as hell," he said. "You guys have a phrase like that? Everybody must, don't you think? Hades? Inferno?"

The Greek just smiled at him.

Eric shouldered his pack, and they started walking again. On the map, the path had been drawn as a straight line, but in reality it meandered. Stacy and Amy were a hundred feet ahead, and sometimes Eric could glimpse them, other times not. Jeff and Mathias had started up the trail like two Boy Scouts, all business. Eric couldn't see them anymore, not even on the longer straightaways. The path was about four feet wide, packed dirt, with thick jungle growth on either side. Big-leafed plants, vines and creepers, trees straight out of a Tarzan comic book. It was dark under the trees, and difficult to see very far into their midst, but now and then Eric could hear things crashing about in the foliage. Birds, maybe, startled by their approach. There was a lot of cawing, and a steady locust-like throbbing underneath it all that could suddenly, for no apparent reason, fall silent, sending a shiver up his spine.

The path seemed to be fairly well traveled. They passed an empty beer bottle, a flattened pack of cigarettes. There were tracks at one point, too, some sort of hoofed animal, smaller than a horse. A donkey, maybe, or even a goat—Eric couldn't decide. Jeff probably knew what it was; he was good at things like that—picking out constellations, naming flowers. He was a reader, a fact hoarder, maybe a bit of a show-off at times: ordering in Spanish even when it was clear that the waiter spoke English, correcting people's pronunciation. Eric couldn't decide how well he liked him. Or, for that matter—and maybe this was more to the point—how well he was liked by Jeff.

They rounded a curve and descended a long, gradual slope with a stream running alongside the trail, and then suddenly there was sunlight in front of them, blinding after all that time in the shade. The jungle fell away, beaten back by what appeared to be some sort of aborted attempt at agriculture. There were fields on either side of the trail, extending for a hundred yards or so, vast tracts of churned-up earth, baking in the sun. It was the end stages of the slash-and-burn cycle: the slashing and burning and sowing and reaping had already happened here, and now this was what followed, the wasteland that preceded the jungle's return. Already, the foliage along the margins had begun to send out exploratory parties, vines and the occasional waist-high bush, looking squat and somehow pugnacious amid all those upturned clods of dirt.

Pablo and Eric fumbled for their sunglasses. In the distance, the jungle resumed, extending like a wall across the path. Jeff and Mathias had already vanished into its shadows, but Stacy and Amy were still visible. Amy had put on her hat; Stacy had tied a bandanna over her hair. Eric called to them, yelling their names, and waved, but they didn't hear him. Or, hearing him, didn't glance back. The little black flies remained behind beneath the trees, but the mosquitoes continued to accompany them, unabated.

They were midway across the open space when a snake crossed the path, right in front of them. It was just a small snake—black, with tan markings, two feet long at the most—but Pablo gave a shout of terror. He jumped backward, knocking Eric down, then lost his own footing and fell on top of him. He was up in an instant, pointing at the spot where the snake had disappeared, chattering in Greek, dancing from foot to foot, a look of horror on his face. Apparently, he had a fear of snakes. Eric rose slowly to his feet, dusting himself off. He'd scraped his elbow when he fell, and there was dirt in the cut; he tried to brush it clean. Pablo kept spewing his Greek, exclaiming and gesturing. All three Greeks were like this; sometimes they tried to mime their meaning or draw something to explain themselves, but mostly they just held forth, making no attempt to clarify what they were saying. It was as if the uttering of it was all that mattered; being understood was beside the point.

Eric waited for Pablo to finish. Toward the end, it seemed as if he were apologizing for knocking him down, and Eric smiled and nodded to express his forgiveness. Then they continued on, though Pablo proceeded at a much slower pace now, nervously scanning the edges of the trail. Eric spent some time trying to picture their arrival at the ruins. The archaeologists with their careful grids, their little shovels and whisk booms, their plastic bags full of artifacts: tin cups the miners had drunk from, the iron nails that had once held their shacks together. Mathias would find his brother; there'd be some sort of confrontation, an argument in German, raised voices, ultimatums. Eric was looking forward to it. He liked drama, conflict, the rush and tumble of other people's emotions. It wasn't all going to be like this, the drudgery of walking through the heat, his elbow throbbing in time with his heartbeat. Once they found the ruins, the day would shift, take on a new dimension.

They reached the far end of the open space, and the jungle resumed. The little black bugs were waiting for them here in the shade. They hovered around them in a humming cloud, as if joyful in the reunion. There was no sign of the stream anymore. The trail curved to the right, then to the left, then became straight again, a long corridor of shade, at the end of which appeared to be another clearing, a circle of sunlight awaiting their approach, so bright, it felt audible to Eric, like a horn, blowing. It hurt to look at it—hurt his eyes, his head. He put his sunglasses back on. Only then did he notice the others clustered together there—Jeff and Mathias and Stacy and Amy—crouching in a loose circle just short of the clearing, passing a water bottle back and forth among themselves, and turning now to watch as he and Pablo went slowly toward them.

The map said that if they reached the Mayan village, they'd gone too far, and there it was, down the slope from where they crouched. Jeff and Mathias had been watching for their turnoff as they walked, but somehow they must've missed it. They'd have to double back along the trail now, moving more slowly this time, looking more closely. The question they were debating was whether or not they should investigate the village first, perhaps even see if there might be someone there who'd be willing to guide them to the ruins. Not that the village appeared very promising. It consisted of perhaps thirty flimsy-looking buildings, nearly identical in size and appearance. One- and two-room shacks, most with thatch roofs, though there were several of tin, too.

Dirt-floored, Jeff guessed. There were no overhead wires visible, so he assumed there was no electricity. Nor running water, for that matter: there was a well in the center of the village, with a bucket attached to a rope. As they crouched there, waiting for Eric and Pablo to reach them, he saw an old woman fill a pitcher at the well, turning a wheel to lower the bucket into its depths. The wheel needed oiling; he could hear it squeaking even from this distance as the bucket dropped and dropped, then paused, filling, before its equally clamorous ascent. Jeff watched the woman balance the pitcher on her shoulder and move slowly back down the dusty street to her shack.

The Mayans had cleared a circular swath of jungle around their village, planting what appeared to be corn and beans in the open space. Men and women and even children were scattered across the fields, bent over, weeding. There were goats about, chickens and some donkeys and a trio of horses in a fenced corral, but no sign of any mechanical equipment: no tractors or tillers, no cars or trucks. When Jeff and Mathias first appeared at the mouth of the trail, a tall, narrow-chested mutt had come trotting quickly toward them, tail aggressively raised. It stopped just short of stone-throwing range and paced back and forth for a few minutes, barking and growling. The sun was too hot for this sort of behavior, though, and eventually it fell quiet, then lost interest altogether and drifted back toward the village, collapsing into the shade beside one of the shacks.

Jeff assumed that the dog must've alerted the villagers to their presence, but there was no overt acknowledgment of this. No one paused in his work to stare; no one nudged his neighbor and pointed. The men and women and children remained bent low over their weeding, moving slowly down the rows of plants. Most of the men were dressed in white, with straw hats on their heads. The women wore dark dresses, shawls covering their hair. The children were barefoot, feral-looking; many of the boys were shirtless, dark from the sun, so that they seemed to blend into the earth they were working, to vanish and reappear from one moment to the next.

Stacy wanted to push forward into the village, to see if they might find someplace cool to sit and rest—perhaps they could even buy a cold soda somewhere—but Jeff hesitated. The lack of greeting, the sense that the village was collectively willing away their appearance, filled him with a feeling of caution. He pointed out the absence of overhead wires, and how this would lead to a lack of refrigerators and air conditioners, which, in turn, would make cold sodas and cool places to sit and rest seem somewhat unlikely.

"But at least we might find a guide," Amy said. She'd removed her camera from his pack and had started to take pictures. She took some of them crouched there, then one of Pablo and Eric walking toward them, then one of the Mayans working in their fields. Her spirits had lifted, Jeff could tell; Stacy had brought her out of it. Her moods came and went; he assumed there was a logic to them, but he'd long ago stopped trying to fathom it. He called her his "jellyfish," rising and falling through the depths. Sometimes she seemed to find this endearing; other times she didn't. She took a picture of him, spending a long moment peering through the viewfinder, making him self-conscious. Then the click. "We could just end up walking back and forth along this trail all day," she said. "And then what? Are we supposed to camp out here?"

"And maybe they'll be able to drive us back to Cobá afterward," Stacy said.

"See any cars or trucks?" Jeff asked.

They all spent a moment staring down into the village. Before anyone could say anything further, Pablo and Eric were upon them. Pablo hugged everyone, then immediately began chattering in Greek, very excitedly, extending his arms full length, as if describing a fish he'd caught. He jumped up and down; he pretended to knock into Eric. Then he held out his arms again.

"We saw a snake," Eric said. "But it wasn't that big. Maybe half that."

The others laughed at this, which seemed to encourage Pablo. He started all over again, the chattering, the jumping, the bumping into Eric.

"He's scared of them," Eric said.

They passed the water bottle around, waited for Pablo to finish. Eric took a long swallow of water, then poured some on his elbow. He had a cut there; everyone clustered around him to examine it. The wound was bloody but not especially deep, three inches long, sickle-shaped, following the curve of his elbow. Amy took a picture of it.

"We're going to find a guide in the village," she said.

"And a cool place to sit," Stacy offered. "With cold sodas."

"Maybe they'll have a lime, too," Amy said. "We can squeeze it on your cut. It'll kill off all the nasty things inside."

She and Stacy both turned from Eric to smile at Jeff, as if taunting him. He didn't respond—what was the point? Clearly, it had already been decided: they were going to the village. Pablo finally stopped talking; Mathias was putting the cap back on the water bottle. Jeff shouldered his pack. "Shall we?" he said.

Then they started down the path toward the village.

There was a moment, just as they emerged from the trees, when the entire village seemed to freeze, the men and women and children in the fields, everyone pausing for the barest fraction of a second to note the six of them approaching down the trail. Then it was over, and it was as if it hadn't happened, though Stacy was certain it had, or maybe not so certain, maybe less certain with each additional step she took toward the village. The work continued in the fields, the bent backs, the steady pulling of the weeds, and no one was looking at them; no one was bothering to observe their advance along the path, not even the children. So perhaps it hadn't happened after all. Stacy was a fantasist—she knew this about herself—a daydreamer, a castle builder. There would be no cool rooms here, no cold sodas. And it was equally probable that there'd been no moment of furtive appraisal, either, no veiled and quickly terminated collective glance.

The dog reappeared, the one who'd been barking at them earlier. He emerged again from the village, but with an entirely different demeanor. Tail wagging, tongue hanging: a friend. Stacy liked dogs. She crouched to pet this one, let him lick her face. The tail wagging intensified, the entire rear half of the mutt's body swinging back and forth. The others didn't stop; they kept walking down the path. The dog was covered in ticks, Stacy noticed. Dozens of them, like so many raisins hanging off his belly: fat, blood-engorged. She could see others moving through his pelt, and she stood up quickly, pushing the dog away from her, but to no avail. That brief demonstration of affection had won the mutt over; he'd adopted her. He pressed close to her body as she walked, winding himself through her legs, whimpering and wagging, nearly tripping her. Hurrying to catch up with the others, she had to resist the urge to kick at the animal, smack him across the snout, send him scurrying. She felt as if the ticks were crawling over her own body now, had to tell herself this wasn't true, actually form the words in her mind: *It's not true.* She wished, suddenly, that she was back in Cancún, back in her room, about to climb into the shower. The warm water, the smell of shampoo, the little bar of soap in its paper wrapper, the clean towel waiting on its rack.

The path widened as it entered the village, became something that could almost be called a road. The shacks lined it on either side. Brightly colored blankets hung over some of the doorways; others were open but equally unrevealing, their interiors lost in shadow. The chickens scampered, clucking. Another dog appeared, joining the first in his adoration of Stacy, the two of them nipping at each other, fighting over her. The second dog was gray, wolflike. He had one blue eye and one brown, which gave his gaze an ominous intensity. In her head, Stacy already had names for them: Pigpen and Creepy.

At first, it appeared that there was no one in the village, that everyone was out working in the fields. Their footsteps sounded loud on the packed dirt, intrusive. No one spoke, not even Pablo, for whom silence had always seemed so unattainable. Then there was a woman, sitting in one of the doorways, with an infant in her arms. The woman had a withered quality about her, gray streaks in her long black hair. They were moving down the center of the dirt road, ten or so feet from her, but she didn't glance up.

"¡Hola!" Jeff called.

Nothing. Silence, averted eyes.

The baby had no hair to speak of, and a raw, painful-looking rash on its scalp. It was hard not to stare at the rash; it looked as if someone had spread a layer of jam across the infant's skull. Stacy couldn't understand why the baby wasn't crying, and it upset her, inordinately, though she couldn't say why. *Like a doll*, she thought—not moving, not crying— and then she realized why its stillness bothered her: there was the sense that the infant might be dead. She glanced away, calling up those words again, forcing them into her head: *It's not true*. Then they were past, and she didn't look back.

They stopped at the well, in the center of the village, peering about, waiting for someone to approach them, not certain what to do if this didn't happen. The well was deep. When Stacy leaned over its edge, she couldn't see its bottom. She had to resist the urge to spit, or pick up a pebble and drop it in, listening for the distant plop. There was a wooden bucket on a slimy coil of rope; Stacy wouldn't have wanted to touch it. Mosquitoes hovered in a cloud around them, as if they, too, were waiting to see what might happen next.

Amy took some pictures: the surrounding shacks, the well, the two dogs. She handed the camera to Eric and had him take one of her and Stacy standing arm in arm. There'd be a whole series of these by the time they got home, the two of them gripping each other, smiling into the camera, pale at first, then sunburned, then peeling. This was the first one without matching hats, and it made Stacy sad for a moment, thinking of it—the boys running off along the plaza, the shock of that tiny hand squeezing her breast.

The dog she'd named Creepy, with his brown and blue eyes, went into a crouch, and a long string of shit spooled out of him onto the ground beside the well. The shit was moving; it was more worms than feces. Pigpen sniffed at it with great interest, and this sight finally jarred Pablo into speech. He began to exclaim in Greek, gesturing wildly. He stepped over to peer at the squirming pile of shit, his lip curled in disgust. He lifted his head to the sky and kept talking, as if speaking to the gods, all the while gesturing at the two dogs.

"Maybe this wasn't such a good idea," Eric said.

Jeff nodded. "We should go. We'll just have to—"

"Someone's coming," Mathias said.

A man was approaching down the dirt track. Coming from the fields, it seemed, wiping his hands on his pants, leaving two brown smudges on the white fabric. He was short, broad-shouldered, and when he removed his straw hat to wipe the sweat from his forehead, Stacy saw that he was almost completely bald. He stopped twenty feet away, appraising them, taking his time. He put his hat back on, returned his handkerchief to his pocket.

"¡Hola!" Jeff called.

The man answered in Mayan, with a question, it appeared, eyebrows raised.

It seemed logical to assume that he was asking them what they wanted, and Jeff struggled to answer him, first in Spanish, then in English, then in pantomime. The man showed no sign of understanding any of this. Stacy had the odd sense, in fact, that he didn't want to understand, that he was willing himself not to comprehend what had brought them here. He listened to Jeff's words, even smiled at his foray into mime, yet there was something distinctly unwelcoming in his bearing. He was polite but not friendly; she could tell that he was waiting for them to leave, that he'd rather they'd never come.

Finally, Jeff seemed to realize this, too. He gave up, turned to them with a shrug. "This isn't working," he said.

No one argued. They shouldered their packs, started back toward the jungle. The Mayan man remained by the well, watching them go.

They passed the woman who'd refused to acknowledge them earlier, and, once again, she kept her gaze averted, the baby, with its mottled cap of red jam, motionless in her arms. *Dead,* Stacy thought, and then, as she forced herself to look away: *It's not true.*

The dogs followed them. So did two children, which was a surprise. There was a squeaking sound, and when Stacy glanced back, she found a pair of boys coming up the trail after them on a bike. The bigger of the two was pedaling, the smaller rode perched on the handlebars. Relative terms, these—*bigger, smaller*—as neither of the boys was very large. They were hollow-chested, slope-shouldered, with knobby knees and elbows, and their bike was far too big for them. It looked heavy; its tires were fat and bulging; it had no seat. The boy in back had to pedal standing up, and he was panting with the effort, sweating. The chain needed oil—that was the squeaking.

The six of them stopped, turned, thinking to ask the boys where the ruins were, but the children stopped, too, forty feet back, scrawny, dark-eyed, watchful as two owls. Jeff called out, waved for them to approach; he even held up a dollar bill to tempt them forward, but the boys just waited there, staring, the smaller of the two still perched on the handlebars. Finally, they gave up, started walking again. A moment later, that steady squeaking resumed, but they paid it no mind. In the fields, the weeding continued. Only the man by the well and the two boys on the bike showed any interest in their departure. Creepy dropped away as soon as they entered the jungle, but Pigpen persisted. He kept rubbing against Stacy, and she kept pushing him away. He seemed to think this was a game, and threw himself into it with greater and greater enthusiasm.

Stacy couldn't help herself; she lost patience. "No," she said, and gave the mutt a slap across his snout. The dog yelped, jumped back, astonished. He stood in the center of the trail, peering at her with what looked like a painfully human expression. Betrayal—this was what his eyes communicated. "Oh, honey," Stacy said, and stepped toward him, holding out her hand, but it was too late; the dog backed away, wary now, his tail tucked between his legs. The others were continuing forward along the shadowed path, striding into the first of the curves; they'd vanish from sight in another moment. Stacy felt a tremor of fear, a childish, lost-alone-in-the-forest sensation, and she turned, broke into a jog, hurrying to catch up. When she glanced back, the dog was still standing in the center of the trail, watching her go. The boys pedaled past him on their squeaking bike, almost brushing against him, but he didn't move, and his mournful gaze seemed to cling to her as she vanished around the curve.

Walking back along the trail, Amy tried to think of a happy ending for their day, but it wasn't easy to come by. They'd either find the ruins or they wouldn't. If they didn't, they'd end up back on the dirt road, with eleven miles or more between them and Cobá, and night falling fast. Maybe they'd received the wrong impression of the road; maybe there was more traffic on it than they thought. That was a happy ending, she supposed, them hitching a ride into Cobá. They could arrive just as the sun was setting and either find a place to spend the night or catch a late bus back to Cancún. Amy wasn't able to muster much faith in this vision, though. She pictured them walking along the road in total darkness, or camping in the open, without tents or sleeping bags or mosquito nets, and decided that perhaps it would be better after all if they could somehow find their way to the ruins.

There'd be Henrich and his new girlfriend and the archaeologists at the ruins. They'd speak English, probably; they'd be welcoming and helpful. They'd find a way to transport them back to Cobá, or, if it was already too late in the day, would happily offer to share their tents. Yes— why not?—the archaeologists would cook dinner for them. There'd be a campfire and drinking and laughter, and she'd take lots of pictures to show people when she got back home. It would be an adventure, the highlight of their trip. This was the happy ending Amy kept in her mind as she made her way back down the trail, with the clearing opening up ahead of them, a circle of sunlight, blinkingly intense, into which they'd soon have to walk.

They paused in the last shadows before the clearing. Mathias took out his water bottle, and they passed it around again. They were all sweating; Pablo had begun to smell. Behind them, the squeaking came to a stop. Amy turned and there were the two boys, fifty feet back, watching them. The mangy dog was there, too, the one who'd taken such a liking to Stacy. He was even farther down the trail, though, almost lost in shade. He, too, had stopped, and was hesitating now, gazing toward them.

Amy was the one who thought of the fields. She felt a flush of pride as the idea surfaced in her head, a childhood feeling, leaning forward in her tiny desk, hand raised, waving for the teacher's attention. "Maybe the path opens off the fields," she said, pointing out into the sunlight.

The others turned, stared toward the clearing, thinking it through. Then Jeff nodded. "Could be," he said, and he was smiling, pleased with the idea, which made Amy even more proud of herself.

She unlooped her camera from her neck, ordered them all into a loose group. Then, with her back to the sun, she framed them in the view-finder, goading them into grins—even frownful Mathias. At the last instant, just before Amy pressed the button, Stacy glanced over her shoulder, back down the trail, toward the boys, the dog, the silent vil-lage, turning away from the camera. But it didn't matter. It was still a nice picture, and Amy knew it now: she'd thought of their solution, the path to their happy ending. They were going to find the ruins after all.

After the packed-down firmness of the trail, the field proved to be a difficult hike. The dirt seemed to have been worked with a harrow in the recent past. It was uneven—turned and furrowed—with sudden, inexplicable patches of mud. The mud stuck to their shoes, gradually accumulating, and they kept having to stop to scrape it off. Eric wasn't in any shape for this sort of adventure. He was hungover, weary from lack of sleep, and beginning to feel the day's heat in an unpleasant way. His heart was racing; his head ached. Waves of nausea came and went. He was just beginning to realize that he wasn't going to make it much farther, and was deciding how he ought to announce this revelation, when Pablo saved him from the indignity by stopping suddenly. The mud had sucked his right shoe straight off his foot. He stood there in the field, balanced, cranelike, on one foot, and started swearing. Eric rec-ognized many of the obscenities from the lessons the Greeks had given him.

Jeff and Mathias and Amy had already pulled ahead—they were walk-ing with what appeared to be a baffling effortlessness along the jungle's margin—but Stacy had tarried alongside Pablo and Eric. She stopped with Eric now to aid the Greek, holding him by the elbow, helping him keep his balance, while Eric crouched to free his shoe from the field's grasp. It emerged, finally, after several strenuous pulls, with a suctioned popping sound, making them all laugh. Pablo put the shoe back on. Then, without a word, he began walking back toward the trail. Stacy and Eric glanced toward the others, who were a good fifty feet ahead now, moving methodically along the tree line. A silent debate followed, very brief, and then Eric held his hand out to Stacy. She took it, smiling, and the two of them started back across the field, following in Pablo's footsteps.

Jeff shouted something to them, but Eric and Stacy just waved and kept walking. Pablo was waiting for them on the trail. He'd opened his pack, taken out the tequila. The cap was off; he offered the bottle to Eric, who—despite himself, knowing better—took a long, wincing swallow and then passed it on to Stacy. Stacy could be an impressive drinker when she put her mind to it, as she did now. She threw her head back, the bottle tilted at a perfect vertical, the tequila going *blub-blub, blub-blub* as it poured straight down her throat. She surfaced for air with a cough that became a laugh, her face flushed. Pablo applauded, slapped her on the shoulder, took back the bottle.

The two Mayan boys were still with them. They'd approached a little closer but hadn't yet left the jungle's shade. They'd climbed off their bike and were standing side by side, the larger of the two holding it by its handlebars. Pablo raised the bottle toward them, calling in Greek, but they didn't move; they just stood, staring. The dog was right beside them, also watching.

Jeff and Mathias and Amy had reached the far wall of the jungle, directly across the field from them. They were just beginning to move along it now, parallel to the trail, searching for the mysterious path. Pablo returned the bottle to his pack, and the three of them stood for a while, watching the others make their way along the muddy field. Eric didn't believe they were going to find the ruins. He didn't, in fact, believe that the ruins even existed. Someone was lying to them, or playing a prank, but whether it was Mathias or Mathias's brother or Mathias's brother's perhaps imaginary girlfriend, he couldn't decide. It didn't matter. He'd been having fun for a while, but now he wanted it to be over, wanted to be safely back on an air-conditioned bus to Cancún, drifting into sleep. He wasn't certain how he was going to accomplish this; all he knew was that he wanted to get there, and that the first thing he had to do was finish walking back to the road on the shortest route possible. This didn't involve tramping through a muddy field.

Eric started forward along the path. They could wait for the others in the shade on the far side of the clearing; perhaps he'd even be able to nap a little. He and Stacy held hands as they walked.

"So . . ." Stacy said. "There was this girl who bought a piano."

"But she didn't know how to play it," Eric responded.

"So she signed up for lessons."

"But couldn't afford them."

"So she got a job in a factory."

"But was fired for being late."

"So she became a prostitute."

"But fell in love with her first client."

This was an old game of theirs, the so-but stories. It was nonsense, the purest form of idleness; they could keep at it for hours at a time, ping-ponging back and forth. It was their own invention; no one else understood it. Even Amy found it annoying. But it was the sort of thing Eric and Stacy were best at: silliness, play. In some deep, not entirely accessible part of his mind, Eric realized that they were two children together, and that someday Stacy was going to grow up, that it was already, in fact, beginning to happen. He didn't think he himself would ever accomplish this; he didn't understand how people did it. He was going to teach children and remain a child forever, while Stacy advanced implacably into adulthood, leaving him behind. He could dream of them getting married someday, but it was just a story he told himself, yet another example of his inherent immaturity. There was a good-bye lurking in their future, a breakup note, a last painful encounter. This was something he tried not to see, something he knew, or suspected he knew, but before which he reflexively closed his eyes.

"So she asked him to marry her."

"But he was already married."

"So she begged him to get a divorce."

"But he was in love with his wife."

"So she decided to kill her."

The dog began to bark, startling Eric. He turned, peered back down the trail. The two boys and the mutt had emerged from the jungle; all three were standing there in the sunlight now. They weren't looking in Eric's direction, though; they were staring off across the open ground at Jeff and Mathias and Amy. Mathias was lifting a large palm frond away from the tree line, tossing it out into the field. As he bent to pick up another one, Jeff turned, shouted something indecipherable, waved for them to approach.

Eric and Stacy and Pablo didn't move. None of them wanted to walk out into the mud again. Mathias kept picking up palm fronds and tossing them aside. Gradually, an opening was revealed in the tree line: a path.

Before Eric could quite absorb this, he noted a flurry of movement back along the trail. It drew his gaze. The larger of the two boys had climbed onto his bike and was pedaling away now, very rapidly, disappearing into the jungle, leaving the smaller boy alone on the trail, watching Jeff and the others with an unmistakable air of anxiety, rocking side to side, his hands clasped together, tucked under his chin. Eric noted all this but couldn't make any sense of it. Jeff was waving for them to come, shouting again. There seemed to be no choice. Sighing, Eric stepped back into the muddy field. Stacy and Pablo did, too, and together they began slogging their way toward the tree line.

Behind them, the dog continued his steady barking.

It had been Mathias who noticed the palm fronds; Jeff had walked right past them. It was only when he'd sensed Mathias hesitating behind him that he turned, following the German's stare, and saw them. The fronds were still green. They'd been artfully arranged, with the ends of their stalks pushed into the dirt, so that they looked like a bush growing there along the tree line, hiding the entrance to the path. One of the fronds had tipped over, though, pulling itself free from the soil. This was what Mathias had noticed. He stepped forward, yanked another one free, and, in an instant, everything was revealed. That was when Jeff turned and called to the others, waving for them to come.

Once they'd cleared away the fronds, they could see the path easily enough. It was narrow and it wound off through the jungle, moving gradually uphill. Mathias and Amy and he crouched at its entrance, in the shade. Mathias took out his water bottle again, and they all drank from it. Then they sat for a stretch, watching Eric and Pablo and Stacy move slowly toward them across the field. Amy was the first to mention what was surely on all their minds.

"Why was it covered?" she asked.

Mathias was sliding his water bottle back into his pack. You had to ask him a question directly to get him to answer; whenever someone addressed the group, he seemed to pretend not to hear. This was fair enough, Jeff supposed. After all, he wasn't really one of them.

Jeff shrugged, feigning indifference. He tried to think of a way to distract her from this topic, but he couldn't, so he kept silent. He was afraid she'd refuse to venture down the path.

He could tell she wasn't going to let it go, though. And he was right. "The boy rode off," she said. "Did you see that?"

Jeff nodded. He wasn't looking at her—he was watching Eric and the others plodding toward them—but he could feel her gaze resting on him. He didn't want her to be thinking about this: the boy riding off, the camouflaged path. It would only frighten her, and she became obstinate and skittish when she was frightened, which wasn't a particularly helpful combination. Something strange was going on here, but Jeff was hoping that if they could just ignore it, it might not amount to anything. He knew this probably wasn't the wisest course, yet it was the best he could come up with at the moment. So it would have to do.

"Someone tried to hide the path," Amy said.

"Seems that way."

"They cut palm fronds and stuck them in the dirt so that it looked like a plant was growing there."

Jeff was silent, and wishing she was, too.

"That's a lot of work," Amy said.

"I guess so."

"Doesn't it seem strange to you?"

"A little."

"Maybe it's not the right path."

"We'll see."

"Maybe it's got something to do with drugs. Maybe it leads to a marijuana field. The village is growing pot, and that boy went back to get them, and they're gonna come with guns, and—"

Jeff finally gave in, turned to look at her. "Amy," he said, and she stopped. "It's the right path, okay?"

It wasn't going to be that easy, of course. She gave him an incredulous look. "How can you say that?"

Jeff waved toward Mathias. "It's on the map."

"It's a hand-drawn map, Jeff."

"Well, it's . . ." He floundered, wordless, waved his hand. "You know—"

"Tell me why the path was covered. Give me one possible scenario where it's the right one, and there's a logical reason for someone to have camouflaged its opening."

Jeff thought for a minute. Eric and the others were nearly upon them. Across the field, the little Mayan boy still stood, staring at them. The dog had finally stopped barking. "Okay," he said. "How's this? The archaeologists have started to find things of value. The mine isn't played out. They're finding silver. Or emeralds, maybe. Whatever they were mining in the first place. And they're worried that someone might come and try to rob them. So they've camouflaged the path."

Amy spent a moment considering this scenario. "And the boy on the bike?"

"They've recruited the Mayans to help them keep people away. They pay them to do it." Jeff smiled at her, pleased with himself. He didn't really believe any of it; he didn't know what to believe, in fact. Yet he was pleased nonetheless.

Amy was thinking it through. He could tell she didn't believe it, either, but it didn't matter. The others had finally reached them. Everyone was sweating, Eric especially, who was looking a little too pale, a little too drawn. The Greek needed to hug them, one by one, of course, wrapping his damp arms around their shoulders. And, just like that, the discussion was over. After all, what other option did they have?

A few more minutes of rest, then they started down the path into the jungle.

The path was narrow enough so that they were forced to walk single file. Jeff led the way, followed by Mathias, then Amy, then Pablo, then Eric. Stacy was the last in line.

"But her lover told the police," Eric said.

Stacy stared at the rear of his head. He was wearing a Boston Red Sox hat; he had it on backward. She tried to imagine that this was his face she was staring at, covered in brown hair, his eyes and mouth and nose hiding behind it. She smiled at this hairy face. It was their game, she knew, and she thought the words, *So she fled to another city,* but she didn't say them. Amy had made fun of her enough times, mimicking her and Eric saying "So" and "But," that Stacy didn't like playing the game in her presence anymore. She didn't say anything, and Eric kept walking. Sometimes this was just how it worked: you threw out a "So" or a "But" and the other person didn't respond, and that was okay. That was part of the game, too, part of their understanding.

She shouldn't have gone at the tequila so aggressively. That had been a stupid idea. She'd been trying to show off, she supposed, trying to impress Pablo with her drinking. Now she felt light-headed, a little sick to her stomach. There was all this green around her—too much, she felt—and that didn't help things: thick leaves on either side, the trees growing so close to the trail that it was hard not to touch them as she walked. An occasional breeze pushed past her down the path, shifting the leaves, making them whisper. Stacy tried to hear what they were say-ing, tried to attach words to the sound, but her mind wasn't working that way; she couldn't concentrate. She was a little drunk, and there was far, far too much green. She could feel the beginning of a headache—flexing itself, eager for a chance to grow. And the green was underfoot, too, moss growing on the trail, making it slippery in places. When the path dipped into a tiny hollow, she almost fell on the slickness. She gave a squawk as she caught her balance, and was dismayed to see that no one glanced back to make sure she was safe. What if she'd fallen, hit her head, been knocked unconscious? How long would it have taken them to realize she was no longer following in their footsteps? They'd have doubled back eventually, she supposed; they'd have found her, revived her. But what if something had slipped out of the jungle and taken her in its jaws before this happened? Because certainly there were creatures in the jungle; Stacy could sense them as she walked, watchful presences, noting her passage along the trail.

She didn't really believe any of this, of course. She liked scaring her-self, but in the way a child does, knowing the whole time that it was only pretend. She hadn't noticed the boy riding off on his bike, nor the fact that the path had been camouflaged. No one was talking about any of this. It was too hot to talk; all they could do was put one foot in front of the other. So the only threats Stacy had with which to entertain her-self were the ones she could think up on her own.

Why had she worn sandals? That was stupid. Her feet were a mess now; there was mud between her toes. It had felt nice, walking across the field—warm and squishy and oddly reassuring, but it wasn't like that anymore. Now it was just dirt, with a vaguely fecal smell to it, as if she'd dipped her feet in shit.

Green was the color of envy, of nausea. Stacy had been a Girl Scout; she'd had to hike through her share of green woods, clad in her green uniform. She still knew some songs from that time. She tried to think of one, but her headache wouldn't let her.

They crossed a stream, jumping from rock to rock. The stream was green, too, thick with algae. The rocks were even slipperier than the trail, but she didn't fall in. She hopped, hopped, hopped, and then she was on the other side.

The mosquitoes and the little black flies were so persistent, so numer-ous, that she'd long ago stopped bothering to swat them. But then, abruptly, just after she crossed the stream, they weren't there anymore. It seemed to happen in an instant: they were all around her, humming and hovering, and then, magically, they were gone. Without them, even the heat felt easier to bear, even the implacable greenness, the smell of shit coming from her feet, and for a short stretch it was almost pleasant, walking one after another through the whispering trees. Her head cleared a bit, and she found words for the rustling leaves.

Take me with you, one of the trees seemed to say.

And then: *Do you know who I am?*

The trail rounded a curve, and suddenly there was another clearing ahead of them, a circle of sunlight a hundred feet down the path, the heat giving a throbbing, watery quality to the view.

A tree on her left seemed to call her name. *Stacy,* it whispered, so clearly that she actually turned her head, a goose-bump feeling running up and down her back. Behind her came another rustling voice: *Are you lost?* And then she was stepping with the others into sunlight.

This clearing wasn't a field. It looked like a road, but it wasn't that, either. It was as if a gang of men had planned to build a road, had chopped away the jungle and flattened the earth, but then abruptly changed their minds. It was twenty yards wide and stretched in either direction, left and right, for as far as Stacy could see, finally curving out of sight. On the far side of it rose a small hill. The hill was rocky, oddly treeless, and covered with some sort of vinelike growth—a vivid green, with hand-shaped leaves and tiny flowers. The plant spread across the entire hill, clinging so tightly to the earth that it almost seemed to be squeezing it in its grasp. The flowers looked like poppies, the same size and color: a brilliant stained-glass red.

They all stood there, staring, shading their eyes against the sunlight. It was a beautiful sight: a hill shaped like a giant breast, covered in red flowers. Amy took out her camera, started snapping pictures.

The cleared ground was a different color than the fields they'd crossed earlier. The fields had been a reddish brown, almost orange in spots, while this was a deep black, flecked with white, like frost rime. Beyond it, the path resumed, winding its way up the hillside. It had grown strangely quiet, Stacy suddenly realized; the birds had fallen silent. Even the locusts had stopped their steady thrumming. A peaceful spot. She took a deep breath, feeling sleepy, and sat down. Eric did, too, then Pablo, the three of them in a row. Mathias was passing his water bottle around again. Amy kept taking pictures—of the hill, the pretty flowers, then of each of them, one after another. She told Mathias to smile, but he was peering up the hillside.

"Is that a tent?" he asked.

They turned to look. There was an orange square of fabric just visible, at the very top of the hill. It was billowing, sail-like, in the breeze. From this distance, with the rise of the hill partly blocking their view, it was hard to tell what it was. Stacy thought it looked like a kite, trapped in the flowering vines, but of course a tent made more sense. Before anyone could speak, while they were still peering up the hill, squinting against the sun, there came an odd noise from the jungle. They all heard it at the same time, while it was still relatively faint, and they turned, almost in unison, heads cocked, listening. It was a familiar sound, but for a few seconds none of them could identify it.

Jeff was the one who finally put a name to it. "A horse," he said.

And then Stacy could hear it, too: hoofbeats, approaching at a gallop down the narrow trail at their back.

Amy still had her camera out. Through her viewfinder, she watched the horse arrive; she took its picture as it burst into the clearing: a big brown horse, rearing to a stop before them. On its back was the Mayan man who'd approached them beside the well in the little village. It was the same man, but he seemed different now. In the village, he'd been calm and distant, even aloof, with something that felt almost condescending in his approach to them, a weary parent dealing with unmannered children. Now all this had vanished, replaced by an air of urgency, even panic. His white shirt and pants were splashed with green stains from riding so rapidly through the trees. He'd lost his hat, and sweat was shining on his bald head.

The horse, too, was agitated: lathered, snorting, rolling its eyes. It reared twice, frightening them, and they backed away, retreating farther into the clearing. The man began to shout, waving his arm. The horse had reins but no saddle; the man was riding bareback, his legs clinging to the big animal's flanks like a pair of pincers. The horse reared once more, and this time the man half-fell, half-jumped to the ground. He was still holding the reins, but the horse was backing away from him, jerking its head, trying to break free.

Amy took a picture of the ensuing tug-of-war, the man struggling to calm the horse as the animal pulled him, step by step, back toward the trail. It was only when she stopped peering through the viewfinder that she noticed the gun on the man's belt: a black pistol in a brown holster. He hadn't been wearing it in the village; she was certain of this. He'd put it on to come chase them. The horse was too frantic; the man couldn't calm it, and finally he just relinquished the reins. Instantly, the animal turned, galloped off into the jungle. They listened to it crashing through the trees, the sound of its hoofbeats gradually diminishing. Then the man was shouting at them again, waving his arms over his head, pointing back down the trail. It was hard to tell what he was trying to say. Amy wondered if it had something to do with the horse, if he somehow blamed them for the animal's frenzy.

"What does he want?" Stacy asked. Her voice sounded frightened—like a little girl's—and Amy turned to look at her. Stacy was holding Eric's arm, standing a little behind him. Eric was smiling at the Mayan, as if he thought the whole encounter must be some sort of joke and was waiting for the man to confess to this.

"He wants us to go back," Jeff said.

"Why?" Stacy asked.

"Maybe he wants money. Like a toll or something. Or for us to hire him as a guide." Jeff reached into his pants pocket, pulled out his wallet.

The man kept shouting, pointing vehemently back down the path.

Jeff removed a ten-dollar bill, held it out to him. "*¿Dinero?*" he said.

The man ignored this. He made a shooing motion with his hand, waving them out of the clearing. They all stood there, uncertain, no one moving. Jeff carefully folded the bill back into his wallet, returned the wallet to his pocket. After a few more seconds, the man stopped shouting; he was out of breath.

Mathias turned toward the flower-covered hill, cupped his hands around his mouth. "Henrich!" he yelled.

There was no answer, no movement on the hillside except the gentle billowing of that orange fabric. In the distance, there was the sound of hoofbeats again, coming closer. Either the man's horse was returning or another villager was about to join them.

"Why don't you hike up the hill, see if you can find him?" Jeff said to Mathias. "We'll wait here, try to sort this out."

Mathias nodded. He turned, started across the clearing. The Mayan began to shout again, and then, when Mathias didn't stop, the man pulled his pistol from its holster, raised the gun over his head, fired into the sky.

Stacy screamed, covering her mouth, backing away. Everyone else flinched, instinctively, half-ducking. Mathias turned to look, saw the man aiming the pistol at his chest now, and went perfectly still. The man waved at him, yelling something, and Mathias came back, his hands in the air, to join the others. Pablo, too, raised his hands, but then, when nobody else did, he slowly lowered them again.

The hoofbeats came closer and closer, and suddenly two more horsemen burst into the clearing. Their mounts were just as agitated as the first man's had been: white-eyed and snorting, sweat shining on their flanks. One of the horses was pale gray, the other black. Their riders dropped to the ground, neither of them making any attempt to hold on to their reins, and the horses immediately turned to gallop back into the jungle. These new arrivals were much younger than the bald man; they were dark-haired, leanly muscular. They had bows slung across their chests, and quivers of thin, fragile-looking arrows. One of them had a mustache. They began speaking with the first man, very rapidly, asking him questions. He still had his pistol pointed in Mathias's general direction, and as they talked, the other two men unslung their bows, each of them nocking an arrow.

"What the fuck?" Eric said. He sounded outraged.

"Quiet," Jeff ordered.

"They're—"

"Wait," Jeff said. "Wait and see."

Amy pointed her camera at the men, took another picture. She could tell it wasn't capturing the drama of the moment, that she'd have to back up to do this, so she could get not only the Mayan men with their weapons but also Jeff and the others, standing there, facing them, everyone looking so frightened now. She retreated a handful of steps, peering through her viewfinder. It felt safer like this, more distant, as if she were no longer part of this strange situation. Four more steps, and Jeff was in the frame, and Pablo, and Mathias, too, with his hands still raised. All she had to do was go a little farther and Stacy and Eric would appear; then she could take the picture and it would be exactly what she wanted. She took another step backward, then another, and suddenly the Mayans were shouting again, all three of them, at her now, the first man pointing his pistol, the other two drawing their bows. Jeff and the others were turning to stare at her in surprise—yes, there was Stacy now, on the right-hand side of the frame—and Amy took another step.

"Amy," Jeff said, and she almost stopped. She hesitated; she started to lower her camera. But she could tell she was nearly there, so she took one last step, and it was perfect: Eric was in the frame now, too. Amy pressed the button, heard it click. She was pleased with herself, still feeling weirdly outside the encounter, and liking the sensation. It was as she was lifting her eye from the viewfinder that she felt the odd pressure around her ankle, as if a hand were gripping it. She glanced down, and realized she'd backed completely across the clearing. What she felt was the flowering vine. A long green tendril was coiled around her ankle. She'd stepped right into a loop of it, and now somehow had pulled it taut.

There was a strange pause; the Mayan men stopped shouting. The two bows remained drawn, but the man with the pistol slowly lowered it. She could feel the others watching her, following her gaze toward her right foot, which had sunk ankle-deep into the vines, as if swallowed. She crouched to free it, and was just rising back up when she heard the Mayan men begin to shout again. They were yelling at her, and then they weren't—they were yelling at one another. An argument, it seemed, the two men with the bows turning against the bald man.

"Jeff," she called.

He raised his hand without looking at her, silencing her. "Don't move," he said.

So she didn't. The bald man was clutching his right ear with one hand, tugging at it, frowning and shaking his head, his left hand still gripping the pistol, pressing it against his thigh. He didn't seem to want to hear what the other two had to say. He pointed to Amy, then the others; he waved down the trail. But there was already something halfhearted in his gestures, the prescience of defeat. Amy could tell that he knew he wasn't going to get his way. She could see him being worn down, see him giving in. He fell silent; the men with the bows did, too. They stood staring at Jeff and Mathias, at Eric and Stacy and the Greek. And at her, too. Then the bald man raised his pistol, aimed it at Jeff, at his chest. He made a shooing motion with his other hand, but now it was in the opposite direction, toward Amy, toward the hill behind her.

No one moved.

The bald man began to shout, waving toward the hill. He lowered his pistol slightly, fired a bullet into the dirt at Jeff's feet. Everyone jumped, started to back away. Pablo had his hands in the air again. The other men were shouting, too, swinging their bows back and forth, aiming first at one of them, then another, herding them, step by step, toward Amy. Jeff and the others were walking backward; they weren't watching where they were going. When they reached the edge of the clearing, they hesitated, each of them, feeling the vines against their feet and legs. They glanced down, stopped. Eric was beside Amy, on her left. Pablo was to her right. Then the others: Stacy, Mathias, Jeff. And beyond Jeff, the path. This was where the bald man was pointing now, gesturing for them to start up it, to climb the hill. His expression looked oddly stricken, close to tears—no, he'd actually begun to cry. He wiped at his face with his sleeve as he waved them onward. It was all so peculiar, so impossible to comprehend, and no one said a word. They moved to the path, Jeff leading the way, the others following.

And then, still silent, all in a line, they began the slow climb up the hill.

Eric was in the rear. He kept glancing over his shoulder as he walked. The Mayan men were watching them climb, the bald one using his hand to shield his eyes against the sun. There were no trees on the hill, just the vine growing over everything, thick coils of it, with its dark green leaves, its bright red flowers. The sun was pouring its heat upon them—there was no shade anywhere—and behind them, down the slope, stood three armed men. None of this made any sense. At first, the bald man had tried to tell them to go back; then he'd ordered them forward. The men with the bows had had something to do with this, clearly; they'd argued with the other man, changed his mind. But it still didn't make any sense. The six of them climbed the trail, sweating with the exertion, walking in total silence, because they were scared and there was nothing for any of them to say.

At some point, they'd have to come back down the hill and cross the clearing, take the narrow path to the fields and then the wider path to the road, but how they'd manage to do this, Eric couldn't guess. It was possible, he supposed, that the archaeologists might be able to explain what had happened. Maybe it was even something simple, something easily solved, something they'd all be laughing about a few minutes from now. A misunderstanding. A miscommunication. A mistake. Eric tried to think of other words that began with *mis,* tried to remember what the prefix meant. He was going to be teaching English in a few weeks, and this was the sort of thing he ought to know. Wrong, he guessed, or bad—something like that—but he wasn't certain. And he'd need to be certain, too, because there'd probably be students who would know;

there were always two or three like that, ready to catch their teachers in an error, eager for the chance. There were books Eric had meant to read this summer, books he'd assured the head of his department he'd already read, but the summer was essentially over now, and he hadn't even glanced at them, not one.

Misstep. Misplace. Misconstrue.

That last one was a good one. Eric wished he knew more words like that, wished he could be the sort of teacher who effortlessly used them, his students straining to understand him, learning just through listening, but he knew this wasn't who he'd ever be. He'd be the boy-man, the baseball coach, the one who winked and smiled at his students' pranks, a favorite among them, probably, but not really much of a teacher at all. Not someone from whom they'd ever learn anything important, that is.

Mischief. Misanthrope. Misconception.

Eric was growing a little less frightened with each step he took, and he was glad for this, because for a moment or two there, he'd been very frightened indeed. When the bald man fired into the dirt at Jeff's feet, Eric had been glancing toward Stacy, making sure she was all right. He hadn't seen the man lower his aim; he'd heard the pistol go off, and for an instant he'd thought the man had shot Jeff, shot him in the chest, killed him. Then everything had happened so fast—they were herded backward, prodded up the trail—and only now was his heart beginning to slow a bit. Someone would figure something out. Or the archaeologists would help them. And all this would come to nothing.

Misrepresent. Mislead. Misguide.

"Henrich!" Mathias called, and they stopped, staring up the hill, waiting for a response.

None came. They hesitated a few more seconds, then started to walk again.

It was a tent. Eric could see it clearly now as they climbed higher, a bright traffic-cone orange, looking a little worse for wear. It must've been there for quite some time, because the vines had already managed to grow up its aluminum poles, using them like a trellis. A four-person tent, Eric guessed. Its doorway was facing away from them.

"Hello?" Jeff called, and they stopped again to listen.

They were close enough now that they could hear the breeze tugging at the tent, a flapping noise, like a sail might make. But there was nothing else, no sound at all, nor any sign of people. In this quiet, Eric noticed for the first time what Stacy had realized earlier: the mosquitoes had vanished. The tiny black flies, too. This ought to have offered him at least a small sense of relief, but for some reason it didn't. It had the exact opposite effect, in fact: it made him anxious, bringing back an odd echo of that fear he'd felt in the clearing as he'd turned, expecting to see Jeff's body lying there, the gunshot echoing back at him from the tree line. It seemed strange to be standing here, sweating, halfway up a hill in the midst of the jungle, and not be harassed by those little insects. And Eric didn't want to feel strange just now; he wanted everything to make sense, to be predictable. He wanted someone to tell him why the bugs had vanished, why the men had forced them up the hill, and why they still stood down there at the base of the trail, staring after them, their weapons in their hands.

Misery didn't count. Nor *miser*. Eric wondered briefly if they had the same root. Latin, he guessed. Which was yet another thing he ought to know but didn't.

The cut on his elbow had begun to ache. He could feel his heart beating inside it again, a little slower now, but still too fast. He tried to picture the archaeologists, all of them laughing over this strange situation, which would turn out to be not so strange after all, once everything had been properly explained. There'd be a first-aid kit in the orange tent, Eric assumed. Someone would clean his wound for him, cover it with a white bandage. And then, when they got back to Cancún—he smiled at the thought of this—he'd buy a rubber snake, hide it under Pablo's towel.

The vines covered everything but the path and the tent's orange fabric. In some places, they grew thinly enough that Eric could glimpse the soil underneath—rockier than he would've expected, dry, almost desertlike—but in others, they seemed to fold back upon themselves, piling layer upon layer, forming waist-high mounds, tangled knoll-like profusions of green. And everywhere, hanging like bells from the vines, were those brilliant bloodred flowers.

Eric glanced back down the hill again, just in time to see a fourth man arrive. He was on a bicycle, dressed in white, like the others, a straw hat on his head. "There's another one," Eric said.

Everyone stopped, turned to stare. As they watched, a fifth man appeared, then a sixth, also on bicycles. The new arrivals all had bows slung over their shoulders. There was a brief consultation; the bald man seemed to be in charge. He talked for a while, gesturing with his hands, and everyone listened. Then he pointed up the hill and the other men turned to peer at them. Eric felt the impulse to look away, but this was silly, of course, a "Don't stare; it's rude" reflex that had nothing to do with what was happening here. He watched the bald man wave in either direction, the clipped gestures of a military officer, and then the men with bows started off along the clearing, moving quickly, two one way, three the other, leaving the bald man alone at the base of the trail.

"What are they doing?" Amy asked, but nobody answered. Nobody knew.

A child emerged from the jungle. It was the smaller of the two boys who'd followed them, the one they'd left behind in the field. He stood next to the bald man, and they both stared up at them. The bald man rested his hand on the boy's shoulder. It made them look as if they were posing for a photograph.

"Maybe we should run back down," Eric said. "Quick. While there's just him and the kid. We could rush them."

"He's got a gun, Eric," Stacy said.

Amy nodded. "And he could call the others."

They were silent again, all of them staring down the hill, struggling to think, but if there was a solution to their present situation, no one could find it.

Mathias cupped his hands, shouted once more toward the tent: "Henrich!"

The tent continued to billow softly in the breeze. It wasn't that far from the base of the hill to the top, a hundred and fifty yards, no farther, and they were more than halfway up it now. Close enough, certainly, for anyone who might be present there to hear them shouting. But no one appeared; no one responded. And, as the seconds slipped past and the silence prolonged itself, Eric had to admit to himself what everyone else was probably thinking, too, though none of them had yet found the courage to say it out loud: there wasn't anyone there.

"Come on," Jeff said, waving them forward.

And they resumed their upward march.

The hill grew flat at its top, forming a wide plateau, as if a giant hand had come down out of the sky and given it a gentle pat in those still-malleable moments following its creation. It was larger than Jeff had expected. The trail ran past the orange tent, and then, fifty feet farther along, it opened out into a small clearing of rocky ground. There was a second tent here, a blue one. It looked just as weathered as the orange one. There was no one about, of course, and Jeff had the sense, even in that first glimpse, that this had been true for some time.

"Hello?" he called again. And then the six of them stood there, just a few yards short of the orange tent, going through the motions of waiting for an answer without really expecting one to come.

It hadn't been that arduous a climb, but they were all a little out of breath. Nobody spoke for a while, or moved; they were too hot, too sweaty, too frightened. Mathias got out his water bottle and they passed it around, finishing it off. Eric and Stacy and Amy sat down in the dirt, leaning against one another. Mathias stepped over to the tent. Its flap was zipped shut, and it took him a few moments to figure out how to open it. Jeff went over to help him. *Zzzzzzzzzzip.* Then they both stuck their heads inside. There were three sleeping bags unrolled on the floor. An oil lamp. Two backpacks. What looked like a plastic toolbox. A gallon jug of water, half-full. A pair of hiking boots. Despite this evidence of occupation, it was clear that no one had been here for quite some time. The musty air would've been evidence enough, but even more striking was the flowering vine. Somehow it had gotten inside the sealed tent and had taken root, growing on some things, leaving others untouched. The hiking boots were nearly covered in it. One of the backpacks was hanging open and the vine was spilling out of it.

Jeff and Mathias pulled their heads from the tent, looked at each other, didn't speak.

"What's inside?" Eric called.

"Nothing," Jeff said. "Some sleeping bags."

Mathias was starting off across the hilltop, heading for the blue tent, and Jeff followed him, struggling to make sense of their situation. Something, obviously, had happened to the archaeologists. Perhaps there'd been some sort of conflict with the Mayans, and the Mayans had attacked them. But then why would they have ordered them up the hill? Wouldn't they have wanted to send them away? It was possible, of course, that the Mayans were worried they'd already seen too much, even from the base of the hill. But then why not kill them outright? It would've been relatively easy to cover this up, Jeff assumed. No one knew where they were. Just the Greeks, maybe, if Pablo had, in fact, written them a note before he left. But even so, it seemed simple enough. Kill them, bury them in the jungle. Feign ignorance if someone ever came searching. Jeff forced himself to remember his fears about their taxi driver, the same fears, unfounded, as it turned out. So why shouldn't this present situation prove to be equally benign?

Mathias unzipped the flap to the blue tent, stuck his head inside. Jeff leaned forward to look, too. It was the same thing: sleeping bags, backpacks, camping equipment. Again, there was that musty smell, and the vines growing on some things but not on others. They pulled their heads out, zipped the flap shut.

Ten yards beyond the tent, there was a hole cut into the dirt. It had a makeshift windlass constructed beside it, a horizontal barrel with a hand crank welded to its base. Rope was coiled thickly around the barrel. From the barrel, it passed over a small wheel, which hung from a sort of sawhorse that straddled the hole's mouth. Then it dropped straight down into the earth. Jeff and Mathias stepped warily to the hole, looked into it. The hole was rectangular—ten feet by six feet— and very deep; Jeff couldn't see its bottom. The mine shaft, he supposed. There was a slight draft rising from it, an eerily chilly exhalation from the darkness.

The others had gotten to their feet now, followed them across the hilltop. Everyone took turns peering into the hole.

"There's no one here," Stacy said.

Jeff nodded. He was still thinking. Perhaps it was something with the ruins? Something religious? A tribal violation? But it wasn't that sort of ruins, was it? It was an old mining camp, a shaft cut into the earth.

"I don't think they've been here for a while," Amy said.

"So what do we do?" Eric asked.

They all looked to Jeff, even Mathias. Jeff shrugged. "The trail keeps going." He waved past the hole, and everyone turned to follow his gesture. The clearing ended just a few yards from them; then the vines resumed, and in the midst of the vines was the path. It wound its way to the edge of the hilltop, vanished over it.

"Should we take it?" Stacy asked.

"I'm not going back the way we came," Amy said.

So they started along the path, single file again, with Jeff taking the lead. For a while, he couldn't glimpse the base of the hill, but then the trail tilted downward, more precipitously here than on their route up, and Jeff saw exactly what he'd been fearing he would see. The others were startled; they stopped all at once, staring, and he stopped, too. But he wasn't surprised. As soon as he'd heard the bald Mayan sending the bowmen running along the clearing, he'd known. One of them was standing at the bottom of the trail, staring up at them, awaiting their approach.

"Fuck," Eric said.

"What do we do?" Stacy asked.

No one responded. It looked from here as if the jungle had been chopped down all the way around the base of the hill, isolating it in a ring of barren soil. The Mayans had spread themselves out along this ring, surrounding them. Jeff knew that there was no point continuing down the hill—the man obviously wasn't going to let them pass—but he couldn't think of any other course to pursue. So he shrugged and waved them forward. "We'll see," he said.

The trail was much steeper here; there were short stretches where they had to drop onto their rear ends and slide down, one after the other. It was going to be a hard climb back up, but Jeff tried not to think of this. As they got closer, the Mayan man slid the bow off his shoulder, nocked an arrow. He shouted toward them, shaking his head, waving them away. Then he called out to his left, yelling what sounded like someone's name. A few seconds later, another one of the bowmen came jogging into view along the clearing.

The two men waited for them at the bottom of the hill, bows taut.

They all stopped on the edge of the clearing, wiping the sweat from their faces, and Pablo said something in Greek. It had the upward lilt of a question, but of course no one could understand him. He repeated it, the same phrase, then gave up.

"So," Amy said.

Jeff didn't know what to do. He believed there was a difference between aiming an arrow at someone and letting that arrow fly—a significant difference, he assumed—and he toyed briefly with the idea of exploring this distinction. He could take a step out into the clearing, and then another, and then another, and at some point the two men would either have to shoot him or let him pass. Perhaps it was merely a question of courage, and he tried to gird himself for the venturing of it, was nearly there, he felt, but then another bowman came jogging toward them from their left, and the moment passed. Jeff took out his wallet, knowing it was pointless; he was simply going through the motions. He emptied it of bills and held the money toward the Mayans.

There was no reaction.

"Let's rush them," Eric suggested again. "All at once."

"Shut up, Eric," Stacy said.

But he didn't listen. "Or go make shields. If we had some shields, we could—"

Another man came running toward them along the clearing, heavier than the others, bearded, someone they hadn't seen before. He was carrying a rifle.

"Oh my God," Amy said.

Jeff put the money back in his wallet, returned the wallet to his pocket. The vine had invaded the clearing here, formed an outpost in its midst. Ten feet in front of the path, there was one of those odd knob-like growths, this one a little smaller than the others, knee-high, thick with flowers. The Mayans had arranged themselves on the far side of it, with their drawn bows. And now the man with the rifle joined them.

"Let's go back up the hill," Stacy said.

But Jeff was staring at the vines, the isolated island, knowing already what it was, knowing it deep, without quite being conscious of this knowledge.

"I wanna go back," Stacy said.

Jeff stepped forward. It was ten feet, and it took him four strides. He walked with his hands held up in front of him, calming the men, trying to show them that he meant no harm. They didn't shoot; he'd known they wouldn't, that they'd allow him to see what was beneath the vines, what he already knew but wasn't letting himself know. Yes, they wanted him to see it.

"Jeff," Amy called.

He ignored her, crouching beside the mound. He reached out, sinking his hand into the flowers, parting them. He grasped a stalk, tugged, pulled it free, glimpsed a tennis shoe, a sock, the lower part of a man's shin.

"What is it?" Amy asked.

Jeff turned, stared at Mathias. Mathias knew, too; Jeff could see it in his eyes. The German stepped forward, crouched beside him, started to pull at the vines, gently at first, then more aggressively, tearing at them, a low moan beginning to rise from his chest. Twenty feet away, the Mayans watched. Another shoe was revealed, another leg. A pair of jeans, a belt buckle, a black T-shirt. And then, finally, a young man's face. It was Mathias's face, only different: it had the same features, the family resemblance vivid even now, with some of Henrich's flesh oddly eaten away, so that his cheekbone was visible, the white socket of his left eye.

"Oh Jesus," Amy said. "No."

Jeff held up his hand, silencing her. Mathias crouched over his brother's body, rocking slightly, that moaning coming and going. The T-shirt was only black, Jeff realized, because it had been stained that color: it was stiff with dried blood. And sticking out of Henrich's chest, pointing up through the thick vines, were three slender arrows. Jeff rested his hand on Mathias's shoulder. "Easy," he whispered. "All right? Easy and slow. We'll stand up and we'll walk away. We'll walk back up the hill."

"It's my brother," Mathias said.

"I know."

"They killed him."

Jeff nodded. His hand was still on Mathias's shoulder, and he could feel the German's muscles clenching through his shirt. "Easy," he said again.

"Why . . ."

"I don't know."

"He was—"

"Shh," Jeff said. "Not here. Up the hill, okay?"

Mathias seemed to be having trouble breathing. He kept struggling to inhale, but nothing went very deep. Jeff didn't let go of his shoulder. Finally, the German nodded, and then they both stood up. Stacy and Amy were holding hands, looking stricken, staring down at Henrich's corpse. Stacy had started to cry, very softly. Eric had his arm around her.

The Mayans kept their weapons raised—arrows nocked, bows taut, rifle shouldered—and watched in silence as Jeff and the others turned to start back up the hill.

The climb helped some—the physical demands of it, the need to concentrate on the steeper stretches, where they almost had to crawl at times, pulling themselves forward with their hands—and as Stacy moved slowly up the hill, she gradually managed to stop crying. She kept glancing back down toward the clearing as she went; she tried not to, but she couldn't help it. She was worried the men were going to come chasing after them. They'd killed Mathias's brother, so it only seemed logical that they'd kill her, too. Kill all six of them, let the vines grow over their bodies. But the men just stood there in the center of the clearing, staring after them.

At the top, things got hard again. Amy started crying, and then Stacy had to, too. They sat on the ground and held hands and wept. Eric crouched beside Stacy. He said things like "It's gonna be okay." Or "We'll be all right." Or "Shh, now, shh." Just words, nonsense really, little phrases to stroke and soothe her, and the fear in his face made her sob all the harder. But the sun burned down upon them and there was no shade to be found and she was worn-out from the climb, and after awhile she began to feel so stunned from it all that she couldn't even cry anymore. When she stopped, Amy did, too.

Jeff and Mathias had wandered off across the hilltop. They were standing on the far side of it, staring down toward the clearing, talking together. Pablo had disappeared into the blue tent.

"Is there any water?" Amy asked.

Eric dug through his pack, pulled out a bottle. They took turns drinking from it.

"It's gonna be okay," he said again.

"How?" Stacy asked, hating herself for speaking. She knew she shouldn't be asking questions like that. She needed to be quiet and let Eric build this dream for them.

Eric thought for a moment, struggling. "Maybe when the sun sets, we can go back down, sneak past them in the darkness."

They drank some more water, considering this. It was too hot to think, and there was a persistent buzzing in Stacy's ears, like static, but higher-pitched. She realized she should get out of the sun, crawl into one of the tents and lie down, but she was frightened of the tents. She knew that whoever had set them up so carefully here upon the hilltop was almost certainly dead now. If Henrich was dead, then the archaeologists must be, too. Stacy couldn't see any way around this.

Eric tried again. "Or we can always just wait them out," he said. "The Greeks will come sooner or later."

"How do you know?" Amy asked.

"Pablo left them a note."

"But how can you be sure?"

"He copied the map, didn't he?"

Amy didn't say anything. Stacy sat there, wishing she'd speak again, that she'd somehow manage to clarify this question, either refute Eric's logic or accept it, but Amy remained silent, peering off across the hilltop at Jeff and Mathias. There was no way to tell, of course. Pablo might've left a note or he might not have. The only way they'd know for certain was if the Greeks were eventually to show up.

"I've never seen a dead body before," Eric said.

Amy and Stacy were silent. How could they possibly respond to a statement like that?

"You'd think something would've eaten him, wouldn't you? Come out of the jungle and—"

"Stop it," Stacy said.

"But it seems odd, doesn't it? He's been there long enough for those vines to—"

"Please, Eric."

"And where are the others? Where are the archaeologists?"

Stacy reached out and touched his knee. "Just stop, okay? Stop talking."

Jeff and Mathias were coming back toward them. Mathias was holding his hands out in front of himself, as if they were covered in paint and he was trying not to get it on his clothes. As they came closer, Stacy saw that his hands and wrists had turned a deep raw-meat red; they look scarred.

"What happened?" Eric asked.

Jeff and Mathias crouched beside them. Jeff reached for the water bottle, poured a tiny bit on Mathias's hands; then Mathias rubbed at them with his shirt, grimacing.

"There's something in the plants," Jeff said. "When he tore them off his brother, he got their sap on his hands. It's acidic. It's burned his skin."

They all peered down at Mathias's hands. Jeff handed the water back to Stacy. She took off her bandanna, started to tilt the bottle over it, thinking the wet cloth might cool her head some, but Jeff stopped her.

"Don't," he said. "We need to save it."

"Save it?" she asked. She felt stupid with the heat: she didn't know what he meant.

He nodded. "We don't have that much. We'll each need a half gallon a day, at least. That's three gallons total, every day. We'll have to figure out a way to catch the rain." He glanced up at the sky, as if searching for clouds, but there weren't any. It had rained every afternoon since they'd arrived in Mexico, and now, when they needed it, the sky was perfectly clear. "We have to get organized," Jeff said. "Now, while we're still fresh."

The others just stared at him.

"We can last without food. It's water that matters. We'll have to keep out of the sun, spend as much time as we can under the tents."

Stacy felt sick, listening to him. He was acting as if they were going to be here for some time, as if they were trapped here, and the idea filled her with panic. She had the urge to cover her ears with her hands; she wanted him to stop talking. "Can't we sneak away when it gets dark?" she asked. "Eric said we could sneak away."

Jeff shook his head. He waved across the hilltop, toward where he and Mathias had been standing. "They keep coming," he said. "More and more of them. They're all armed, and the bald one sends them out along the clearing. They're surrounding us."

"Why don't they just kill us?" Eric asked.

"I don't know. It seems like it's something to do with the hill. Once you step onto the hill, you're not allowed to step off it. Something like that. They won't step on it themselves, but now that we're on it, they won't let us leave. They'll shoot us if we try. So we have to figure out a way to survive until someone comes and finds us."

"Who?" Amy asked.

Jeff shrugged. "The Greeks, maybe—that would be quickest. Or else, when we don't come home, our parents will—"

"We're not supposed to leave for another week," Amy said.

Jeff nodded.

"And then they'd have to come searching for us."

Again, he nodded.

"So you're talking—what, a month?"

He shrugged. "Maybe."

Amy looked appalled by this. Her voice jumped a notch. "We can't live here for a month, Jeff."

"If we try to leave, they'll shoot us. That's the one thing we know for certain."

"But what will we eat? How will we—"

"Maybe the Greeks will come," Jeff said. "They could come tomorrow, for all we know."

"And then what? They'll just end up trapped here with us."

Jeff shook his head. "We'll keep someone posted at the base of the hill. To warn them away."

"But those men won't let us. They'll force them—"

Again, Jeff shook his head. "I don't think so," he said. "It wasn't until you stepped beyond the clearing that they made us climb the hill. In the beginning, they were trying to keep us away. I think they'll try to stop the Greeks from coming up, too. All we have to do is figure out a way to communicate to them, to let them know what's happened, so that they can go get help."

"Pablo," Eric said.

Jeff nodded. "If we can get him to understand, then he can warn them off."

They all turned and stared at Pablo. He'd emerged from the blue tent and was wandering around the hilltop. He seemed to be talking to himself, very softly, muttering. He had his hands in his pants pockets, his shoulders hunched. He didn't sense them watching him.

"Planes might fly over, too," Jeff said. "We can signal to them with something reflective. Or maybe pull up some of the vines, dry them out, start a fire. Three fires in a triangle—that's supposed to be a signal for help."

He stopped talking then; he didn't have any more ideas. And neither Stacy nor the others had any ideas at all, so they just sat without speaking for a stretch. In the silence, Stacy gradually became aware of a strange chirping sound—steady, insistent, barely audible. A bird, she thought, then knew immediately she was wrong. No one else seemed to notice the noise, and she was turning to track its source when Pablo started yelling. He was jumping up and down beside the mine shaft, pointing into it.

"What's he doing?" Amy asked.

Stacy watched him pressing his hand to his head, to his ear, as if he were miming talking on a phone, and she sprang to her feet, started quickly toward him. "Hurry," she said to the others, waving for them to follow. She'd realized suddenly what that steady chirping was: some-how—miraculously, inexplicably—there was a cell phone ringing at the bottom of the hole.

Amy didn't believe it. She could hear the noise coming from the hole, and—along with the others—she had to admit it sounded like a cell phone, yet even so, she had no faith in it. Jeff had told her not to pack her own phone before they left; it would be too expensive to use in Mexico. But that didn't mean there weren't local networks, of course, and why shouldn't it be possible that what they were hearing was a phone linked to one of these? It should be possible—there was no reason for it not to be possible—and Amy struggled to convince herself of this. It wasn't working, though. Inside, in her heart, she'd already dropped into a place of doom, and the plaintive beeping coming from the darkness wasn't enough to pull her free. When she peered into the hole, what she imagined was not a phone calling out to them, but a baby bird, open-beaked, begging to be fed—*chirrrp . . . chirrrp . . . chirrrp*—a thing of need rather than assistance.

The others were enthusiastic, however, and who was Amy to question this? She stayed silent; she feigned hope along with the rest of them.

Pablo had already uncoiled a short length of rope from the windlass. He was wrapping it around his chest, tying it into a knot. It seemed he wanted them to lower him into the hole.

"He won't be able to answer it," Eric said. "We have to send someone who speaks Spanish." He reached for the rope, but Pablo wouldn't relinquish it. He was tying one knot after another across his chest: big, sloppy tangles of hemp. It didn't look like he knew what he was doing.

"It doesn't matter," Jeff said. "He can bring it back up, and we'll try calling from here."

The chirping stopped, and they stood over the hole, waiting, listening. After a long moment, it started up again. They all smiled at one another, and Pablo moved to the edge of the shaft, eager to begin his descent. The flowering vine had twined itself around the windlass, growing on the rope, the axle, the crank, the sawhorse and its little wheel; Jeff pulled much of it off, careful not to get the sap on his skin. Mathias had vanished into the blue tent. When he reappeared, he was carrying an oil lamp and a box of matches. He set the lamp on the ground beside the hole, scratched one of the matches into flame, and carefully lighted the wick. Then he handed the lamp to Pablo.

The windlass was a primitive piece of equipment: jerry-built, flimsy-looking. It sat beside the shaft on a small steel platform, which appeared to have been bolted somehow into the rock-hard dirt. Its barrel was mounted on an axle that was rusting in places and in definite need of greasing. The crank didn't have a brake to it; if it became necessary to hold it in place midway down or up, this would have to be accomplished by brute strength. Amy didn't believe the apparatus could support Pablo's weight; she thought he'd step into the open space above the hole and the entire contraption would give way. He'd drop into the darkness—fall and fall and fall—and they'd never see him again. But, after the exchange of many hand signals and gestures and pats of encouragement, when he finally began his descent, the windlass groaned, settling into its mount, and then started to turn, creaking loudly as Jeff and Eric strained against its hand crank, slowly lowering the Greek into the shaft.

It was working. And, despite herself, Amy felt her heart lift. Maybe it was a cell phone after all. Pablo would find it down there in the darkness; they'd hoist him back up and then call for help: the police, the American embassy, their parents. The beeping had stopped once more, and this time it didn't resume, but it didn't matter. It was down there. Amy was beginning to believe now—she wanted to believe, had given herself permission to believe—they were going to be saved. She stood beside the hole, peering over its edge, with Stacy on her right and Mathias across from her, watching Pablo drop foot by foot into the earth. His oil lamp illuminated the walls of the shaft: the dirt was black and pitted with rocks toward the top, but it became brown and then tan and then a deep orange-yellow as he descended. Ten feet, fifteen, twenty, twenty-five, and they still couldn't see the bottom. Pablo smiled up at them, dangling, one hand reaching out to steady himself against the shaft's wall. Amy and Stacy waved to him. But not Mathias. Mathias was staring at the slowly uncoiling rope.

"Stop!" he shouted suddenly, and everyone jumped.

Jeff and Eric were straining against the crank, both of them sweating already, their hair sticking to their foreheads. Amy could see the muscles standing out on Jeff's neck—taut, tendoned—and it gave her a sense of the immense tension on the rope, gravity grasping at the Greek, dragging him downward.

Mathias was growing frantic now, yelling, "Pull him up! Pull him up!"

Jeff and Eric hesitated, uncertain. "What?" Eric said, blinking at him stupidly.

"The vine," Mathias shouted, his voice urgent, waving for them to start reeling Pablo back up. "The rope."

And then they saw it. Jeff had stripped most of the vine off the windlass, but not all of it. The tendrils he'd left behind had burrowed their way into the spool of rope and now, as the windlass turned, they were being crushed, their milky sap oozing out, darkening the rope's hemp, eating away at it.

Pablo shouted up to them, a short string of Greek words, a question, and Amy had a brief glimpse of him, swinging gently back and forth there, twenty-five feet down the shaft, the oil lamp in his hand; then she was rushing with Stacy and Mathias toward the crank, all of them struggling to help, getting in one another's way, putting their weight into it, the sap visibly burning into the rope now—implacably, too fast, faster than they could work. Pablo was just beginning to bump his way upward when there was an abrupt, gut-dropping jerk, and they fell forward onto one another, the windlass spinning wildly behind them, free of its weight. There was a long silence—too long, far too long—and then a thump they seemed to feel more than hear, a jump in the earth beneath them, which was followed an instant later by the shattering pop of the lamp. They scrambled to the hole, peered into it, but there was nothing for them to see.

Darkness. Silence.

"Pablo?" Eric called, his voice echoing down the shaft.

And then, sounding impossibly far away, but somehow close, too—suffocatingly close—as if it were coming from inside Amy's own body, the Greek began to scream.

The screaming filled Eric with a sense of panic. Pablo was down in the hole, in the darkness, in terrible pain, and Eric couldn't think what to do, where to turn, how to make it better. They needed to help him, and it was taking too long. It ought to be happening now, instantly, but it wasn't; it couldn't. They had to come up with a plan first, and none of them seemed to know how to do this. Stacy just stood beside the windlass, wide-eyed, biting her hand. Amy was peering down into the hole. "Pablo?" she kept calling. "Pablo?" She was shouting, but even so, it was hard to hear her over his screams, which refused to stop, which went on and on and on, without diminishment or pause.

Mathias ran off toward the orange tent, disappeared inside. Jeff was pulling the rope back up from the shaft. He uncoiled it from the windlass, spreading it out in big looping circles across the little clearing. Then he began to work down its length, carefully removing all traces of the vine from it, examining the rope foot by foot, searching for sections where the sap might've weakened the hemp. It was a slow process, and he was going about it in an excruciatingly methodical manner, as if there were no rush at all, as if he couldn't even hear the Greek's screams. Eric stood beside him, too stunned to be of any assistance, motionless, yet feeling as if he were running inside—in full, headlong flight—his heart beating itself into a blur behind his ribs. And the screaming wouldn't stop.

"See if you can find a knife," Jeff said.

Eric stared down at him. *A knife?* The word hung in his head, inert, as if it belonged to a foreign language. How was he supposed to find a knife?

"Check the tents," Jeff said. He didn't look up at him; he kept his gaze focused on the rope, crouched low over it, searching out the burned spots.

Eric went to the blue tent, unzipped its flap, stepped inside. It smelled musty, like an attic, the air still and hot. The blue nylon filtered the sunlight, muting it, giving everything a dreamlike, watery tint. There were four sleeping bags, three of them unrolled, looking as if they'd only recently disgorged their owners' bodies. *Dead now,* Eric thought, and pushed the words aside. There was a transistor radio, and he had to resist the impulse to turn it on, to see if it worked, if he could find a station, music maybe, something to drown out Pablo's screams. There were two backpacks, one dark green, one black, and he crouched beside the first of them, began to rifle through it, feeling like a thief, an old instinct, from another world entirely, that sense of transgression inherent in handling a stranger's belongings. *Dead now,* he thought again, summoning the words this time, searching for courage in them, but they didn't make it any better, only turned it into a different sort of violation. The green backpack seemed to belong to a man, the black one to a woman. Other people's clothes: he could smell cigarette smoke on the man's T-shirts, perfume on the woman's. He wondered if they belonged to the woman whom Mathias's brother had met on the beach, the one whose promised presence had drawn them all here—doomed them, perhaps.

The vine was growing on some of the objects: thin green tendrils of it, with tiny pale red flowers, almost pink. It was more prominent in the woman's pack than the man's, twining itself among her cotton blouses, her socks, her dirt-stained jeans. He found a windbreaker in the man's backpack, gray, with blue stripes on the sleeves, a double of one he himself owned, hanging safely back in his closet at his parents' house, so out of reach now, awaiting his return. *A knife,* he had to remind himself, and he turned away from the tangle of clothes, searching through other pockets, unzipping them, emptying their contents onto the tent's floor. A camera, still loaded with film. Half a dozen spiral notebooks—

journals, it looked like—filled nearly to capacity with the man's jagged handwriting, blue ink, black ink, even red in places, but all in a language Eric not only couldn't decipher but couldn't even recognize: Dutch perhaps, or something Scandinavian. A deck of playing cards. A first-aid kit. A Frisbee. A tube of sunblock. A folded pair of eyeglasses with wire rims. A bottle of vitamins. An empty canteen. A flashlight. But no *knife.*

Eric emerged from the tent, carrying the flashlight, squinting at the sun's sudden brightness, that sense of space abruptly opening around him after the airless confines of the tent. He turned on the flashlight, realized it didn't work. He shook it, tried again: nothing. Pablo stopped screaming—for the space of two deep breaths—then he started up again. The stopping was almost as bad as the screaming, Eric decided, then immediately changed his mind: the stopping was worse. He dropped the flashlight to the ground, saw that Mathias had reappeared, bringing a second oil lamp from the orange tent, a large knife, another first-aid kit. He and Jeff were busily cutting the burned sections from the rope, working as a team, silently, efficiently. Mathias would cut away the weak spots; then Jeff would tie the rope back together again, grimacing as he tugged the knots tight. Eric stood above them, watching. He felt stupid: he should've taken the first-aid kit from the blue tent, too, should've at least checked to see what was inside. He wasn't thinking. He wanted to help, wanted to stop Pablo's screams, but he was stupid and useless and there was no way to change this. He felt the urge to pace, yet he just kept standing there, staring, instead. Stacy and Amy looked exactly like he felt: frantic, anxious, immobile. They all watched Jeff and Mathias work at the rope, cutting, tying, tugging. It was taking so long, so impossibly long.

"I'll go," Eric said. It wasn't something he'd thought out before speaking; it emerged from his panic, from his need to hurry things along. "I'll go down and get him."

Jeff glanced up at him; he seemed surprised. "That's okay," he said. "I can do it."

Jeff's voice sounded so calm, so bizarrely unruffled, that for an instant Eric had difficulty understanding his words. It was as if he first had to translate them into his own state of terror. Eric shook his head. "I'm lighter," he said. "And I know him better."

Jeff considered these two points, seemed to see their wisdom. He shrugged. "We'll make a sling for him," he said. "You may have to help him into it. Then we'll pull it up. After we get him out, we'll drop the rope back down and pull you up, too."

Eric nodded. It sounded so simple, so straightforward, and he was trying to believe that it would be like that, wanting to believe it, but not quite accomplishing it. He felt the urge to pace again, and only managed to hold himself still through a jaw-tightening act of will.

Pablo stopped screaming. One breath, two breaths, three breaths, then he started up again.

"Talk to him, Amy," Jeff said.

Amy looked frightened by this prospect. "Talk to him?" she asked.

Jeff motioned her toward the hole. "Just stick your head over the side. Let him see you. Let him know we haven't abandoned him."

"What should I say?" Amy asked, still looking scared.

"Anything—soothing things. He can't understand you anyway. It's just the sound of your voice."

Amy moved to the hole. She dropped to her hands and knees, leaned forward over the shaft. "Pablo?" she called. "We're coming to get you. We're fixing the rope, and then Eric's coming to get you."

She kept going on like this, describing how it would happen, step by step, how they'd help him into the sling and pull him back up to the surface, and after awhile Pablo stopped screaming. Jeff and Mathias were almost done; they'd reached the last section of rope. Jeff tied the final knot, then pulled on one end while Mathias held on to the other, the two of them using all their weight, a momentary tug-of-war, tightening the knot, testing its strength. There were five splices on the rope now. The knots didn't look very strong, but Eric tried not to notice this. It felt good to be the one going, the one doing, and if he thought too long about the knots, about their apparent tenuousness, he knew he might end up changing his mind.

Mathias was winding the rope back onto the windlass, double-checking it for burned spots as he went. He threaded the end of it back over the sawhorse's little metal wheel. Then Jeff fashioned a sling for Eric, helped him slide it over his head, tucking it snugly under his armpits.

"It's going to be all right, Pablo," Amy was yelling. "He's coming. He's almost there."

Stacy crouched to light the second oil lamp, then handed it to Eric, its flame flickering weakly in the tiny glass globe.

Eric was standing beside the hole now, staring into the darkness.

Mathias and Jeff positioned themselves behind the crank, leaning against its handle. The rope went taut; they were ready. The hardest part was the step into open air, wondering if the rope would hold, and for an instant Eric wasn't certain he had the courage for it. But then he realized it wasn't possible not to: the moment he'd pulled the sling over his head, he'd set something into motion, and now there was no way he could stop it. He stepped off the edge of the shaft, dangling beneath the sawhorse, the rope biting into his armpits, and then—the windlass creaking and trembling with every turn—they began to lower him.

Before he was ten feet down, the temperature started to drop, chilling the sweat on his skin—chilling his spirits, too. He didn't want to go any farther, and yet was dropping foot by foot even as he admitted this to himself, that he was scared, that he wished he'd let Jeff be the one to go. There were wooden supports hammered into the walls of the shaft, haphazardly, at odd angles, buttressing the dirt. They looked like old railroad ties, soaked in creosote, and Eric could detect no apparent plan in their positioning. Twenty feet from the surface, he was astonished to glimpse a passage opening up into the wall before him, a shaft running perpendicular to the one he was descending. He lifted the oil lamp to get a better view. There were two iron rails running down its center, dull with rust. A dented bucket lay against one of the rails, at the far limit of his lamp's illumination. The shaft curved leftward, out of sight, into the earth. A steady stream of cold air spilled out of it, thick-feeling, moist, and it made the flame in the lamp rise suddenly, then flicker, almost going out.

"There's another shaft," he called up to the others, but there was no response, just the steady creak of the windlass unwinding him into the darkness. There were skull-size stones embedded in the walls of the shaft: smooth, dull gray, almost glassy in appearance. The vine had even gained a foothold here, clinging to some of the wooden supports, its leaves and flowers much paler than on the hillside above, almost translucent. When he looked up, he could see Stacy and Amy peering down at him, framed by the rectangle of sky, everything growing a little smaller with each shuddering foot he descended. The rope had begun to swing slightly, pendulumlike, and the lamp swayed, too, its shifting light making the walls of the shaft seem to rock vertiginously. Eric felt a lurch of nausea, had to stare down at his feet to calm it. He could hear Pablo moaning somewhere beneath him, but for a long time the Greek remained lost in darkness. Eric was having difficulty guessing how far he'd dropped—fifty feet, he guessed—and then, just as the bottom came into view, still shadowed, a deeper darkness, upon which Pablo's crumpled form—his white tennis shoes, his pale blue T-shirt—was coming into focus, the rope jerked to a halt.

Eric hung there, swaying back and forth. He lifted his eyes, peered up toward that small rectangle of sky above him. He could see Stacy's and Amy's faces, and then Jeff's, too.

"Eric?" Jeff called.

"What?"

"It's the end of the rope."

"I'm not at the bottom."

"Can you see him?"

"Pretty much."

"Is he okay?"

"I can't tell."

"How far are you above him?"

Eric looked down, tried to estimate the distance between himself and the bottom. He wasn't very good at this sort of thing; all he could do was pull a number out of the air. It was pointless, like guessing how many pennies someone had in his pocket. If he were right, it would simply be a matter of chance. "Twenty feet?" he said.

"Is he moving?"

Eric stared down again toward the Greek's dim figure. The longer he looked, the more he could make out, not just the shoes and T-shirt but Pablo's arms, too, his face and neck, looking oddly pale in the darkness. Eric's lamp picked up bits of broken glass around the Greek's body, pieces of its shattered cousin. "No," Eric called. "He's just lying there."

There was no response. Eric looked up, and the faces had disappeared from the hole. He could hear them talking, not the words, just the murmur of their voices, which had a back-and-forth feel to them, discursive, strangely unhurried. They sounded even farther away than they actually were, and Eric felt a brief wobble of panic. Maybe they were walking off; maybe they were going to leave him here. . . .

He glanced down just in time to see Pablo lift his hand, hold it out toward him, a slow, underwater gesture, as if even this slight movement were difficult to accomplish.

"He lifted his hand," he called.

"What?" It was Jeff's voice; his head reappeared over the hole. Stacy's did, too, and Amy's, and Mathias's. No one was holding the windlass.

No one had to, Eric realized. *I'm at the end of my rope,* he thought. He couldn't help it: The words were just there inside his head. A joke, but mirthless.

"He lifted his hand," he shouted again.

"We're pulling you up," Jeff called. And all four heads vanished from the hole.

"Wait!" Eric shouted.

Jeff's face reappeared, then Stacy's, then Amy's. They were so tiny, silhouetted against the sky. He couldn't make out their features, but somehow he knew who was who. "We have to figure out a way to make the rope longer," Jeff called.

Eric shook his head. "I want to stay with him. I'm gonna jump."

There was that murmur of voices once more, a consultation far above him. Then Jeff's voice echoed down the shaft. "No—we'll pull you up."

"Why?"

"We might not be able to make it longer. You'd be trapped down there."

Eric couldn't think of anything to say to that. Pablo was already down there. If they couldn't make the rope longer . . . well, that meant . . . He glimpsed what followed, shied away from it.

"Eric?" Jeff called.

"What?"

"We're pulling you up."

The heads disappeared once more, and then, a second later, the rope gave a jerk as they began to turn the windlass. Eric looked down. His lamp was swaying again, so it was hard to tell, but it seemed as if Pablo was staring up at him. His hand was no longer raised. Eric started to yank at the sling, kicking his legs. He wasn't thinking; he was being stupid, and he knew it. But he couldn't leave Pablo there. Not alone, not hurt, not in that darkness. He lifted his left arm toward the sky, the sling scraping his skin as it slid upward, over his head. He was still hooked under his other arm, rising slowly, the bottom of the shaft slipping into darkness, and he had to switch the oil lamp from one hand to the other. Then he let go of the rope and dropped into the open air, the flame fluttering out as he fell.

It was farther to the bottom than he'd imagined, yet the bottom seemed to come too soon, materializing out of the darkness, slamming up into him before he had a chance to prepare himself, his legs collapsing, jarring the air from his lungs. He landed to Pablo's left—he'd had the presence of mind to aim for this spot before the lamp blew out—but he wasn't able to hold his balance once he'd hit the bottom. He fell, bounced back off the wall of the shaft, landed on the Greek's chest. Pablo bucked beneath him, began to scream again. Eric struggled to push himself up and away, but it was difficult in the darkness to find his bearings. Nothing was where it seemed it ought to be; he kept reaching out with his hands, expecting to find the ground or one of the walls but hitting open air instead. "I'm sorry," he said. "Oh, Jesus, Jesus Christ, I'm so sorry." Pablo was screaming beneath him, flailing with one arm, while the lower half of his body remained perfectly still. It frightened Eric, this stillness; he could guess what it meant.

He managed to rise to his knees, then pull back into a crouch. There was a wall behind him, and one to his left and another to his right, but across from him, on the far side of Pablo, he could sense open space: another shaft, cutting its way into the earth beneath the hill. Once again, there was a current of cold air pouring forth from it, but something more, too, some sense of pressure, of a presence: watching. Eric spent a moment straining to peer into the darkness, to make out whatever shape or form might be lurking within it, but there was nothing there, of course, just his terror fashioning phantoms, and finally he managed to convince himself of this.

Eric heard Jeff yell something, and he tilted his head back, looking up toward the mouth of the hole. It was far above him now, a tiny window of sky. The rope was swinging gently back and forth in the intervening space, and Jeff was shouting again, but Eric couldn't hear his words, not over Pablo's screaming, which echoed off the shaft's dirt walls, doubling and tripling, until it began to seem as if there were more than one of him lying there, as if Eric were trapped in a cave full of shrieking men.

"I'm okay!" he yelled upward, doubting if they could hear him.

And was he okay? He spent a moment assessing this, tallying up the various pains his body was beginning to announce. He must've banged his chin, because it felt as if he'd been punched there, and his lower back had definitely registered the fall. But it was his right leg that called out most aggressively for attention, a tight, tearing sensation just beneath his kneecap, accompanied by an odd feeling of dampness. Eric groped with his hand, found a large piece of glass embedded there. It was about the size of a playing card—petal-shaped, gently concave—and had sliced neatly through his jeans, burying itself half an inch into his flesh. Eric assumed it was from Pablo's shattered lamp; he must've landed on it when he fell. He girded himself now, clenching his teeth, then pulled the glass free. He could feel blood seeping down his shin, strangely cool—a lot of blood, too—his sock growing spongy with it.

"I cut my leg," he shouted, then waited, listening, but he couldn't tell if there was a response.

It doesn't matter, he thought. *I'll be all right.* It was the sort of empty reassurance only a child would find comforting, and Eric knew this, yet he kept repeating it to himself nonetheless. It was so dark, and there was that cold air pouring across him from the shaft, that watchful presence, and his right shoe was slowly filling with blood, and Pablo's screaming wouldn't stop. *I'm at the end of my rope,* Eric thought. And then, again: *It doesn't matter. I'll be all right.* Just words, his head was full of words.

He was still holding the lamp in his left hand; somehow, he'd managed to keep it from breaking. He set it on the ground beside him, reached out, found the Greek's wrist, grasped it. Then he crouched there in the darkness, saying, "Shh, now, shh. I'm here, I'm right here" as he waited for Pablo to stop screaming.

They could hear Eric shouting, but they couldn't make out his words over Pablo's screaming. Jeff knew that the Greek would stop eventually, though—that he'd tire and fall silent—and then they'd be able to find out what had happened down there, whether Eric had jumped or fallen, and if he, too, was hurt now. For the time being, it didn't really matter. What mattered was the rope. Until they figured out how to lengthen it, there was nothing they could do for either of them.

Jeff thought of the clothes first, of emptying the backpacks the archaeologists had left behind and knotting things together—pants and shirts and jackets—into a makeshift rope. It wasn't a good idea, he knew, but for the first few minutes it was all he could come up with. He needed twenty feet, probably more to be safe, maybe even thirty, and that would be a lot of clothes, wouldn't it? He doubted if they'd be strong enough to support a person's weight, or if the knots would even hold.

Thirty feet.

Jeff and Mathias stood beside the windlass, both of them straining to think, neither of them speaking, because there was nothing to say yet, no solution to share. Amy and Stacy were on their knees beside the hole, peering into it. Every now and then, Stacy would call Eric's name, and sometimes he'd shout something back, but it was impossible to under-stand him: Pablo was still screaming.

"One of the tents," Jeff said finally. "We can take it down, cut the nylon into strips."

Mathias turned, examined the blue tent, considering the idea. "Will it be strong enough?" he asked.

"We can braid the strips—three strips for each section—then knot the sections together." Jeff felt a flush of pleasure, saying this, a sense of success amid so much failure. They were trapped here on this hill, with little water or food, two of them out of reach down a mine shaft, at least one of them injured, but for a moment, none of it seemed to matter. They had a plan, and the plan made sense, and this gave Jeff a brief burst of energy and optimism, setting them all into motion. Mathias and he started emptying the blue tent, dragging the sleeping bags out into the little clearing, then the backpacks, the notebooks and radio, the camera and first-aid kit, the Frisbee and the empty canteen, tossing everything into a pile. Then they began to take down the tent, yanking up its stakes, dismantling its thin aluminum poles. Mathias did the cutting. There was a brief debate about the desired width and they settled on four inches, the knife slicing easily through the nylon, Mathias working with strong, quick gestures, cutting ten-foot strips for Jeff to braid. Jeff was halfway through the first section, taking his time with it, keeping a tight weave, when Pablo finally stopped screaming.

"Eric?" Stacy called.

Eric's voice came echoing back up to them. "I'm here," he shouted.

"Did you fall?"

"I jumped."

"Are you okay?"

"I cut my knee."

"Bad?"

"My shoe's full of blood."

Jeff laid down the nylon strips, stepped to the mouth of the shaft. "Put pressure on it," he yelled into the hole.

"What?"

"Take off your shirt. Wad it up, press it against the cut. Hard."

"It's too cold."

"Cold?" Jeff asked. He thought he'd misheard. His entire body was slick with sweat.

"There's another shaft," Eric called. "Off to the side. There's cold air coming from it."

"Wait," Jeff shouted. He went over to the pile from the blue tent, dug through it, found the first-aid kit, opened it. There wasn't much of use inside. Jeff couldn't say what he'd been hoping to find, but whatever it might've been, it certainly wasn't here. There was a box of Band-Aids, which were probably too small for Eric's wound. There was a tube of Neosporin that they could put on when they hauled him back up. There were bottles of aspirin and Pepto-Bismol, and some salt tablets, a thermometer, and a tiny pair of scissors.

Jeff carried the bottle of aspirin back to the shaft, stripped off his shirt. "What happened to the lamp?" he shouted.

"It went out."

"I'm going to drop my shirt down. I'm knotting a bottle of aspirin inside it. And the box of matches, too. All right?"

"Okay."

"Use the shirt to put pressure on your cut. Give three of the aspirin to Pablo and take three yourself."

"Okay," Eric said again.

Jeff knotted the aspirin and the matches into the shirt, then leaned out over the hole. "Ready?" he called.

"Ready."

He dropped the shirt, watched it vanish into the darkness. It took a long time to land. Then there was a soft, echoing thump.

"Got it," Eric called.

Mathias was done cutting strips, and he'd taken up the braiding Jeff had abandoned. Jeff turned to Amy and Stacy, who were both still peering into the shaft. "Help him," he said, nodding toward Mathias, and they walked over to the dismantled tent, crouched beside the German. Mathias showed them how to braid, and they started on their own sections.

Down in the shaft, a faint glow appeared, gaining strength: Eric had managed to light the lamp. Jeff could see him now, crouched over Pablo, the two of them looking very tiny.

"Is he okay?" Jeff called.

There was a pause before Eric answered, and Jeff could see him examining the Greek, holding out the oil lamp, bent low over his body. Then he lifted his head, shouted up toward him. "I think he broke his back."

Jeff turned from the shaft, glanced at the others. They'd stopped working and were staring back at him. Stacy had her hand over her mouth; she seemed as if she were about to start crying again. Amy got to her feet and came toward him. They both peered down into the hole.

"He's moving his arms," Eric called to them, "but not his legs."

Jeff and Amy looked at each other. "Check his feet," Amy whispered.

"I think he might've, you know . . ." Eric paused, seemed to search for the right words. Finally: "It smells like he shit himself."

"His feet," Amy whispered again, nudging Jeff. For some reason, she wouldn't shout it herself.

"Eric?" Jeff yelled.

"What?"

"Take off one of his shoes."

"His shoes?"

"Take it off—his sock, too. Then scrape the bottom of his foot with your thumbnail. Do it hard. See if there's a reaction."

Amy and Jeff leaned over the shaft, watching Eric crouch beside Pablo's feet, pull off his tennis shoe, his sock. Stacy came over to watch, too. Mathias had resumed his braiding.

Eric lifted his head toward them. "Nothing," he called.

"Oh God," Amy whispered. "Oh Jesus."

"We need to make a backboard," Jeff said to her. "How can we make a backboard?"

Amy shook her head. "No, Jeff. No way. We can't move him."

"We have to—we can't just leave him down there."

"We'll only make it worse. We'll jostle him and he'll—"

"We'll use the tent poles," Jeff said. "We'll strap him to them, and then—"

"*Jeff.*"

He stopped, stared at her. He was thinking about the tent poles, trying to imagine them as a backboard. He didn't know if it would work, but he couldn't think of anything else for them to use. Then he remembered the backpacks, their metal frames.

"We have to get him to a hospital," Amy said.

Jeff didn't respond to this, just kept watching her, taking the backpacks apart in his mind, using the tent poles for added support. How did she imagine them getting him to a hospital?

"This is bad," Amy said. "This is so, so bad." She'd started to cry but was struggling not to, wiping the tears away with the heel of her hand, shaking her head. "If we move him . . ." she began, but didn't finish.

"We can't leave him down there, Amy," he said. "You know that, don't you? It's not possible."

She considered this for a long moment, then nodded.

Jeff leaned over the hole, shouted, "Eric?"

"What?"

"We have to make a backboard before we can bring him up."

"Okay."

"We'll do it as fast as we can, but it might take a little while. Just keep talking to him."

"There's not much oil left in the lamp. Only a little."

"Then blow it out."

"Blow it out?" Eric sounded frightened by this idea.

"We'll need it later. When we come down. We'll need it to get him on the backboard."

Eric didn't respond.

"All right?" Jeff called.

Perhaps Eric nodded; it was hard to tell. They watched him bend over the lamp, and then—abruptly—they couldn't see him anymore. Once again, the bottom of the shaft was hidden in darkness.

Stacy and Amy resumed the braiding of the nylon strips while Jeff and Mathias struggled to make a backboard. The boys were muttering together, arguing over the possibilities. They had the tent poles, a backpack frame, and a roll of duct tape Mathias had found among the archaeologists' supplies, and they kept putting things together, then taking them apart again. Stacy and Amy worked in silence. There ought to have been something soothing in the task—so simple, so mindless, their hands moving right to left to right to left—but the longer Stacy kept at it, the worse she began to feel. Her stomach was sour from the tequila she'd chugged; she was cotton-mouthed, her skin prickly from the heat, her head aching. She wanted to ask for some water but was afraid that Jeff would say no. And she was growing hungry, too, light-headed with it. She wished she could have a snack, drink something cool, find a shady place to lie down, and the fact that none of this was possible gave her a tight, breathless feeling of near panic. She tried to remember what she and Eric had in their pack: a small bottle of water, a bag of pretzels, a can of mixed nuts, a pair of too-ripe bananas. They'd have to share, of course; everyone would. They'd put all their food together and then ration it out as slowly as they could.

Left to right to left to right to left to right . . .

"Shit," she heard Jeff say quite distinctly from across the clearing; then they began to tear apart their latest attempt at a backboard, the aluminum poles clinking dully as they knocked one against another. Stacy couldn't even look at the two of them. Pablo had broken his back, and she just couldn't face it. They needed help. They needed a team of paramedics to come in a helicopter and fly him to a hospital. Instead, they were going to pull him up on their own, bumping and jostling him all the way to the surface. And when they got him out—then what? He'd lie in the orange tent, she supposed, moaning or screaming, and there wasn't a thing they'd be able to do for him.

Aspirin. Pablo's back was broken, and Jeff had dropped him a bottle of aspirin.

Jeff took a break, walked across the clearing, stared down the hill. Everyone stopped to watch him. *They're gone,* Stacy thought with a brief jump of hope, but then Jeff turned and came back toward them, not saying a thing. He crouched again beside Mathias. She heard the clinking poles, a ripping sound as they tore off another piece of tape. The Mayans were still there, of course; Stacy knew this. She could picture them ringing the base of the hill, staring up the slope with those frighteningly blank expressions. They'd killed Mathias's brother. Shot him with their arrows. And now Mathias was kneeling there, holding the aluminum poles for Jeff to tape, absorbed in the difficulty of it, the solving of the problem. She couldn't begin to understand how he was managing this, couldn't understand how any of them were managing what they were doing. Eric was down at the bottom of the shaft, in the darkness, his shoe full of blood, and she was braiding strips of nylon, one hand moving over the other, tightening the weave as she went.

Left to right to left to right to left to right . . .

The sun was beginning its implacable slippage toward the west. How long had this been happening? Stacy didn't know what time it was; she'd left her watch back in her hotel room, forgotten it on the table beside the bed. Realizing this, she felt a momentary tug of anxiety, thinking that the maid might steal it, a graduation present from her parents. She was always expecting hotel maids to steal her things, and yet in all the traveling she'd done it hadn't happened, not once. Perhaps it wasn't as easy to get away with as it seemed, or maybe people were simply more honest than she assumed. In her head, she could hear the watch ticking, could picture it lying on the glass tabletop, patiently counting off the seconds, the minutes, the hours, waiting for her return. The maids turned down their beds for them in the early evening, placed tiny chocolates on their pillows, leaving the radio playing so softly that sometimes Stacy didn't notice it until after they'd turned out the lights.

"What time is it?" she asked.

Amy paused in her work, checked her watch. "Five-thirty-five," she said.

When they finished with the braiding, they'd need to haul up the rope and knot the sections of nylon onto its end. Then someone would have to descend into the hole with the improvised backboard and help Eric lift Pablo onto it, somehow securing him to the metal frame so that they could pull him safely back to the surface. After that, they'd drop the rope down yet again and ferry the other two, one after the other, to the top.

Stacy tried to imagine how long all this might take, and she knew it was too long, that they were running out of time. Because if it was 5:35 now, creeping toward 5:40, then they had only another hour and a half before dark.

In the end, they had to braid a total of five strips. They knotted the first three onto the rope, then dropped it back down the shaft to see if it was long enough, but Eric shouted up to them, saying it was still out of reach. So they braided a fourth section, only to realize when it came time to attach their improvised backboard that they'd need two separate strips hanging from the bottom of the rope, one to connect to the head of the aluminum frame, the other to its foot.

While Mathias was quickly braiding this final addition, Jeff took Amy aside. "Are you okay with this?" he asked.

They were standing together on the square of dirt where the blue tent had formerly sat. The sun was almost at the horizon, but it was still bright out, still hot. That was how it was here, Amy knew: there was no transition between day and night, no gentle easing into evening. The sun rose almost immediately into a noontime intensity, which it didn't relinquish until the moment it touched the sky's western edge. And then you could count the day into darkness—that was how fast night came on. The only lamp they had was the one with Eric, and it was low on oil. Fifteen minutes, she guessed, and they'd be working blind.

"Okay with what?" she asked.

"You'll be the one to go down," Jeff said.

"Down?"

"Into the shaft."

Amy just stared at him; she was too startled to speak. He'd taken one of the archaeologists' shirts to replace the T-shirt he'd thrown down to Eric, and it looked odd on him, making him seem almost like another person. The shirt had a sheen to it—it was meant to pass for khaki, but it didn't; it was some sort of polyester, with buttons down the front and large pockets on each side of the chest. It looked like something a hunter might wear on safari, Amy thought. Or a photographer, maybe, with rolls of film jammed into those peculiar pockets. Or a soldier, perhaps. Somehow it made Jeff seem older—larger, even. His nose was pink and peeling, and though he looked tired and sun-worn, there was a jittery quality to him, an aura of heightened alertness.

"Mathias and I have to turn the crank," he said. "So it's either you or Stacy. And Stacy, you know . . ." He trailed off, shrugged. "It just seems like you should be the one."

Still Amy was silent. She didn't want to go, of course, was terrified of the idea, of dropping into the earth, into the darkness. She hadn't even wanted to come here—that was what she wanted to say to Jeff. If it had been up to her, they never would've left the beach in the first place. And then, when they'd discovered the hidden path, she'd tried to warn him, hadn't she? She'd tried to tell him that they shouldn't take it, and he'd refused to listen. This was all his fault, then, wasn't it? So shouldn't he be the one to descend into that hole? But even as she was asking herself these questions, Amy was remembering what had happened at the base of the hill, how she'd retreated across the clearing, peering through her camera's viewfinder, her foot slipping into the tangle of vines. If she hadn't done that, maybe the Mayans wouldn't have forced them up the hill. They wouldn't be here now—Pablo wouldn't be lying at the bottom of the shaft with a broken back; Eric's shoe wouldn't be full of blood. They'd be walking somewhere miles from this place, every step carrying them farther away, all six of them imagining that the mosquitoes and the tiny black flies and the blisters forming on their feet were things perfectly worthy of complaint.

"You were a lifeguard, weren't you?" Jeff asked. "You ought to know how to handle this sort of thing."

A lifeguard. It was true, too, in a way. Amy had spent a summer working at a pool in an apartment complex in her hometown. A tiny oval pool, with a seven-foot deep end, no diving allowed. She'd sat in a lawn chair, sunning herself from ten until six, five days a week, warning children not to run, not to splash or dunk one another, and telling the adults that they weren't supposed to bring alcohol into the pool area. Both groups largely ignored her. It was a small complex, teetering on the edge of solvency, full of her town's downwardly mobile—drinkers and divorcées—a depressing place. There weren't that many children, and on some days no one came to the pool at all. Amy would sit in her chair, reading. If it was especially quiet, she'd often slip into the shallow end and float there on her back, her mind going empty. She'd had to take a lifesaving class, of course, before she was hired. And there must've been a lesson about spinal injuries, how to secure someone on a backboard. But, if so, she retained no memory of it.

"You'll use our belts," Jeff said.

What Amy wanted to do was run down the hill. She had an image of herself attempting this, bursting into the clearing, confronting the men waiting there. She'd tell them what had happened, find a way to communicate everything that had gone so wrong here, miming it out for them. It would be difficult, of course, but somehow she'd get them to see her fear, to make them feel it, too. And they'd relent. They'd get help. They'd let them all depart. Mathias's brother was lying on the opposite side of the hill, his corpse pierced with arrows, but still Amy managed, for a brief instant, to believe in this fantasy. She didn't want to be the one who was lowered into the shaft.

Jeff took her hand. He was opening his mouth to say something—to convince her, she knew, or tell her that she didn't have a choice—when the chirping resumed from the bottom of the hole.

Everyone but Mathias ran to the shaft, peered into it. Mathias was nearly finished braiding, and he kept at it, not even pausing.

"Eric?" Jeff yelled. "Can you find it?"

Eric didn't answer for a moment. They could sense him stirring down there, searching for the source of the sound. "It keeps moving," he called. "Sometimes it seems like it's to my left. And then it's to my right."

"Shouldn't it light up as it rings?" Amy asked Jeff, her voice low, almost a whisper.

Jeff shouted, "Is there a light? Look for a light."

Again, they could sense Eric moving about. "I don't see it," he called. And then, a second later, just as they were realizing this for themselves: "It's stopped."

They all waited to see if the sound would start again, but it didn't. The sun touched the western horizon and everything took on a reddish hue. In a few minutes, it would be dark. Mathias was done with his braiding. They watched him join this final section to the others, then attach their makeshift backboard to the two dangling strands. He finished just as the day began its sudden descent into night. Then Jeff held the crank while Mathias and Stacy lifted the backboard out over the shaft's mouth. They spent a moment staring at it as it dangled there: Mathias had covered the aluminum frame with one of the archaeologists' sleeping bags, cushioning it. They piled all four of their belts on top of the sleeping bag. Amy knew that though she hadn't yet agreed to Jeff's proposition, the question had somehow been decided. Everything was ready, and they thought she was, too. Mathias joined Jeff beside the windlass, taking hold of its crank. Stacy stood there, hugging herself, watching.

"Just climb on it," Jeff said.

So that was what Amy did. Girding herself, thinking brave thoughts, she stepped out into the shaft's opening, crouching on the aluminum frame, clutching at the braided strands of nylon. The backboard creaked beneath her weight, rocking back and forth, but it held. And then—before Amy even had a chance to collect herself, or begin to second-guess her decision—the windlass started to turn, dropping her from the day's gathering darkness into the deeper darkness of the hole.

It had taken them a long time, but now, finally, they were coming. Eric didn't know how long, exactly, it had been, perhaps not quite as long as it had seemed, but a long time nonetheless. Even under the best of circumstances, he wasn't very good at reckoning the passage of time—he lacked an internal clock—but here in the hole, in the darkness, under the stress of everything that had happened thus far today, it was far more difficult than usual. All he knew was that it was becoming night up there, that the blue rectangle of sky had taken on a brief blush of red before fading into a blue-gray, a slate gray, a gray-black. They'd made a backboard and Amy was crouched on it now, dropping toward him.

Hours, Eric supposed. It must've been hours. Pablo had been

screaming and then he'd stopped, and Stacy had shouted down to him, and they'd talked back and forth, and Jeff had told him to blow out the lamp. Then they'd all vanished to make the backboard and lengthen the rope—it had taken them a long time, too long—and he'd first crouched, then sat beside Pablo, gripping his wrist all the while. Talking, too, off and on, to keep the Greek company, to raise his spirits and try to trick him—trick both of them, maybe—into believing that everything was going to be all right.

But everything wasn't going to be all right, of course, and no matter how hard Eric worked to throw a tone of optimism into his voice—and he did work; he consciously struggled for it, an echo of the Greeks' playful bantering among themselves—he couldn't elude this difficult fact. There was the smell, for one thing. The smell of shit—of urine, too. Pablo had broken his back, lost control of his bowels, his bladder. He'd need to have a catheter put in, a bag hanging from the side of his bed, nurses to empty it and keep him clean. He'd need surgery, and quickly—right now, earlier than now—he'd need doctors and physical therapists hovering about him, charting his progress. And Eric couldn't see how any of this was going to happen. They'd worked all afternoon to build a backboard and with it they were finally going to get him out of this hole, but what would that accomplish? Out of the hole, up there among the tents and the flowering vines, his back would still be broken, his bladder and bowels leaking urine and shit into his already-sodden pants. And there was nothing they could do about it.

Eric's knee had stopped bleeding finally. There was a steady, throbbing ache, which jumped in volume whenever he shifted his weight. Jeff's T-shirt was stiff with dried blood; Eric set it on the ground beside him. His shoe still felt damp.

Eric told Pablo how people healed—implacably—how the worst part was the accident itself, then the body went to work, mobilizing, rebuilding. Even now, even as they were talking, it was beginning to happen. He told Pablo about the bones he'd broken as a child. He described falling on a wet sidewalk and cracking his forearm—he couldn't remember which bone, the radius, maybe, or the ulna; it didn't matter. He'd had a cast for six weeks, the end of the summer; he could remember the stink of it when they cut it off, sweat and mildew, his arm looking pale and too thin, his terror of the whirling saw. He'd broken his collarbone playing Superman, flying headfirst down a playground slide. He'd broken his nose falling off a pogo stick. And he described all of these accidents for Pablo now, in detail, the pain of each one, the course of his eventual recovery: his implacable, inevitable recovery.

Pablo couldn't understand a single word of this, of course. He moaned and muttered. Occasionally, he'd lift the arm Eric wasn't holding and seem to reach for something at his side, though Eric couldn't guess what, since there was nothing there but darkness. Eric ignored this movement—the moaning and muttering, too—he just kept talking, working at it, his voice high and falsely cheerful. He couldn't think of anything else to do.

He told Pablo of other accidents he'd witnessed: a boy who'd skateboarded into traffic (a concussion and a handful of broken ribs), a neighbor who'd tumbled off his roof while cleaning out the gutters (a dislocated shoulder, a pair of broken fingers), a girl who'd mistimed her jump from a rope swing, landing not in the river, as intended, but upon its rocky bank (a shattered ankle, three lost teeth). He talked about the town where he'd been raised, how small it was, how ugly and provincial, yet somehow picturesque in its ugliness, somehow worldly in its provincialism. When a siren sounded, people went to their front doors, stepped out onto their porches, shaded their eyes to see. Children jumped on bicycles, raced after the ambulance or fire truck or police car. There was gawking involved, of course, but also empathy. When Eric had broken his arm, neighbors had come calling, bearing gifts: comic books for him to read, videos to watch.

He kept hold of Pablo's wrist with his right hand while he talked, squeezing sometimes to emphasize certain points, never letting go. His left hand moved back and forth between the oil lamp and the box of matches, touching one and then the other in a continuous, restless circuit, moving lightly across them, as if they were beads on a rosary. And there was something prayerful about the gesture, too; it was accompanied by a pair of words in his head. Yet, even as he told his tales to Pablo in his confident, assertively optimistic voice, he was silently repeating the two words, chanting them internally while his hand shifted from lamp to matches to lamp to matches: *Still there, still there, still there, still there . . .*

He described for Pablo what it had felt like to ride his bicycle in pursuit of the sirens, the flashing lights. The excitement—that giddy feeling of drama and disaster. He told him of happy endings. Of seven-year-old Mary Kelly, who knew how to climb a tree but not how to get down, her fear making her scramble higher and higher, crying as she went, pulling her tiny body upward, forty feet, into the very crown of an ancient oak, a crowd gathering beneath her, calling to her, urging her back down, while a wind came up, gradually increasing, making the branches sway, the entire tree seeming to dip and rise. He imitated for Pablo the collective gasp when she almost slipped, dangling for an excruciatingly long string of seconds before she managed to regain her foothold, crying all the while, the sirens approaching, the boys on their bicycles. Then the fire truck with its ladder slowly angling skyward, the cheers when the paramedic leaned deep into the foliage, grasped the little girl by her arm, yanked her toward him, throwing her over his shoulder.

Eric had the sudden sense, in the darkness, of a hand touching the small of his back. He jumped, almost yelped, but caught himself. It was just the vine. Somehow, it had managed to take root down here, too, at the bottom of the shaft. He must've leaned into it as he talked, creating the impression of its having reached out and touched him, cradling him at the base of his spine, almost caressing him. It was impossible to keep his bearings here; he was as good as blind. All he had to orient himself was Pablo's wrist and—*still there, still there, still there*—the oil lamp and the box of matches. He slid forward to escape the vine's touch—it was creepy, and it made him shiver; he didn't like it—shifting until he was right up against Pablo's broken body. When he moved, there was a sharp, tearing pain from the cut in his knee, and it started to bleed again. He patted at the ground, searching for Jeff's T-shirt, then pressed it once more to the wound.

He circled back to the girl on the rope swing; Marci Brand, thirteen years old. She'd had braces and a long brown ponytail. He told Pablo how they'd all laughed at first, seeing her fall, he and the other children. There'd been something comical about it, cartoonlike. They'd watched her drop, heard that awful slapping sound as she hit the rocks; everyone must've known she was hurt. But they'd laughed, all of them, as if to deny this, to undo it, stopping only when they saw her try to stand, then crumple awkwardly, falling onto her side and sliding down the rocky bank into the water. Her mouth was cut—she'd hit her face against the stones—and a murky cloud of blood slowly formed around her in the water as she floated there, thrashing her arms. Her eyes were clenched shut, Eric remembered, her expression contorted. She was grimacing, but not crying; she didn't make a sound, not even when they pulled her out, dragging her back up onto the bank while one of them rode off on his bicycle to get help. Later, they all felt guilty about having laughed, especially when it looked as if she might not be able to walk again. But she did, eventually—*implacably, inexorably*—with a slight limp, perhaps, although this was barely noticeable, not noticeable at all, really, unless you knew the story, unless you were watching for it.

Now and then, Eric thought he could see things in the darkness—floating shapes, balloonlike, faintly luminescent. They seemed to approach, then hover right in front of him before slowly withdrawing again. Some had a bluish green tint; others were a faint yellow, almost white. These were tricks his eyes were playing on him, he knew, physiological reactions to the darkness, but he couldn't help himself: whenever they appeared to come especially close, he'd relinquish his grip on Pablo's wrist so that he could try to touch them. As soon as he'd lift his hand, though, the shapes would vanish, only to reappear at some new spot, farther away, and resume their slow, gently bobbing approach. He took the T-shirt away from his cut knee. The wound had stopped bleeding again. Immediately, he reached for the lamp, the matches: *still there, still there. . . .*

He told Pablo other stories, too, tales that hadn't ended so happily—*implacably, inexorably*—changing them for the wounded man's benefit. Little Stevie Stahl, who was swept into a storm sewer while playing in a flooded field, was no longer discovered by a volunteer scuba diver, half-buried in silt, bloated beyond recognition. No: he reappeared five minutes later and almost a mile away, spit out into the river, cut and bruised and crying, it was true, but otherwise, miraculously, unharmed. And Ginger Ruby—who'd set her uncle's garage on fire while playing with a book of matches, and then, disoriented by the smoke and her rising panic, fled away from the door through which she could've easily escaped, and died crouching against the back wall, behind a row of garbage cans—was, in Eric's retelling of the story, saved by a fireman, brought out to the cheers of the gathered crowd, gasping and coughing and covered with soot, her shirt and hair scorched, but otherwise (yes, *miraculously*) unharmed.

The cold air coming from the open shaft on the far side of Pablo's body wasn't constant. Sometimes it would stop, seem to hold its breath, and the temperature in the hole would instantly begin to rise. Eric would start to sweat, his shirt growing damp with it, and then, abruptly, the cold air would return. This constant fluctuation unsettled Eric, frightened him, made the darkness within the shaft seem threateningly animate. Each time the draft paused, he felt as if it had been blocked by someone—or something—a presence that was hesitating just in front of him, examining and appraising him. Once, he even thought he heard it sniffing, taking in his scent. His senses were playing tricks again, he knew. But still, he had to resist the urge to light the lamp, his hand pausing, wavering, then resuming its steady back and forth: *still there, still there, still there.*

He told Pablo of his friend Gary Holmes, who'd dreamed of becoming a pilot. Gary had badgered and cajoled and begged his parents, wearing them down year by year, until they finally gave him flying lessons for his sixteenth birthday. Every Saturday, he'd ride his bicycle out to the local airport and spend the afternoon there, entering this new world. Three months into it, Eric was playing soccer—a youth league, four separate games going on at once, the fields lying parallel to one another. A small plane flew over, very low, buzzing them, the players pausing for a reflexive instant as the aircraft's shadow swept across them, everyone ducking involuntarily, then peering upward. The plane flew on, banked, made another pass, the games stuttering to a more complete halt. The referees blew their whistles; they were waving their arms, struggling to restore order, when the plane banked a second time, its engine stuttering, coughing, falling silent. And then—a handful of seconds later, the time it takes to breathe, exhale, breathe again—from somewhere within the wooded area west of the fields came the slamming, splintering, crunching sound of the crash. Not in the version Eric shared with Pablo, though. No, as Eric told the story, someone had understood what was happening on that very first low pass. One of the coaches, then another. They began to shout, pointing, the referees joining in with their whistles, everyone yelling suddenly, running. The plane was in distress; it was attempting an emergency landing. They needed to clear the fields. And they did it. By the time the plane had banked, returned for its second pass, everyone was crowded back against the sidelines. The plane landed roughly, bouncing, crashing through one of the wooden goals, its front wheels digging into the soft earth, nearly flipping it, so that it finally came to rest tipped forward on its nose, its propeller bent, its windshield cracked. Eric hesitated for a moment here, struggling to imagine what Gary and his instructor's injuries might've been, how that plane's abrupt return to earth would've battered the two bodies in its cockpit. A shattered kneecap, he decided. A dislocated shoulder, a cracked pelvis, a mild concussion. He waved these aside even as he listed them. They all healed, he assured Pablo, as such injuries always do—yes, once again—*implacably, inexorably.*

The others were busy up above, braiding the strips of nylon they'd cut from the blue tent, building their backboard; they didn't have time to think. But Eric was down here in the dark, with the smell of Pablo's shit and urine, the rising and falling of his moans, his muttering. So it was probably natural that he was the first of them to begin to wonder if the Greek might not survive this adventure, if his body had moved beyond the realm of *implacable* and *inexorable,* if he was, after all, going to die in the coming hours or days while they hovered helplessly about him.

It seemed as if Pablo might've fallen asleep—or lost consciousness. He'd stopped muttering, anyway, stopped moaning, stopped reaching out into the darkness for whatever it was that he imagined to be waiting there for him to grasp. Eric fell silent, too, sat beside Pablo, holding his wrist with one hand, touching the lamp, the matches with the other. Time seemed to pass even more slowly without the sound of his voice echoing back at him from the shaft's narrow walls. His thoughts returned to Gary Holmes, to the photograph of the mangled plane on the front page of the local paper, the memorial service in the high school auditorium.

Gary had been a friend of his—not a close one, but more than an acquaintance, and, a month after the funeral, Gary's mother had stopped by Eric's house. "Eric?" his own mother had called. "There's someone here to see you."

Eric had hurried downstairs, to find Mrs. Holmes standing in the front hall. She'd come to ask if he wanted Gary's bicycle. It was an odd, awkward encounter; Eric's mother had stood there watching them talk, looking tearful. She kept reaching out to touch Mrs. Holmes's shoulder. Eric had felt startled by the request, and strangely embarrassed—after all, he hadn't been that close to Gary. He tried to decline the offer, only to change his mind when he saw how stricken Mrs. Holmes looked at the first, hesitant shake of his head. Yes, he said. Of course he'd take the bike. He thanked her, and then his mother was crying in earnest. So was Mrs. Holmes.

The bicycle was still at the airport, locked to the chain-link fence where Gary had left it that final day. Eric's father dropped him off there early one morning, on his way to work, and Eric claimed the bike, hunching over it with the slip of paper Mrs. Holmes had given him, squinting to decipher her handwriting, the three numbers for the combination lock. He had to try it a half dozen times before it worked, and then he rode off, straight to school, a fifteen-mile trip, arriving a few minutes late, the first bell having already rung, the halls silent and empty. The bicycle's seat had been too high for him, making it difficult to pedal; the chain needed oil; the rims were rusting from having sat out in the weather for the past month. It wasn't a thing to feel proud of, and he already had his own bike anyway—perhaps it was this, or else simply that he was late, but he didn't lock the bicycle when he arrived at school; he tossed it down against the rack and hurried inside. He left it there that night, too, still unlocked, taking the bus home instead. And in the morning, it was gone.

There was that pressure against Eric's back once more, a hand touching him. He felt his heart jump in his chest even as he struggled to reassure himself. It was just the vine. He must've slouched back into it again. He shifted toward Pablo, only to realize that he was already as close to the Greek as he could get. The vine had moved somehow, crept toward him, drawn by his warmth, perhaps. It made him uneasy, a little scared, to think of the vine like this—something volitional, almost sentient—it made him want to flee the hole altogether. He thought about shouting upward, calling to the others, but he stopped himself at the last instant, worried that he'd wake Pablo from his sleep.

Gary's mother had gone from house to house, passing on her son's possessions to boys who didn't know what to do with them. Boys who lost her son's sweaters and jackets, his baseball mitt and swim goggles, who gave them away or discarded them outright, who buried them in closets and trunks and basements. This was the way death always worked, Eric supposed; the living did everything possible to sweep all evidence of it from sight. Even Gary's closest friends continued forward with their lives, unmarred in any significant way by his absence, climbing from grade to grade, then leaping off into college, forgetting him as they went, remembering instead that photograph of the crumpled plane, the abrupt silence on the soccer fields before its crash.

Eric had to pee. But he was afraid to stand up and step toward the wall of the shaft to do this, irrationally frightened that the Greek or the lamp or the matches would no longer be there when he returned. He unbuckled his belt to ease the pressure on his bladder, tried to distract himself with word games, making up a vocabulary test for his future students, beginning with the *A*'s, ten words, a little quiz to start the week, five points for the definitions, five for the spelling.

Albatross, he thought. *Avarice. Annunciation. Alacrity. Armament. Adjacent. Arduous. Accentuate. Accommodate. Allegation.*

He was just turning to the *B*'s—*Boisterous. Bravado. Bandoleer. Botanist*—when that electronic chirping began again, waking Pablo, startling them both. Eric let go of the Greek's wrist, stood up, the wound on his knee making him stagger-step, like a clubfoot. The chirping seemed to be coming from his right, yet when he limped toward it, he realized he was wrong. It was coming from behind him now. He started to turn, but then wasn't so certain. It seemed to be circling him, drifting along the walls of the shaft.

"Eric?" Jeff yelled down. "Can you find it?"

Eric craned his head back. He could see them leaning into the rectangle of blue sky. He called up, told them how it was moving on him, first in one direction, then another.

"Is there a light?" Jeff shouted. "Look for a light."

The sound seemed to be coming from the opening beyond Pablo's body now, just inside the mouth of the shaft. Eric limped past Pablo, the air growing noticeably cooler. The chirping retreated, as if to draw him down the shaft. He hesitated, frightened suddenly. "I don't see it," he called. And then the chirping fell silent. "It's stopped," he yelled. He counted to ten inside his head, waiting for it to start again, but it didn't. When he peered up at the mouth of the hole, the heads had vanished and the sky had taken on a reddish tint. The sun was beginning to set.

He hobbled back to Pablo's body. He could sense him moving in the darkness, shifting his head, but he remained silent. He didn't resume his moaning or muttering, and this frightened Eric.

"Pablo?" Eric said. "You okay?" He wanted the Greek to start speaking again, but he just lay there, motionless now. Eric reached for the lamp, found it, reached for the matches, and . . . they weren't there. He patted at the rocky floor of the shaft, in a slowly widening circle, with a sense of growing panic. He couldn't find the box.

There was a creaking sound above him, and he looked up. The sky was rapidly growing dark, but he could see something silhouetted against it, an oblong shape, almost filling the hole. They'd finished their backboard, were setting it into place. He kept patting at the ground, reaching farther and farther away from himself, then returning to the lamp, starting outward again. But the matches weren't there.

The creaking grew louder, steadier, and he glanced up again. They were lowering the backboard into the shaft. "Eric?" he heard Amy call.

"What?" he yelled.

"Light the lamp!" She was on the backboard, he realized, dropping slowly toward him.

He stood up, limped a step, thinking that he might've been holding the matches when the chirping began, might've carried them with him as he started off to discover the source of the sound, only, absentmindedly, to set them down again. It didn't make sense, and he didn't really believe in it, but then he took another step and his foot hit something, kicking it, and he knew by the noise it made, by the way it felt against his foot, that it was the box of matches. He lowered himself carefully to his hands and knees, began to pat the ground, searching.

The creaking continued. The sky had grown dark now; he couldn't see the backboard any longer, but he could sense its approach. "Light the lamp, Eric," Amy called again. She was closer now, and there was an urgency to her voice. She sounded scared.

He kept patting at the ground. He was in a corner of the shaft that the vine had colonized fairly aggressively; his hands kept getting tangled in its tendrils, giving him the eerie sensation that the plant was purposefully impeding him. When he finally found the box of matches, it was buried underneath the vine, almost completely covered by it. Eric had to tug it free, tearing at the plant, its sap sticking damply to the fingers of his left hand, cool at first, then suddenly burning.

"Eric?" Amy shouted again. She was almost upon him.

"Just a sec," he called. He hobbled back to the lamp, crouched over it, lifted its glass globe. He didn't realize how badly his hand was trembling until he struck the first match: he was shaking so much that it immediately fluttered out. He had to take a moment, two deep breaths, working to calm himself, then try again. This time, he was successful— he lighted the lamp—and there Amy was, barely fifteen feet up, peering anxiously down at them, dropping, dropping, dropping.

He had to turn away from the lamp's brightness after so many hours sitting in the dark, but, even so, the flame was somehow fainter than he'd remembered—or than he'd hoped, perhaps. Much of the shaft remained shadowed, impenetrably so. His hand was burning from the vine's sap. He wiped it on his pants, but it didn't help.

When the backboard came within reach, he took hold of it, guiding it slightly to the right so that it would come to rest at Pablo's side, but then, with three feet still to go, it jerked to a halt, almost toppling Amy off her perch.

"Amy?" Jeff called from above.

"What?" she shouted.

"Have you reached them?"

"Almost. A few more feet."

There was a brief silence while this information was absorbed. Then: "How many?"

Amy leaned, peered down off the backboard at Pablo's broken body. "I don't know. Three?"

"It's the end of the rope," Jeff called. There was a pause. Then: "Can you still do it?"

Amy and Eric looked at each other. The whole point of the backboard was to keep Pablo's spine straight while he was lifted: without it, there'd be twisting or bending, which would, of course, cause further damage to his injured body. But if they decided to wait, it meant winching the backboard back up, taking it off the rope, braiding another length of nylon, reattaching the backboard, dropping the whole thing down the shaft once more, all of this attempted in complete darkness.

"What do you think?" Amy asked Eric. She was still crouched on the backboard, though she could've easily slid to the ground. It seemed as if she didn't want to attempt this, as if she felt it might commit her to a task she was still hoping she could evade.

Eric struggled for something that might approximate thought; it wasn't easy. He noticed a shovel leaning against the far wall of the shaft—a camp shovel, the type that could be folded up and carried in a backpack—and he spent a long moment staring at it, trying to imagine a way in which it might be useful to them. He couldn't come up with anything, though, and when the words *grave digger* popped into his head, he almost flinched, as if he'd picked up something hot.

"We can undo the backboard," he said. "Put him on it, then lift it up and tie it back on."

"By ourselves?" Amy asked. It was clear she didn't think this was possible.

Eric shook his head. "They'll have to lower someone else to help. Stacy, I guess. Two of us to lift him, one to tie the knots."

They thought about this for a moment, imagining all the steps, the time it would take.

"We'll need to blow out the lamp," Eric said. "Wait for her in the dark."

Amy shifted her weight, and the backboard began to swing. Eric extended his hand, stopped it. He thought she was going to climb off it, but she didn't.

"Or we can just lift him ourselves," he said.

Amy was silent, staring down at Pablo. Eric wished she'd say something. He couldn't do this by himself.

"It's only a few feet."

"If he twists—"

"I could take his shoulders. You take his feet. One, two, three—easy as that."

Amy frowned, uncertain.

Eric lifted the lamp, tilted it, examining its reservoir, the diminishing pool of oil. "We have to decide," he said. "The light's not going to last."

"Amy?" Jeff called.

They both craned their heads to look, but it had grown too dark up there to see him.

"We're gonna try it," she yelled.

Eric held the backboard steady while she climbed off, then he set the oil lamp on the ground. Amy gathered the belts from the sleeping bag, dropped them next to the lamp. Pablo was watching them, his eyes moving back and forth from one to the other.

"We're going to pick you up," Amy said to him. She made a lifting motion with her hands, palms open, then pointed to the backboard. "We're going to put you onto here, and then hoist you up and out."

Pablo stared at her.

Eric moved to the Greek's head; Amy stood at his feet.

"His hips," Eric said.

Amy hesitated. "You sure?"

"If you lift from his feet, he'll bend at the waist."

"But if I lift at his hips, won't he end up arching his back?"

They both stared down at Pablo, picturing these two different scenarios. It was a bad idea, Eric knew. They should send the backboard back up, have them lengthen the rope. Or at least have Stacy come join them. He glanced toward the lamp. It was nearly out of oil.

"At his knees," Eric said.

Amy considered this, but not long enough. A handful of seconds, and then she crouched over Pablo's knees. Eric bent, sliding his hands under the Greek's shoulders. He could feel the cut on his leg stretching, tearing, beginning to bleed again. Pablo groaned, and Amy started to pull away, but Eric shook his head.

"Quickly," he said. "On three."

They counted together: "One . . . two . . . three."

And then they lifted.

It was a disaster—far worse than Eric had feared. It seemed to take forever, and yet it happened so fast. They'd barely gotten him off the ground before Pablo began to scream—even more loudly than before, if possible, a pure shriek of pain. Amy almost gave up, almost set him back down on the ground, but Eric shouted at her—"No!"—and she kept going. Pablo's body sagged at the waist; he began to thrash his arms. His scream went on and on. His body was too heavy for Amy; she couldn't keep up with Eric. The Greek's shoulders were level with the backboard now, but his knees were still a good foot beneath it, and it looked as if Amy might not be able to lift them any higher. The bend at Pablo's waist increased. His right arm, flailing, hit the backboard, and it began to swing wildly back and forth.

"Lift!" Eric shouted at Amy, and she tried to hoist Pablo's legs higher, lunging, the Greek's torso twisting, his screams going higher.

Afterward, Eric wasn't even certain how they managed it. It was as if he'd had some sort of blackout in those final moments. He had the impression that they'd been reduced, finally, to making a lurching sort of toss toward the swaying backboard, throwing the Greek's body onto it. All he knew was that he felt terrible, as if he'd absentmindedly stepped on an infant. Amy had begun to cry, was standing there, looking stricken.

"It's okay," Eric said. "He'll be okay." He didn't think she could hear him, though, because Pablo was still screaming. Eric had the urge to vomit, his tongue going thick, bile rising in his throat. He forced himself to breathe. His leg was bleeding again, draining wetly into his shoe, and, once more, he was abruptly conscious of his bladder. "I have to pee," he said.

Amy didn't even look at him. She stood with her hand over her mouth, watching Pablo shriek, the lower half of his body perfectly still while his arms flailed about, the backboard continuing to swing to and fro. Eric limped to the wall, unzipped, began to urinate. By the time he was through, Pablo had started to quiet. His eyes were tightly clenched; there were beads of sweat standing on his forehead.

"We have to tie him down," Amy said. She'd stopped crying, was wiping at her face with her sleeve.

There were four belts on the ground beside the oil lamp; Eric stripped off his, added it to the pile. Amy picked up two of them, buckled them together so that they formed one long strap. She draped this over Pablo's chest, sternum-high, pulled it tight, knotted it in place. The Greek's eyes remained shut. Eric put two more belts together, handed them to Amy, and she repeated the procedure, securing Pablo at his thighs.

"We need another one," Eric said, holding up the last remaining belt.

Amy leaned over Pablo, carefully undid his buckle, started to pull his belt free of its loops. The Greek still didn't open his eyes. Eric handed her the belt he was holding, and she used these last two to tie Pablo across his forehead. Then they stepped back to examine their work.

"It's okay," Eric said again. "He'll be okay." Inside, he felt wretched, though. He wanted Pablo to open his eyes, wanted him to start muttering again, but Pablo just lay there, swaying slightly on the backboard, the beads of sweat continuing to form on his forehead, growing larger and larger, and then suddenly collapsing, rolling sideways down his skull. Eric could feel the blood filling his shoe. His elbow was hurting, his hand burning. There was a bruise on his chin, and his back was itching—he was covered with bug bites from their long walk through the jungle. He was thirsty, hungry; he wanted to go home—not simply back to the relative safety of their hotel, but *home*. And it wasn't possible, he knew. Nothing was going to be okay. Pablo was terribly hurt, and they were part of this, part of his pain. Eric felt like weeping.

Amy lifted her head toward the darkness above them. "Ready!" she yelled. And then: "Go slow!"

They were just starting to raise him, the windlass beginning to creak, the backboard climbing past Eric's face, moving upward—above him, beyond his reach now—when the lamp dimmed, flickered, and went out.

Jeff," Stacy said, her voice quiet, almost a whisper, but tense, too—he could hear an urgency in it.

He and Mathias were working the windlass's crank, struggling to keep it slow and steady, and he answered without looking at her. "What?"

"The lamp went out."

Now he turned, Mathias and he both, pausing to stare at the mouth of the shaft. It had gone dark, like everything else around them. The sky was clear; there was starlight but the moon hadn't risen yet. Jeff tried to recall if he'd seen it in the preceding nights—what stage it was at, what time it ought to appear—but all that came to him was the image of a cantaloupe slice hanging just above the horizon on one of their first evenings at the beach. Whether it had been rising or sinking, waxing or waning, he couldn't guess. "Call to them," he told her.

Stacy leaned over the hole, cupped her hands around her mouth, shouted, "What happened?"

Eric's voice came echoing up the shaft: "It's out of oil."

Jeff was trying to keep everything in his head, but it wasn't working. He wished he had a sheet of paper, and the time to write things down, make a list, bring a little order to the chaos into which they'd stumbled. In the morning, he could use one of the archaeologists' notebooks, but for now he had to keep going over everything in his mind, feeling at each moment as if he were forgetting some crucial detail. There was water and food and shelter to think about. There were the Mayans at the base of the hill, and Henrich's corpse stuck full of arrows. There was Pablo with his broken back. There were the other Greeks, who might or might not be coming to their rescue. And there was the lamp to add to it all—the lamp without any oil to light it.

He and Mathias resumed their cranking of the windlass. "Let us know when you see him," Jeff said to Stacy.

Thinking wasn't important right now, he told himself; thinking would only confuse things, make him hesitate, slow him down. Thinking could wait until the morning, until daylight. What he needed to do was pull everyone out of the shaft, set them up in the orange tent, and then try, somehow, to get some sleep.

The windlass creaked and creaked as the rope slowly coiled around the barrel. Stacy remained silent; Pablo was still hidden in darkness. Jeff could smell him, though, quite suddenly: an outhouse odor, his shit, his urine. All the time they'd been cutting and braiding the strips of nylon, taping the aluminum poles together, he'd kept trying to tell himself that maybe Eric was wrong, maybe Pablo's back wasn't broken after all. They'd laugh about it later—tomorrow morning, when the Greek was up and limping about—how they'd jumped to their doomsday conclusion. But now, with that stench coming toward him from the shaft, he knew better.

Stop, he told himself. *Just get everyone out. Into the tent. And then to sleep.*

"I see him," Stacy whispered.

"When he clears the hole," Jeff said, "you'll have to grab the back-board, guide it toward the ground."

They kept working at the crank.

"Okay," Stacy said, and they paused, turning to look. The backboard was hanging above the shaft, just beneath the sawhorse, Pablo a dark form upon it, perfectly still, like a mummy. Stacy was gripping the sleeping bag, one of the aluminum poles. "Lower it a little," she told them.

They reversed the crank, and as the backboard began to descend again, Stacy pulled at it, guiding it toward the edge of the hole.

"Careful," she said. "Slow."

They eased him down onto the ground, then Mathias and Jeff stepped toward him, everyone crouching beside the backboard. Maybe it was just the darkness, or his own fatigue, but Pablo looked even worse than Jeff had feared. His cheeks were sunken, his face gaunt and strikingly pale, almost luminescent in the darkness. And his body seemed smaller, as if his injury had somehow diminished him, atrophy already setting in. His eyes were shut.

"Pablo?" Jeff said, touching his shoulder.

The Greek's eyelids fluttered open, and he stared up at Jeff, then at Stacy and Mathias. He didn't say anything. After a moment, he closed his eyes again.

"It's bad, isn't it?" Stacy asked.

"I don't know," Jeff said. "It's hard to tell." And then, because this seemed like a lie: "I think so."

Mathias remained silent, staring down at Pablo, his face somber. A breeze had come up, and with the sun gone, the night was starting to grow cooler. Jeff's sweat was drying, goose bumps rising on his arms.

"Now what?" Stacy asked.

"We'll put him in the tent. You can sit with him while we pull the others out." Jeff glanced at her, wondering if she was going to protest, but she didn't. She was still staring down at Pablo. Jeff leaned over the hole, shouted into it: "We're carrying him to the tent. Then we'll come back. Okay?"

"Hurry," Amy yelled.

They had trouble untying the knots connecting the backboard to the nylon braids, and finally Mathias just took the knife and cut it free. Then he and Jeff carried Pablo across the hilltop toward the orange tent, moving slowly, trying not to jostle him, while Stacy followed behind them, whispering, "Careful . . . careful . . . careful."

They set him down outside the tent, and Jeff unzipped the flap. He pushed his way inside to clear a space for the backboard, but instantly—as soon as he breathed in the stale air—he knew it was the wrong idea. He turned, stepped back outside. "We can't put him there," he said. "His bladder—he's gonna keep leaking urine."

Mathias and Stacy stared down at Pablo. "But we can't just leave him out here," Stacy said.

"We'll have to rig up some sort of shelter." Jeff waved back across the hilltop. "We can use what's left of the blue tent."

The other two considered this, silent. Pablo's eyes were shut; his breathing had developed a burr, a phlegmy roughness.

"We'll pull Amy and Eric up, then figure it out. Okay?"

Stacy nodded. Then Jeff and Mathias ran back toward the shaft.

Pablo started to shiver. One moment, he was just lying there, eyes shut—not sleeping, Stacy could tell, but quiet—and the next, he was trembling so violently that she began to wonder if he was having some sort of seizure. She didn't know what to do. She wanted to call out for Jeff, but she could hear the windlass creaking. They were pulling Amy or Eric up from the hole, and she knew she couldn't interrupt them. The belts were still buckled tightly around Pablo's body—at his thighs, his chest, his forehead—and she wished she could loosen them, yet she wasn't certain if this were allowed. She touched Pablo's hand, and he opened his eyes, stared at her. He said something in Greek, his voice sounding hoarse, weak. He was still trembling; struggling against it, she could tell, but unable to stop.

"Are you cold?" Stacy asked. She hugged herself, tucked her head into her shoulders, mimed a shiver.

Pablo shut his eyes.

Stacy stood up, darted into the tent. It was even darker inside than out, but—groping on her hands and knees—she managed to find one of the sleeping bags. She rose with it, intending to hurry back outside and drape it across Pablo's body, then felt a sudden hesitation, the temptation to lie down instead, curl into herself here in this musty stillness, hide. It lasted only an instant, this temptation. Stacy knew it was pointless—there'd be no hiding here—and she pushed past the moment. When she stepped back outside, the Greek was still shivering. Stacy laid the sleeping bag across his body, then sat down next to him, reaching to take his hand. She felt she ought to speak, ought to find some words to soothe him, but she couldn't think of a single thing to say. He was lying with a broken back in his own shit and urine, surrounded by strangers who didn't speak his language. How could she possibly hope to make this better?

There was a slight breeze, and the tent billowed in it. The vines seemed to be moving, too: shifting, whispering. It was too dark to see anything; there was just her and Pablo and the tent, and—somewhere out of sight across the hilltop—the creak, creak, creak of the windlass. Soon Amy or Eric would appear out of the shadows, coming to sit with her and Pablo, and then things would be easier. That was what Stacy told herself: *This is the hardest moment, right here, all alone with him.*

She didn't like the rustling sounds. It seemed as if more were happening out there than the wind could account for. Things were moving about; things were creeping closer. Stacy thought of the Mayans, with their bows and arrows, and had to repress the urge to flee, to drop Pablo's hand and sprint across the hilltop, toward Jeff and the others. But this was silly, of course, as silly as her fantasy of hiding in the tent. There was nowhere for her to run. If the sounds were what she feared, then attempting to flee would only prolong her terror, draw out her suffering. Better to end it now, swiftly, with an arrow from the darkness. She sat clenched, waiting for it, listening for the soft twang of the bowstring, while that furtive rustling among the vines continued, but the arrow didn't arrive. Finally, Stacy couldn't bear it any longer—the suspense, the anticipation. "Hello?" she called.

Jeff's voice came toward her from across the hilltop: "What?" The windlass had stopped its squeaking.

"Nothing," she yelled. And then, as the windlass resumed its turning, she repeated the word, in a whisper now: "Nothing, nothing, nothing."

Pablo stirred, stared up at her. His hand felt cold to her, oddly damp, like something found rotting in a cellar. He licked his lips. "Nottin?" he said with a rasp.

Stacy nodded, smiled. "That's right," she said. "It's nothing." And then she sat there, waiting for the others to join her, struggling to believe it was true, that it was nothing—the wind, her imagination—that she was pulling monsters out of the night. "It's nothing," she kept whispering. "It's nothing. It's nothing. It's nothing."

Amy had asked Eric if she could hold his hand. She wasn't frightened, she'd explained; it was just so dark down there in the hole, and she needed some sort of contact, needed more than the sound of his voice to reassure her of his presence beside her. He'd agreed, of course, and though at first it had felt a little awkward, sitting on the rocky floor of the shaft, holding hands with her best friend's boyfriend, she'd soon grown comfortable with it.

This was while they were waiting for Jeff and Mathias to return from the orange tent and lower the rope back into the hole. She and Eric spent the whole time talking—assiduously—as if they sensed some danger in even the briefest silence. The danger of thinking, Amy supposed, of stopping and assessing where they were, what they were dealing with. She felt as if they were sitting on some perilously high cliff, sensing the earth so far beneath them but trying not to look down and see it. Talking felt safer than thinking, even if they ended up talking about precisely what would've occupied their thoughts, because with talking there was at least the chance for reassurance, for them to bolster and encourage each other in a way that was impossible to do on one's own. And there was the chance to lie, too, if this were necessary. They talked about Eric's knee (it hurt when he put any weight on it, but it had stopped bleeding again, and Amy assured him it was going to be okay). They talked about how thirsty they were and how long their water would last (very thirsty, and only another day or so, though they both agreed that they'd probably be able to catch enough rain to tide them over). They talked about whether the other Greeks would come in the morning (probably, Eric said, and Amy seconded this, though she knew they were only hoping it was true). They talked about the possibility of their signaling a passing plane, or of one of them sneaking past the Mayans in the middle of the night, or of the Mayans simply losing interest at some point, vanishing back into the jungle, leaving the path open for their departure.

The one thing they didn't talk about was Pablo. Pablo and his broken back.

They talked about what they were going to do when they finally managed to return to their hotel, the very first thing, debating the merits of their various choices, until it became too painful to think about any longer—the meals they both dreamed of eating made them feel too hungry; the icy beer made them feel too thirsty, the shower too dirty.

The cold draft came and went, yet it did nothing to clear the shaft of the smell of Pablo's shit. Amy had to breathe through her mouth, but even so, the stench managed to reach her; she began to feel as if it were some sort of paint into which she'd been dipped, as if she'd never be free of it. Eric asked her if she could see things in the darkness, floating lights, bobbing slowly toward them. "Over there," he said, and his hand fumbled for her chin, turned her head to her left, held it still. "A bluish sphere, like a balloon. Can't you see it?" But she couldn't; there was nothing there.

Jeff yelled down that they were back. All they had to do was knot together a sling, and then they'd pull them up.

Amy and Eric discussed who should go first, both of them offering this opportunity to the other. Amy insisted that Eric should be the one. He was wounded, after all, and he'd already spent so many hours alone in the hole. She swore she wasn't frightened, said it would only be a minute or two, that she didn't mind at all. But Eric wouldn't hear of it; he refused outright, and, finally, with secret relief—because she *was* frightened, because she *did* mind—Amy accepted his decision.

The windlass started to squeak. Jeff and Mathias were lowering the rope.

It was too dark to make out the sling's approach. They sat staring upward, seeing nothing, and then the creaking stopped. "Got it?" Jeff yelled.

Eric and Amy stood up, still clasping hands, and held their free arms out, swinging them slowly to and fro until Amy felt the cool nylon of the sling; it seemed to materialize out of the darkness at her touch. "Here it is," she said, and she guided Eric to it. They stood for a moment, both of them gripping the sling. Amy shouted upward, "Got it!"

"Tell us when," Jeff called back.

Amy could hear Eric breathing beside her. "Are you sure?" she asked.

"Definitely," he said. And then he laughed, or pretended to. "Just don't forget to send it back down."

"How do I do it?"

"Pull it over your head. Tuck it under your arms."

She let go of his hand, pushed her arms through the sling's opening, her head. Eric helped her, adjusting it beneath her armpits.

"You're sure it's okay?" she asked again.

Somehow, she could sense him nodding in the darkness, cutting her off. "Want me to shout?"

"I can," she said. Eric didn't respond. He stood beside her, with one hand resting lightly on her shoulder, waiting for her to call out. She craned back her head, yelled, "Ready!"

And then the windlass began its squeaking, and suddenly she was rising into the air, her feet dangling free, Eric's hand falling from her shoulder, vanishing into the darkness behind her.

The chirping began again. At first, it seemed to be coming from above Eric; then it was right in front of him, nearly at his feet. He reached toward the sound, patting with his hands, but found only more of the vine, its leaves slick to his touch, slimy even, like the skin of some dark-dwelling amphibian.

The windlass paused in its creaking, leaving Amy dangling somewhere up above him.

"Can you see it?" Jeff yelled.

Eric didn't answer. The chiming had moved away now, toward the open shaft in front of him, then into it, down it, growing fainter.

"Eric?" Amy called.

There was a pale yellow balloon bobbing to his left. It wasn't real, of course, just a trick of his eyes, and he knew this. So why should the chirping be real? He wasn't going to follow the sound down the shaft, wasn't going to move, was determined to keep crouching here, with one hand on the oilless lamp, the other on the box of matches, waiting for the sling to come dropping back toward him.

"I can't see it," he shouted up at them.

The windlass resumed its creaking.

The wound on his knee throbbed steadily. He had a headache—he was hungry, thirsty. And tired now, too. He was trying not to think about everything he and Amy had discussed, trying to fill his mind with static, because it was so much harder now, all alone down here, to keep believing in the hopeful scenarios they'd created. The Mayans weren't going to leave—which of them had been the one to propose such a foolish idea? And how did they imagine they'd ever be able to signal a plane for help, it flying so far above them, so quickly, so tiny in the sky? *Chiropractor,* he thought, struggling to mute these questions. *Credentials. Collision. Celestial. Cadaver. Circumstantial. Curvaceous. Cumulative. Cavalier. Circumnavigate.*

The chirping stopped. And then, a moment later, so did the windlass. Eric could hear them helping Amy out of the sling.

What if the Greeks didn't come? Or, having come, were simply trapped here on the hill with them? *Derisive,* he thought. *Dilapidated. Decadent.* And what if it didn't rain? What would they do then for water? *Delectable,* he thought *Divinity. Druid.* Jeff had told him that he had to wash the cut on his elbow, that even something as small as that could get infected very quickly in this climate, and now he had a much deeper wound on his knee, with no chance of cleaning it. It could become gangrenous. He could lose his leg. *Dovetail,* he thought. *Disastrous. Devious.*

And Pablo . . . what about Pablo and his broken back?

The creaking resumed, and Eric stood up. *Effervescent,* he was thinking. *Eunuch.* He had the matches in one hand, the lamp in the other, and he lifted his arms, held them blindly out before him, waiting to receive the sling.

Stacy and Amy sat next to each other on the ground, a few feet away from Pablo's backboard. They were holding hands, watching Jeff examine Eric's knee. Eric had gingerly lowered his pants, grimacing as he pulled them free of his wound, the fabric tearing at the dried blood. Jeff crouched over him, struggling unsuccessfully in the darkness to get a sense of how badly Eric had been injured. Finally, he gave up; it would have to wait till morning. All that mattered for now was that it had stopped bleeding.

Mathias was building a shelter for Pablo, using the duct tape to fashion a flimsy-looking lean-to from what remained of the blue tent's nylon and aluminum poles.

"One of us should probably stay on watch while the others sleep," Jeff said.

"Why do we need someone on watch?" Amy asked.

Jeff nodded toward Pablo. They'd removed the belts, and he was lying on the backboard, eyes shut. "In case he wants something," Jeff said. "Or . . ." He shrugged, glanced across the clearing, toward the trail that led down the hill. *The Mayans,* he was thinking, but he didn't want to say it. "I don't know. It just seems smarter."

Everyone was silent. Mathias tore off a strip of tape, using his teeth.

"Two-hour shifts," Jeff said. "Eric can skip his." Eric was sitting there, looking dazed, his pants bunched around his ankles. Jeff couldn't tell if he was listening. "I'm thinking we should probably start collecting our urine, too. Just to be safe."

"Our urine?" Amy asked.

Jeff nodded. "In case we run out of water before it rains. We can hold ourselves over for a little while by—"

"I'm not going to drink my urine, Jeff."

Stacy nodded in agreement. "There's no way," she said.

"If we reach the point where it's either drinking urine or dying of—"

"You said the Greeks would come tomorrow," Amy protested. "You said—"

"I'm only trying to be careful, Amy. To be smart. And part of being smart is thinking about the worst-case scenario. Because if it comes to that, we'll wish we'd planned for it. Right?"

She didn't answer.

"Our urine's only going to get more and more concentrated as we become dehydrated," Jeff continued. "So now's the time to start saving it."

Eric shook his head, rubbed tiredly at his face. "Jesus," he said. "Jesus fucking Christ."

Jeff ignored him. "Tomorrow, once it's light, we'll figure out how much water we have and how we should go about rationing it. Food, too. For now, I think we should each just take a single swig and then try our best to get some sleep." He turned to Mathias, who was still working on the lean-to. "You have that empty bottle?"

Mathias stepped toward the orange tent. His pack was lying in the dirt beside it. He unzipped it, rummaged about for a moment, then pulled out his empty water bottle. He handed it to Jeff.

Jeff held it up before the others; it was a two-liter bottle. "If you have to pee, use this. Okay?"

Nobody said anything.

Jeff placed the bottle beside the doorway to the tent. "Mathias and I will finish Pablo's shelter. Then I'll take the first watch. The rest of you should try to get some sleep."

They talked only long enough to agree that they shouldn't talk, that they'd just end up agitating themselves, lying in the darkened tent, whispering back and forth. Stacy was in the middle, between Eric and Amy, on her back, holding hands with both of them. They'd left enough space for Mathias on the far side of Amy. There were two sleeping bags remaining in the tent, but it was too hot to think of using them. They'd pushed them and everything else—the backpacks, the plastic toolbox, the hiking boots, the jug of water—into a pile against the tent's rear wall. They'd talked, briefly, about drinking some of the water, whispering conspiratorially, hunched over the plastic jug. Amy was the one who'd suggested it, saying it as if it were a joke, her hand poised above the cap. It was hard to tell if she'd meant it—maybe she would've taken a long, gulping swallow if they'd agreed—but when they'd shaken their heads, insisting it wouldn't be fair to the others, she'd set the jug quickly aside, laughing. Stacy and Eric had laughed, too, but it had sounded odd in the darkness, the musty closeness of the tent, and they'd quickly fallen silent.

Eric removed his shoes, and then Stacy helped him pull his pants the rest of the way off. She and Amy remained fully clothed. Stacy didn't feel safe enough to disrobe; she wanted to be ready to run. She assumed Amy felt the same way, though neither of them admitted to it.

Not that there would be anywhere to run, of course.

Stacy lay very still, listening to the other two breathe, trying to guess if they were close to sleep. She wasn't; she was tired to the point of tears, but she didn't believe she'd ever be able to find any rest here. She could hear Jeff and Mathias talking softly outside the tent, without being able to tell what they were saying. After awhile, Amy let go of her hand, rolling away from her, onto her side, and Stacy almost cried out, calling her back. Instead, she shifted closer to Eric, pressing against him. He turned his head toward her, started to speak, but she put a finger to his lips, silencing him. She laid her head on his shoulder, snuggling. She could smell his sweat, and she stuck out her tongue, licked his skin, tasted the salt. Her hand was resting on his stomach, and without really thinking, she slid it down his body, slipping beneath the waistband on his boxers. She touched his penis, tentatively, the sleepy softness of it, let her fingers rest on top of it. She wasn't thinking of sex—she was too tired, too frightened for this to be any sort of motivation. What she was searching for was reassurance. She was fumbling for it, not knowing how to find it, trying this particular route only because she couldn't think of any other. She wanted to make him hard, wanted to jerk him off, wanted to feel his body arch as the sperm spurted out of him. She believed she'd find some comfort in this, some illusory sense of safety.

So that was what she did. It didn't take long. His penis slowly stiffened beneath her touch, and then she began to stroke him, fast, grimacing with the effort. His breath deepened, with a rasp hiding in it, and then—just as her arm was beginning to ache with the exertion—rose to a moan as he climaxed. Stacy heard the first, thick shot of semen splatter wetly to the tent's floor beside him. She could feel his body relax in the aftermath, could even feel the moment when he fell asleep, the tension easing from his muscles. It was infectious, that abrupt sense of relief, that sudden abatement, like an emptiness sweeping through her, and in the face of it, her fear seemed, if only temporarily, to retreat a step. That was enough, though; it was all she needed. Because in that brief moment—somehow, miraculously—with her hand still clasping Eric's sticky, slackening penis, Stacy, too, slipped into sleep.

Amy heard the whole thing. She lay there listening to Stacy's furtive rustling, its rhythmic push and pull, growing faster and faster, tugging Eric's breathing along behind it, the steady climb in volume, the suppressed moan, the silence that followed. In another context, she would've found the whole thing funny, would've teased Stacy in the morning, maybe even said something at the moment of climax, clapped, shouting, "Bravo! Bravo!" But here, in the stuffy darkness of the tent, she simply lay on her side with her eyes shut, enduring it. She could tell when they fell asleep, and she felt a moment's envy, a yearning for Jeff to be here, holding her, soothing her out of consciousness. Then the flap zippered open, and Mathias entered in his stocking feet. He stepped over her body and lowered himself into the empty space beside her. It was startling, how rapidly he joined the other two in sleep, as if it were a shirt he'd pulled over his head, adjusting it, tucking it into his pants, brushing out the wrinkles, before, his eyes drifting shut, he began to snore. Amy counted his snores. Some were so deep, they echoed in the air above her, while others were like whispers she had to strain to hear. When she reached one hundred, she sat up, crawled to the tent's flap, unzipped it, and slipped out into the night.

It wasn't as dark outside as in; Amy could see Jeff's shape beside the longer shadow of the lean-to, could sense him lifting his head to look at her. He didn't say anything; she assumed he didn't want to wake Pablo. She picked up the plastic bottle, unbuttoned her pants, and—crouching right there in front of the tent, with Jeff watching her through the darkness—started to urinate. It took her a moment to guide the mouth of the bottle beneath her stream, and she peed on her hand in the process. The bottle was already bottom-heavy with someone else's piss—Mathias's, Amy guessed—and there was something disturbing about this, the sound of her urine spurting into his, sloshing and spattering and merging. She wasn't going to drink it, she assured herself; it would never come to that. She was just humoring Jeff, showing him what a good sport she could be. If he wanted her to pee in the bottle, that was what she'd do, but in the morning the Greeks would arrive, and none of it would matter anymore. They'd send them off to get help, and by nightfall everything would be resolved. She capped the bottle, returned it to its spot beside the doorway, then pulled her pants back up, buttoning them as she moved toward Jeff.

The moon had risen, finally, but it was tiny, a faint silver sliver hanging just above the horizon. It didn't give off much light; she could make out the shapes of things, but not their details. Jeff was sitting cross-legged, looking oddly at peace—content, even. Amy dropped to the ground beside him, reached out and took his hand, as if she hoped by touching him she might claim some of his calm for herself. She was making a conscious effort not to glance beneath the lean-to. *He's asleep,* she told herself. *He's fine.*

"What are you doing?" she whispered.

"Thinking," Jeff answered.

"About?"

"I'm trying to remember things."

Amy felt a catch at this, a dropping sensation inside her chest, as if she'd reached for a light switch in a darkened room and encountered someone's face instead. She remembered visiting her mother's father, an old man with a smoker's cough, as he lay on his deathbed, tubed and monitored, clear fluids dripping into him, dark ones dripping out. Amy was six, maybe seven; she didn't let go of her mother's hand, not once, not even when she was prodded forward to kiss the dying man good-bye on his stubbled cheek.

"What are you doing, Dad?" her mother had asked the old man when they'd first arrived.

And he'd said, "Trying to remember things."

It was what people did, Amy had decided, as they waited for death; they lay there struggling to remember the details of their lives, all the events that had seemed so impossible to forget while they were being suffered through, the things tasted and smelled and heard, the thoughts that had felt like revelations, and now Jeff was doing this, too. He'd given up. They weren't going to survive this place; they were going to end just like Henrich, shot full of arrows, the vines coiling and flowering around their bones.

But no: it wasn't like that, not for Jeff. She should've known better.

"There's a way to distill urine," he said. "You dig a hole. You put the urine in it, in an open container. You cover the hole with a waterproof tarp, weigh it down to hold it in place. In its center you place a stone, so that the tarp droops there. And beneath that spot, in the hole, you leave an empty cup. The sun heats the hole. The urine evaporates, then condenses against the tarp. The water droplets slide down to the center and drip into the cup. Does that sound right to you?"

Amy just stared at him. She'd stopped following almost from the start.

It didn't matter, though; she knew Jeff wasn't really talking to her. He was thinking out loud, and might not even have heard her if she'd bothered to answer. "I'm pretty sure it's right," he said. "But I feel like I'm forgetting something." He fell silent again, considering this. She couldn't make out his face in the dim light, but she could picture it easily enough. There'd be a slight frown, a wrinkling of his forehead. His eyes would appear to be squinting at her, intensely, but this would be an illusion. He'd be looking through her, past her. "It doesn't have to be urine," he said finally. "We could cut the vine, too. Place it in the hole. The heat will suck the moisture right out of it."

Amy didn't know what to say to this. Ever since their arrival here, there'd been a jitteriness to Jeff, a heightened quality to his voice, his gestures. She'd assumed it was merely a symptom of anxiety, the same fear, the same nervousness the rest of them were feeling. But maybe it wasn't, she realized now; maybe it was something more unexpected. Maybe it was excitement. Amy had the sudden sense that Jeff had been preparing for something like this all his life—some crisis, some disaster—studying for it, training, reading his books, memorizing his facts. Trailing along behind this thought was the realization that if anyone was going to get them out of here, it would be Jeff. She knew this ought to have made her feel more safe rather than less, but it didn't. It unsettled her; she wanted to pull away from him, creep back into the tent. He seemed happy; he seemed glad to be here. And the possibility of this made her feel like weeping.

I'm not going to drink the urine, she wanted to say. *Even distilled, I'm not going to drink it.*

Instead, she lifted her head, sniffed the air. There was the faint, slightly musky scent of wood burning, a campfire smell, and she felt her stomach stir in response to it. She was hungry, she realized; they hadn't eaten since the morning. "Is that smoke?" she whispered.

"They've built fires," Jeff said. He lifted his arm, made a circular motion, encompassing them within it. "All around the base of the hill."

"To cook with?" she asked

He shook his head. "So they can see us. Make sure we don't try to sneak past in the dark."

Amy took this in, along with all its implications, the sense of being under siege. There were questions she knew she should be asking him, doors opening off of this particular hallway, leading to rooms that needed to be explored, but she didn't think she had the courage for his answers. So she kept silent, her fear chasing off her hunger, her stomach going tight and fluttery.

"There'll be dew in the morning," Jeff said. "We can tie rags to our ankles, walk through the vines, and the rags'll pick up the moisture. We can squeeze it out of them. Not much, but if—"

"Stop it," she said. She couldn't help herself. "Please, Jeff."

He fell silent, staring at her through the darkness.

"You told us the Greeks will come," she said.

He hesitated, as if choosing between different possible responses. Then, very quietly, he said, "That's right."

"So it doesn't matter."

"I guess not."

"And it'll rain, too. It always rains."

Jeff nodded, without saying anything. He was humoring her, Amy knew. And that was okay; she wanted him to humor her, wanted him to tell her it was all right, that they'd be rescued tomorrow, that they'd never have to dig a hole to distill their urine, never have to tie rags to their ankles and shuffle up and down the hillside collecting dew. A mouthful of dew, squeezed from dirty rags—how could they possibly have reached the point where this was a topic of conversation?

They sat in silence, still holding hands, her right clasped in his left. She remembered walking out of a movie once, their second date, how Jeff had reached to slide his arm through hers. It had been raining; they'd shared an umbrella, pressing close together as they walked. He was shier than she would've guessed; even that evening, standing so near, the rain spattering against the taut fabric only inches above their heads, he hadn't dared to kiss her good night. This was still to come, another week or so in the future, and it was nice that way; it gave weight to the other things, the smaller gestures, his arm hooking hers as they stepped out from beneath the brightly lighted marquee onto the rain-slick streets. She almost spoke of it now, but then stopped herself, worried he might not have any memory of the moment, that what had felt so touching to her, so joyous, had been an idle gesture on his part, a response to the inclement weather rather than a timid advance toward her heart.

A wind came up, briefly, and for a moment Amy felt almost chilly. But then it stopped, and the heat returned. She was sweating; she'd been sweating since she'd stepped off the bus, so many hours ago now, a different epoch altogether. Pablo shifted his head, muttered something, then fell silent. It took effort not to look at him; she had to shut her eyes.

"You should be sleeping," Jeff said.

"I can't."

"You're going to need it."

"I said I can't." Amy knew she sounded angry, peevish—she was doing it again, complaining, ruining everything, spoiling this moment of quiet they'd managed to forge together, this false sense of peace—and she wished she could take back the words, soften them somehow, then lie down with her head in Jeff's lap so that he might soothe her into sleep. Her left hand was sticky with urine. She lifted it to her nose, sniffed. Then she opened her eyes and, without meaning to, looked at Pablo. They'd taken the sleeping bag off him. He was lying on his back beneath the little lean-to, his arms folded across his chest. His eyes were closed. *Sleeping,* she reassured herself. *Resting.* You couldn't see the damage—it was inside him, his shattered vertebrae, his crushed spinal cord—but it was easy enough to imagine. He looked shrunken, aged. He looked withered and diminished. Amy couldn't understand how this transformation could have happened so rapidly. She remembered him standing beside the hole, holding that imaginary phone to his ear, waving for them to approach; it seemed impossible that this ragged figure could belong to the same person. His pants were gone; he was naked from the waist down, and his legs looked wrong, askew somehow, as if he'd been carelessly dropped here. Amy could see his penis, nearly hidden in the darkly shadowed growth of his pubic hair. She looked away.

"You took off his pants," she said.

"We cut them off."

Amy pictured the two of them, Jeff and Mathias, leaning over the backboard with the knife, one of them cutting, the other holding Pablo's legs still. But no: Pablo's legs wouldn't have needed to be held still, of course—that was the whole point. Mathias was like Jeff, Amy supposed: head down, eyes focused, a survivor. His brother was dead, but he was far too disciplined to grieve. He would've been the one to wield the knife, she decided, while Jeff crouched beside him, setting the strips of denim aside, already imagining how he could use them, the ones that weren't too soiled, how they could tie them to their ankles in the morning and gather the dew to drink. She knew that if she were Mathias, she'd still be at the bottom of the hill, clutching her brother's rotting body, sobbing, screaming. And what good would this do any of them?

"We have to be able to keep him clean," Jeff said. "That's how it will happen, I think. If it does."

There was that breeze again, chilling her. Amy shivered. She was breathing through her mouth, trying not to smell the fires burning at the base of the hill. "If what does?" she asked.

"If he dies here. It'll be an infection, I'm guessing. Septicemia, maybe—something like that. There's nothing, really, we can do to stop it."

Amy shifted slightly, her hand slipping free of Jeff's grasp. You weren't supposed to speak the words, but he'd gone and done it anyway, so casually, a man flicking his hand at a fly. *If he dies here.* Amy felt the need to say something, to assert some other reality—more benign, more hopeful. The Greeks were going to arrive in the morning, she wanted to tell him. By this time tomorrow, they'd all be saved. No one was going to have to drink any urine, any dew. And Pablo wasn't going to die. But she remained silent, and she knew why, too. She was afraid Jeff might contradict her.

Jeff yawned, stretching, his arms rising over his head.

"Are you tired?" she asked.

He made a vague gesture in the darkness.

Amy waved toward the tent. "Why don't you go to sleep? I can sit with him. I don't mind."

Jeff glanced at his watch, pushing a button to make it glow, briefly. Pale green: if she'd blinked, she would've missed it. He didn't speak.

"How much longer do you have?" she asked.

"Forty minutes."

"I'll add it to mine. I can't sleep anyway."

"That's all right."

"Seriously," she persisted. "Why should we both be up?"

He looked at his watch again, that green luminescence; she could almost see his face in its glow, the jut of his chin. He turned toward her. "I'm thinking of going down the hill," he said.

Amy knew what he was saying, but she didn't allow herself to admit it. "Why?"

He waved beyond her, past the tent. "There's a spot where the fires are a little farther apart. It might be possible to sneak by."

She pictured Mathias's brother, the arrows in his body. *No,* she thought. *Don't.* But she didn't speak. She wanted to believe that he could do it, that he could move, ghostlike, across the clearing, creeping slowly, silently, invisibly past the Mayans standing guard there. Then into the jungle, through the trees—running.

"I figure they're watching the trails. If I make my way straight down through the vines . . ." He fell silent, waiting for Amy's reaction.

"You have to be careful," she said. It was the best she could do.

"I'm just gonna check it out. I'll only try it if it seems clear."

She nodded, not certain if he could see her. He stood up, then bent to tie one of his shoelaces.

"If I don't come back," he said. "You'll know where I am."

Running, he meant. Heading for help. But what she pictured was Henrich's corpse again, the bones showing through on his face. "Okay," she said, thinking, *No.* Thinking, *Don't.* Thinking, *Stop.*

Then she sat there, next to Pablo, and watched as he walked away, without another word, vanishing into the darkness.

Eric woke, briefly, as Jeff moved past the tent. He lay on his back, wondering where he was. He was thirsty and his leg ached, and it was darker than it seemed like it ought to be. Then it came to him, everything, the whole day, all in a flash. The Mayans with their bows, his descent into the shaft, Amy and he tossing Pablo's body onto the backboard. This last bit was too much for him, too horrible; he shoved the image aside, feeling wretched.

Stacy had rolled away from him, and he could hear someone snoring on the far side of the tent. Mathias, he supposed. He wondered what time it was, how Pablo was doing, and thought about getting up to check on him. But he was too tired; the impulse came and went, and then his eyes were drifting shut again. He slid his hand in under the waistband of his boxers, scratched at his groin; it felt sticky. Only then did he remember Stacy jerking him off. There was something else down there, too, in the darkness, something soft, tentative but insistent, like a spiderweb, brushing against his leg. He tried to kick it away, rolled onto his side, slipped back into sleep.

Jeff headed straight through the vines, angling downhill. The Mayans had built fires all along the margin of the clearing, evenly spaced, and close enough together so that the light from one merged into the light of the next. But there were two that were just slightly farther apart, with a narrow strip of shadow between them. It wasn't much; Jeff knew it wouldn't be sufficient on its own. There'd have to be another factor to help him, a lapse in vigilance, one of the Mayans drowsing, perhaps, or two of them talking quietly together, telling a story. What he needed was ten seconds, maybe twenty, time enough for him to approach the clearing, cross it, then vanish into the jungle.

It was harder to move through the vines than he'd anticipated. They grew knee-high in most spots, but in some stretches they climbed almost to his waist. They clung to him as he passed, tangled their tendrils about his legs. It was slow going, and arduous, too—he kept having to stop to catch his breath. He knew he'd need to conserve his strength for the bottom of the hill, in case it came to a sprint, him crashing through the jungle, the Mayans yelling, pointing their bows toward him, the hiss of their arrows.

It was after one of these pauses, when he started forward again, while he was still only halfway down the hill, that the birds began to cry out, screeching, marking his passage through the vines. Jeff couldn't see them in the darkness. He stopped walking, and they fell silent. But then, as soon as he took another step, they began to call again. Their cries were loud, dissonant; there seemed to be a whole flock of them nesting on the hillside. Jeff had a sudden memory of himself as a child, visiting the birdhouse at the zoo, his fear of the noise, the echoing, the abrupt flappings. His father had pointed to the wire net hanging from the ceiling far above them, had struggled to calm him, but it hadn't been enough for Jeff; he'd cried, made them leave. There was no point in going on, Jeff knew: the Mayans would know he was coming now. But he continued downhill anyway, the shrieking of the birds following him through the darkness.

As he neared the bottom, he saw the Mayans waiting for him. There were three men standing by the fire on the left, two by the one on the right. One of them had a rifle; the others had their bows out, arrows nocked. Jeff hesitated, then stepped out into the margin of cleared ground, the light from the fires flickering softly off his body. The men with the bows didn't seem to be looking at him; they were scanning the hillside above, as if they expected the others to be coming, too. The man with the rifle raised it, aimed it at Jeff's chest. In the same instant, the birds fell silent.

The Mayans were standing with their backs to the fires—to preserve their night vision, Jeff assumed. Their faces were shadowed, so he wasn't certain if they were the same men who'd confronted them earlier, or some more recent arrivals. There was a large black pot hanging on a tripod over the fire to the right, steam rising thickly from it, the smell of chicken stewing, tomatoes. Jeff's stomach stirred hungrily; he couldn't help himself: He stood for a long moment, staring at the pot. Someone was singing softly in the shadows beyond it, a woman's voice, but then one of the bowmen whistled shrilly, and the singing stopped. No one spoke. The Mayans watched him, waiting to see what he might do.

Jeff wished he could speak to them, ask them what it was they wanted, why they were keeping him captive on this hillside, what it would take to purchase his freedom, but he didn't know their language, of course, and doubted, somehow, that they would deign to answer him even if he did. No, they'd just keep staring, weapons raised, waiting. Jeff could either stride bravely toward them and be shot like Mathias's brother or turn and make his way slowly back up through the vines, the shrieking birds, the darkness. There was no other option.

So he started back up the hill.

The return was much easier, too, for some inexplicable reason, than his descent had been. There was the exertion of the climb, of course, the impeding pull of gravity, but the vines caused him much less difficulty now, seeming almost to part for his passing, rather than grabbing and snaring at his legs. And, even more puzzling, the birds remained silent. Jeff wondered about this as he made his way higher up the hillside. It was possible, he supposed, that they'd flown off while he and the Mayans were standing at the base of the hill, in their mute confrontation, but if so, he couldn't understand why he hadn't heard their wing beats. And why hadn't he noticed the birds earlier, too, while it was still day? There had to be quite a few of them, judging by the volume of their calls as he'd made his way down the hill, and it seemed strange that he wouldn't have registered their presence. The only explanation he could think of was that they'd arrived at dusk, while he and Mathias were too busy raising Pablo from the shaft to take note of them. Obviously, the birds spent their nights here, though, which would mean he'd be able to find their nests in the morning. And their eggs, too, perhaps. At the very least, he'd be able to string up some snares to catch the adult birds, and Jeff found a measure of relief in this. They could distill their urine and gather dew and hope for rain, yet none of that was going to help them feed themselves. Jeff had been postponing confronting this problem, not wanting to think of it because he'd sensed he wouldn't find a solution, and now, like an unexpected gift, one seemed to have presented itself.

They'd have to use something thin, he thought, but strong, like fishing line. He was too tired, though, to think beyond this point. It didn't matter; they had plenty of time. All he needed to do now was get back to the tent, drop into sleep. In the morning, when it grew light, he was certain that everything would be clearer: the many things that still had to be done, and the ways in which he ought to do them.

Stacy had the third shift. Amy roused her, jostling her shoulder, whispering that it was time. Stacy was thirsty, open-eyed but still not quite awake; it was too dark inside the tent to see. She could tell that Eric was still lying there, with his back to her, and then there was Amy crouching over her, shaking her, and then Jeff and Mathias. The boys were all asleep. Mathias was snoring softly.

Amy kept whispering the same thing: "It's time." Stacy struggled first to grasp the words, then their meaning, then suddenly she understood. She was awake; she was getting up and leaving the tent, zippering it shut behind her.

Awake, but still dazed. She had to go back for Amy's watch, stepping carefully over Jeff, Amy already slipping into sleep, mumbling something, holding out her hand. It took Stacy several fumbling tries before she managed to unbuckle the watch's strap. Then she was back outside, alone with Pablo, sitting beside him, growing more and more awake with each passing moment. She slid Amy's watch onto her own wrist, and it felt warm against her skin, a little damp.

Pablo was asleep. She could hear him breathing, and it didn't sound right. There was too much fluid in it, a raggedness, and Stacy thought of his lungs, wondered what was happening inside him, the crises that were building, the systems failing. She stared at him dreamily, not really focusing, and several minutes passed before she noticed his legs in the darkness, his crotch, exposed. She had the momentary impulse— absurd and inappropriate and quickly repressed—to reach forward and touch his penis. The sleeping bag was lying on the ground beside the backboard, and she stood up to drape it across him, lowering it stealthily, gently, trying not to wake him.

He stirred, shifted his head, but his eyes remained shut.

This ought to have been the time for Stacy to attempt some appraisal of her situation—to glance back over the day or reach forward into the coming hours—and though she was conscious of this, though she understood the wisdom of such a course, she couldn't bring herself to attempt it. She sat listening to the liquid sound of Pablo's breathing, and her mind remained empty, not asleep, but not fully awake yet, either. Her eyes were open—she was aware of her surroundings, would've known if Pablo had stopped breathing suddenly, or called out for her—but she didn't quite feel as if she were present. She thought of a mannequin, propped in a store window, staring out at the street; that was how she felt.

She kept checking Amy's watch, squinting to read its numbers in the darkness. Seven minutes passed, then three, then six, then two, and then she forced herself to stop looking, knowing it was only going to stretch out her time here, eating it in such little bites.

She tried singing inside her head to help speed things along, but the only things she could think of were Christmas carols. "Jingle Bells," "O Tannenbaum," "Frosty the Snowman." She didn't know all the lines, and even silently, the words rising and falling in her mind, she didn't like the sound of her voice. So she stopped, stared vacantly down at Pablo.

Against her will, she checked the time again. She'd been awake for twenty-nine minutes; she had an hour and a half to go. For a moment, she panicked, wondering whom she was supposed to rouse when she was through, but then she figured it out, feeling proud of herself for her cleverness. Amy had been the one to shake her shoulder, pulling her from sleep, and Jeff had gone first, so that must mean Mathias was next. She glanced at the watch and another minute had passed.

I just hope Pablo doesn't wake up, she thought, and, at that very instant— as if these words inside her head had roused him—he did.

He lay perfectly still for a long moment, peering up at Stacy. Then he coughed, rolling his head away from her. He lifted his hand, as if to cover his mouth, but didn't seem to have the strength; he only made it to his throat. His hand hung in the air for a few seconds, hovering over his Adam's apple, then dropped slowly back to his chest. He licked his lips, turned toward her again, said something in Greek; it sounded like a question. Stacy smiled at him, but she felt false doing it, a liar, and she thought he must know it, must guess everything the smile was trying to hide, how hopeless things were. She couldn't stop herself, though; the smile was there and it wouldn't go away. "It's okay," she said, but that wasn't enough, of course, and Pablo spoke again, asking the same question. He paused, then repeated it once more, and his arms began to move, both of them, emphasizing his words, his hands patting the air. This made the stillness of his legs beneath the sleeping bag that much more difficult to ignore, and Stacy felt a rising sense of panic. She didn't know what she was supposed to do.

He kept speaking: the same question, over and over again, his hands cutting the air above his chest.

Stacy tried nodding, but then stopped, worried suddenly that he might be asking "Am I going to die?" She tried shaking her head then, only to realize that this was equally perilous, because couldn't he also be asking "Am I going to recover?" She was still smiling—she couldn't stop herself—and she sat staring down at him, feeling each moment closer and closer to tears, but not wanting to cry, desperately not wanting it, wanting to be strong, to make him feel safe, if only because she was with him, because she was his friend, and would've helped him if she could. She wondered how much Pablo understood of his situation. Did he realize that his back was broken? That he'd almost certainly never walk again? And that he very well might die here before they could get him to help?

He kept waving his arms at her, kept asking that same question over and over, his voice rising now, as if in impatience or frustration. There were six or seven words to the question, Stacy guessed, though it was hard to tell because they sounded enjambed, each flowing into the next, and there was that watery fricativeness lurking behind them, rounding their edges. She tried to guess what the words might mean, but her mind wouldn't help. It kept offering her "Am I going to die?" "Am I going to recover?" And she sat beside him, alternately feeling as if she ought to shake her head, or nod, but doing neither, not moving at all, while her liar's smile slowly stiffened on her face. She wanted to check her watch again, wanted someone to emerge from the tent and help her, wanted Pablo to slip back into silence, into sleep, for his eyes to drift shut, his arms to go still. She took his hand, gripped it tightly, and this seemed to help some, to calm him. And then, without thinking, Stacy started to sing her Christmas carols, very softly, humming the lines she didn't know. She did "Silent Night," "Deck the Halls," "Here Comes Santa Claus." Pablo fell quiet. He smiled up at her, as if he recognized the songs; he even seemed to join her for "Rudolph the Red-Nosed Reindeer," mumbling along with her in Greek. Then his eyes drifted shut and his hand went slack in hers; he fell back asleep, his breathing going deep, that watery sound rising from his chest.

Stacy stopped singing. She felt stiff; she wanted to stand up and stretch, but she was afraid to let go of Pablo's hand, worried that she might wake him. She shut her eyes—*just resting,* she told herself—and listened to his breathing, wishing it didn't sound like that, counting his inhalations, matching them with her own: *one, two, three, four . . .*

Suddenly, Mathias was beside her, crouching in the darkness, his hand on her forearm, that cool touch, and she was blinking at him, confused, slightly alarmed, wondering who he was, what he wanted, until everything came back with a snapping sensation, and she realized she'd fallen asleep. She felt flustered, embarrassed, derelict in her duty. She struggled into a sitting position. "I'm sorry," she said.

Mathias seemed startled by this. "For what?" he asked.

"I fell asleep."

"It's okay."

"I didn't mean to," she said. "I was singing to him, and he—"

"Shh." Mathias gave her arm a pat. Then he took his hand away, producing a tilting sensation in her chest, a subtle shift in gravity; she felt herself leaning toward him, had to jerk herself back. "He's fine," Mathias said. "Look." He nodded toward Pablo, who was still asleep, his mouth slightly open, his head canted away from them. He didn't seem fine, though; he seemed ravaged, as if something were sitting on his chest, slowly sucking the life from him. "It's been two hours," Mathias said.

Stacy lifted her arm, peered down at Amy's watch. He was right; she was done now. She could shuffle back to the tent and sleep till morning. But she still felt ashamed. She didn't move. "How did you wake up?" she asked.

He shrugged, dropped from his crouch into a sitting position at her side. "I can do that. Tell myself when to wake up. Henrich could, too. And our father. I don't know how."

Stacy turned, watched his profile for a moment. "Listen," she said finally, stumbling a bit, groping for the words. No one had taught her how to do this. "About your brother. I wanted, you know . . . to tell you how—"

Mathias waved her into silence. "It's all right," he said.

"I mean, it must be—"

"It's okay. Really."

Stacy didn't know what else to say. She wanted to offer him her sympathy, wanted him to tell her how he felt, but she couldn't find the words to make this happen. She'd known him for a week, had barely spoken to him in this time. She'd seen him staring at her that night she'd kissed Don Quixote, had felt frightened by his gaze, anxious that she was being judged, and then he'd surprised her by being so nice in the bus station, when her hat and sunglasses were stolen—he'd stopped and crouched and touched her arm. She had no idea who he was, what he was like, what he thought of her, but his brother was lying dead at the base of the hill, and she wanted to reach toward him somehow, wanted him to cry so that she could soothe him—to take him in her arms, maybe, rock him back and forth. But he wasn't going to cry, of course; she could see the impossibility of this. He was sitting right beside her, yet he felt too far away to touch. She had no idea what he was feeling.

"You should go to sleep," he said.

Stacy nodded but didn't move. "Why do you think they did it?" she asked.

"Who?"

She waved toward the base of the hill. "The Mayans."

Mathias was silent for a long moment, considering this. Then he shrugged. "I guess they didn't want him to leave."

"Like us," she said.

"That's right." He nodded. "Like us."

Pablo stirred, shifting his head, and they both stared down at him. Then Mathias reached out, patted her arm again, the cool touch of his fingertips.

"Don't," he said.

"Don't what?"

He made a wringing motion with his hands. "Twist yourself up. Try to be like an animal. Like a dog. Rest when you have the chance. Eat and drink if there's food and water. Survive each moment. That's all. Henrich—he was impulsive. He mulled over things, and then he lunged at them. He thought too much and too little, all at the same time. We can't be like that."

Stacy was silent. His voice had risen toward the end, sounding angry, startling her.

Mathias made an abrupt gesture, waving it all away. "I'm sorry," he said. "I'm just talking. I don't even know what I'm saying."

"It's okay," Stacy said, thinking, *This is how he cries*. She was about to reach toward him, when he shook his head, stopping her.

"No," he said. "It's not. Not at all."

Nearly a minute passed then, while Stacy tried out words and phrases inside her head, searching for the right combination but not finding it. Pablo's ragged breathing was the only thing to break the silence. Finally, Mathias waved her toward the tent again.

"You really ought to go back to sleep."

Stacy nodded, stood up, feeling stiff, a little dizzy. She touched his shoulder. She rested her hand there for a moment, squeezed, then crept back toward the tent.

Amy jerked awake, her pulse in her throat. She sat up, struggling to orient herself, to understand what had yanked her so abruptly out of sleep. She thought it must've been a noise, but if so, it seemed to be one only she had heard. The others were still lying motionless, eyes shut, their breath coming deep and steady. She could count the bodies in the darkness: Eric's and Stacy's and Jeff's. Mathias would be outside, she supposed, keeping watch over Pablo. So everyone was accounted for.

She sat listening, waiting for the noise to come again, her heart slowly calming.

Silence.

It must've been a dream, then, though Amy couldn't remember any details of it; there was simply that instant sense of panic as she sat up, her blood feeling too thick for her veins, moving too fast. She lay back down, shut her eyes. But she was awake now, still listening, still frightened—even though she couldn't have said of what—and thirsty, too, her lips sticking together with a gummy, crusty feeling, a foul, cottony taste in her mouth. Gradually, as she rested there, wishing for sleep but sleep not coming, her thirst began to triumph over her fear, a big dog barking a smaller dog into silence. She reached with her foot, stretching like a ballerina, and touched the plastic water jug sitting against the back wall of the tent. If she could just have a sip of water, a single small swallow to wash that dreadful taste from her mouth, Amy believed she'd be able to fall back asleep. And wasn't that important? They'd need to be rested in the morning, need to be up and about doing whatever it was that Jeff felt ought to be done to ensure their survival here. Walking through the vines with rags tied to their ankles. Digging a hole to distill their urine. One very tiny mouthful—was this too much to ask? Of course, they'd agreed not to drink anything more until morning. When they were all awake and rested, they'd gather around and ration out their food and water. But what good did this do Amy now, with her gummy lips, her sewer mouth, while the others lay on either side of her, blissfully sunk in sleep?

She sat up again, squinted toward the rear of the tent, struggling to discern the jug in the darkness. She couldn't do it; she could see the pile of things there, a shadowy mass, but couldn't make out the individual items, the backpacks, the toolbox, the hiking boots, the plastic jug. She'd felt it with her foot, though: she knew where it was. All she'd need to do would be crawl a few feet, groping with her hands to find it. Then it would simply be a matter of unscrewing its cap, raising the jug to her lips, tilting back her head. One small swallow—who could begrudge her this? If Eric, say, were to wake now, begging for a drink, Amy would gladly offer him one, even if she herself weren't thirsty. And she was certain the others would feel the same, would act toward her with a similar spirit of generosity. She could wake them right now, ask their permission, and they'd say "Yes, of course." But why should she disturb them when they all seemed to be sleeping so soundly?

She shifted a little closer, still straining to glimpse the jug, careful not to make any noise.

Amy wasn't going to steal any water, of course—no, not even a sip. Because that was what it would amount to, wouldn't it? A theft. They didn't have much water, and—despite Jeff's schemes—they couldn't be certain of getting more. So if she were to take a swallow now while the others slept, even the smallest, the daintiest of sips, it would be that much less water for all of them to share. Amy had seen enough survival movies—the plane crashes, the castaways, the space travelers trapped on distant planets—to know how there was always someone who grabbed, wild-eyed and swearing, who wrestled for the last ration, who gulped when others sipped, and she wasn't going to be that person. Selfish, thinking only of her own needs. They'd each taken their allotment of water before they went to sleep, passing the jug from hand to hand, and that was it, they'd agreed, that was all they'd have till morning. If the others could wait, why shouldn't she?

She edged a little closer. She just wanted to see the jug, maybe touch it, heft it in her hand, reassure herself with its weight. What harm was there in this? Especially if it might help her slip back into sleep?

The thing was, though, they hadn't really agreed, had they? It wasn't as if they'd discussed it, or voted on it. Jeff had simply made the decision, then imposed it on them, and they'd been too tired to do anything but bow their heads and accept this. If Amy had been more rested, or less frightened, she might've spoken up, might've demanded a larger ration right then and there. And the others might've added their voices, too.

No, you couldn't really call it an agreement.

And what was going to happen in the morning? They'd pass the jug around again, wouldn't they? They'd all take their allotted sip. But since Amy was thirsty now, why shouldn't she claim her portion a few hours earlier than the others? This wouldn't be grabbing or stealing; it would be like taking an advance on one's salary. When the jug was handed to her in the morning, she'd simply shake her head, explain that she'd grown thirsty during the night—terribly thirsty—and so had already consumed her morning's ration.

She shifted another foot forward, and she could see it now, make out its shape amid the large jumble there against the tent's rear wall. All she'd need to do was tilt forward onto her hands and knees, stretch her arm out, grasp the jug by its handle. She sat for a long moment, hesitating. In her mind, she was still debating, was even beginning to lean away from the idea, telling herself that she should just wait till morning like everyone else, that she was being a baby, and then suddenly—even as she was thinking these thoughts—her body was moving closer to the jug, her hand reaching for it, lifting it toward her, unscrewing its cap. Everything was happening in a rush now, as if someone might call out to stop her. She lifted the jug to her mouth, took her small sip, but it wasn't enough, not nearly enough, and she raised the jug higher, pouring the water down her throat: a long, gulping swallow, then a second one, the water spilling down her chin.

She lowered the jug, wiping her mouth with the back of her hand. She was twisting the cap back onto the jug when she glanced guiltily at the shadowed forms of the others, Eric and Stacy both lost in sleep, Jeff peering toward her through the darkness. They stared at each other for a long moment. She thought he was going to speak, berate her in some way, but he didn't. It was dark enough that she could almost convince herself that his eyes weren't open after all, that it was just a trick of perception, her conscience tugging at her, but then he shook his head, once— less in admonition, it seemed to Amy, than revulsion—and rolled away from her.

Amy returned the jug to its resting place against the rear wall, crawled back to her spot. "I was thirsty," she whispered. She felt like crying, but she was angry, too, a terrible cocktail of emotion: guilt and fury and shame. And relief, too: the water in her mouth, her throat, her stomach.

Jeff didn't respond. He remained perfectly silent, perfectly still, and this felt worse to Amy than anything he might've said. She wasn't worth the trouble of a response—that was what he was telling her.

"Fuck off," Amy said, not loudly, but loudly enough. "All right, Jeff? Just fuck off." She could feel tears coming now; she didn't try to stop them.

"What?" Stacy asked, befuddled, still asleep.

Amy didn't answer her. She lay curled into herself, crying softly, wanting to lash out and hit Jeff, pummel his shoulders, wanting him to turn and tell her it was okay, that she hadn't done anything wrong, that he understood, forgave her, that it was nothing, nothing at all, but he lay there with his back to her—sleeping now, she thought, like Stacy and Eric, all of them leaving her alone here, awake in the dark, her face damp with tears.

The sun had risen. That was the first thing Eric noticed when he opened his eyes, the light filtering through the orange nylon of the tent. It already felt hot, too—that was the second thing—he was sweaty, dry-mouthed. He lifted his head, glanced about. Stacy was sleeping at his side. And then, beyond her, was Amy, curled into a tight ball. Mathias was gone. Jeff, too.

Eric thought about sitting up, but he was still tired, and his body ached. He lowered his head, shut his eyes again, spent a few moments cataloging the various sensations of pain his body was offering him, starting at the top and moving downward. His chin felt bruised; it hurt when he opened and shut his mouth. His elbow was sore; when he probed at the cut, it was hot to his touch. His lower back was stiff, the pain radiating down his left leg each time he shifted his body. And then there was his knee, which didn't hurt nearly as much as he'd anticipated, which felt a bit numb, actually. He tried to bend it, but his leg wouldn't move; it was as if something were sitting upon it, holding it to the floor of the tent. He lifted his head to look, and was startled to see that the vine had grown dramatically in the night, reaching out from the pile of supplies at the rear of the tent to spread across his left leg, up his left side, almost to his waist.

"Jesus," Eric said. It wasn't fear he felt, not yet; it was closer to disgust.

He sat up and was just reaching to yank the plant off his body, when Pablo began to scream.

Jeff was at the base of the hill, too far away to hear the screams. He'd emerged from the tent shortly before dawn, urinated into the plastic bottle. By the time he'd finished, it was more than half-full. Later, after the sun rose, they could dig a hole, attempt to distill what they'd collected. Jeff wasn't certain it would work—he still felt as if he were forgetting some crucial detail—but at the very least it would occupy them for a few hours, keep their minds off their thirst and hunger.

He capped the bottle, set it back on the ground, then moved toward the little lean-to. Mathias was sitting cross-legged beside it; he nodded hello as Jeff approached. It wasn't light yet, but the darkness had already begun to diminish somewhat. Jeff could see Mathias's face, the stubble growing on his cheeks. He could see Pablo, too, unconscious on his backboard, a sleeping bag covering him from the waist down, could see him well enough to read the damage in his face, the sunken quality, the shadowed eye sockets, the slack-looking mouth. Jeff lowered himself to the ground beside Mathias and they sat in silence for a stretch. Jeff liked that about the German, his separateness, the way he'd always wait for someone else to be the first to speak. He was easy to be around. There was no pretense; things were exactly what they appeared to be.

"He looks pretty bad, doesn't he?" Jeff said.

Mathias's gaze moved slowly up Pablo's body, came to rest on his face. He nodded.

Jeff ran his hand through his hair. He could feel how greasy it was; his fingers came away slippery with it. His body was giving off a sour, yeasty smell. He wished he could shower, wished for it with an abrupt, almost tearful urgency, a childhood feeling—of frustration, of knowing that he wasn't going to get what he desired, no matter how hard he might work to attain it. He pulled back from the feeling, the yearning, forced himself to focus on what was rather than on what he wished to be, the here and now in all its painful extremity. His mouth was dry; his tongue felt swollen. He thought of the water jug, but he knew they'd have to wait until everyone was awake. This reflection led, inevitably, to the memory of Amy, her furtive thievery during the night. He'd need to speak to her; she couldn't keep doing things like that. Or maybe not; maybe he should let it go. He tried to think of a way to address the theft indirectly, but he felt dirty and tired and thirsty, and his mind refused to help him. His father was good at that sort of thing, telling a story rather than delivering a lecture. It was only afterward that you realized what he was saying: *Don't lie.* Or: *It's okay to be frightened.* Or: *Do the right thing even if it hurts.* But his father wasn't here, of course, and Jeff wasn't like him; Jeff didn't know how to be subtle in that way. He felt a jolt of emotion at this thought, missing his father even more than the unattainable shower, missing both his parents, wishing they were here to make things right. He was twenty-two years old; he'd spent nine-tenths of his life as a child, could still reach back and touch the place. It frightened him, in fact, how accessible it was. He knew that being a child now, waiting for someone else to save him, would be as easy a way to die as any other.

He'd keep silent, he decided. He'd only speak if Amy did it again.

He told Mathias about the hole with the tarp over it to distill their urine. He described how they could collect the dew, with rags tied to their ankles. "Now would be the time for it, too," he said. "Just before the sun rises."

Mathias turned, glanced toward the east. It wasn't true what they said, about the darkest moment being right before the dawn. It was lighter already, a graying quality to the sky, but there was still no sign of the sun.

"Or maybe not," Jeff continued. "Maybe we should wait. Let everyone get their sleep. We have enough water for today. And it may rain, too."

Mathias made an ambiguous gesture, half nod, half shrug, and then they sat for a minute in silence. Jeff listened to Pablo's breathing. It was too thick—gluey with phlegm. They'd have him pumped full of antibiotics if he were in a hospital; they'd be suctioning clear his airway. That was how bad it sounded.

"We should put up a sign, I guess," Jeff said. "Just to be safe. In case the Greeks come when no one's there. A skull and crossbones or something."

Mathias laughed, very softly. "You sound like a German."

"What do you mean?"

"Always doing the practical thing, even when it's pointless."

"You think a sign is pointless?"

"Would a skull and crossbones have stopped you from climbing the hill yesterday?"

Jeff mulled over that, frowning. "But it's worth a try, isn't it?" he asked. "I mean, couldn't it stop someone else, even if it wouldn't have stopped us?"

Mathias laughed again. "*Ja,* Herr Jeff. By all means. Go make your sign." He waved him away. "*Gehen,*" he said. "Go."

Jeff stood up, headed off. The contents of the blue tent were still tumbled beside the shaft—the backpacks, the radio, the camera and first-aid kit, the Frisbee, the empty canteen, the spiral notebooks. Jeff dug through first one of the backpacks, then the other, until he found a black ballpoint pen. He took it and one of the notebooks, carried them back across the hilltop to the debris remaining from Mathias's hurried construction of the lean-to. From this, he retrieved the roll of duct tape, a three-foot aluminum pole. Mathias watched him—smiling, shaking his head—but he didn't say anything. It was growing subtly lighter; the sun was about to rise, Jeff could tell. As he set off along the trail, the Mayans' fires came into view, still burning on the far edge of the clearing, flickering palely in the fading darkness.

Halfway down the hill, he felt the urge to defecate: powerful, imperative. He set down everything he was carrying, then stepped into the vines and quickly lowered his pants. It wasn't diarrhea, but something one notch short of it. The shit slipped wetly out of him, snakelike, collapsing into a small pile between his feet. There was a strong smell rising off it, sickening him. He needed to wipe himself, but he couldn't think of anything to use. There was the vine growing all around him, with its flat, shiny leaves, but he knew what happened when these were crushed in any way, the acid sting of their sap. He shuffled back to the trail, only half-rising, his pants still bunched around his ankles, and ripped a sheet of paper from the notebook. He crumpled it, rubbed roughly. They should probably dig a latrine, he realized, somewhere downhill from the tent. Downwind, too. They could leave one of the other notebooks beside it, for toilet paper.

Dawn had begun to break, finally. It was an extraordinary sight—clear pink and rose above a line of green. Jeff crouched there, watching, the shit-stained sheet of paper still held in his hand. Then the sun, all in an instant, seemed to leap above the horizon: pale yellow, shimmering, too bright to look at.

It was as he was stepping back into the vines to kick some dirt over his shit—pulling his pants up, fumbling for his zipper—that he felt his fingers begin to burn. In the growing light, he could see that there was a pale green fuzz sprouting across his jeans. His shoes, too. It was the vine, he realized; tendrils of it had taken root on his clothes during the night, so tiny that they still looked more like the spread of a fungus than a plant—diaphanous, veil-like, nearly invisible. When Jeff brushed them away, they crumpled, leaking their stinging sap, singeing his hands.

He stared at the green fuzz a long moment, not certain what to make of it. That the vine could grow so quickly seemed extraordinary, an important development, and yet what did it mean? He couldn't think, couldn't decide, had to give up finally. He forced himself to look away, to continue forward into the day. He tossed the wad of paper onto the little pile of shit. The dirt was too packed, too dry for him to kick any free; he had to crouch and chop at it with a rock, sweat rising on his skin from the effort. He loosened one handful of the pale yellow soil, then another, scattering them across the mess he'd made, partially obscuring it, burying the stench; it was good enough.

Then it was back to the trail, where he stooped to retrieve the tape and pen, the notebook and the aluminum pole. He was just turning to resume his downward journey, when he hesitated, thinking, *There should be flies. Why aren't there flies?* He crouched again, puzzling over this, staring back toward his half-covered pile of shit, as if waiting for the insects to appear, belatedly, buzzing and swirling. But they didn't, and his mind kept jumping—too rapidly, without pause, like a burglar rifling a desk, yanking open drawers, dumping their contents to the floor.

Not just here but on Pablo, too. Flies hovering over his smell, crawling across his skin.

And mosquitoes.

And gnats.

Where are they?

The sun continued to rise. The heat, too—so fast.

Maybe the birds, Jeff thought. *Maybe they've eaten all the insects.*

He stood up, stared across the hillside, searching for the birds, listening for their calls. They ought to be awake now, flitting about, greeting the dawn. But there was nothing. No movement, no sound. No flies, no mosquitoes, no gnats, no birds.

Droppings, he thought, and scanned the surrounding vines, searching among the bright red flowers, the flat, hand-shaped leaves, for the white or amber splatter of bird shit. But, once again, there was nothing.

Maybe they live in holes, burrows they gouge from the earth with their beaks. He remembered reading of birds who did this; he could almost picture the creatures, earth-colored, taloned, hook-beaked. But he could see no sign of tunneled dirt, no shadowed openings.

He noticed a pebble at his feet, perfectly round, no larger than a blueberry, and he crouched, picked it up, popped it into his mouth. This was something else he'd read: how people lost in the desert would sometimes suck on small stones to keep their thirst at bay. The pebble had an acrid taste, stronger than he'd expected; he almost spit it out, but he resisted the impulse, using his tongue to push the tiny stone behind his lower lip, like a pinch of tobacco.

You were supposed to breathe through your nose, not your mouth; you lost less moisture that way.

You were supposed to refrain from talking unless it was absolutely necessary.

You were supposed to limit your eating, and avoid alcohol.

You were supposed to sit in the shade, at least twelve inches off the ground, because the earth acted like a radiator, sucking your strength from you.

What else? There was too much to remember, too much to keep track of, and no one here to help him.

He'd heard the birds last night. Jeff was certain he'd heard them. He was tempted to stride off across the hillside, searching for their burrows, but knew that he ought to wait, that it wasn't important. The sign first. Then back up to the tent, so that they could ration out the day's water and food. Then the hole to distill their urine, and the latrine—they'd need to get the digging done before it got much hotter. Then, after all that, he could find the birds, search for their eggs, string up some snares. It was crucial not to lunge at things, not to become overwhelmed. One task and then another, that was how they'd make it through.

He started down the trail.

The Mayans were waiting for him at the bottom, four of them, three men and a woman. They were crouching beside the still-smoldering remains of their campfire. They watched him approach, the men rising as Jeff neared the foot of the hill, reaching for their weapons. One of them was the man who'd first tried to stop Jeff and the others, the bald man with the holstered pistol. He held the gun in his hand now, hanging casually at his side but ready to be raised. Ready to be aimed, fired. His two companions each had a bow, arrows loosely nocked. There were half a dozen more Mayans along the far tree line, Jeff saw, wrapped in blankets, straw hats hiding their faces, sleeping. One of them stirred, as if sensing Jeff's approach. He jostled the man lying beside him, and they both sat up to stare.

Jeff stopped at the mouth of the trail, set everything down. He crouched with his back to the Mayans. It filled him with a fluttery sense of panic—he kept imagining the bows being raised, the arrows pulled taut—but he thought it might make him appear less threatening. He tore a blank page out of the rear of the notebook, uncapped the pen, and began to draw the first of his signs, a skull and crossbones, stark and simple, appropriately ominous. He went over and over it with his pen, making the drawing as dark as possible.

He tore off another page, wrote "SOS" on it.

Then a third page: "HELP."

And a fourth: "DANGER."

He pried up a softball-size stone, used it to pound the aluminum pole into the dirt, right at the edge of the clearing, blocking the trail. Then he duct-taped his signs to the pole, one beneath another. He turned finally, as if to see the Mayans' reaction. The two along the tree line had lain down again, their hats over their faces, and the woman by the fire had her back to him now. She was stirring the embers with her left hand, setting a small pot onto an iron tripod with her right: breakfast, Jeff assumed. The other three were still watching him, but with a much more casual air. They almost seemed to be smiling—good-humoredly, he thought. Or was there an air of mockery, too? Jeff turned, banged at the pole a few more times with his stone. Someone would have to come and sit by it later in the day, after the bus arrived in Cobá, but for now this ought to suffice. Just as a precaution, in case the Greeks somehow managed to appear earlier than expected. If they'd hitchhiked, say. Or rented a car.

Jeff retrieved the pen and the notebook and the roll of tape and was just about to start back up the trail, when he changed his mind. He set everything down again and—very hesitantly, very carefully—stepped out into the clearing, lifting his hands, patting at the air. The Mayans raised their weapons. Jeff pointed to his right, trying to show them that he just wanted to walk along the clearing's margin, keeping close to the vines: he wasn't going to try to flee. The Mayans kept staring at him, the bows drawn, the pistol aimed at his chest, but they didn't say anything, made no overt attempt to stop him, so Jeff took this as permission. He started slowly along the base of the hill.

The Mayans followed him, leaving the trail momentarily unguarded. Then, after about a dozen yards, the man with the pistol shouted something to the woman behind them, and she rose from her cooking, kicked at one of the sleeping men along the tree line. He pushed himself into a sitting position, rubbing his eyes. He stared after Jeff for a long moment, then roused one of his companions. They reached for their bows, stood up, shuffled sleepily toward the watch fire.

Jeff continued along the edge of the clearing, the Mayans keeping pace with him, their weapons raised. His mind was jumping again—the latrine, the hole to distill their urine, Amy stealing the water. He wondered if the signs would have any meaning to the Greeks, if they'd just walk right past them. He checked the sky—a pale blue now, perfectly clear—and wondered if it would darken later in the afternoon, if the customary showers would sweep over them, brief but intense, so inexplicably absent yesterday. He tried to think how they ought to go about collecting the rain if it did fall—they could use the remains of the blue tent, maybe, fashion it into a giant nylon funnel, but leading into what? There was no point gathering the water if they couldn't store it; they needed containers, bottles, urns. And this was the problem that was occupying Jeff when he glimpsed the first waist-high mound of vines and finally realized why he'd set off along the clearing, what he was looking for here, what—without admitting it to himself—he'd known that he'd eventually find.

The mound lay ten feet out into the clearing, a small island of green amid the dark, barren soil. Jeff stopped while he was still a few yards short of it, feeling a little frightened, almost turning back. But no, though he knew what it was—he was sure he knew—he still had to see for certain. He stepped toward it, dropped into a crouch, started to tear at the vines, forgetting the danger of their sap until he felt his palms begin to burn. By then, he already had the thing half uncovered; he could stop, wiping his hands in the dirt.

It was another body.

Jeff stood up, used his foot to part the remaining vines. It was a woman, perhaps even the one Henrich had met on the beach, the one whose beauty had enticed him here, luring him to his death. She had dark blond hair, shoulder-length, but beyond that it was difficult to say, as most of her flesh had already been eaten away. Her face was a blankly staring skull. Her clothes were gone, too; she was just a skeleton and hair, some mummified strips of meat, a tarnished silver bracelet still encircling her bony wrist, a belt buckle, zipper, and copper button resting in the otherwise-empty hollow of her pelvis. She couldn't be Henrich's love, of course; she was too far gone. Such a degree of dissolution had to have taken months to accomplish, even in this climate. Or maybe not, Jeff realized, bending to remove more of the vine, carefully this time, gently. Maybe it was the plant that had done it, eaten away at the flesh, fed off its nutrients.

The Mayans stood twenty feet away, watching him.

Jeff pulled more of the vine free, and the skeleton's left arm came loose, fell from its socket, dropped with a clatter to the ground. The vine wasn't growing out of the soil, he noticed; it was clinging directly to the bones. Jeff considered this for a moment, his mind jumping to the mystery of the clearing itself: how had the Mayans managed to keep it free of vegetation? The vine sprouted so quickly; in a single night it had taken root on his clothing, his shoes. And yet the earth he was standing upon was utterly barren. He scooped up a handful of dirt, examined it closely. Dark, rich-looking soil, flecked with white crystals. *Salt,* he thought, touching it with the tip of his tongue to make sure. *They've sowed it with salt.*

It was at this instant, up on the hill, that Pablo began to scream. Far away—too far away—Jeff didn't hear a thing.

He stood, dropped the handful of dirt, continued walking. His three companions followed, keeping themselves between him and the far tree line. He passed another watch fire, seven Mayans clustered around it, eating their morning meal. They paused as he approached, lowering their tin plates into their laps. He could smell the food, see it. It was some sort of stew—chicken, tomatoes, rice—perhaps left over from the night before, and Jeff's stomach clenched hungrily. He had the urge to beg from them, to drop to his knees and extend his open palms in supplication, but he resisted it, sensing the futility of such a gesture. He kept moving forward, sucking dryly on the pebble in his mouth.

He could already see the next mound.

When he reached it, he crouched, carefully pulled some of the vines away.

Another corpse.

This one seemed to belong to a man, though it was hard to tell, since it was even more reduced than the blond woman's. The bones had collapsed in a loose pile; they no longer bore any obvious relationship to a skeleton. Jeff guessed at the corpse's gender more from the size of its skull than anything else—it was large, almost boxlike. One of the flowering vines had pushed its way into the eye sockets, entering the right one, emerging from the left. There were buttons again, and a thin worm-like length of zipper from the man's pants. A pair of wire-rimmed glasses, a plastic comb, a ring of keys. Jeff counted three small arrowheads, stripped of their shafts. And then, lying in the dirt, nearly hidden beneath the tangle of bones, there was a scramble of credit cards, a passport. It was the contents of a wallet, of course. Which must've been made of leather, Jeff guessed, since there was no sign of it now. What remained was the inorganic, the synthetic—the metal and plastic and glass—everything else had been eaten. And that was the right word for it, too: *eaten.* Because it was the flowering vine that had done this, Jeff realized, not a passive force—not rot or dissolution—but an active one.

Jeff crouched over the body, examining the passport. It belonged to a Dutchman named Cees Steenkamp. Inside, his picture revealed him to be broad-browed, with thinning blond hair and an expression that could either be read as aloof or melancholic. He'd been born on November 11, 1951, in a town named Lochem. When Jeff looked up, he found the three Mayans watching him. It was possible, of course, that they were the ones who'd killed this man, shooting him with their arrows. Jeff felt the urge to extend the man's passport toward them, to show them the photo of Cees Steenkamp, his large, slightly bovine eyes staring so sadly out at the world: dead now, murdered. But he knew it wouldn't matter, wouldn't change anything. He was beginning to grasp what was happening here, the whys and wherefores, the forces at play. Guilt, empathy, mercy: these weren't what this was about. The photo would mean nothing to these men, and Jeff, increasingly, could understand this—even sympathize, perhaps. Half a dozen yards beyond the Mayans, there was a cloud of gnats swirling in the air, hovering over the jungle's edge, as if held back from approaching any nearer by some invisible force. And this, too, made sense to Jeff.

He slid the passport into his pocket, continued walking, the three Mayans mutely accompanying him. They passed other watch fires, everyone pausing at Jeff's approach, staring at him as he shuffled by. It took him nearly an hour to make his way around the base of the hill, and he found another five mounds before he was through. More of the same: bones, buttons, zippers. Two pairs of glasses. Three passports—an American's, a Spaniard's, a Belgian's. Four wedding rings, some earrings, a necklace. More arrowheads, and a handful of bullets, flattened from striking bone. And then, of course, there was Henrich, though at first Jeff had difficulty recognizing him. His body was in the right location, but it had changed dramatically overnight. The flesh was completely gone, as was most of his clothing, eaten by the vine.

Yes, Jeff understood now, or was beginning to understand. But it wasn't until he completed the circle, returning to his starting point at the base of the trail, that the true depths of their situation began to open before him.

His signs had vanished.

At first, Jeff assumed the Mayans must've taken them down, but this didn't fit into the picture he was forming in his mind, and he stood for a long moment, staring about, searching for some other possibility. He could see the hole where he'd pounded the pole into the dirt; he could see the stone he'd used as an improvised mallet, the notebook, the pen, the roll of tape. But the signs were nowhere to be found.

Just as he was about to give up, he noticed a glint of metal beside the trail, three feet from its margin, buried under the vines. He stepped toward it, crouched, began probing with his hands beneath the knee-high vegetation. It was the aluminum pole, still warm to the touch from its time in the sun. The vines had wrapped themselves so tightly around it that Jeff had to strain to tug it free. The signs he'd drawn had been torn from their duct tape; the plants were already starting to dissolve the paper, eating away at it. Yet even now, having glimpsed this, Jeff still couldn't stop himself from clinging to the old logic, the ways of the world beyond this vine-covered hill: perhaps the Mayans had thrown stones at the pole, he thought, knocking it off the trail. Then he noticed something else beneath the thickly coiled vegetation, a blackened sheet of metal. He kicked the vines clear of it, reached to drag the thing out into the open. It was a baking pan, a foot square, three inches deep. Someone had scratched a single word onto its soot-encrusted bottom, gouging deeply, cutting a groove into the metal.

¡PELIGRO!

Jeff stood for a long moment, contemplating this.

Danger.

The day was growing steadily warmer. He'd left his hat behind in the tent, and he could feel the sun beginning to scorch his neck, his face. His thirst had climbed to a new level. It was no longer simply a desire for water; there was pain involved now, a sense of damage being done to his body. The pebble he'd been sucking was proving useless to combat this, and he spit it out, only to be startled by a leap of movement amid the vegetation as the tiny stone dropped into the vines. Something had seemed to dart, snakelike, at the pebble, too quickly for Jeff to see it clearly, just the abrupt blur of motion.

The birds, he thought.

But no, of course not, it wasn't the birds—and he knew this. Because though he'd yet to understand where the noise had come from last night, he'd already realized that there weren't any birds on the hillside. No birds, no flies, no mosquitoes, no gnats. He bent, picked up another pebble, tossed it into the profusion of vines beside him. Once more, there was that jump of movement, nearly too fast to glimpse, and Jeff knew what it was now—knew what had pulled down his sign, too—and felt almost sickened by the knowledge.

He threw another pebble. This time there was no movement, and that made sense to Jeff, too. It was exactly what he'd expected. If it had kept happening, it would've simply been a reflex, and that wasn't what this was about.

He turned, stared toward the Mayans, who were standing in the center of the cleared ground, watching him, their weapons lowered finally. They seemed slightly bored by what they were seeing, and Jeff supposed he could understand this also. After all, he'd done nothing here that they hadn't witnessed on other occasions. The posting of the sign, the circumnavigation of the hill, the discovery of the bodies, the slowly dawning awareness of what sort of world he'd become trapped in: they'd seen it all before. And not only that; they could probably guess what was still to come, too, could've told Jeff, if they'd only shared a language, how the approaching days would unfold, how they'd begin and how they'd end. It was with these thoughts in his head that Jeff returned to the trail and began his slow climb up it to tell the others of all he'd discovered.

Stacy had opened her eyes to the sound of screaming. Eric was writhing about beside her, obviously in some sort of distress, and it took her a moment to realize that it wasn't his cries that were filling the tent. The noise was coming from outside. It was Pablo. Pablo was screaming. And yet something was wrong with Eric, too. He was leaning on his elbow, staring toward his legs, kicking them, saying, "Oh fuck, oh my God, oh Christ." He kept repeating the words, and Pablo kept screaming, and Stacy couldn't understand what was happening. Amy was on the other side of her, just coming awake, looking even more confused, even more lost than Stacy felt herself.

The three of them were alone in the tent; there was no sign of Jeff or Mathias.

Eric's left leg was covered with the vine.

"What is it?" Stacy said. "What's going on?"

Eric didn't seem to hear her. He sat up, leaning forward, and began to yank at the vine, struggling to pull it free from his body. The plant's leaves ripped and crumpled as he tugged at them, sap oozing out, beginning to burn him, to burn her, too, when she reached to help him. The vine had wound itself around his left leg, climbing all the way to his groin. *His sperm,* Stacy thought, remembering the hand job she'd given him the night before. *It was drawn to his sperm.* Because it was true: the vine had wrapped itself not only around Eric's leg but also his penis, his testicles. Eric was struggling to free himself from its hold, pulling gingerly now, still repeating that string of words: "Oh fuck, oh my God, oh Christ . . ."

Pablo's screaming grew louder, if this were possible; the tent seemed to be shaking beneath it. Stacy could hear Mathias yelling now, too. Calling for them, she thought, but she couldn't focus on this, was simply aware of it in a distant way while she continued to yank at the vine, her hands not merely burning but feeling abraded, lacerated; the tips of her fingers had begun to bleed. Amy was getting up, hurrying toward the flap, unzipping it, stepping out. She left the flap hanging open behind her, and sunlight poured through the opening, flooding the tent, the heat entering, too, making Stacy, even in the midst of all this chaos, abruptly aware of her thirst. Her mouth was webbed with it; her throat felt swollen, cracked.

It wasn't just Eric's semen, she realized. It was his blood, too. The vine seemed to have fastened, leechlike, to his wounded knee.

Outside, quite suddenly, Pablo stopped screaming.

"It's inside me," Eric said. "Oh Jesus—it's fucking inside me."

And it was true. Somehow the vine had pushed itself into his wound, opening it, widening it, thrusting a tendril into his body. Stacy could see it beneath his skin, the ridged rise of it, three inches long, like a thick finger, probing. Eric tried to pull it free, but he was too panicky, too quick, and the vine broke, oozing more sap, burning him, leaving the tendril snagged beneath his skin.

Eric started yelling. At first, it was just noise, but then there were words, too. "Get the knife!" he shouted.

Stacy didn't move. She was too stunned. She sat and stared. The vine was inside him, under his skin. Was it moving?

"Get the fucking knife!" Eric screamed.

And then she was up, on her feet, rushing for the tent flap.

Amy had awakened a few seconds after Stacy. She hadn't realized what was happening with Eric; Pablo's screaming was too loud for her to take note of anything else. Then Mathias was yelling for them, and for some reason Eric and Stacy weren't responding. They were thrashing about; they seemed to be wrestling. Amy couldn't make any sense of this—she was still half-asleep, and not thinking very clearly. Pablo was screaming; nothing else mattered. She jumped up and hurried outside to see what was happening. The screaming was loud, full of obvious pain, and it showed no sign of stopping, but she wasn't particularly worried by this. After all, Pablo's back was broken—why shouldn't he be screaming? It might take some time, but they'd calm him down, just as they had the night before, and then he'd slip back into sleep.

Outside, she stood blinking for a long moment, the sun too bright for her to see. She felt dizzy from it, disoriented, and was about to duck back inside the tent to search for her sunglasses, when Mathias turned toward her with a look of panic. It was as if a hand had grabbed Amy, shaken her roughly; she felt a rush of fear.

"Help me!" Mathias called. He was crouched beside the backboard, bent over the Greek's legs, and he had to shout to be heard above the screaming.

Amy stepped quickly toward him, seeing and not seeing at one and the same time. The sleeping bag was lying crumpled on the ground beside Mathias, leaving Pablo bare beneath the waist. Or no, not bare, not bare at all, because his legs were completely covered by the flowering vine, covered so thickly that it almost looked as if he'd pulled on a pair of pants made of the stuff. Not an inch of skin was visible from his waist to his feet. Mathias was pulling at it, yanking long tendrils off and throwing them aside, sap shining slickly on his hands and wrists. Pablo had lifted his head enough to watch; he kept trying to rise onto his elbow, but he couldn't seem to manage it. The tendons were taut on his neck with the effort, and his mouth hung open in a perfect O, screaming. The sound was so loud, so terrible, that, moving toward them, Amy felt as if she were wading through an actual physical barrier, a zone of inexplicably heightened gravity. Then she, too, was on her knees, tearing at the vine, ignoring the sap seeping across her hands, cool at first, slightly slippery, but then burning with such intensity that she might've stopped if it hadn't been for the screaming, the incessant screaming, the screaming that seemed to have entered her, to be inside her body now—

resonating, echoing—growing louder with each passing second, impossibly louder, excruciatingly louder, far more painful than the burning. She needed to stop it, to silence it, and the only way she could think to do this was to keep pulling at the vines—tugging, yanking, tearing—freeing Pablo's body from their grip. And still she was seeing and not seeing, the legs coming into view finally, a flash of white beneath the knee, not the white of skin, but deeper, brighter—shiny and wet—a bone white. She kept clearing the vine away, buffeted by Pablo's screaming, seeing and not seeing, not bone white, but bone itself, the flesh stripped cleanly from it, blood beginning to pool now, pool and drip, as the plant was pulled free, revealing more white, more bone white, more bone, his lower leg nothing but bone, the skin and muscle and fat gone, eaten, blood dripping from the Greek's knee, dripping and pooling, a long tendril wrapped completely around his shinbone, gripping it, refusing to relinquish its hold, a trio of flowers hanging from the length of green, red flowers, bright red, bloodred.

"Oh my God," Mathias said.

He'd stopped pulling at the vines, was crouched now, staring in horror at Pablo's mutilated legs, and suddenly Amy's not seeing wasn't working anymore; it was just seeing now—the bones, the flowers, the pooling blood—and the screaming didn't matter any longer, nor the burning; there were only the bones shining so whitely up at her, and a sense of pressure in her chest, her stomach rising, a surge of nausea. She jumped up, took three quick steps away from the lean-to, and vomited into the dirt.

Pablo stopped screaming. He was crying now—she could hear him crying, whimpering. She didn't turn around; she stood, bent over, with her hands on her knees, a long string of drool hanging from her mouth, swinging slightly, a little puddle of bile spreading between her feet, all that precious water she'd stolen in the night, gone now, draining slowly into the dirt. She wasn't done yet; she could feel more coming, and she shut her eyes, waiting for it.

"He woke up and just started screaming," Mathias said.

Amy didn't move, didn't glance toward him. She coughed once, spit, her eyes still closed.

"I pulled off the sleeping bag. I didn't—"

Then it was there, worse than the first surge; she bent low, a thick torrent spewing from her mouth. It was painful; she felt as if she were vomiting part of herself up, part of her body. Mathias fell silent—

watching, Amy assumed. And, an instant later, inside the tent, Eric began to yell. Just shouting at first, just noise, but then words, too.

"Get the knife!" he screamed.

Amy lifted her head, puke still dripping from her mouth, down her chin, across her shirt. She turned toward the tent. They all did—even Pablo, pausing in his whimpering, lifting his head, straining to see.

"Get the fucking knife!"

Then Stacy appeared, stooping past the tent flap, hesitating for an instant just beyond it, staring at Amy, at the string of drool hanging from her mouth, the puddle of vomit between her feet. Stacy squinted, the sun too bright for her—*seeing and not seeing,* Amy thought—turned toward the lean-to, toward Mathias.

"I need the knife," she said.

"Why?" Mathias asked.

"It's inside him. Somehow . . . I don't know . . . it's gotten inside."

"What has?"

"The vine. Through his knee. It pushed inside." Even as she spoke, her gaze drifted toward Pablo, who'd resumed his whimpering, but more softly now. *Seeing and not seeing:* the exposed bones, the pooling blood, the vine still half-covering his legs.

From inside the tent came Eric's voice, shouting, sounding frightened: "Hurry!"

Stacy glanced back toward the open flap, then at Pablo again, then at Mathias. Amy could tell that she wasn't taking it in, wasn't understanding what had happened, any of it. Her face was slack, her voice flat. *Shock,* Amy thought.

"I think he wants to cut it out," Stacy said.

Mathias turned, rummaged for a moment through the debris beside the lean-to, the remaining strips of blue nylon, the jumble of aluminum poles. When he stood up, he had the knife in his hand. He was just starting for the tent, when he stopped suddenly, staring toward Amy, toward her feet, toward the ground beyond them. Stacy, too, turned to look, and—instantly—went equally still. Their faces shared an identical expression, a mix of horror and incomprehension, and even before Amy spun to see what it was, she felt her heart begin to accelerate, adrenaline rushing through her body. She didn't want to see, but that was over, the not seeing; that wasn't an option any longer. There was movement behind her, a shuffling sound, and Stacy lifted her right hand, covered her mouth, wide-eyed.

Amy turned.

To look.

To *see.*

She was in the center of the little clearing before the tent. There were fifteen feet of dry, rocky dirt in any direction, and then the vines began, a knee-high wall of vegetation. Emerging from this mass of green, directly in front of her, was what Amy took at first to be a giant snake: impossibly long, dark green, with bright red spots running along its length. Bloodred spots, which weren't spots at all, of course, but flowers, because—although it moved like a snake, slithering toward her in wide S-shaped curves—that wasn't what it was. It was the vine.

Amy stepped backward, quickly, away from the puddle. She kept going until Mathias was in front of her, the knife held low at his side.

Pablo was watching from the backboard, silent now.

Eric called from the tent again, but Amy hardly heard him. She watched the vine snake its way across the clearing to her little pool of vomit. It hesitated there, as if sniffing at the muck, before sliding into it, folding itself into a loose coil. Then, audibly, it began to suck up the liquid, using its leaves, it seemed. They flattened across the surface of the puddle, siphoning it dry. Amy couldn't say how long this took. Not long, though—a handful of seconds, perhaps, half a minute at most— and when it was over, when the puddle was dry, just a damp shadow on the rocky soil, the vine began, with that same slithering motion, to withdraw across the clearing.

Stacy started to scream. She looked from one to the other of them, pointing toward the vine, horror-struck, screaming. Amy stepped toward her, took her in her arms, hugging her, stroking her, struggling to quiet her, both of them watching as Mathias pushed past them, carrying the knife into the tent.

Eric had stopped shouting when he heard Stacy begin to scream. His hands and legs and feet were burning from the vine's sap, and there was that three-inch tendril still inside him, under his skin, just to the left of his shinbone, running parallel to it. *Moving,* he thought, though maybe it was his body doing this—the muscles, spasming. He wanted it out of him—that was all he knew—and he needed the knife to get it out, to cut it free from his flesh.

But what was happening out there? Why was Stacy screaming?

He called to her, shouting, "Stacy?"

And then, an instant later, Mathias was ducking in past the flap, coming toward him with the knife, a clenched expression on his face. It was fear, Eric realized.

"What is it?" he asked. "What's happening?"

Mathias didn't answer. He was scanning Eric's body. "Show me," he said.

Eric pointed toward his wound. Mathias crouched beside him, examined it for a moment, the long bump beneath his skin. It was moving again, wormlike, as if intent on burrowing into Eric. Outside, Stacy finally stopped screaming.

Mathias held up the knife. "You want to?" he asked. "Or me?"

"You."

"It's going to hurt."

"I know."

"It's not sterilized."

"Please, Mathias. Just do it."

"We might not be able to stop the bleeding."

It wasn't his muscles, Eric realized. It was the vine; the vine was moving of its own accord, pushing its way deeper into his leg, as if it had somehow sensed the knife's presence. He felt the urge to cry out, but he bit it back. He was sweating, his entire body slick with it. "Hurry," he said.

Mathias straddled Eric's leg, sitting on his thigh, clamping it to the floor of the tent. His body blocked Eric's view; Eric couldn't see what he was doing. He felt the bite of the knife, though, and yelped, tried to jerk away, but Mathias wouldn't let him; the weight of his body held him in place. Eric shut his eyes. The knife sliced deeper, moved down his leg with a strange zippering sensation, and then he felt Mathias's fingers digging into him, grasping the length of vine, prying it free. Mathias threw it away from them, toward the pile of camping supplies at the rear of the tent. Eric heard it smack wetly against the tarped floor.

"Oh Jesus," he said. "Oh fuck."

He could feel Mathias applying pressure to his wound, struggling to staunch the fresh flow of blood, and he opened his eyes. Mathias's back was bare; he'd taken off his shirt, was using it as a makeshift bandage.

"It's all right," Mathias said. "I got it."

They stayed like that for several minutes, not moving, each of them struggling to catch his breath, Mathias using all his weight to press against the incision. Eric thought Stacy would come to check on him, but she didn't. He could hear Pablo crying. There was no sign of the girls.

"What happened?" he asked finally. "What happened outside?"

Mathias didn't answer.

Eric tried again. "Why was Stacy screaming?"

"It's bad."

"What is?"

"You have to see. I can't—" Mathias shook his head. "I don't know how to describe it."

Eric fell silent at this, taking it in, struggling to make sense of it. "Is it Pablo?" he asked.

Mathias nodded.

"Is he okay?"

Mathias shook his head.

"What's wrong with him?"

Mathias made a vague gesture with his hand, and Eric felt a tightening sensation in his chest: frustration. He wished he could see the German's face.

"Just tell me," he said.

Mathias stood up. He had his T-shirt in his hand, crumpled into a ball; it was dark now with Eric's blood. "Can you stand?" he asked.

Eric tried. His leg was still bleeding, and it was hard to put weight on it. He managed to pull himself to his feet, though, then nearly fell. Mathias grabbed him by the elbow, held him up, helped him hobble slowly toward the open flap of the tent.

Jeff found the four of them in the little clearing, sitting beside the orange tent. When they saw him approaching, they all started to talk at once.

Amy seemed to be on the edge of tears. "What are you doing here?" she kept asking him.

It turned out that he'd been gone so long, they'd begun to think he might've found a way to flee, that he'd sneaked past the guards at the base of the hill and sprinted off into the jungle, that he was on his way to Cobá now, that help would soon be coming. They'd talked through this scenario in such depth, playing out the various steps of his journey, imagining the time line—Would he be able to flag down a passing car once he'd reached the road, or would he have to hike the entire eleven miles? And was it only eleven miles? And would the police come immediately, or would they need time to gather a large enough force to overcome the Mayans?—that Amy seemed to have pushed past the murky realm of possibility into the far clearer, sharper-edged one of probability. His escape wasn't something that might be happening; it had become something that *was* happening.

Over and over again, the same question: "What are you doing here?"

When he told her he'd been down at the base of the hill, that he'd walked completely around it, she stared at him in incomprehension, as if he'd said he'd spent the morning playing tennis with the Mayans.

There was something wrong with Eric. He kept standing up, limping about, talking over everyone else, then dropping back down, his wounded leg extended in front of him. He was wearing shorts now—rifled, Jeff assumed, from one of the backpacks. He'd sit for a bit, rocking slightly, staring at the dried blood on his knee and shin, only to jump back up again: talking, talking, talking. The vine was inside him: that was what he was saying, repeating it to no one in particular, not waiting for a response, not seeming even to expect one. They'd gotten it out, but it was still inside him.

Stacy was the one who explained it to Jeff, what had happened to Eric, the vine pushing its way in through his wound while he slept, Mathias cutting it free with the knife. At first, she seemed much calmer than the other two, surprisingly so. But then, in mid-sentence, she suddenly jumped topics. "They'll come today," she said, her voice low and urgent. "Won't they?"

"Who?"

"The Greeks."

"I don't know," Jeff began. "I—" Then he saw her expression, a tremor moving across her face—*terror*—and he changed direction. "They might," he said. "This afternoon, maybe."

"They have to."

"If not today, then in—"

Stacy interrupted him, her voice rising. "We can't spend another night here, Jeff. They *have* to come today."

Jeff went silent, staring at her, startled.

She watched Eric for a moment, his pacing and muttering. Then she leaned forward, touched Jeff's arm. "The vine can move," she said, whispering the words. As she spoke, she glanced toward the low wall of vegetation that surrounded the little clearing, as if frightened of being overheard. "Amy threw up, and it reached out." She made a snakelike motion with her arm. "It reached out and drank it up."

Jeff could feel them all watching him, as if they expected him to deny this, to insist upon its impossibility. But he just nodded. He knew it could move—knew far more than that, in fact.

He got Eric to sit still so that he could examine his leg. The cut on his knee had closed again; the scab was dark red, almost black, the skin around it inflamed, noticeably hot to the touch. And beneath this wound was another, running perpendicular to it, moving down the left side of Eric's shinbone, so that it looked as if someone had carved a capital *T* into his flesh.

"It seems okay," he said. He was just trying to calm Eric, to slow him down; he didn't think it seemed okay at all. They'd smeared some of the Neosporin from the first-aid kit on the cuts—Eric's leg was shiny with it—and there were flecks of dirt stuck in the gel. "Why didn't you bandage it?" Jeff asked.

"We tried," Stacy said. "But he kept tearing it off. He says he wants to be able to see it."

"Why?"

"It'll grow back if we don't keep watching," Eric said.

"But you got it out. How would it—"

"All we got was the big piece. The rest is still inside me. I can feel it." He pointed at his shin. "See? How puffy it is?"

"It's just swollen, Eric. That's natural. That's what happens after you've been hurt."

Eric waved this aside, a tautness entering his voice. "That's bullshit. It's fucking growing in there." He pushed himself up onto his feet, limped off across the clearing. "I've got to get out of here," he said. "I've got to get to a hospital."

Jeff watched him pace, startled by his agitation. Amy still looked as if she might begin to cry at any moment. Stacy was wringing her hands.

Mathias was wearing a dark green shirt; he must've pulled it from one of the backpacks. This whole time, he hadn't spoken. But now, finally, in his quiet voice, with its almost unnoticeable accent, he said, "That's not the worst of it." He turned, looked toward Pablo.

Pablo. Jeff had forgotten about Pablo. He'd given him a quick glance when he'd first come walking back into the clearing, seen him lying so still beneath his lean-to, his eyes shut. *Good,* he'd thought, *he's sleeping.* And then that was it; there'd been Amy repeating her strange question—

"What are you doing here?"—and Stacy worrying over the Greeks' arrival and Eric insisting the vine was growing inside him, all of it distracting him, making no sense, pulling his mind from where it ought to be.

The worst of it.

Jeff stepped toward the lean-to. Mathias followed him; the rest of them watched from across the clearing, as if frightened to approach any closer. Pablo was lying on his backboard, the sleeping bag covering him from the waist down. He didn't look any different, so Jeff couldn't understand why he was feeling such a strange intimation of peril. But he was: a sense of imminent danger, a tightness in his chest.

"What?" he asked.

Mathias crouched, carefully pulled back the sleeping bag.

For a long moment, Jeff couldn't take it in. He stared, he saw, but he couldn't accept the information his eyes were offering him.

The worst of it.

It wasn't possible. How could it be possible?

On both legs, from the knees down, Pablo's flesh had been almost completely stripped away. Bone, tendon, gristle, and ropy clots of blackened blood: this was all that remained. Mathias and the others had tightened a pair of tourniquets around the Greek's thighs, clamping shut the femoral arteries. They'd used some of the strips of nylon from the blue tent. Jeff bent low to examine them; it was an effort at escape—he could admit this to himself—a way of not having to look at the exposed bones. He needed to occupy his mind for a moment, distract it, give it time to adjust to this new horror. He'd never tied a tourniquet before, but he'd read about them, and knew—in the abstract at least—how to apply them. You were supposed to loosen them at regular intervals, then retighten them, but Jeff couldn't remember the exact time frame, or even what it was supposed to accomplish.

It didn't matter, he supposed.

No: He *knew* it didn't matter.

"The vines?" he said.

Mathias nodded. "When we pulled them off, the blood started to spurt. They were holding it back somehow, and once they were gone . . ." He made a spraying motion with his hands.

Pablo's eyes were shut, as if he were asleep, but his hands seemed to be clenched, the skin across his knuckles drawn to a taut whiteness. "Is he conscious?" Jeff asked.

Mathias shrugged. "It's hard to tell. He was screaming at first; then he stopped and shut his eyes. He's rolled his head back and forth, and he shouted once. But he hasn't opened his eyes again."

There was an oddly sweet smell coming off of Pablo, stomach-turning once you began to notice it. This was decay, Jeff knew. It was the Greek's legs beginning to rot. He needed to be operated on, needed to get to a hospital—and sooner rather than later. Help would have to arrive by tonight for him to survive. If it didn't, they'd spend the coming days watching Pablo die.

Or maybe there was a third option.

Jeff was fairly certain help wasn't going to arrive before nightfall. And he didn't want to sit and watch Pablo die. But this third option . . . he knew the others wouldn't be ready for it, not nearly—not in concept, not in practice. And he'd need their help, of course, if he was going to attempt it.

So it was with the idea of preparing them, of hardening them, that he turned from Pablo's mutilated body and began to speak of his own discoveries that morning.

Given everything she'd seen of the vine's capabilities since dawn—how it had pushed its way into Eric's leg, stripped Pablo of his flesh, snaked across the clearing to suck dry Amy's vomit—Stacy felt little surprise at Jeff's revelations. She listened to him with a strangely numb sensation; her only noticeable emotion was a low hum of irritation toward Eric, who continued to pace about the little clearing, paying no attention whatsoever to Jeff and his story. Stacy wanted him to sit down, to stop obsessing on what she was certain was the purely imaginary presence of the plant inside his body. The plant wasn't inside his body; the very idea seemed absurd to her, pointlessly frightening. Yet assuring Eric of this had no effect at all. He just kept pacing, stopping now and then to probe wincingly at his wounds. The only thing one could do was struggle to ignore him.

The vine was the reason they were being held captive here: that was the gist of what Jeff was telling them. The Mayans had cut the clearing around the base of the hill in an attempt to quarantine the plant, sowing the surrounding soil with salt. Jeff's theory was that the vine spread through contact. When they touched it, they picked up its seeds or spores or whatever served as its means of reproduction, and if they were to cross the cleared swath of ground, they'd carry these with them. This was why the Mayans refused to allow them off the hill.

"What about birds?" Mathias asked. "Wouldn't they—"

"There aren't any," Jeff said. "Haven't you noticed? No birds, no insects—nothing alive here but us and the plant."

They all stared about the clearing, as if searching for some refutation of this. "But how would they know to stay away?" Stacy asked. She pictured the Mayans stopping the birds and mosquitoes and flies, just like they'd attempted to stop the six of them, the bald man waving his pistol toward the tiny creatures, shouting at them, keeping them at bay. How, she wondered, could the birds have known to turn aside when she hadn't?

"Evolution," Jeff said. "The ones who've landed on the hillside have died. The ones who've somehow sensed to avoid it have survived."

"All of them?" Amy asked, clearly not believing this.

Jeff shrugged. "Watch." His shirt had plastic buttons on its pockets; he reached up, yanked one off, tossed it out into the vines.

There was a jumping movement, a blur of green.

"See how quick it is?" he asked. He seemed oddly pleased, as if proud of the plant's skill. "Imagine if that were a bird. Or a fly. It wouldn't have a chance."

No one said anything; they were all staring out into the surrounding vegetation, as if waiting for it to move again. Stacy remembered that long arm swaying toward her across the clearing, the sucking sound it made as it drank up Amy's vomit. She realized she was holding her breath, felt dizzy with it, had to remind herself to exhale . . . inhale . . . exhale.

Jeff pulled the button off his other pocket and tossed it, too. Once more, there was that darting flash. "But here's the amazing thing," he said, and he reached up to his collar, plucked a third button from the shirt, threw it out into the vines.

Nothing happened.

"See?" He smiled at them. There was that sense of pride again; he couldn't seem to help himself. "It *learns*," he said. "It *thinks*."

"What're you talking about?" Amy asked, as if affronted by Jeff's words. Or scared, maybe—there was an edge to her voice.

"It pulled down my sign."

"You're saying it can read?"

"I'm saying it knew what I was doing. Knew that if it wanted to succeed in killing us—and maybe others, too, whoever else might come along—it had to get rid of the sign. Just like it had gotten rid of this one." He kicked at the metal pan with that single Spanish word scraped across its bottom.

Amy laughed. No one else did. Stacy had heard everything Jeff was saying, but she wasn't following his words, wasn't grasping that he meant them literally. *Plants bend toward the light:* that was what she was thinking. She even, miraculously, remembered the word for this reflex—a darting glance back toward high school biology, the smell of chalk dust and formaldehyde, sticky bumps of dried gum hanging off the underside of her desk—a little bubble rising toward the surface of her mind, breaking with a popping sound: *phototropism.* Flowers open in the morning and shut at night; roots reach toward water. It was weird and creepy and uncanny, but it wasn't the same as thinking.

"That's absurd," Amy said. "Plants don't have brains; they can't think."

"It grows on almost everything, doesn't it? Everything organic?" Jeff gestured at his jeans, the pale green fuzz sprouting there.

Amy nodded.

"Then why was the rope so clear?" Jeff asked.

"It wasn't. That's the reason it broke. The vine—"

"But why was there any rope left at all? This thing stripped the flesh off Pablo's legs in a single night. Why wouldn't it have eaten the rope clean, too?"

Amy frowned at him; she clearly didn't have an answer.

"It was a trap," Jeff said. "Can't you see that? It left the rope because it knew whoever came along would eventually decide to look in the hole. And then it could burn through, and—"

Amy threw up her hands in disbelief. "It's a *plant,* Jeff. Plants aren't conscious. They don't—"

"Here," Jeff said. He reached into his pockets, emptied them one after another onto the dirt at his feet. There were four passports, two pairs of glasses, wedding rings, earrings, a necklace. "They're all dead. These are the only things left. These and their bones. And I'm telling you that the vine did this. It killed them. And right now, even as we're speaking, it's planning to kill us, too."

Amy shook her head, vehement. "The *vine* didn't kill them. The Mayans did. They tried to flee and the Mayans shot them. The vine just claimed their bodies once they'd been shot. There's no thought involved in that. No—"

"Look around you, Amy."

Amy turned, glanced about the clearing. Everyone did, even Eric. Amy lifted her hands: "What?"

Jeff started across the clearing, stepped into the surrounding vegetation. Half a dozen strides and he reached one of those odd waist-high mounds. He crouched beside it, began yanking at the vines. *He's going to get burned,* Stacy thought, but she could tell he didn't care. As he pulled at the plants, she began to glimpse bits of yellowish white beneath the mass of green. *Stones,* she thought, knowing better even as she fashioned the word in her head. Jeff reached into the center of the mound, pulled out something vaguely spherelike, held it toward them. Stacy didn't want to see what it was; that was the only explanation she could devise for how long it took her to recognize the object, which was otherwise so instantly identifiable, that smiling Halloween image, that pirate flag flapping from the mast of Jeff's arm, poor Yorick of infinite jest. He was holding a skull toward them. She had to repeat the word inside her head before she could fully absorb it, believe in it. *A skull, a skull, a skull . . .*

Then Jeff waved across the hilltop, and all their heads swiveled in unison to follow the gesture. Those mounds were everywhere, Stacy realized. She started to count them, reached nine, with many more still to number, and flinched away from the task.

"It's killed them all," Jeff said. He strode back toward them, wiping his hands on his pants. "The *vine,* not the Mayans. One by one, it's killed them all."

Eric had finally stopped pacing. "We have to break out," he said.

Everyone turned to stare at him. He was flipping his hand quickly back and forth at his side, as if he'd just caught it in a drawer and was trying to shake the pain out. That was how jumpy he'd become, how anxious.

"We can make shields. Spears, maybe. And charge them. All at once. We can—"

Jeff cut him off, almost disdainfully. "They have guns," he said. "At least two, maybe more. And there are only five of us. With what? Thirteen miles to safety? And Pablo—"

Eric's hand started to go faster, blurring, making a snapping sound. He shouted, "We can't just sit here doing nothing!"

"Eric—"

"It's inside me!"

Jeff shook his head, very firmly. His voice, too, was firm, startlingly so. "That's not true. It might feel like it is, but it's not. I promise you."

There was no reason for Eric to believe this, of course. Jeff was simply asserting it—even Stacy could see that. But it seemed to work nonetheless. She watched Eric surrender, watched the tension ease from his muscles. He lowered himself to the ground, sat with his knees hugged to his chest, shut his eyes. Stacy knew it wasn't going to last, though; she could tell he'd soon be back up on his feet, pacing the length of the clearing. Because even as Jeff turned away, thinking that he'd solved this one problem and could now move on to the next, she saw Eric's hand drifting down toward his shin again, toward the wound there, toward the subtle swelling around its margins.

They each took a swig of water. They sat in the clearing beside Pablo's lean-to, in a loose circle, and passed the plastic jug from hand to hand. Amy didn't think of her vow from the night before—her intention to confess her midnight theft and refuse the morning's ration—she accepted her allotted swallow without the slightest sense of guilt. She was too thirsty to do otherwise, too eager to wash the sour taste of vomit from her mouth.

The Greeks are coming: this was what she kept telling herself, imagining their progress with each passing moment, the two of them laughing and capering in the Cancún bus station, buying the tickets with their names printed on them—Juan and Don Quixote—the delight they'd feel at this, slapping each other's shoulders, grinning in that impish way of theirs. Then the bus ride, the haggling for the taxi, the long walk along the trail through the jungle to the first clearing. They'd skip the Mayan village, Amy decided—somehow they'd know better—they'd find the second trail, and hurry down it, singing, perhaps. Amy could picture their faces, their utter astonishment, when they emerged from the trees and glimpsed the vine-covered hill before them, with her or Jeff or Stacy or Eric standing at its base, waving them away, miming out their predicament, their peril. And the Greeks would understand, too. They'd turn, rush back into the jungle, go for help. All this was hours away, Amy knew. It was still so early. Juan and Don Quixote weren't even at the bus station yet; maybe they weren't even awake. But they were going to come. She couldn't allow herself to believe otherwise. Yes, it didn't matter if the vine was malevolent, if—as Jeff asserted—it could think and was plotting their destruction, because the Greeks were hurrying to their rescue. Any moment now they'd be rousing themselves, showering and breakfasting and studying Pablo's map. . . .

Jeff had them empty their packs so they could inventory the food they'd brought.

Stacy produced her and Eric's supplies: two rotten-looking bananas, a liter bottle of water, a bag of pretzels, a small can of mixed nuts.

Amy unzipped Jeff's knapsack, pulled out two bottles of iced tea, a pair of protein bars, a box of raisins, a plastic bag full of grapes going brown.

Mathias set down an orange, a can of Coke, a soggy tuna fish sandwich.

They were all hungry, of course; they could've easily eaten everything right then and there and still not been satisfied, not nearly. But Jeff wouldn't let them. He crouched above the little pile of food, frowning down at it, as if hoping that he might, simply through his powers of concentration, somehow manage to enlarge it—double it, triple it—miraculously providing enough food for them to survive here for as long as might be necessary.

As long as might be necessary. That was the sort of phrase he'd use, too, Amy knew—objective and detached—and she felt a brief push of anger toward him. The Greeks would show up this afternoon. Why was he so stubbornly refusing to acknowledge this? They'd find a way to warn the two of them off, turn them back for help; rescue would arrive by nightfall. There was no need to ration food. It was alarmist and extreme. Later, Amy believed, they'd tease him about it, mimic the way he'd picked up the tuna fish sandwich, unwrapped it, then used the knife to cut it into five equal sections. Amy spent a few moments imagining this scenario—all of them back on the beach in Cancún, laughing at Jeff. She'd hold her finger an inch away from her thumb to show everyone how small the pieces had been, how absurdly small—yes, it was true, no bigger than a cracker—she could fit the whole thing in her mouth. And this was what she was doing now, too, even as she busied herself picturing that happier scene still to come—tomorrow, showered and rested, on the beach with their brightly colored towels—she opened her mouth, placed the little square of sandwich inside it, chewed a handful of times, swallowed, and it was gone.

The others were tarrying over theirs—taking tiny, mouselike bites—and Amy felt a lurch of regret. Why hadn't she thought to do this, to draw the process out, elongate what couldn't really even be called a snack into something that might almost resemble a meal? She wanted her ration back, wanted a new one altogether, so that she might find a way to consume it more gradually. But it was gone; it had dropped irretrievably into her stomach, and now she had to sit and wait while the others lingered over theirs, nibbling and sniffing and savoring. She felt like crying suddenly—no, she'd felt like crying all morning, maybe ever since they'd arrived here on this hill, but now it was only more so. She was thrashing about in deep, deep water, trying to pretend all the while that this wasn't true, and it was wearing her down—the thrashing, the pretending—she didn't know how much longer she could keep it up. She wanted more food, more water, wanted to go home, wanted Pablo not to be lying there beneath the lean-to with the flesh stripped from his legs. She wanted all this and more, and none of it was possible, so she kept thrashing and pretending, and any moment now she knew it would become too much for her, that she'd have to stop thrashing, stop pretending, and give herself over to the drowning.

They passed the plastic jug of water around and everyone took another swallow to wash the food down.

"What about Pablo?" Mathias asked.

Jeff glanced toward the lean-to. "I doubt he can stomach it."

Mathias shook his head. "I mean his pack."

They scanned the clearing for Pablo's knapsack. It was lying next to Jeff; he reached, unzipped it, pulled out three bottles of tequila, one after another, then upended the bag, shaking it. A handful of tiny cellophane packets tumbled out: saltines. Stacy laughed; so did Amy, and it was a relief, too. It felt good, almost normal. Her head seemed to clear a little, her heart to lighten. Three bottles of tequila—what had Pablo been thinking? Where had he imagined they were going? Amy wanted to keep laughing, to prolong the moment in the same way that the others had stretched out their paltry portion of tuna fish, but it was too slippery, too quick for her. Stacy stopped and then it was just Amy, and she couldn't sustain it on her own. She fell silent, watched Jeff slide the bottles back into the knapsack before adding the saltines to their small cache of food. She could see him making calculations in his head, deciding what they ought to eat and when. The perishables first, she assumed—the bananas and grapes and orange—rationing them out bite by bite. In her mouth, the aftertaste of the tuna was mixing with the lingering residue of vomit. Her stomach ached, felt oddly bloated; she wanted more food. It wasn't enough, what Jeff had given them; this seemed obvious to her. He had to offer them something further—a cracker at least, a slice of orange, a handful of grapes.

Amy glanced around the loose circle they'd formed. Eric wasn't part of it; he was hobbling back and forth again, pacing, stopping now and then to bend and examine his leg. Mathias was watching Jeff arrange the pile of food; Stacy was working on her last meager morsel of sandwich, taking a tiny nibble, then chewing for a long time with her eyes shut. The Greeks were coming—they'd be here in a handful of hours—it was ridiculous for them to be rationing in such a manner, and somebody needed to speak this truth. But it wasn't going to be any of the others, Amy realized. No, as usual, she would have to be the one: the complainer, the whiner, the squeaky wheel.

"One of us ought to go down the hill and watch for the Greeks," Jeff said. "And I was thinking we should dig a latrine—now, before the sun rises any higher. And—"

"Is that all we get?" Amy asked.

Jeff lifted his head, looked at her. He didn't know what she was talking about.

Amy waved at the pile of food. "To eat," she said.

He nodded. That was it, just a single curt dip of his head. Apparently, her question wasn't even worth a spoken response. There was to be no discussion, no debate. Amy turned to the others, expecting support, but it was as if they hadn't heard her. They were all watching Jeff, waiting for him to continue. Jeff hesitated another moment, his gaze resting on Amy, making sure she was done. And she was, too. She shrugged, looked away, surrendered to the will of the group. She was a coward in that way, and she knew it. She could complain, she could pout, but she couldn't rebel.

"Mathias and I will do the digging," Jeff said. "Eric should probably try to rest—in the tent, out of the sun. That means one of you two will have to go down the hill, while the other one stays here with Pablo." He looked at Stacy and Amy.

Stacy wasn't paying attention, Amy could tell; her eyes were still shut, savoring the last of her tuna. Amy was conscious, beyond her hunger and thirst and general sense of discomfort, of a growing need to urinate. She'd been holding it in all morning, not wanting to empty her bladder into the bottle again, hoping she could find a moment to sneak off and pee in the dirt somewhere. This was what prompted her to speak, more than anything else; she wasn't thinking about what it would be like down the hill, all alone, facing the Mayans across that barren stretch of land—no, she was thinking about crouching on the trail, out of sight from the others, her jeans pulled down around her ankles, a puddle of piss slowly forming beneath her.

"I'll go," she said.

Jeff nodded his approval. "Wear your hat. Your sunglasses. And try not to move around too much. We'll want to wait a couple hours before we take any more water."

Amy realized that he was dismissing her. She stood up, still thinking only of her bladder, the relief that awaited farther down the hill. She put on her hat, her sunglasses, looped her camera around her neck, then set off across the clearing. She was just starting along the trail, when Jeff called out after her, "Amy!"

She turned. He'd stood up, was jogging toward her. When he reached her side, he took her by the elbow, spoke in a low voice. "If you see the chance to run," he said, "don't hesitate. Take it."

Amy didn't say anything. She wasn't going to try to run—it seemed like a preposterous idea to her, a pointless risk. The Greeks were coming; even now, they were probably waking up, showering, packing their knapsacks.

"All you have to do is get into the jungle—just a little ways. Then drop to the ground. It's thick enough that they probably wouldn't be able to find you. Wait awhile, and then make your way out. But carefully. It's when you move that they'll see you."

"I'm not going to run, Jeff."

"I'm just saying if you have the—"

"The Greeks are coming. Why would I try to run?"

Now it was Jeff who didn't say anything. He stared at her, expressionless.

"You act like they're not coming. You won't let us eat or drink or—"

"We don't know that they're coming."

"Of course they're coming."

"And if they do come, we can't be certain they won't just end up on the hill here with us."

Amy shook her head at that, as if the very idea were too outlandish to consider. "I wouldn't let them."

Again, Jeff didn't speak. There was the hint of a frown on his face now.

"I'll warn them away," Amy insisted.

Jeff continued to watch her in silence for a long moment, and she could sense him debating, toying with the idea of saying something further, setting it down, picking it back up again. When he finally spoke, his voice dropped even lower, almost to a whisper. "This is serious, Amy. You know that, don't you?"

"Yes," she said.

"If it was just a matter of waiting, I'd feel okay. As hard as it might be, I'm pretty sure we'd make it. Maybe not Pablo, but the rest of us. Sooner or later, someone would come—we'd just have to tough it out until then. And we would, too. We'd be hungry and thirsty, and maybe Eric's knee would get infected, but we'd be all right in the end, don't you think?"

She nodded.

"But it's not just waiting now."

Amy didn't respond. She knew what he was saying, but she couldn't bring herself to acknowledge it.

Jeff's gaze remained intent upon her, forcing eye contact. "You understand what I mean?"

"You mean the vine."

He nodded. "It's going to try to kill us. Like all these other people. And the longer we stay here, the better its chances."

Amy stared off across the hilltop. She'd seen what the vine could do. She'd seen it come squirming toward her across the clearing so that it could suck up her little puddle of vomit. She'd seen Pablo's legs stripped free of flesh. Yet all this was so far beyond what she took to be the immutable laws of nature, so far beyond what she knew a plant ought to be capable of, that she couldn't quite bring herself to accept it. Strange things had happened—dreadful things—and she'd witnessed them with her own eyes, but even so, she continued to doubt them. Looking at the vine now, tangled and coiled across the hill, its dark green leaves, its bloodred flowers, she could muster no dread of it. She was scared of the Mayans with their bows and guns; she was scared of not getting enough to eat or drink. But the vine remained just a plant in her mind, and she couldn't bring herself to fear it in the way she knew she ought to. She couldn't believe that it would kill her.

She fell back to her place of safety: "The Greeks will come," she said.

Jeff sighed. She could tell that she'd disappointed him, that she'd once again turned out to be less than he'd needed her to be. But it was all she could do—she couldn't be better or braver or smarter than she was—and she could see him thinking this, too, resigning himself to her failure. His hand dropped from her elbow.

"Just be careful, okay?" he said. "Stay alert. Scream if anything happens—loud as you can—and we'll come running."

With those parting words, he sent her down the hill.

Eric was back in the orange tent. It was a bad idea, he knew; it was the worst possible place for him to be, but he couldn't bring himself to leave. He felt passive and inert, and yet—within this outer shell of sluggishness—full of panic. Trapped, out of control, and being in the tent only made it worse. But Jeff had told him to get into the shade and try to rest, so that was what he was doing.

He sensed it wasn't the right thing, though.

It was growing hot, the sun climbing implacably upward, beating down on the tent's orange nylon, so that soon the cloth itself began to seem as if it were radiating light and heat, rather than merely filtering it. Eric lay on his back, sweaty, greasy-haired, trying to bring his breathing under control. It was too fast, too shallow, and he believed that if he could only quiet it down some, deepening his inhalations, letting the air fill his chest, everything else would follow—his heart would slow, and then maybe his thoughts would, too. Because that was the main problem just now: his thoughts were moving too fast, jumping and rearing. He knew that he was on the edge of hysteria—that he'd maybe even drifted over into the thing itself. He was having some sort of anxiety attack, and he couldn't seem to find a way back from it. There was his breathing and his heart and his thoughts, and all of them had inexplicably slipped beyond his control.

He kept sitting up to examine his wounded leg—bending close, squinting, pushing at the swollen tissue with his finger. The vine was inside him. Mathias had cut it out, but there was still some in there. Eric could feel it—he was certain of it—yet the others refused to listen. They were ignoring him, dismissing him, and the vine was starting to grow; it was starting to grow and eat, and when it was done, Eric would be just like Pablo, his legs stripped clean of flesh. He and the Greek weren't going to leave this place alive; they were going to end up as two more of those green mounds scattered across the hillside.

The tent was where it had happened—so why was he back in the tent? Jeff was the reason: he'd told him to come inside here, to rest, as if rest were still possible now. But that was because Jeff didn't believe him. He'd spent a few seconds looking at Eric's knee, and that wasn't long enough, not nearly; he hadn't *seen* it. Or maybe you couldn't see it, no matter how long you looked; maybe that was the problem. Eric knew the truth because he could feel it; there was something awry inside his leg, something moving that wasn't himself, but a thing foreign to him, with goals all its own. Eric wished he could see it, wished Jeff and the others could see it, too; everything would be better if they could only see it. He shouldn't be here in the tent, where it had happened, where it might happen again. He shouldn't be alone.

He surprised himself by standing up. He limped to the flap and stooped through it, into the sunlight. Stacy was beside the lean-to. They'd constructed a little sunshade for her, using some of the leftover poles and nylon from the other tent, fashioning this debris into a battered-looking sort of umbrella. She was sitting in the dirt beneath it, cross-legged, facing Pablo at an oblique angle, so that she could watch over him without actually having to look at him. No one wanted to look at Pablo anymore, and Eric understood this—he didn't want to look at the Greek, either. What troubled him was the sense that the others were beginning to include him, too, in their zone of not seeing. Even now, as he dropped to the ground beside her, Stacy's gaze remained averted.

Eric reached, took her hand, and she let him, but passively, her muscles limply inert, so that it felt as if he were holding an empty glove. They sat for a few moments without speaking, and in this brief silence Eric almost managed to achieve a sort of peace. They were just two people resting in the sun together—why shouldn't it be this simple? It didn't last, though, this momentary serenity; it fell away from him with the suddenness of something made of glass, shattering, and his heart leapt abruptly into his throat. He could feel the sweat rising on his skin, his grip on Stacy's hand becoming slippery with it. He had to resist the urge to jump up and begin to pace. He could hear Pablo's breathing—wet-sounding, unhealthy, like someone dragging a saw back and forth through a tin can—and he risked a quick glance at him, immediately regretting it. Pablo's face had taken on an odd grayness, his eyes were closed and deeply sunken, and there was a thin string of dark liquid draining from the corner of his mouth, vomit or bile or blood—Eric couldn't tell which. *Someone should wipe it away,* he thought, but he made no move to do this. And under the sleeping bag, of course, were Pablo's legs, or what was left of them—the bones, the thick clots of blood, the yellow tendons.

Eric knew the Greek couldn't survive like this, stripped clean of flesh, knew Pablo was going to die, and wished only that it would happen sooner rather than later, now even—*a blessing, a release,* he thought—all the lies people utter around death in order to comfort themselves, to bury their grief with the body, but here, suddenly, they were true. *Die,* Eric said in his head. *Do it now, just die.* And all the while—yes, *implacably, inexorably*—the Greek's breathing continued its ragged course.

Eric could hear the faint murmur of Jeff's and Mathias's voices, but he couldn't make out what they were saying. They were out of sight, somewhere farther down the hill, digging the latrine.

He squeezed Stacy's hand; she still hadn't looked at him. "So . . ." he began, tentatively, not certain if it was the right path, "there was this guy, and he had a vine growing inside him."

Silence. *She's not going to answer,* he thought. And then she did. "We got it out," she said, her voice quiet. Eric had to lean to hear her.

"You're supposed to say 'but.'"

Stacy shook her head. "I'm not playing. I'm telling you he cut it out. It's not inside you anymore."

"But I can still feel it."

She finally looked at him. "Just because you can feel it doesn't mean it's there."

"But what if it is?"

"We can't do anything about it."

"So you admit it might be."

"I'm not saying that."

"But I can *feel* it, Stacy."

"I'm saying no matter what might be true, we just have to wait it out."

"So I'm going to end up like Pablo."

"Stop it, Eric."

"But it's inside me—it's in my blood. I can feel it in my chest."

"Please stop."

"So I'm going to die here."

"*Eric.*"

He fell silent, startled by the jump in her voice. She was crying. When had she begun to cry?

"Please stop, sweetie," she said. "Can you do that? Can you calm down?" She wiped at her face with the back of her hand. "I really need you to calm down."

Eric was silent. *In my chest*—where had that come from? He hadn't realized it till he said it, but it was true. He could feel the vine inside his chest, a subtle yet definite pressure against his lower rib cage, pressing outward.

Stacy pulled her hand free from his grip, pushed herself to her feet, stepped across the clearing. She bent over Pablo's pack, rummaged through it, dragged out one of the glass bottles, then started back toward him, opening it as she came. "Here," she said, standing over him, offering him the tequila.

Eric didn't take it. "Jeff said we shouldn't drink."

"Well, Jeff isn't here, is he?"

Still not moving, Eric eyed the bottle, the amber liquid within it. He could smell the tequila, could feel its pull, which was mixed—illogically but inextricably—with his larger sense of thirst. He lifted his hand, took the bottle from her. It was the one they'd drunk from the previous afternoon, after their aborted crossing of the muddy field—a different world altogether, peopled by other versions of themselves, untouched and unknowing. He remembered Pablo standing before them, so full of laughter, offering the bottle, and with this image in his mind—more dream, it seemed, than memory—Eric tilted back his head and took a long swallow of the liquor. It was too much; he gasped, coughed, tears briefly blurring his vision. But it was good, too; it was the right thing. Without waiting to recover—just his breath, that was all he needed—he lifted the bottle to his lips again.

The only thing he'd eaten since yesterday morning was that tiny square of tuna fish and bread—he was dehydrated, exhausted—and he could feel the tequila within seconds, pleasantly enervating, letting him breathe, finally. It happened so quickly, like the plunge of a needle into a vein, a numbness, a slurred quality to his thoughts. He wiped his mouth on his forearm and surprised himself by laughing.

Stacy was still standing over him, the absurd-looking umbrella resting on her shoulder, enclosing him within its circle of shade. "Not too much," she said, and when he raised the bottle for another swallow, she bent quickly and pulled it from his grasp.

She capped it, put it back in Pablo's bag. Then she sat beside him, letting him take her hand again. The tequila burned in his chest, made his ears ring. *Maybe they're right,* he thought. *Maybe I'm overreacting.* He could still feel something moving, wormlike, in his leg, and that odd pressure continued in his lower chest, but he could see now, as the liquor quieted the tumble of his thoughts, that none of this necessarily had anything to do with the vine. It was possible that he was simply frightened, that he was paying too much attention to his body. There was always something odd to feel if only you stopped and searched for it.

"The miserable misery of the miser," he said, the words coming to him suddenly, for no apparent reason.

"What?" Stacy asked.

Eric shook his head, waving it aside. There were three bottles of tequila, and he struggled to tilt his thoughts forward into the coming hours, rationing out the liquor sip by sip, like a bag dripping solace into a vein. The Greeks would be here soon, and everyone was going to be okay. What he needed to do now was sit, holding Stacy's hand, and in a little while he'd be able to ask her for the bottle again. In that way, one small sip at a time, he believed he could make it through the coming day.

They didn't have a shovel.

Jeff had found a sharp rock, shaped like a giant spearhead, big enough that he had to get down on his knees and use both hands to chop at the dry, hard-packed soil. Mathias used one of the metal stakes from the blue tent, stabbing the earth with it, grunting each time he swung his arm. When a sufficient amount of dirt was loosened in this manner, they stood up to kick it free, then paused for a few moments—catching their breath, wiping the sweat from their faces—before starting the whole process all over again.

It was hard work, and not going nearly as well as Jeff had hoped. He had an image in his mind: a hole four feet deep, just wide enough for someone to squat over it, one foot on either side, its walls dropping into the earth, perfectly perpendicular. It was possible Jeff had read a book that described such a thing, or seen a drawing of it somewhere, but this wasn't what he and Mathias were creating here. At even a slight depth, the walls of their latrine began to collapse and crumble, so that it widened as quickly as it deepened. For it to be narrow enough to allow someone to squat above it, the hole would have to stop while it was still only two feet deep, which defeated the whole purpose, of course. A latrine that shallow wasn't really a latrine at all; they might as well just continue to fumble through what Jeff had done earlier that morning, shuffling off into the vines and shitting, covering the mess with a parting kick of dirt.

Thinking this, Jeff realized the truth, what he should've known from the very start: it was a stupid idea. They didn't need a latrine, even a well-made one. Sanitation wasn't high on their list of problems just now, and no matter what might happen to them here, they'd be gone long before it became an issue of any urgency. Rescued, perhaps. Or dead. Jeff and Mathias were digging now not because it made any sense to be doing so, but because Jeff was floundering about, looking for something solid to cling to, some action to take, anything to keep from simply having to sit, helpless, and wait. Realizing this, accepting it, Jeff stopped digging, dropped back on his haunches. Mathias did, too.

"What are we doing?" Jeff asked.

Mathias shrugged, gesturing toward the sloppy, shallow ditch they'd managed to gouge out of the earth. "Digging a latrine."

"And is there any point in that?"

Mathias shook his head. "Not really."

Jeff tossed his stone into the dirt, wiped his hands on his pants. His palms burned—that green fuzz was growing on his jeans again. They all had it—on their clothes, their shoes—he'd seen each of them, at one moment or another, reaching to brush it away as they'd crouched together in the clearing.

"We could use it for the urine," Mathias said. "To distill it." He made a motion with his hands, spreading an imaginary tarp across the hole.

"And is there any point in that?" Jeff asked.

Mathias bridled at this, lifting his head. "You were the one who—"

Jeff nodded, cutting him off. "I know—my idea. But how much water will we get out of it?"

"Not much."

"Enough to make up for whatever we're sweating right now, digging like this?"

"I doubt it."

Jeff sighed. He felt foolish. And—what else? Tired, maybe, but more than this: defeated. Perhaps this was despair, which he knew was the worst thing of all, the opposite of survival. Whatever it was, the feeling was on him now, and he didn't know how to shake it. "If it rains," he said, "we'll have plenty of water. If it doesn't, we'll die of thirst."

Mathias didn't say anything. He was watching him closely, squinting slightly.

"I was trying to make work," Jeff said. "Give us things to do. Keep up our morale." He smiled, mocking himself. "I was even planning to drop back down into the shaft."

"Why?"

"The beeping. The cell phone sound."

"There's no oil for the lamp."

"We could make a torch."

Mathias laughed, incredulous. "A torch?"

"With rags—we could soak them in tequila."

"You see?" Mathias asked. "How German you are?"

"You're saying there's no point?"

"None worth the risk."

"What risk?"

Mathias shrugged, as if it were self-evident. And perhaps it was. "Look at Pablo," he said.

Pablo. *The worst thing.* Jeff hadn't mentioned his idea yet, his plan to save the Greek, and he hesitated even now, wondering at his motives, how pure they were, how mixed. The possibility that he was simply, yet again, making work for them hovered at the edge of his mind, then was quickly dismissed. They could save him if they tried; he was certain of it. "You think he's going to make it?" he asked.

Mathias frowned. When he spoke, his voice went low, almost inaudibly so. "Not likely."

"But if help came today—"

"Do you believe help is coming today?"

Jeff shook his head, and they were silent for a stretch. Mathias picked at the dirt with his stake. Jeff was working up his courage. Finally, he cleared his throat, said the words. "Maybe we could save him."

Mathias kept probing at the dirt, not even bothering to glance up. "How?"

"We could amputate his legs."

Mathias went still, watching Jeff now, smiling at him, but uncertainly. "You're joking."

Jeff shook his head.

"You want to cut off his legs."

"He'll die if we don't."

"Without anesthesia."

"There wouldn't be any pain. He has no feeling beneath his waist."

"He'd lose too much blood."

"The tourniquets are already in place. We'd cut below them."

"With what? You don't have any surgical instruments, any—"

"The knife."

"You'd need a bone saw—a knife wouldn't do a thing."

"We could break the bones, then cut."

Mathias shook his head, looking appalled. It was the most emotion Jeff had ever seen on his face. "No, Jeff. No way."

"Then he's dead."

Mathias ignored this. "What about infection? Cutting into him with a dirty knife?"

"We could sterilize it."

"We don't have any wood. Or water to boil. Or a pot, for that matter."

"There are things to burn—those notebooks, the backpacks full of clothes. We could heat the knife directly in the flames. It'll cauterize as it cuts."

"You'll kill him."

"Or save him—one or the other. But at least there's a chance. Would you rather sit back and watch him die over the coming days? It's not going to be quick—don't trick yourself into thinking that."

"If help comes—"

"Today, Mathias. It would have to come today. With his legs exposed like that, septicemia's going to set in—maybe it already has. Once it gets going, there'll be nothing anyone can do."

Mathias started picking at the dirt again, hunched into himself. "I'm sorry I brought us here," he said.

Jeff waved this aside; it seemed beside the point. "We chose to come."

Mathias sighed, dropped the tent stake. "I don't think I can do it," he said.

"I'll do it."

"I mean agree to it—I can't agree to it."

Jeff was silent, absorbing this; he hadn't expected it, had thought that Mathias would be the easiest to convince, the one to help him sway the others. "Then we should put him out of his misery," Jeff said. "Get him drunk—pour the tequila down his throat, wait for him to pass out. And, you know . . ." He made a sharp gesture with his arm, waving it through the air, a blow. It was harder than he would've thought to put the thing into words.

Mathias stared at him; Jeff could tell he didn't understand. Or didn't want to, maybe, was going to force him to say it outright. "What?" he asked.

"End it. Cut his throat. Smother him."

"You can't be serious."

"If he were a dog, wouldn't you—"

"But he's not a dog."

Jeff threw up his hands in frustration. Why had this become so difficult? He was just trying to be practical. Humane. "You know what I mean," he said.

He wasn't going to continue with this. He'd offered his idea; what more could he do? He felt that weight again, that leaden quality. The sun was climbing higher. They ought to be in the tent, in the shade; it was foolish for them to be out in the open like this, sweating. But he made no attempt to move. He was pouting, he realized, punishing Mathias for not embracing his plan. He disliked himself for this, and disliked Mathias for witnessing it; he wished he could stop. But he couldn't.

"Have you spoken to the others?" Mathias asked.

Jeff shook his head.

Mathias brushed some of the green fuzz off his jeans, then wiped his hands in the dirt, thinking it all through. Finally, he stood up. "We should vote," he said. "If the others say yes, then I will, too."

And with that, he started back up the hill toward the tent.

They gathered, once again, in the clearing. First Mathias reappeared, and then, a few moments later, Jeff. They sat on the ground beside Eric and Stacy, forming a little half circle around the lean-to. Pablo lay there with his eyes shut, and—even as they spoke of his situation—no one seemed willing to look at him. They were avoiding using his name, too; rather than speaking it, they'd say "he," and throw a vague wave toward his broken body. Amy was still down at the base of the hill, watching for the other Greeks, but even after they started talking, when it became clear that there was a purpose to this conversation, that something important—something dreadful— was in the process of being decided, no one mentioned her absence. Stacy thought of her, wondered if she ought to be fetched—Stacy wanted this to happen, to have Amy beside her, holding her hand, the two of them thinking their way through this together—but she couldn't bring herself to speak. She wasn't good in situations like this. Fear made her passive, silent. She tended to cower and wait for bad things to pass her by.

But they wanted her opinion. Wanted both hers and Eric's. If they said yes, then it would happen: Jeff would cut off Pablo's legs. Which was horrible and unimaginable, but also, according to Jeff, the only hope. So, by this logic, if they said no, there'd be no hope. Pablo would die. This was what Jeff told them.

No hope—there was a precursor to these words, a first hope that had to be relinquished in order for the second, also, to be risked. They weren't going to be rescued today: that was what Jeff was telling them. And this was what Stacy found herself focusing on, even though she knew she should've been thinking about Pablo—they were going to have to spend another night here in the orange tent, surrounded by the vine, which could move, which could burrow into Eric's leg, and which—if she were to believe Jeff—wanted them all dead. She didn't see how she could do this.

"How do you know?" she said. She could feel the fear in her voice, and it had a redoubling effect: hearing it frightened her all the more.

"Know what?" Jeff asked.

"That they aren't coming."

"I didn't say that."

"You said—"

"That it didn't seem likely they'll be coming *today*."

"But—"

"And if they don't come today, and we don't act, he"—and here there was that vague wave toward the lean-to—"won't make it."

"But how do you know?"

"His bones are exposed. He's going to—"

"No—that they aren't coming."

"It's not about knowing; it's about not knowing. About the risk of waiting rather than acting."

"So they might come."

Jeff gave her an exasperated look, throwing up his hands. "And they might *not* come. That's the whole point."

They were circling, of course, not saying anything, really, just throwing words at each other; even Stacy could see this. He wasn't going to give her what she wanted—couldn't give it to her, in fact. She wanted the Greeks to come, wanted them to be here already, wanted to be rescued, safe, and all Jeff could say was that it might not happen, not today at least, and that if it didn't, they had to cut off Pablo's legs.

He wanted to do it; Stacy could see this. And Mathias didn't. But Mathias wasn't speaking. He was just listening, as usual, waiting for them to decide. Stacy wished he'd say something, that he'd struggle to convince her and Eric not to agree, because she didn't want Jeff to cut off Pablo's legs, couldn't believe that it was a good idea, but she didn't know how to argue this. She sensed she couldn't just say no, that she'd have to tell Jeff why. She needed someone to help her, and there was no one to do it. Eric had become slightly drunk, was sleepy-eyed with it; he was much calmer than he had been, it was true, but not entirely present anymore. And Amy was far away, down the hill, watching for the Greeks.

"What about Amy?" Stacy said.

"What about her?"

"Shouldn't we ask what she thinks?"

"She only matters if it's a tie."

"If what's a tie?"

"The vote."

"We're *voting?*"

Jeff nodded, made an *of course* gesture with his hand, full of impatience, as if this were the only logical course and he couldn't see why she was expressing such surprise.

But she was surprised. She thought they were just talking about it, searching for a consensus, that nothing would be done unless they all agreed. That wasn't how it was, though; it would only take three of them, and then Jeff would cut off Pablo's legs. Stacy struggled to put her reluctance into words, fumbling, searching for an entry. "But . . . I mean, we can't just . . . It doesn't seem—"

"Cut them off," Eric said, his voice loud, startling her. "Right now."

Stacy turned to look at him. He looked sober suddenly, clear-eyed. And vehement, too, certain of himself, of the course he was advocating. Stacy could still say no, she knew. She could say no and then Jeff would have to go down the hill and ask Amy what she thought. He'd convince her, probably; even if Amy tried to hold out, he'd eventually wear her down. He was stronger than the rest of them. Everyone else was tired and thirsty and longing to be in some other place, and somehow he didn't seem to be any of those things. So what was the point of arguing?

"You're sure it's the right thing?" she asked.

"He'll die if we leave him as he is."

Stacy shuddered at that, as if Pablo's potential death were being laid at her feet—her fault, something she might easily have averted. "I don't want him to die."

"Of course not," Jeff said.

Stacy could feel Mathias's gaze upon her. Watching her, unblinking.

He wanted her to say no, she knew. She wished she could, too, but knew she couldn't.

"Okay," she said. "I guess you should do it."

Amy was taking pictures.

As she'd set off from the clearing, she'd grabbed her camera—reflexively, with no conscious motive—just picking it up and hanging it around her neck. It was only while she was crouched beside the path, midway down the hill, in that moment of relaxation and clarity that followed the release of her bladder, that she'd realized why she'd reached for it. She wanted to photograph the Mayans, to collect evidence of what was happening here, because they were going to be rescued—she kept insisting upon this to herself—and, after this happened, there would inevitably be an investigation, and arrests, and a trial. Which meant there'd need to be evidence, of course, and what better evidence could there possibly be than photographs of the perpetrators?

She started shooting as soon as she reached the bottom of the hill, focusing on the men's faces. She enjoyed the feeling it gave her, a sneaky sort of power, the hunted turning on her hunters. They were going to be punished; they were going to spend the rest of their lives in jail. And Amy was going to help this happen. She imagined the trial while she aimed and snapped, the crowded courtroom, the hush as she testified. They'd project her photos on a giant screen, and she'd point at an image of the bald man, that pistol on his hip. *He was the leader,* she'd say. *He was the one who wouldn't let us go.*

The Mayans paid her no attention. They weren't watching, hardly even seemed to glance her way. Only when she stepped out into the clearing, searching for a better angle on the group of men clustered around the nearest campfire, did two of them stir, raising their bows in her direction. She took their picture, stepped quickly back into the vines.

After awhile, the sense of power started to slip away from her, and she had nothing good to replace it with. The sun kept climbing, and Amy was too hot, too hungry, too thirsty. But she'd already been all these things when she'd first arrived, so this wasn't what the shift was about. No, it was the Mayans' indifference to her presence there, so busy with her camera, that finally began to wear her down. They were clustered around their smoldering campfire, some of them napping in the slowly diminishing line of shade at the edge of the jungle. They were talking and laughing; one of them was whittling a stick, just carving it down into nothing, a bored man's task, a way to occupy his hands while time ticked sluggishly by. Because that was it, wasn't it? That was what they were so clearly doing here: they were waiting. And not in any suspense, either, not in any anxiety as to the outcome of their vigil. They were waiting with no apparent emotion at all, as one might sit over the course of an evening, watching a candle methodically burn itself into darkness, never less than certain of the outcome, confident that the only thing standing between now and the end of waiting was time itself.

And what does that mean? Amy wondered.

Maybe the Mayans knew about the Greeks. Maybe Juan and Don Quixote had already come, had walked by the opening to the trail, kept on until they reached the village, only to be turned back, oblivious, never even thinking to check the tree line. Neither Amy nor the others had mentioned this possibility, yet it seemed so obvious now, once she'd thought of it, so impossible to overlook. They weren't coming, she realized suddenly, with the weight of certainty: no one was coming. And if this were true, then there was no hope. Not for Pablo, certainly, nor for the rest of them. And the Mayans must have understood this—it was the source of their boredom, their lassitude—they knew that it was simply a matter of waiting for events to unfold. Nothing was asked of them but that they guard the clearing. Thirst and hunger and the vine would do the rest, as they had so many times before.

Amy stopped taking pictures. She felt dizzy, almost drunk; she had to sit down, dropping into the dirt at the foot of the trail. *It's only the sun,* she told herself. *My empty stomach.* She was lying, though, and she knew it. The sun, her hunger, they had nothing to do with it. What she was feeling was fear. She tried to distract herself from this realization, taking deep breaths, fussing with her camera. It was just a cheap point-and-shoot; she'd bought it more than ten years ago, with money she'd earned as a baby-sitter. Jeff had given her a digital camera for the trip, but she'd made him take it back. She was too attached to this one to think of relinquishing it yet. It wasn't very reliable—it took bad pictures more often than not, sun-bleached or shadowed, and almost always blurrily out of focus—but Amy knew she'd have to break it or lose it or have it stolen before she'd accept the prospect of a replacement. She checked how many shots she had left—three out of thirty-six. That would be it, then; she hadn't brought any extra rolls, hadn't thought they'd be gone long enough to need them. It seemed odd to think that there was an exact number of pictures she'd taken in her life, and that nearly all of them had been with this camera. There were x number of her parents, x of trees and monuments and sunsets and dogs, x of Jeff and Stacy. And, if what she was feeling just now was correct—if the Mayans were correct, if Jeff was correct—then it was possible that there were only three more to take in her entire life. Amy tried to decide what they should be. There ought to be a group shot, she supposed, using the timer, all of them clustered around Pablo on his backboard. And one of her and Stacy, of course, arm in arm, the last in the series. And then—

"Are you okay?"

Amy turned, and there Stacy was, standing over her, with that makeshift umbrella on her shoulder. She looked wretched—gaunt and greasy-haired. Her mouth was trembling, and her hands, too, making the umbrella rattle softly, as if in a slight breeze.

Am I okay? Amy thought, struggling for an honest answer. Her dizziness had been followed by an odd sense of calm, a feeling of resignation. She wasn't like Jeff, wasn't a fighter. Or maybe she simply couldn't fool herself as easily as he did. The threat of dying here didn't fill her with an urgency to be up and doing; it made her tired, made her feel like lying down, as if to hurry the process along. "I guess so," she said. And then, because Stacy looked so much worse than she herself felt: "Are you?"

Stacy shook her head. She gestured behind her, up the hill. "They're . . . you know . . ." She trailed off, as if unable to find the words. She licked her lips, which had become deeply cracked in the past twenty-four hours—chapped, rawly split—a castaway's lips. When she tried again, her voice was a whisper. "They've started."

"Started what?"

"Cutting off his legs."

"What're you talking about?" Amy asked. Though she knew, of course.

"Pablo's," Stacy whispered, lifting her eyebrows very high, as if this news were a surprise to her, too. "They're using the knife."

Amy stood up without knowing what she intended to do. She didn't feel herself reacting yet, was numb to the news. But she must've been feeling something, because her expression changed in some way. She could see Stacy reacting to it, stepping back from her, looking scared.

"I shouldn't have said yes, should I?" Stacy asked.

"Yes to what?"

"We voted on it, and I—"

"Why didn't anyone tell me?"

"You were down here. Jeff said it only mattered if there was a tie. But there wasn't. Eric said yes, and then I . . ." There was that same frightened expression again. She stepped forward now, reached out to clutch Amy's forearm. "I shouldn't have, should I? You and Mathias and I— we could've stopped them."

Amy couldn't bring herself to accept that this was happening. She didn't believe that it was possible to cut someone's legs off with a knife, didn't believe that Jeff would ever attempt such a thing. Perhaps they'd only been talking about it, were still talking about it now; perhaps she could stop them if she hurried. She pulled herself free of Stacy's grip. "Stay here," she said. "Watch for the Greeks. Okay?"

Stacy nodded, still with that fear in her face, that trembling coming and going in the muscles around her mouth. She sat down, dropping awkwardly in the center of the path, as if some supporting string had been cut.

Amy waited another moment, watching her, making sure she was all right. Then she started hurriedly up the hill.

Jeff and Mathias were the ones who did it. They didn't ask Eric to help, which was a good thing, because he knew he wouldn't have been able to. He kept pacing about the clearing while they worked, pausing to watch and then turning quickly away, finding both states unbearable, the seeing and the not seeing.

First, they put the belts back on. They found them lying in the dirt beside the backboard, three tangled snakes, abandoned there the night before. Jeff and Mathias needed only two of them; they bound the Greek at his chest and waist. Pablo's eyes remained shut through all this jostling; he hadn't opened them, not once, since he'd stopped screaming earlier that morning. Even when Jeff prodded him now, calling his name, wanting to mime out what they were about to attempt, the Greek refused to respond. He lay there with a clenched expression on his face, everything—his mouth, his eyes—closed against the world. He seemed beyond their reach somehow, not quite present any longer. Past caring, Eric supposed, long past.

Next, they built a fire, a small one—it was all they could manage. They used three of the archaeologists' notebooks, a shirt, a pair of pants. They crumpled two sheets of paper for kindling, then added the notebooks whole. The clothing, they doused with tequila. The fire was almost smokeless; it burned with a low blue flame. Jeff set the knife in its midst, along with a large rock, shaped like an ax head. While these heated—the stone making a snapping sound as it took on a deep reddish glow—Jeff and Mathias crouched over Pablo, murmuring back and forth, pointing first at one leg, then the other, planning their operation. Jeff looked grim and downcast suddenly, as though he'd been coerced into this undertaking despite his better intentions, but if he was having any second thoughts, he wasn't allowing them to slow the procedure down.

Eric was standing right over them when they started. Jeff used a small towel he'd found in one of the backpacks to pull the stone from the fire; he wrapped it around his hand, glovelike, to protect himself from the heat. Moving quickly, in one fluid motion, he scooped up the stone, raised it over his head, turned toward the backboard. Then he slammed it down with all his strength against the Greek's lower leg.

Pablo's eyes jerked open; he began to scream again, writhing and bucking beneath his bonds. Jeff seemed hardly to notice; his face showed no reaction. He was already dropping the stone back into the fire, reaching for the knife. Mathias, too, remained expressionless, focused on his task. It was his job to keep the fire burning hot, to feed in new notebooks if they were needed, to sprinkle more alcohol, to stir and blow upon the embers.

Jeff was hunched over the backboard, muscles taut with the strain of his labor, sawing and chopping. There was the stench of the hot knife against Pablo's flesh, a cooking smell, meat burning. Eric glimpsed the shattered bone below the Greek's left knee, the bloody marrow spilling out, Jeff's knife pushing and cutting and prying. He saw the bottom half of Pablo's leg come free, the foot and ankle and shin bones a separate thing now, cut off, gone forever. Jeff sat back on his haunches, catching his breath. Pablo continued to scream and writhe, his eyes rolling, flashing white. Mathias took the knife from Jeff, returned it to the fire. Jeff picked up the little towel, started to wrap it around his hand again. As he reached for the glowing stone, Eric turned quickly away, started off across the clearing. He couldn't watch any longer, had to flee.

But there was nowhere to go, of course. Even on the far side of the clearing, with his back turned to the scene, he could still hear what was happening, the crunch of the stone slamming into Pablo's other leg, and the screaming—louder now, it seemed, higher-pitched.

Eric glanced over his shoulder—he couldn't stop himself.

Mathias was holding the black pan, the one Jeff had brought back from the bottom of the hill, with that word carved across its bottom—*peligro*. Eric watched him place it in the fire. They were going to use it to cauterize the Greek's wounds, pressing it flat across his stumps, one after the other.

Jeff was bent low over the backboard, working with the knife, a steady sawing motion, his shirt soaked through with sweat.

Pablo was still screaming. And there were words now, too. They were impossible to understand, of course, but Eric could hear the pleading in them, the begging. He remembered how he'd fallen on the Greek when he'd jumped down into the shaft, that feeling of his body bucking beneath him. And he thought of how Amy and he had thrown Pablo onto the backboard, that clumsy, lurching, panic-filled toss. He could feel the vine moving inside him, in his leg, and his chest, too—that insistent pressure at the base of his rib cage, pushing outward. It was all wrong; everything here was wrong, and there was no way to stop it, no way to escape.

Eric turned away again, but he couldn't maintain it. He had to glance back almost immediately.

Jeff finished with the knife, dropped it into the dirt at his side. Eric watched him pick up the towel; he wrapped it around his hand, turned to pull the pan from the fire. Mathias had to help him now. He squatted beside the backboard, bent to lift Pablo's left leg, what remained of it, grasping it with both hands just above the knee. Pablo was crying, talking to the two of them, Mathias and Jeff both, using their names. Neither of them showed any sign of hearing, though; they wouldn't look at him. The pan was glowing orange now, and the letters scratched into its bottom were a deeper color, almost red, so that Eric could still read the word they spelled there, even as Jeff swung it free of the flames. He watched Jeff spin, place the pan against the base of Pablo's stump, holding it in place, pressing hard, using all his weight. Eric could hear the flesh burning, a spitting, snapping sound. He could smell it, too, and was appalled to feel his stomach stirring in response—not in nausea, either, but, shockingly, in hunger.

He turned away, dropped into a crouch, shutting his eyes, pressing his hands to his ears, breathing through his mouth. He remained like this for what seemed like an impossibly long time, concentrating on the sensation of the vine inside his body, that insistently probing spasm in his leg, that pressure in his chest, trying to feel them as something else, something benign, some trick of perception, as Stacy kept insisting they must be: his heartbeat, his overtired muscles, his fear. He couldn't do it, though, and he couldn't wait any longer, either; yet again, he had to look.

When he turned, he found Jeff and Mathias still crouched over the backboard. Jeff was pressing the pan into Pablo's right stump now. There was that same sickeningly enticing smell in the air. But silence now—Pablo had gone still, stopped screaming. He seemed to have lost consciousness.

Then there was the sound of footsteps approaching. Amy was coming up the path. She entered the clearing at a run, out of breath, her skin shining with sweat.

Too late, Eric thought, watching her stagger to a stop, staring—seeing—a look of horror on her face. *She's come too late.*

Jeff didn't know what to feel. Or no: He knew what he thought, and then he knew what he felt, and he couldn't seem to bring the two into line. It had gone well, maybe even better than he'd expected—this was what he thought. They'd gotten the legs off fairly quickly, each of them a few inches below the knee, saving the joint. They'd cauterized the stumps thoroughly enough so that when they removed the tourniquets, there was only a minimal amount of bleeding. *Seepage,* really, would be the word for it, nothing too serious. Pablo had lost consciousness toward the end, more from shock, it seemed, than anything else. It wasn't pain—Jeff was almost certain of this—he shouldn't have been able to feel a thing. But he'd been awake; he'd been able to lift his head and see what they were doing, and that must've counted as its own sort of anguish. He was safer now, Jeff believed, though still in peril. All they'd done was buy him some time—not much, maybe another day or two. But it was something, and Jeff believed that he ought to feel proud of himself, that he'd done a brave deed. So he couldn't understand why he felt so sick at heart, almost breathless with it, as if holding back the threat of tears.

Amy wasn't helping much. None of them were. Mathias seemed reluctant to look at him, was hunched into himself beside the remains of their little fire, completely withdrawn. Eric had resumed his pacing, his fretful probing at his leg and chest. And Amy, without even bothering to take the time to understand what he'd accomplished—while they were still removing the tourniquets, carefully smearing Neosporin on the seared stumps—had immediately begun to attack him.

"Oh Jesus," she'd said, startling him. He hadn't heard her approach. "Jesus fucking Christ. What've you done?"

Jeff didn't bother to answer. It seemed clear enough.

"You cut off his legs. How could you fucking—"

"We didn't have a choice," Jeff said. He was bent over the second stump, spreading the gel across it. "He was going to die."

"And you think this will save him? Chopping off his legs with a dirty knife?"

"We sterilized it."

"Come on, Jeff. Look what he's lying on."

It was true, of course: The sleeping bag they'd used to cushion the backboard was soaked through with the leakage from Pablo's bladder. Jeff shrugged it away. "We've bought him some time. If we're rescued tomorrow, or even the next day, he'll—"

"You cut off his *legs*," Amy said, almost shouting.

Jeff finally turned to look at her. She was standing over him, sunburned, her face smudged with dirt, a half-inch-deep layer of green fuzz growing across her pants. She didn't look like herself anymore; she looked too ragged, too frantic. He supposed it must be true for all of them, in one way or another. He certainly had stopped feeling like himself at some point in the past twenty-four hours. He'd just used a knife and a stone to cut off a man's legs—a friend's, a stranger's, it was hard to say any longer. He didn't even know Pablo's real name. "What chance do you think he would've had, Amy?" he asked. "With his bones exposed like that?"

She didn't answer; she was staring to his right, at the ground, with an odd expression on her face.

"Answer me," he said.

Was she starting to cry? Her chin was trembling; she reached up, touched it with her hand. "Oh God," she whispered. "Oh Christ."

Jeff followed her gaze. She was peering down at Pablo's severed limbs, the remains of his feet and ankles and shins, the bloodstained bones held together with a few remaining cords of flesh. Jeff had dropped them beside the backboard, carelessly, planning to bury them when he was through cauterizing Pablo's stumps. But it wasn't going to come to that, apparently. The vine had sent another long tendril snaking out into the clearing. It had wrapped itself around one of Pablo's severed feet and was dragging the bones away now, back through the dirt. As Jeff watched, a second tendril slithered forward, more quickly than the first, and laid claim to the other foot.

They were all staring now—Eric and Mathias, too. And then Mathias was in motion, jumping to his feet, the knife in his hand. He stepped on the first length of vine, bent to slash at it with the blade, severing it from its source. He swooped toward the second one, slicing again. Even as he did this, though, a third tendril slithered into the clearing, and then a fourth, reaching for the bones. Amy screamed— once, short and loud—then clapped her hand over her mouth, retreating toward Jeff. Mathias bent and slashed, bent and slashed, and the vine kept coming, from all directions now.

"Leave it," Jeff said.

Mathias ignored him. Cutting and stomping and tearing at the vines, faster and faster, but still too slow, the tendrils fighting back, wrapping themselves around his legs, hindering his movements.

"*Mathias*," Jeff said, and he stepped toward him, grabbed his arm, pulled him away. He could feel the German's strength, the taut, straining muscles, but also his fatigue, his surrender. They stood side by side, watching as the vine pulled the severed limbs into itself, the white of the bones dragged into the larger mass of green, vanishing altogether.

They were still standing like this, all four of them, perfectly motionless, when, from across the hilltop, there came that familiar chirping again, the sound of a cell phone plaintively ringing at the bottom of the shaft.

Stacy sat beneath her jerry-rigged umbrella, in her little circle of shade, cross-legged, hunched into herself. She kept having to resist the temptation to glance at her wrist, kept having to remind herself that her watch wasn't there, that it was resting on a table beside a bed in Cancún, in her hotel room, where she ought to be right now, too, but wasn't. Or perhaps not: perhaps her fears had finally come true and a maid had stolen the watch. In which case, it would be where? With her hat, she supposed, and her sunglasses, adorning some stranger, some woman laughing over lunch at a restaurant on the beach. Stacy could feel the absence of these possessions in a way that was almost physical, an ache inside her chest, a bodily yearning, but it was her glasses that she missed most of all. There was too much sun here, too much glare. Her head throbbed with it—throbbed with hunger, too, and thirst, and fatigue, and fear.

Behind her, up the hill, they were amputating Pablo's legs. Stacy tried not to think of this. He was going to die here; she couldn't see any way around it. And she tried not to think of that, too.

Finally, she couldn't help it: She gave in, glanced at her wrist. There was nothing there, of course, and her thoughts began to circle once again—the night table, the maid, the hat and sunglasses, the woman eating lunch at the beach. This woman would be rested and fed and clean, with a bottle of water at her elbow. She'd be careless, carefree: happy. Stacy felt a wave of hatred for this imaginary stranger, which quickly metastasized, jumping to the boy who'd squeezed her breast outside the bus station, to the—probably fictional—felonious maid, to the Mayans sitting across from her with their watchful faces, their bows and arrows. One of the boys was there now, the one who'd followed them on the bike yesterday, the little one, riding on the handlebars. He was sitting in an elderly woman's lap, staring toward Stacy, expressionless, like all the other Mayans, and Stacy hated him, too.

Her khakis and T-shirt were covered with the pale green fuzz from the vine, her sandals also. She kept brushing it away, burning her hands, but the tiny tendrils quickly grew back. They'd already eaten several holes in her T-shirt. One, just above her belly button, was as big as a silver dollar. It was only a matter of time, Stacy knew, before her clothes would be hanging off her in shreds.

She hated the vine, too, of course, if it was possible to hate a plant. She hated its vivid green, its tiny red flowers, the sting of its sap against her skin. She hated it for being able to move, for its hunger, and its malevolence.

Her feet were still caked with mud from the long walk across that field the previous afternoon, and the mud continued to give off its faint scent of shit. *Like Pablo,* Stacy thought, her mind jumping up the hill, to what was happening there, the knife, the heated stone. She shuddered, shut her eyes.

Hate and more hate—Stacy was drowning in it, dropping downward, with no bottom in sight. She hated Pablo for having fallen into the shaft, hated him for his broken back, his fast-approaching death. She hated Eric for his wounded leg, for the vine moving wormlike beneath his skin, for his panic in the face of this. She hated Jeff for his competence, his coldness, for turning so easily to that knife and heated stone. She hated Amy for not stopping him, hated Mathias for his silences, his blank looks, hated herself most of all.

She opened her eyes, glanced about. A handful of minutes had passed, but nothing had changed.

Yes, she hated herself.

She hated herself for not knowing what time it was, or how much longer she'd have to sit here.

She hated herself for having stopped believing that Pablo was going to live.

She hated herself for knowing that the Greeks weren't going to come, not today, not ever.

She tilted back her umbrella, risked a quick look at the sky. Jeff was hoping for rain, she knew, depending on it. He was working to save them; he had plans and schemes and plots, but they all had the same flaw, the same weakness lurking within them—they all involved a degree of hope. And rain didn't come from hope; rain came from clouds, white or gray or the deepest of black—it didn't matter—they had to be there. But the sky above her was a blinding blue, stubbornly so, without a single cloud in sight.

It wasn't going to rain.

And this was just another thing for Stacy to hate herself for knowing.

They decided to drop back into the hole.

It was Jeff's idea, but Amy didn't argue. The Greeks weren't coming today. Everyone was admitting this now—to themselves at least, if not to the others—and thus the cell phone, the perhaps mythical cell phone calling to them from the bottom of the shaft, was the only thing left to pin their hopes on. So when Jeff proposed that they try one final time to find it, Amy startled him by agreeing.

They couldn't leave Pablo alone, of course. At first, they were going to have Amy sit with him while Eric and Mathias worked the windlass, lowering Jeff into the shaft. But Jeff wanted her to go, too. He was planning on making some sort of torch out of the archaeologists' clothes, soaking them in tequila, and he wasn't certain how long the light would last from this. Two sets of eyes down there would be more efficient than one, he said, allowing the search to be more thorough, more methodical.

Amy didn't want to go down into the hole again. But Jeff wasn't asking what she wanted; he was telling her what *he* wanted, describing it as something that had already been decided, a problem they needed to solve.

"We could carry it to the hole," Mathias said, meaning the backboard, meaning Pablo, and they all thought about this for a moment. Then Jeff nodded.

So that was what they did. Jeff and Mathias lifted the backboard out from under the little lean-to, carried it across the hilltop to the mouth of the shaft—carefully, working hard not to jostle Pablo. There were some terrible smells coming off the Greek's body: the by-now-familiar stench of his shit and urine, the burned-meat stink of his stubs, and that sweeter scent, lingering underneath everything else, that first ominous hint of rot. No one said anything about it; no one said anything about Pablo at all, in fact. He was still unconscious, and appeared worse than ever. It wasn't just his legs Amy had to avoid looking at; it was also his face. When she'd first applied to medical school, she'd gone on some campus tours, and she'd seen the cadavers the students dissected: gray-skinned, sunken-eyed, slack-mouthed. That was what Pablo's face was beginning to look like, too.

They set him down beside the shaft. The chirping had stopped, but now, as soon as they arrived, it started up again, and they all stood there, staring into the darkness, heads cocked, listening.

It rang nine times. Then it stopped.

Mathias checked the rope. He unspooled it from the windlass, the whole thing, laying it out in a long zigzag across the little clearing, searching its hemp for weakness.

Amy stood beside the hole, peering into it, trying to gather her courage, remembering her time down there with Eric, just the two of them, the things they'd spoken of to keep their fear at bay, the lies they'd told each other. She didn't want to return again, would've said no if only she could've thought of a way to do so. But now that they'd carried Pablo all the way across the hilltop, she couldn't see how she had a choice.

Eric crouched, began to probe at the wound on his leg, muttering to himself. "We'll cut it off," he said, and Amy turned to stare at him, startled, not certain if she'd heard correctly. Then he was up and pacing once more. The vine had eaten holes in his shirt, almost shredding it. He was covered in his own blood, spattered and dripped and smeared with it. They all looked bad, but he looked the worst.

Jeff was making his torch. He used a tent pole, wrapping duct tape around its bottom for a grip so the aluminum wouldn't grow too hot for him to hold. He knotted some of the archaeologists' clothes around the top—a pair of denim shorts, a cotton T-shirt—tying them tight. Amy couldn't see how it was going to work, but she didn't say anything, was too worn-out to argue about it. If they had to attempt this, she wanted just to do it and get it done.

Mathias stood up, wiping his hands on his pants. The rope was fine. They all watched as he carefully wound it back around the windlass. When he was done, Jeff slid the sling over his head, tucking it under his arms. He was holding the box of matches, the already-opened bottle of tequila, his flimsy-looking torch. Mathias and Eric stepped to the windlass, leaning against the hand crank with all their weight. And then, without the slightest hint of hesitation, Jeff stepped into the open air above the shaft. He didn't say anything in parting to Amy; they hadn't talked about a plan. She was supposed to follow him into the hole—that was all she knew. The rest, they'd have to make up once they got down there.

There was that familiar creaking of the windlass. Mathias and Eric strained against its pull, letting the rope out, turn by turn, sweating with the labor of it. Amy leaned over the shaft, watched Jeff drop into the darkness; he seemed to grow smaller as he descended. She could see him for longer than she would've anticipated, as if he were somehow drawing the sunlight with him into the depths. He grew shadowy, ghostlike, but she could still discern him long after it seemed he should've vanished altogether. He didn't return her gaze, didn't lift his face to her, not once, kept his eyes focused downward, toward the bottom of the hole.

"Almost there," Mathias said. It wasn't clear whom he was talking to, perhaps himself; that was how quiet his voice was.

Amy turned, glanced at him, at the windlass. The rope was nearly played out, just a few more rotations to go. When she looked back into the shaft, Jeff was gone. The rope went down and down and down into the darkness, swaying slightly as it uncoiled, and she could no longer see its end. She had to resist the urge to call out to Jeff, the sense that he'd vanished not merely from sight but altogether.

The windlass finally stopped its creaking. Eric and Mathias joined Amy beside the hole, all three of them staring into it. Amy could hear the other two working to catch their breath. "All right?" Mathias called.

"Pull it up," Jeff yelled back. His voice seemed far away, full of echoes, not quite his own.

Mathias rewound the windlass by himself, and it went quickly, weightless, the creaking sounding different now, higher-pitched, with an odd hint of laughter in it, which was a creepy thing to hear. It made Amy shiver, hug herself. *Say no,* she was thinking. *You can say it. Just say it.* But then Eric was handing her the sling, helping her into it, and she still hadn't spoken. *It's not that bad,* she told herself. *You've already done it once. Why shouldn't you do it again?* And those were the words she kept in her head as she stepped out into the open air, swaying there for a moment, before she began her slow descent into the hole.

It was different in daylight. Better in some ways, worse in others. She could see more, of course, as she moved downward—could see the shaft, with the rocks and timbers embedded in its walls, the vine growing here and there in long, looping strands, like decorations for a party. But the light also heightened the feeling of transit, of crossing a border as she dropped, moving from one world into another. It was an oppressive sensation. Day into night, sight into blindness, life into death: These were the connotations. Looking up wasn't the right idea, either—it only made things worse—because, even at this relatively shallow depth, the daylight already seemed impossibly far away. And, just as Jeff had appeared to grow smaller as he descended, now the hole looked to be shrinking, as if threatening to close altogether, like a mouth, swallowing her into the earth. She gripped the sling, concentrated on slowing her breathing, struggling to calm herself. The sling was damp—from Jeff's body, Amy assumed, his sweat. Or maybe it was her own. She was beginning to sway back and forth, almost touching the walls of the shaft, and she tried to stop herself, but that only seemed to make it worse, a wobbly, seasick feeling stirring in her gut. She still had the taste of vomit in her mouth, and this didn't help things, made it seem all the more possible, even with her stomach empty, that she might throw up here, puke spewing from her, splattering down on Jeff, waiting in the darkness below.

She shut her eyes.

Somehow, the feeling passed.

The air was growing cooler and cooler, cold even. Amy had forgotten about this, would've worn something warmer had she remembered, plundering a sweater from one of the archaeologists' backpacks. She began to shiver, even as she continued to sweat. Nerves, she knew: fear.

By the time she opened her eyes again, Jeff had come into view. Murkily: He was there, and not there. It was like seeing him underwater, or through smoke. He had his head tilted back. Amy couldn't make out his face, but there was something about his posture that made her certain he was smiling up at her. Despite herself—despite her fear, despite her sweating and shivering and general sense of discomfort—she smiled back.

Her feet touched the floor of the shaft. The sling went slack; the creaking stopped. And it was odd, because the sudden silence gave her a panicky sensation, a tightness in her chest. "Well," she said, just for the sound of the words, to break that eerie quiet. "Here we are."

Jeff was helping her out of the sling. "It's incredible," he said. "Isn't it? How far down do you think we are?"

Amy was too startled by the obvious excitement in his voice, the pleasure, to answer him. He was enjoying this, she realized. Even with everything that had happened in the past twenty-four hours, somehow he was managing to find pleasure in this. He was like a little boy, with a little boy's passions: the illicit joys of things underground—caves and hideouts and secret tunnels.

"Farther than I've ever been," he said. "No doubt about that. You think it could be a hundred feet?"

"*Jeff,*" she said. It was strange: they were in darkness, but there was light, too. Or some hint of it, some residue dropping toward them from above. As her eyes kept adjusting, she could see more and more, the walls and floor of the shaft, and Jeff, too—his face. She could see him peering at her, his puzzled expression.

"What?" he asked.

"Let's just find the phone, okay?"

He nodded. "Right. The phone."

Amy watched him crouch, begin to prepare his torch. He uncapped the tequila, started to sprinkle the liquor over the knot of clothing, slowly, letting it soak in. He took his time, pouring a small trickle, then pausing, then pouring some more. Amy could smell the tequila; she was so emptied out—hungry, thirsty, tired—that the scent alone made her feel slightly drunk. She could see a sock and a shoe lying on the floor of the shaft, a few feet to Jeff's right, and it took a long moment to realize that they were Pablo's. They were the ones Eric had removed yesterday so that he could scrape the bottom of Pablo's foot to see if his spine was broken. They'd forgotten them in the flurry of their departure last night, and now they were already covered with a thin growth of vine. Amy almost bent to retrieve them, thinking Pablo would want them, but then she caught herself, feeling stupid. And wretched, too, because—

morbidly—she'd started to smile. No need for socks and shoes anymore, of course, not for Pablo, not ever again.

"There was a shovel there last night," she said, surprising herself with the words. She hadn't thought them out first, hadn't even been conscious of noticing the shovel's absence until she'd heard herself remark upon it. She pointed toward the far wall of the shaft, where the shovel had been leaning. It wasn't there anymore.

Jeff turned, followed her gesture. "Are you sure?" he asked.

She nodded. "It was the kind you can fold up."

Jeff stared for another moment, then returned to his torch, dribbling more tequila across it. "Maybe they took it," he said.

"They?"

"The vines."

"Why would they do that?"

"Mathias and I were trying to dig a hole earlier, using a rock and a tent stake—for a latrine, and to distill our urine. Maybe they don't want us to be able to do that."

Amy was silent. There was so much to contest in this that she felt something like panic in the face of it, a buzzing sensation rising in her head. She didn't know where to begin. "You're saying they can see? They could *see* you digging?"

Jeff shrugged. "They have to have some way of sensing things. How else would they be able to reach out and take Pablo's feet like that?"

Pheromones, Amy was thinking. *Reflexes.* She didn't want the vine to be able to see, was horrified by the prospect of this, wanted its actions to be automatic, preconscious. "And it can communicate?" she said.

Jeff stopped with the bottle, capped it; the clothes were thoroughly saturated now. "What do you mean?"

"They saw you digging up there, and then they told the ones down here to hide the shovel." She wanted to laugh, the idea seemed so absurd. But something was keeping her from laughing, that buzzing in her head.

"I guess," Jeff said.

"And they *think?*"

"Definitely."

"But—"

"They dragged down my sign. How could they have known to do that without—"

"They're *plants,* Jeff. Plants don't see. They don't communicate. They don't think. They—"

"Was there a shovel there last night?" He gestured toward the shaft's far wall.

"I think so. I—"

"Then where is it now?"

Amy was silent. She couldn't answer this.

"If something moved it," Jeff said, "don't you think it makes sense to assume it was the vine?"

Before she could respond, the chirping resumed. It was coming from her left, down the open shaft. Jeff fumbled quickly with the box of matches, plucked one out, struck it into flame, held it to the knot of clothing. The alcohol seemed to grab at the match, sucking its light into itself with a fluttering sound, a cloud of pale blue fire materializing around the torch. Jeff lifted it up, held it before them; it gave off a weak, tenuous glow, which seemed constantly on the verge of going out. Amy could tell it wouldn't last long.

"Quick," he said, waving her toward the open shaft.

The chirping continued—it was up to three rings now—and the two of them rushed forward, hurrying to find it before it fell silent again. Five rapid strides and they were into the shaft, a steady stream of cold air pushing against them, making the torch in Jeff's hand shudder weakly. Amy felt a moment's terror, leaving that small square of open sky behind, the ceiling dropping low enough for Jeff to have to crouch as he moved forward. The darkness seemed to press in on them, to constrict somehow with each step they took, as if the walls and ceiling of the shaft were shifting inward. The vine, oddly, in such a lightless place, appeared to be growing in great profusion here, covering every available surface. They were wading through it, knee-deep, and it was hanging toward them from above, too, brushing against Amy's face; if she hadn't been so desperate to find the phone, she would've immediately turned and fled.

There came a fourth chirp, still in front of them, drawing them more deeply into the shaft. Amy could sense a wall somewhere ahead—even in the darkness, even without being able to glimpse it yet—somehow she knew that the shaft came to an end in another thirty feet or so. The chirping had an echo to it, but it still seemed clear to her that the phone was by this far wall, lying on the floor, buried beneath the vines. They'd need to get on their hands and knees to search for it. She was nearly running now, her eagerness to find the phone before it stopped ringing combining with her terror of this place, both of them working together to push her onward.

Jeff was moving more cautiously, hanging back. She was leaving him and his torch behind her, the vine brushing against her body, but softly, caressingly, seeming almost to part to allow her passage.

"Wait," Jeff said, and then he stopped altogether, holding the flickering torch out before him, trying to see more clearly.

Amy ignored him; all she wanted was to get there, to find it, to leave. She could see the wall now, or something like it: a shadow materializing in front of her, a blockage.

"Amy," Jeff said, louder now, his voice echoing back at her from the approaching wall. She hesitated, slowing, half-turning, and it came to her suddenly that the vine was moving, that this was the sense of constriction she was feeling; it wasn't simply the darkness deepening, the shaft narrowing. No, it was the flowers. Hanging from the ceiling, the walls, rising toward her from the floor, the flowers on the vine were moving, opening and closing like so many tiny mouths. Realizing this, she nearly stopped altogether. But then the phone chirped a fifth time, drawing her on; she knew there wouldn't be many more rings. And it was close now, too—right against the wall, she guessed. All she had to do was drop onto her—

"Amy!" Jeff yelled, startling her. He was moving again, hurrying toward her, the torch held up before him. "Don't—"

"It's right here," she said. She took another step. It was silly, but she wanted to be the one to find it. "It's—"

"*Stop!*" he shouted. And then, before she could respond, he was right beside her, grabbing her arm, jerking her back a step, pulling her close to him. She sensed his face beside her own, felt its warmth, heard him whisper, "There's no phone."

"What?" she asked, confused. A sixth chirp sounded right then, seeming to emerge from the vines directly in front of them. Amy tried to pull free. "It's—"

Jeff yanked her back, his grip tight, hurting her. He bent, whispered again, right into her ear. "It's the vine," he said. "The flowers. They're making the noise."

She shook her head, not believing, not wanting to believe. "No. It's right—"

Jeff leaned forward with the torch, shoving it down toward the floor of the shaft, into the mass of vines a few feet in front of them. The vines flinched away from the fire, parting as the torch approached, creating an opening in their midst. They moved so quickly, they seemed to hiss. Jeff crouched, pushing the flames downward into what ought to have been the floor but was open darkness instead, the draft increasing suddenly, stirring Amy's hair, disorienting her. Jeff was waving the torch back and forth now, widening the hole he'd created, and it took Amy several seconds to realize what she was seeing, what this darkness was, why there was no floor here. It was the mouth of another shaft, dropping straight down; the vines had been growing across it, hiding it from sight. *A trap,* she realized. They'd been luring her and Jeff forward, hoping they'd step into open air here, fall into the darkness.

There was a sharp whistling sound, like a whip might make, and one of the vines lashed out, wrapped itself around the aluminum handle of Jeff's torch, yanked it from his grip. Amy watched it fall, its light fluttering, almost failing, but still burning even as it hit bottom, thirty feet beneath them. She had a glimpse of white—*bones,* she thought—and what might've been a skull staring up at her. The shovel was there, too, and more of the vine, a writhing, snakelike mass of it, recoiling from the little knot of fire burning in its midst. Then the flames flickered, dimmed, went out.

It was dark after this, terribly dark, darker than Amy would've thought possible. For a moment, all she could hear was Jeff's breathing beside her, and the faint thump of her own heartbeat in her ears, but then that whistling sound came again, louder this time, denser, and she knew even before they began to grab at her that it was the vines she was hearing. They seemed to come from every direction at once, from the walls and the floor and the ceiling, smacking against her body, wrapping themselves around her arms and legs—even her neck—pulling her toward the open shaft.

Amy screamed, scrambling backward, tearing at them with her hands, yanking free one limb, only to feel another immediately become ensnared. The vine wasn't strong enough to overpower her in this manner— it tore too easily, its sap bleeding across her skin, burning her—but it kept coming, more and more of it. She spun and kicked and continued to scream, panicking now, losing her sense of direction, until finally, in the darkness, she could no longer tell which way led to safety, which to the shaft's open mouth.

"Jeff?" she called, and then she felt his hand grasping her, pulling her, and she surrendered, following him, the vines thrashing at both of them, grabbing and tearing and burning.

Jeff shouted something, but she couldn't understand it. He was dragging her backward, the two of them stumbling, falling over each other, onto their hands and knees amid the vines, which caught at them, trying to hold them down, and then they were up again, and there was a faint hint of light in front of them, and they were sprinting for it, Jeff pulling Amy by her arm, the vines falling away behind them, going still again, motionless, silent.

Amy saw the sling hanging from its rope. And then, up above, that little window of sky. When she craned backward, peering toward it, she could see Eric and Mathias, the shadowed outline of their two heads, staring down at her.

"Jeff?" Mathias called.

Jeff didn't bother answering. He was looking back toward the open shaft behind them. It was just darkness there now, with that steady push of cold air, but he seemed reluctant to take his eyes from it. "Get in the sling," he said to her.

Amy could hear how short of breath he was. She was, too, and she stood beside him for a long moment, not moving, struggling to regain herself.

Jeff crouched, grabbed the bottle of tequila, uncapped it. He picked up Pablo's sock, spilled some of the liquor across it.

"What're you doing?" she whispered.

There was the sound of something stirring now from within the dark mouth of the shaft, almost inaudible, but growing steadily louder. Jeff started to stuff Pablo's sock down the neck of the tequila bottle, using his forefinger to push it deep. The sound kept increasing in volume, still too soft to hear clearly, but oddly familiar—like the shuffle of cards—strange and horrifying and almost human.

"*Hurry,* Amy," Jeff said.

She didn't argue; she reached for the sling, ducked her arms through it, her head.

Mathias called again: "Jeff?"

"Pull her up!"

Amy tilted her head back, looked. The heads were still visible, peering down at her from that tiny rectangle of sky. She knew they couldn't see her in the darkness, though. She saw Mathias cup his hands around his mouth. "What happened?" he yelled.

Jeff was fumbling with the box of matches. "Now!" he shouted.

The sound was louder—a little louder with every passing second—and as it climbed in volume, it grew steadily more familiar. Amy knew what it was; it was in her head, this knowledge, but just out of reach. She didn't want to hear any more, didn't want the knowledge to reveal itself. The sling gave a jerk, and then that creaking began again, dropping toward her from above, blotting out this other sound, the one she didn't want to know, and she was in motion, rising into the air, her feet swinging free of the shaft's floor. Jeff didn't even glance at her. His gaze moved back and forth, from the box of matches to the darkness where that sound lurked, even now continuing to gain in volume, as if intent on following her upward into the light, capturing her, dragging her back down.

Beneath her, Amy saw Jeff's hand flick, a match burst into flame. He held it to Pablo's sock, the tequila catching instantly, coming alight with the same pale blue fire as the torch. Jeff rose to his feet, held the bottle out to his side for a moment, making sure it was burning steadily. Then, side-armed, like a grenade, he threw it down the open shaft. Amy heard the bottle shatter, and a glow swept outward, illuminating Jeff more fully.

A Molotov cocktail, she thought. It seemed odd to her that she should know the name for this; she pictured Poles throwing them impotently at Russian tanks, a futile, desperate gesture. Beneath her, Jeff stood perfectly still, staring off into the shaft; the fire was already dimming, and she kept rising so steadily. Soon, she knew—quite soon—she'd lose sight of him altogether. The flames ought to have stopped that dreadful noise, that sound she recognized yet didn't want to know, and at first this seemed to be the case, but then the noise resumed again, more quietly, and yet in a manner that somehow seemed to envelop her completely. It took Amy a moment to realize that the sound wasn't coming from beneath her any longer; it was all around her now, and above her, too. Jeff was slipping from sight, the fire dying out, the shadows reclaiming him, and as she lifted her eyes to see how much farther she had to climb, a hint of movement caught her gaze, held it fast. It was the plants hanging from the walls of the shaft, paler, more spindly versions of their cousins up above. Their tiny flowers were opening and closing. This was what was making that terrible noise, Amy realized—it was coming so much more softly now, insidiously—the sound she finally had no choice but to recognize, to acknowledge, the sound she also guessed was being echoed all across the hillside.

They're laughing, she thought.

Once they'd pulled them both back up from the shaft, there wasn't much left to do. Jeff was out of plans, for once; he seemed a little dazed by what he'd witnessed down there. They carried Pablo back to his lean-to; then they all sat together—everyone but Stacy, who was still at the base of the hill, waiting for the Greeks—and passed around the plastic jug of water. Eric noticed that Jeff's hands were shaking as he reached to take his allotted swallow, and he felt an odd sense of pleasure in this. After all, his own hands were shaking—they had been for quite some time now—so it felt good to see the others beginning to join him. *The miserable misery of the miser,* he thought. For some reason, he couldn't get the words out of his mind, and he had to keep resisting the urge to speak them.

"They were laughing at us," Amy whispered.

No one said anything. Mathias capped the jug, stood up and returned it to the tent. Jeff had told them what had happened as soon as he'd emerged from the hole, how it was the plants who'd been making that cell phone noise, trying to lure them into a trap, and even this disappointment, with its accompanying freight of terror, had held some solace for Eric. Because now they were going to *see;* now, having witnessed the vine's power, they were going to believe him when he said it was still in his body, growing, eating him from the inside out. He could still feel it, certainly; he couldn't *stop* feeling it. There was a burrowing sensation in his leg, something small and wormlike in the flesh beside his shinbone, constantly in motion, probing and chewing. It seemed to be working its way toward his foot. And then, higher up, in his chest, there was no movement at all, only a steady pressure, impossible to ignore. Eric imagined some sort of void there, just beneath his ribs, a natural cavity within his body that was slowly being filled by the vine, the plant twisting back upon itself as it grew, shoving his organs aside, taking up more and more space with each passing moment. He believed that if he were to cut himself at this spot, just the smallest of incisions, the plant would tumble outward into the light, smeared with his blood, like some horrific newborn, writhing and twisting, its flowers opening and closing, a dozen tiny mouths begging to be fed.

Pablo moaned—it almost sounded like a word, as if he were calling out for something—but when they turned to look, his eyes were still shut, his body motionless. *Dreaming,* Eric thought, yet he knew immediately that it wasn't so, that it was worse, far worse. It was delirium, the stumble before the fall.

Dreaming, delirium, dying . . .

"Shouldn't we give him some water?" Amy asked.

Her voice sounded odd to Eric. *Her hands must be shaking, too,* he thought. No one answered her. They sat for several long moments staring in silence at Pablo, waiting for him to open his eyes, to stir, but he did neither. The only sound was the wet, phlegmy rattle of his breathing. Eric had the memory of himself lying half-asleep somewhere, early in the morning, listening as someone dragged furniture back and forth across the floor of the room above him, rearranging it. He'd been visiting a friend, sleeping on a couch. Oddly, Eric couldn't remember the friend's name. He could see the empty beer bottles lined up on the coffee table, could smell the mustiness of the pillow he'd been given, could hear the furniture being pushed and shoved from one side of the room above him to another, but he was so tired, so parched, so famished that somehow he couldn't remember who his host had been. That was the noise he was hearing now, though—there was no doubt of this—that was what Pablo's breathing sounded like, a table being dragged across a wooden floor.

Amy persisted: "He hasn't had any water, not since—"

"He's unconscious," Jeff said, cutting her off. "How are we supposed to give him water?"

Amy frowned, silenced.

One by one, they all stopped watching Pablo—shutting their eyes, glancing away, not looking back. Eric's gaze drifted around the clearing, aimlessly, only to catch, finally, on the knife. It was lying beside the lean-to. Its blade was dull with the Greek's blood, completely stained from point to hilt. It wasn't that far away—to reach it, all Eric had to do was shift a foot or two to his left, then lean, stretching, and suddenly it was in his hand. Its grip felt warm from the sun, comfortingly so, the right thing for him to be holding. He tried to wipe the blade clean on his T-shirt, but the blood had dried and wouldn't come off. Eric was dehydrated enough that he had to work with his tongue before he could gather enough saliva to spit. Even this didn't help, though; as soon as he started to scrub at the blade, his T-shirt—eaten to a muslinlike transparency by the green fuzz of the vine—began to shred into nothingness.

It didn't matter, he decided. It wasn't infection that he was worried about.

He leaned forward and cut a three-inch-long slit in his leg, just to the left of his shin, slightly beneath the incision Mathias had made earlier that morning. It hurt, of course, especially since he had to push deep, probing down into the muscle, prying the flesh back with the edge of the knife, so that he could hunt for the tiny piece of vine he knew must be in there. The pain was intense—*loud,* was how it felt—but also strangely consoling: it felt bracing, clarifying. Blood was pooling in the slit, spilling outward, running down his leg, making it difficult to see, so he reached with his free hand, stuck his forefinger into the wound, digging, searching by feel, the pain like a man running up a flight of stairs now, sprinting, skipping steps. The others were watching him, too startled to speak. The worming sensation continued, despite the pain; Eric could feel the thing fleeing downward, away from his finger. He started in once more with the knife, cutting deeper, and then Jeff was on his feet, moving quickly toward him.

Eric glanced up, the blood running thickly down his lower leg, beginning to collect in his shoe again. He was expecting solicitude, an offer to help, and was astonished to see the disgust on Jeff's face, the impatience. Jeff reached, grabbed for the knife, yanking it from Eric's grip. "Stop it," he said, tossing the knife away, sending it skittering into the dirt. "Don't be a fucking idiot."

There was silence in the clearing. Eric turned to the others, assuming one of them might offer something in his defense, but they avoided his eyes, their faces set, echoing Jeff's disapproval.

"Don't you think we've got enough problems?" Jeff asked.

Eric made a helpless gesture, waving his bloody hands at his bloody shin. "It's inside me."

"All you're going to do is get yourself infected. Is that what you want? An infected leg?"

"It's not just my leg. It's my chest, too." Eric touched the spot on his chest, the dull ache there, laying his palm against it. He believed he could feel the vine pressing subtly back.

"Nothing's inside you. Understand?" Jeff asked, his voice matching the hardness in his face—the frustration, the fatigue. "You're imagining it, and you just—you just fucking have to stop." With that, he turned and strode back into the center of the clearing.

He started to pace, and everyone watched him. Pablo continued to drag that heavy table along the wooden floor, and suddenly the name Mike O'Donnell popped into Eric's head. That was his friend: red-haired, gap-toothed, a lacrosse player. They'd known each other in high school, had gone to different colleges, gradually grown apart. He'd been living in an old row house outside of Baltimore, and Eric had spent a weekend there. They'd gone to an Orioles game, had bought horrible tickets from a scalper, ended up not being able to see a thing. All this was only two or three years ago, but it seemed impossibly far away now, another life altogether from the one he was living here, sitting in this little clearing, listening to the dreadful rasp of Pablo's breathing—*dreaming, delirium, dying*—wanting to push his finger into his open wound again, but resisting the urge, telling himself, *It's not there,* and struggling to believe it.

Jeff stopped pacing. "Somebody should go relieve Stacy," he said.

No one moved; no one spoke.

Jeff turned first to Amy, then to Mathias. Neither of them met his eyes. He didn't even bother to look at Eric. "All right," he said finally, waving his hand, dismissing the three of them—their inertia, their lassitude, their helplessness—his disgust seeming generalized now, all-encompassing. "I'll do it."

And then, without another word or glance, he turned and walked out of the clearing.

They should've eaten something, Jeff realized as he picked his way down the hill. It was well past noon now; they should've divided up the two bananas, cut them into five equal portions, chewed and swallowed, and called it lunch. Then the orange for dinner—maybe some of the grapes, too—these were the things that wouldn't keep, that were already beginning to spoil in the heat. And then what? Pretzels, nuts, protein bars—how long could this last them? A couple more days, Jeff assumed, and after that the fasting would begin, the starving. There was no point in worrying about it, he supposed, not when there wasn't anything he could do to change the situation. Wishing or praying—increasingly this was all that was left for them, and, in Jeff's mind, wishing or praying was the same as doing nothing at all.

He should've brought the knife with him. Eric was going to keep cutting himself, unless the others stopped him, and Jeff didn't trust Amy and Mathias to do this. He was losing them, he knew. Only twenty-four hours and already they were acting like victims—slope-shouldered, blank-faced. Even Mathias seemed to have retreated somehow, over the course of the morning, grown passive, when Jeff needed him to be active.

He should've known it wasn't a cell phone in the shaft; he should've anticipated such a turn of events, or something like it. He wasn't thinking as clearly as he ought to, and he knew this would only lead to peril. The vine could've easily eaten the rope, but it hadn't. It had left it untouched on the windlass, which meant that it had wanted them to drop back into the hole, and Jeff should've seen this, should've understood that it could only mean one thing, that the chirping sound was a trap. The vine could move and think and mimic different noises—not just the cell phone but the birds, too. Because it must've been the vine that had cried out like that to warn the Mayans as he'd crept down the hill the previous evening, and he should've realized this also.

He was getting sloppy. He was losing control, and he didn't know how to reclaim it.

Stacy came into sight, sitting hunched under her sunshade, facing the clearing, the Mayans, the jungle beyond. She didn't hear Jeff approach, didn't turn to greet him, but it wasn't until he was nearly upon her that he understood why. She was sitting cross-legged, slumped forward, the umbrella propped on her shoulder, her eyes shut, her mouth hanging ajar: she was sound asleep. Jeff stood for nearly a minute, staring down at her, his hands on his hips. His first flash of anger at her negligence passed in an instant; he was too worn-out to sustain it. He knew it didn't really matter, not in any practical sense. If the Greeks had arrived, they would've called out as soon as they'd glimpsed her sitting here, would've roused her while they were still far enough away to be stopped. And, more to the point, the Greeks hadn't arrived, probably weren't ever going to. So there was no place for anger here; it came and went, brief as a shudder.

Her umbrella was angled the wrong way, its circle of shade only covering the upper half of her body, leaving her lap, her crossed legs, exposed to the noontime sun. Her feet, in their mud-stained sandals, were burned all the way up to the ankle—a deep, raw-meat red. They were going to blister later, then peel, a painful process. If it were Amy, this would involve a prodigious amount of complaining—tears, even, at times—but Stacy, Jeff knew, probably wouldn't even notice, let alone mention it. This was part of that spacey quality of hers, a sort of disassociation from her body. Jeff often found it hard to resist comparing her to Amy. He'd met them together, had lived in the same dorm with them his freshman year, one floor down, directly beneath their room. He'd come up late one evening to complain about a pounding noise and found them in their pajamas, crouched above a small pile of wood with a hammer and nails and a sheet of instructions written in Korean. It was a bookshelf Amy had purchased over the Internet, very cheap, not realizing she'd have to put it together herself. Jeff ended up building it for them; in the process, they'd all become friends. For a short period, it wasn't even clear which of them he was courting, and he supposed that this was part of what made it so difficult for him to stop looking at them in a comparative way, weighing their differences, one against the other.

In the end, Amy had won him with her personality—she was so much more solid than Stacy, more grounded, more dependable, despite her complaining—but, in a purely physical sense, Stacy had actually been the one he'd found more attractive. It was something about her dark eyes, and the way she could look at you with them, all of a sudden, a glance that seemed almost painfully open, hiding nothing. She was sexy, alluringly so, where Amy was merely pretty. There'd even been a brief period, shortly after he and Amy had started dating in earnest, when Jeff had entertained the brief, tawdry fantasy of having an affair with Stacy. Because what had happened on the beach with Don Quixote wasn't an isolated occurrence. Stacy had a tendency toward that sort of thing; she was promiscuous in a sly, helpless way, almost despite herself. She liked to kiss strange boys, to touch and be touched, especially when she'd been drinking. Eric knew about some of these misadventures, but not others. They had fights over the ones he did discover, screaming and cursing viciously at each other, only—always—to make up in the end, with Stacy offering tearful, apparently heartfelt promises, which she'd inevitably break, sometimes within days. It seemed strange to remember all this now, especially his fantasy of betrayal, and difficult to recall exactly how he'd managed to entertain it. Or why, for that matter. Far away: that was how it felt.

The odd thing about Stacy was that, despite the aura of sexuality she exuded, there was also something strikingly childish about her. Partly this was a matter of personality—that flightiness, that preference for play and fantasy over anything that might possibly feel like work—but it was just as much something physical, something in the features of her face, the shape of her head, which was noticeably round, and a little too large for her body, more like a little girl's than a grown woman's. It was a quality Jeff doubted she'd ever grow out of. Even if she survived this place, even if she lived on into a wrinkled, stooping, shuffling, trembling old age, she'd probably still retain it. And, of course, it was especially heightened now, with her looking so defenseless, sunk so deeply in sleep.

She shouldn't be here, Jeff thought. The words rose in his head unsought, startling him. It was true, of course: None of them should've been there. Yet they were, and without much prospect, it increasingly appeared, of ever managing to be anywhere else again. It had been his idea to come to Mexico, his idea to accompany Mathias on his search for Henrich. Was this what those words were pointing toward, some hesitant shouldering of responsibility? The vine had taken root on Stacy's sandals, clinging to the leather like a garland, and as Jeff began to flirt with this idea, he crouched before her, reaching to pull the plant free.

She woke to his touch, jerking away, scrambling to her feet, dropping her umbrella: frightened. "What happened?" she asked, almost shouting the words.

Jeff made soothing motions in the air; he would've touched her, too—grasped her hand, hugged her—but she took a step backward, moving beyond his reach. "You fell asleep," he said.

Stacy shielded her eyes, struggling to orient herself. The vine was growing on her clothes, too, Jeff saw. A long tendril hung off the front of her T-shirt; another trailed down the left leg of her khakis, twining itself around her calf. Jeff bent, picked up her sunshade, held it out to her. She stared at it, as if she were having trouble recognizing it—what it was, how it related to her—then she took it, propped it on her shoulder. She retreated another step. *As if she's frightened of me,* Jeff thought, and felt a flicker of irritation.

He waved up the hill. "You can go back now."

Stacy didn't move. She lifted her sunburned foot, scratched absentmindedly at it. "It was laughing," she said.

Jeff just stared at her. He knew what she meant, but he couldn't think of a way to respond. Something about her, about this encounter here, was making him conscious of his fatigue. He had to resist the urge to yawn.

Stacy gestured around them. "The vine."

He nodded. "We went back down into the shaft. To look for the cell phone."

Stacy's expression changed in an instant—everything did, her posture, the sound of her voice—animated by hope. "You found it?"

Jeff shook his head. "It was a trap. The vine was making the noise." He felt as if he'd struck her; the effect of his words upon her was that dramatic. She slumped, her face going slack, losing color.

"I heard it laughing. The whole hillside."

Jeff nodded. "It mimics things." And then, because she seemed in such need of reassurance: "It's just a sound it's learned to make. It's not really laughter."

"I fell asleep." Stacy seemed surprised by this, as if she were talking of someone else. "I was so scared. I was . . ." She shook her head, unable to find the right words, then finished weakly: "I don't know how I fell asleep."

"You're tired. We all are."

"Is he okay?" Stacy whispered.

"Who?"

"Pablo. Is he"—and here again, there was that fumbling search for the proper words—"all right?"

It was odd, but it took Jeff a moment to grasp what she was talking about. He could look down and see the blood spattered on his jeans, but he had to struggle before he could remember whom it belonged to, or how it had gotten there. *Tired,* he thought, though he knew it was more than that. Inside, he was in full flight, just like the rest of them. "He's unconscious," he said.

"His legs?"

"Gone."

"But he's alive?"

Jeff nodded.

"And he's going to be okay?"

"We'll see."

"Amy didn't stop you?"

Jeff shook his head.

"She was supposed to stop you."

"We were already done."

Stacy fell silent at that.

Jeff could feel his impatience building again, his frustration with her; he wanted her to leave. Why wouldn't she leave? He knew what she was going to say next, guessed at it, waited for it, but was still taken aback when it came—affronted.

"I don't think you should've done it," she said.

He gave a brusque wave, swatting the words aside. "A little late for that, isn't it?"

Stacy hesitated, watching him. Then, seemingly despite herself: "I just wanted to say it. So you'd know. That I wish I'd voted the other way. That I didn't want you to cut them off."

Jeff couldn't think how to respond to this. All the options that presented themselves were unacceptable. He wanted to shout at her, to shake her by her shoulders, slap her across the face, but he knew that nothing good would come from any of this. Everyone seemed so intent on failing him here, on letting him down; they were all so much weaker than he ever would've anticipated. He was simply trying to do the right thing, to save Pablo's life, to save them all, and no one seemed capable of recognizing this, let alone finding the strength within themselves to help him do any of the difficult things that needed to be done. "You should get back," he said finally. "Tell them to give you some water."

Stacy nodded, tugging at the tiny vine that clung to her T-shirt. She pulled it free, and the fabric tore open in a long slit. She wasn't wearing a bra; Jeff had a brief glimpse of her right breast. It looked surprisingly like Amy's: the same size, the same shape, but with a darker nipple, a deep brown, whereas Amy's was the faintest of pink. Jeff glanced quickly away, the gesture assuming a life of its own, inertia carrying him onward, turning him around, so that, without really meaning to, he ended up with his back to her. He stared across the clearing at the Mayans. Most of them were lying in the shade along the edge of the jungle now, trying to hide from the day's heat. Several were smoking, talking among themselves; others appeared to be napping. They'd let the fire burn down, banking the embers with ashes. No one was paying Jeff or Stacy any attention, and he had the brief illusion that he could just stride across the clearing, walk right through their midst, vanish into the shadows beneath the trees, and that none of them would stir to stop him. He knew it for what it was, though, a fantasy, could imagine easily enough the scramble for their weapons as he started forward, the shout of warning, the twang of bowstrings, and he felt no impulse to attempt it.

He could see the little boy from the day before, the one who'd followed them as they'd left the village, riding on the handlebars of that squeaky bike. He was standing near the remains of the campfire, trying to teach himself to juggle. He had three fist-size stones, and he'd toss them one after another into the air, striving for that smooth circular motion one saw clowns give to balls and swords and flaming torches. He lacked their grace, though, couldn't begin to approximate it; he kept dropping the stones, only to pick them up and immediately try again. After half a dozen repetitions of this, he sensed Jeff's gaze. He turned, stared at him, holding his eyes, and this, too, seemed to become a sort of game, a challenge, both of them refusing to look away. Jeff certainly wasn't going to be the one to surrender; he was pouring all his frustration into the encounter, all his fury, becoming so focused upon it that he hardly registered the sound of Stacy turning and starting away from him, her footsteps diminishing with each passing second, before they faded, finally, into silence.

Stacy found Amy and Eric in the clearing beside the tent. Amy was sitting on the ground, with her back to Pablo, clasping her knees to her chest. Her eyes were shut. Eric was pacing; he didn't even glance at Stacy when she appeared. There was no sign of Mathias.

Stacy's thirst was her first concern. "Jeff said I could have some water," she announced.

Amy opened her eyes, stared at her, but didn't speak. Neither did Eric. There was a cooking smell in the clearing, a dark circle of soot where Mathias had built his fire, and Stacy thought, *They made lunch.* Then she remembered the reason for the fire, and she half-glanced toward Pablo, half-saw him lying there beneath his lean-to (his sunken eyes, the glistening pink-and-black stubs of his legs . . .), before she recoiled, turning toward the tent, fleeing. The flap was hanging open, and she ducked quickly past it, leaving her sunshade lying on the ground outside.

The light was dimmer here; it took a moment for Stacy's eyes to adjust. Mathias was lying on one of the sleeping bags, curled onto his side. His eyes were closed, but Stacy could sense, somehow, that he wasn't asleep. She crept to the rear of the tent, passing right by him, and crouched to pick up the jug of water. She twisted off its cap, took a long swallow, wiped her mouth with the back of her hand. It wasn't enough, of course—the entire jug wouldn't have been enough—and she toyed briefly with the idea of taking another sip. She knew it would be wrong, though, and felt guilty merely at the thought of the transgression, so she capped the bottle. When she turned to leave, she found

Mathias peering toward her, with that typically unreadable expression of his.

"Jeff told me I could," she said. She was worried he might think she was stealing the water.

Mathias nodded. He remained silent, staring.

"Is he okay?" Stacy whispered, gesturing out toward Pablo.

Mathias hesitated long enough for it to begin to seem as if he wasn't going to answer her. Then he gave a slow shake of his head.

Stacy couldn't think of anything more to say. She took another step toward the open flap, then stopped again. "Are you?" she asked.

Mathias's face shifted, edging toward a smile that didn't happen. For an instant, she thought he might even laugh, but that didn't happen, either. "Are you?" he asked.

She shook her head. "No."

And then, nothing: he just kept staring at her with that look, which was one small notch beyond blank, hinting at a weary sort of amusement without actually expressing it. Finally, she realized he was waiting for her to leave. So that was what she did; she stooped back out into the sunlight, zipping the flap shut behind her.

Eric was still pacing. Stacy noticed that his leg was bleeding again, and she thought about asking him why, but then she realized she didn't want to know. She wished he'd go into the tent with Mathias and lie down, and would've forced him to do it, too, if she could've only thought of a way. They all ought to be in the tent, probably; that would be what Jeff would want. In the shade, resting, conserving their strength. But it felt like a trap inside. You were closed in; you couldn't see what was happening, what might be coming. Stacy didn't want to be in there, and she assumed the others felt the same way. She didn't understand how Mathias could bear it.

She retrieved her sunshade, sat in the dirt a few feet to Amy's right. Eric continued to pace, the blood leaking slowly down his leg; his shoe squeaked with it every time he took a step. Stacy wanted him to stop, wanted him to find some sort of calm for himself, and she spent a while willing this to happen. *Sit down, Eric,* she thought. *Please sit down.* It didn't work, of course; even if she'd spoken the words, shouted them, it wouldn't have worked.

The worst part of being out in the clearing wasn't the sun, or the heat. It was the sound of Pablo's breathing, which was loud, ragged, oddly irregular. Sometimes it would stop for a stretch of seconds—just fall silent—and, despite herself, Stacy would always end up glancing toward the little lean-to, thinking the same two words: *He died.* But then, with a rattling gasping rasp that always made her flinch, the Greek's breathing would resume once more, though not before she'd been forced to look at him again, to see those glistening, blistered stumps, those eyes that refused to open, that thin thread of dark brown liquid seeping from the corner of his mouth.

There was the vine, too, of course; they were surrounded by it. Green, green, green—no matter which direction Stacy turned, it lay waiting in her line of vision. She kept trying to tell herself that it was just a plant, only a plant, nothing more than a plant. This was what it looked like now, after all; it wasn't moving, wasn't making that dreadful laughing sound. It was simply a pretty tangle of vegetation, with its tiny red flowers and its flat, hand-shaped leaves—soaking up the sunlight, harmlessly inert. This was what plants did; they didn't move, didn't laugh, *couldn't* move, *couldn't* laugh. But Stacy wasn't equal to the fantasy. It was like clenching an ice cube in her hand and willing it not to melt; the longer she held to it, the less she had. She'd seen the vine move, seen it burrowing into Eric's leg, seen it reach out to suck dry Amy's vomit, and she'd heard it, too, heard it laughing—the whole hillside laughing. She couldn't help but sense it watching now, observing them, planning its next sally.

She shifted closer to Amy, positioning her flimsy umbrella so that it covered them both in shade. When she took Amy's hand, she was startled by how damp it felt. *Scared,* she thought. And then she asked that question again, the same one she'd offered Mathias in the tent: "You okay?"

Amy shook her head, started to cry, gripping Stacy's hand.

"Shh," Stacy whispered, trying to soothe her. "Shh." She put her arm around Amy's shoulders, felt her weeping deepen, her body starting to jump with it, to hicccup. "What is it, sweetie?" she said. "What's the matter?"

Amy pulled her hand free, wiped her face with it. She began to shake her head, then couldn't seem to stop.

Eric was still pacing, lost in his own world, not even looking at them. Stacy watched him as he moved back and forth, back and forth, across the little clearing.

Finally, Amy managed to speak. "I'm just tired," she said, whispering the words. "That's all. I'm so tired." Then she started to cry again.

Stacy sat with her, waiting for it to pass. But it didn't. Finally, Stacy couldn't bear it any longer. She stood up, strode to the far side of the clearing. Pablo's pack was lying there; she reached into it, pulled out one of the remaining bottles of tequila. She carried it back toward Amy, breaking its seal—it was the only thing she could think to do. She sat again beneath the umbrella, took a long, burning swallow of the liquor, then held out the bottle. Amy stared down at it, still crying, blinking through her tears, wiping at them with her hand. Stacy could sense her debating, could feel her almost deciding against it, then surrendering. She took the bottle, put it to her lips, threw her head back, the tequila sloshing forward into her mouth, down her throat. She surfaced with a gasping sound—part cough, part sob.

Eric was sitting beside them suddenly, holding out his hand.

Amy gave him the bottle.

And so this was how they moved forward into the afternoon as the sun slowly began to wester. They huddled close together in that little clearing—surrounded by the massed and coiled vine, its green leaves, its red flowers—and passed the gradually emptying bottle back and forth among themselves.

It didn't take long for Amy to become drunk.

They started slowly, but it didn't matter. Her stomach was so empty that the tequila seemed to burn its way straight to her core. At first, she simply grew flushed, almost giggly with it, a little dizzy, too. Next came the slurred quality—to her words, her thoughts—and then, finally, the weariness. Eric had already drifted into sleep at her side, the trio of wounds on his leg continuing to leak their thin strings of blood down his shin. Stacy was awake—talking, even—but she'd somehow begun to seem increasingly far away; it was difficult to follow her words. Amy shut her eyes for a moment and began to think about nothing at all, which felt blissful: exactly the right way to be.

When she opened her eyes again, feeling stiff—wretched, actually—the sun was much lower in the sky. Eric was still asleep; Stacy was still talking.

"That's the thing, of course," she was saying. "Whether or not there was another train to catch. It shouldn't make a difference, but I'm sure it does to her; I'm sure she thinks about it all the time. Because if it was the last train of the day, if she would've had to spend the night in this strange city where she didn't even really know the language yet—well, that makes it a little better, doesn't it?"

Amy had no idea what Stacy was talking about, but she nodded anyway; it seemed like the right response. The tequila bottle was resting in front of Stacy, capped, lying on its side, half-full. Amy knew she should stop, that she'd been stupid to drink what she already had, that it would only dehydrate her, making everything that much more difficult to bear here, that night was coming and they ought to be sober to meet it, but none of this held any sway over her. She thought it all through, acknowledged its wisdom, then held out her hand for the bottle. Stacy passed it to her, still talking.

"I think so, too," she said. "If it's the last train, you run for it; you jump. And she was an athlete, remember—a good one. So she probably didn't even consider the possibility of falling, probably didn't even hesitate. Just ran, leapt. I didn't know her, really, so I can't say how it happened. I'm just speculating. I did see her once after she got back, though. Maybe a year later—which is pretty quick, when you consider everything. And she was playing basketball. Not with the team anymore, of course. But out on the playground. And she seemed, you know—she seemed okay. She was wearing sweatpants, so I couldn't see what they looked like. But I saw her run up and down the court, and it was almost normal. Not normal, exactly, but almost."

Amy took two quick swigs of the tequila. It was warm from sitting in the sun, and somehow this made it go down a little more easily than usual. They were big swallows, but she didn't cough. Stacy held her hand out for the bottle and Amy passed it back to her. She took a tiny sip, very ladylike, then capped the bottle and set it in her lap.

"She seemed happy—that's what I'm trying to say. She seemed all right. She was smiling; she was out there doing what she liked to do, even if, you know . . ." Stacy trailed off here, looking sad.

Amy was drunk and half-asleep, and she still had no idea what Stacy was talking about. "Even if?"

Stacy nodded gravely. "Exactly."

After that they sat for a stretch in silence. Amy was about to ask for the bottle again, when Stacy brightened suddenly.

"Want to see?" she asked.

"See?"

"How she ran?"

Amy nodded, and Stacy handed her the umbrella, the bottle. Then she stood up, started quickly across the little clearing, pretending to play basketball: dribbling, passing, feinting. After a jump shot, she jogged back, her hands high in the air, playing defense. Then, once more, she darted quickly to the other side, a fast break, a little leap for the layup. She ran with an odd hitch to her stride, almost a limp, and seemed slightly off balance, like some sort of long-legged wading bird. Amy took a long swallow from the bottle, watching, perplexed.

"You see?" Stacy said, breathing hard, still immersed in her imaginary game. "They saved the knees—that's the important thing. So she could still run pretty good. Just a little awkward. But like I said, this was only after a year or so. She might be even better now."

They saved the knees. Amy understood now: sprinting for a train, jumping, falling. *They saved the knees.* She took another swig of tequila, ventured a glance toward Pablo. His breathing had quieted somewhat, grown softer, slower, though that unsettling rasp—wet sounding, phlegm-filled—remained an essential part of it. He looked terrible, of course. How could he not? He had a broken back, and two seared stubs for legs. He'd lost a lot of blood, was dehydrated, unconscious, probably dying. And he stank, too—of shit and urine and charred flesh. The vine had begun to sprout on the sleeping bag, which had become sodden with the various fluids seeping off of him. They should do something about this, Amy realized, probably get rid of the sleeping bag altogether, lift Pablo clear of his backboard, yank the fetid thing out from under him. She understood that this would be the right thing to do, that it was what Jeff would probably have them attempt if he were here, but she made no move to undertake it. All she could think of was the previous evening—she and Eric at the bottom of the shaft, heaving Pablo toward the swaying backboard. She knew she wasn't going to try to pick the Greek up again, not now, not ever.

"Without the knees," Stacy was saying, "you have to swing them. Like this."

Amy turned to watch as Stacy moved around the edge of the clearing, stiff-legged, swaying, her face focused, concentrating. She was good at this sort of thing; she always had been, was a natural mimic. She looked like Captain Ahab, pacing the deck on his peg-leg. Amy laughed; she couldn't help it.

Stacy turned toward her, pleased. "I don't have the other one yet, do I? With the knees? Let me try again." She resumed her imaginary basketball game, just dribbling at first, trying out different leg movements, searching for the right effect. Then, abruptly, she seemed to get it, an awkward sort of grace, like a ballerina with numb feet. She ran to the far end of the clearing, did another layup, before coming quickly back toward Amy, playing defense.

Eric stirred. He'd been lying on his side, curled into a ball, and now he sat up, watching Stacy. He didn't look well. Amy supposed this was true for all of them. He was hollow-eyed, unshaven. He looked like a refugee: hungry, worn-out, fleeing some disaster. His shirt hung off him in tatters; the wounds on his legs seemed incapable of closing. He watched Stacy dribbling and passing and shooting, his expression oddly vacant, a waiting-room look, someone in an ER, staring at a television whose volume was too low to hear, waiting for a nurse to call his name.

"She's playing basketball," Amy said. "But with fake legs."

Eric turned his head, transferring that empty gaze from Stacy to Amy's face.

"There was this girl," Amy said. "She fell under a train. But she could still play basketball." She knew she wasn't saying it right, was just confusing the matter. It didn't seem to matter, though, because Eric nodded.

"Oh," he said. He held out his hand, and she passed him the bottle.

They watched Stacy play another point, and then, when she finally stopped—out of breath, sweating with the exertion—Amy applauded. She was feeling better and better for some reason, and determined not to let the feeling slip away. "Do the stewardess!" she called.

Stacy tensed her face into a stiff, exaggerated smile, and then she began, silently, to work her way through a preflight orientation, demonstrating how to use a seat belt, where the exits were, how to don an oxygen mask, all of her gestures clipped and robotic. She was mimicking the stewardess from their flight into Cancún. She'd done it for them the night they'd arrived, after they'd dropped their things off at their rooms and met on the beach, where they sat together in a loose circle, sipping bottles of beer. This was before they'd met the Greeks, before Mathias, too. They were still pale, a little weary from the trip, but pleased to be there—a happy time. And they'd laughed, all of them, at Stacy's performance, drinking their beer, feeling the sand beneath them, still warm from the day's sun, and listening to the sound of the surf, the music drifting toward them from the hotel terrace—yes, a happy time. And perhaps Amy was trying to reclaim that now by asking Stacy to mimic the stewardess once again, trying to prod them back toward that innocence, that ignorance of this terrible place into which they'd somehow stumbled. It wasn't working, of course. Not that it was Stacy's fault: She had the smile down, the tense gestures—she *was* the stewardess. It was Eric and Amy who'd changed, who were failing this effort at reclamation. They watched; Amy even managed a laugh, but there was a sadness in it that she couldn't keep out.

They saved the knees, she thought.

That first night on the beach, they'd each offered their contributions. They were good at this sort of thing, had all come from the same type of background—summer camps and ski trips—they knew what to do under a starry sky, or around a campfire, how to entertain one another. They each had their appointed roles. Stacy did her mimicry. Jeff taught them things, told them facts he'd read in the guidebook on the flight down. Eric made up funny stories, imagining how their trip might unfold, creating outrageous scenarios, making them laugh. And Amy sang. She had a nice voice, she knew; not a particularly strong one, but quietly adept, perfect for those campfires, those starry skies.

Stacy returned across the clearing now, sat beside them; she took back the umbrella. Her shirt was torn, Amy noticed; she could see her breast. It was true for all of them: their clothes were rapidly being eaten into shreds by that green webbing of vine. There was nothing you could do about it; you brushed it away, but a few minutes later it was back again. And every time you swiped at it, the vine bled its sap onto your skin, burning you. Their hands looked scarred—it hurt to pick things up. They could dig into the backpacks, she supposed, find themselves new shirts and pants, but there was something creepy about this, wearing other people's things, dead people's, those mounds of green scattered across the hillside, and Amy hoped she'd be able to avoid this eventuality as long as possible. It felt like a surrender in some way, a defeat; as long as rescue seemed imminent, what was the point in replacing her clothes?

Eric kept rubbing at his chest. There was a spot right at the base of his rib cage that he couldn't seem to stop touching. He'd press at it, then dig with his fingers, then gently massage it. Amy knew what he was doing, knew that he thought the vine was inside him, and it was beginning to make her anxious, his constant probing; she wanted him to stop.

"Tell us something funny, Eric," she said.

"Funny?"

She nodded, smiling, trying to prod him on, to distract him from that feeling inside his chest, distract all three of them. "Make up a story."

Eric shook his head. "I can't think of anything."

"Tell us what'll happen when we get home," Stacy said.

They watched him take another swallow of tequila, his eyes watering from it. He wiped at his face with the back of his hand, then recapped the bottle. "Well, we'll be famous, won't we? At least for a while?"

They both nodded. Of course they'd be famous.

"The cover of *People* magazine, maybe," Eric continued, warming to the idea. "*Time,* too, probably. And then somebody'll want to buy the film rights. We'll have to be smart there, stay together, all of us signing something, some document, agreeing to sell the story as a group—we'll get more money that way. We'll need a lawyer, I guess, or an agent."

"They'll make a movie out of it?" Stacy asked. She looked excited by the idea, but surprised, too.

"That's right."

"Who'll play me?"

Eric peered at Stacy, considered. Then he smiled, waving at her chest. "Your tit's hanging out, you know."

Stacy glanced down, adjusted her shirt. There wasn't really enough of it left to cover her breast, but she didn't seem to care. "Seriously. Who'll play me?'

"First, you have to decide who you are."

"Who I am?"

"'Cause they'll have to change us some, you know. Make us more into characters. They'll need a hero, a villain—that sort of thing. See what I'm saying?"

Stacy nodded. "And which am I?"

"Well, there are two female parts, right? So one of you will have to be the good girl, the prissy one, and the other one'll have to be the slut." He thought about this, then shrugged. "I guess Amy would be the prissy one, don't you think?"

Stacy frowned, taking this in. She didn't say anything.

"So you'd, you know—you'd be the slut."

"Fuck you, Eric." She sounded angry.

"What? I'm just saying—"

"You're the villain, then. If I have to be the—"

Eric shook his head. "No way. I'm the funny guy. I'm the Adam Sandler character. Or Jim Carrey. The one who shouldn't be there, who came along by mistake, who keeps stumbling into the others, tripping over things. I'm the comic relief."

"Then who's the villain?"

"Mathias is the villain—definitely. Those scary Germans. They'll have him lure us here on purpose. The vine'll be some sort of Nazi experiment gone awry. His father was a scientist, maybe, and he's brought us here to feed daddy's plants."

"And the hero?"

"Jeff—no doubt about that. Bruce Willis, stoically saving the day. An ex–Boy Scout." He turned to Amy. "Was Jeff a Boy Scout? I bet Jeff was a Boy Scout."

Amy nodded. "An Eagle Scout."

They laughed at this, all three of them, though it wasn't a joke. He really had been an Eagle Scout. His mother had a framed clipping from the local paper hanging in their front hall; it showed Jeff in his uniform, shaking hands with the governor of Massachusetts. Amy felt an odd tightness in her chest when she thought of this, a sudden sense of warmth toward him, a protectiveness. She remembered the way it had been down in the shaft, the vines whipping through the dark, grabbing at her, pulling her toward that hole. She'd glimpsed the bones at the bottom before the torch fluttered out; other people had died there—she might've, too. And it wasn't because of any skill or foresight on her own part that she'd survived. Jeff had saved her. Jeff would save them all, if they'd only let him. They shouldn't be laughing at him.

"It's not funny," she said, but her voice came out too quietly, and the other two were too drunk. They didn't seem to hear her.

"Who's going to play me?" Stacy repeated.

Eric waved the question aside. "It doesn't matter. Somebody who looks good with her tit hanging out of her shirt."

"You'll be the fat one," Stacy said, sounding angry again. "The fat, sweaty one."

They were going to start fighting now, Amy realized—she recognized the tone. Another exchange or two like that, and they'd begin to shout at each other. She didn't think she could handle this—not here, not now. So she tried to distract them. "What about me?" she asked.

"You?" Eric said.

"Who's going to play me?"

Eric pursed his lips, considering this. He uncapped the bottle, took another sip, then held it out toward Stacy, a peace offering. She accepted it, tilting her head back, taking a big swallow, almost chugging. She giggled as she lowered the bottle, pleased with herself, her eyes shining strangely, looking glazed.

"Someone who can sing," Eric said.

"That's right." Stacy nodded. "So they can have musical numbers."

Eric was smiling. "A duet with the Boy Scout."

"Madonna, maybe."

Eric snorted. "Britney Spears."

"Mandy Moore."

They were both laughing. "Sing for us, Amy," Eric said.

Amy was smiling, feeling confused, ready to be affronted. She couldn't tell if they were laughing at her or if it was something she should find funny, too. She was just as drunk as they were, she realized.

"Sing 'One is the loneliest number,'" Stacy said.

"Yeah," Eric nodded. "That's perfect."

They were both grinning at her now, waiting. Stacy offered her the bottle, and Amy took a swallow from it, shutting her eyes. When she opened them again, they were still waiting. So she started to sing: "One is the loneliest number that you'll ever do. Two can be as bad as one. It's the loneliest number since the number one. No is the saddest experience you'll ever know. Yes, it's the saddest experience you'll ever know. 'Cause one is the loneliest number that you'll ever do. One is the loneliest number, worse than two . . ." She trailed off, feeling out of breath, dizzy with it. She handed the bottle to Eric. "I can't remember the rest," she said. It wasn't true; she just didn't want to sing anymore. The lyrics were making her sad, and for a while there she'd been feeling okay—or almost okay, at least. She didn't want to feel sad.

Eric took a long swallow. They were two-thirds of the way through the bottle now. He clambered to his feet, stepped across the clearing, a little unsteady in his gait. He bent, picked something up, then came teetering back toward them. He had the bottle in one hand; in the other, he was holding the knife. Amy and Stacy both stared at it. Amy didn't want it to be there, but she couldn't think of anything to say that might make him put it down. She watched him spit on its blade, try to clean it on his shirt. Then he waved the knife toward her. "You can sing it at the end. When you're the last one left."

"'The last one left?'" Amy asked. She wanted to reach out and take the knife from him, tried to order her arm to rise, to move in his direction, yet nothing happened. She was very, very drunk, she knew—and so tired, too. She wasn't equal to this.

"When everyone else is killed off," Eric said.

Amy shook her head. "Don't. That's not funny."

He ignored her. "The Boy Scout'll live—he's the hero; he has to survive. You'll just think he's dead. You'll sing your song, and he'll pop back to life. And then you'll escape somehow. He'll build a hot-air balloon out of the tent and you'll float away to safety."

"I'll die?" Stacy said. She seemed alarmed by the possibility, wide-eyed with it. She was beginning to slur her words. "Why do I have to die?"

"The slut has to die. No question. Because you're bad. You have to be punished."

Stacy looked hurt by this. "What about the funny guy?"

"He's the first—he's always the first. And in some stupid way, too. So people will laugh when he goes."

"Like how?"

"He gets cut, maybe, and the vine pushes its way into his leg. It eats him from the inside out."

Amy knew what he was going to do next, and she raised her hand, finally, to stop him. But she was too late. He was doing it—it was done. He'd lifted his shirt, cut a four-inch slit along the base of his rib cage. Stacy gasped. Amy sat with her arm held out, uselessly, before her. A horizontal line of blood crested the lip of Eric's wound, swept downward across his stomach, soaking into the waistband of his shorts. He watched it, frowning, probing at the cut with the point of the knife, prying it farther open, the bleeding increasing.

"*Eric,*" Stacy cried.

"I thought it would just come tumbling out," he said. It had to be painful, but he didn't seem to mind. He kept pushing at the wound with the knife. "It's right under here. I can feel it. It must sense me cutting, somehow, must pull back into me. It's hiding."

He felt with his left hand, pressing at the skin above the wound; it looked like he was about to cut himself again. Amy leaned forward, snatched the knife from him. She thought he'd resist her, but he didn't; he just let her take it. The blood kept coming, and he made no effort to staunch it.

"Help him," Amy said to Stacy. She dropped the knife into the dirt at her side. "Help him stop it."

Stacy looked at Amy, openmouthed. She was panting; she seemed to be on the verge of hyperventilating. "How?"

"Pull off his shirt. Press it to the cut."

Stacy set down her umbrella, stepped toward Eric, started to help him out of his T-shirt. He'd become very passive; he lifted his arms like a child, letting her tug the shirt up and off him.

"Lie down," Amy ordered, and he did it, on his back, the blood still coming, pooling in the tiny hollow of his belly button.

Stacy balled up the T-shirt, held it to the wound.

Things had gotten bad again, and Amy knew there was no way to alter this, no way to force the afternoon back into its false air of tranquillity. There'd be no more mimicry now, no more joking, no more singing. She and Stacy sat in silence, Stacy leaning forward slightly, applying pressure to stop the bleeding. Eric lay on his back, uncomplaining, strangely serene, staring up at the sky.

"It's my fault," Amy said. Stacy and Eric both turned to look at her, not understanding. She wiped at her face with her hand; it felt gritty, sweat-stained. "I didn't want to come. When Mathias first asked us, I knew I didn't want to. But I didn't say anything; I just let it happen. We could be on the beach right now. We could be—"

"Shh," Stacy said.

"And the man in the pickup. The taxi driver. He told me not to go. He said it was a bad place. That he'd—"

"You didn't know, sweetie."

"And after the village, if I hadn't thought of checking along the trees, we never would've found the path. If I'd kept silent—"

Stacy shook her head, still pressing the T-shirt to Eric's abdomen. The blood had soaked all the way through now; it wasn't stopping. Her hands were covered with it. "How could you've known?" she asked.

"And I'm the one, aren't I? The one who stepped into the vines? If I hadn't, that man might've forced us to leave. We might've—"

"Look at the clouds," Eric said, cutting her off, his voice sounding dreamy, oddly distant, as if he were drugged. He lifted his hand, pointed upward.

And he was right: clouds were building to the south, thunderheads, their undersides ominously dark, heavy with the promise of rain. Back in Cancún, at the beach, they'd be gathering their things, returning to their rooms. Jeff and she would make love, then slip into sleep, a long nap before dinner, the rain blurring their window, an inch-deep puddle forming on their tiny balcony. Their first day, they'd seen a gull sitting in it, partially sheltered from the downpour, staring out to sea. Rain meant water, of course. Amy knew they should be thinking of ways to gather it. But she couldn't; her mind was empty. She was drunk and tired and sad; someone else would have to figure out how to collect the rain. Not Eric, of course, with his blood rapidly soaking through that T-shirt. And not Stacy, either, who looked even worse than Amy felt: sunstruck, shaky, all dazed behind the eyes. They were useless, the three of them, with their silly stories, their singing, their laughter in a place like this; they were fools, not survivors.

And how was it possible, with such little warning, that the sun had sunk so low? It was nearly touching the horizon. In another hour—two at the most—it would be night.

When did it first begin to go wrong? Afterward, the next morning, when *all of them* suddenly meant one less than it had before, Eric would spend a long time trying to unravel this. He didn't believe it was the drinking, nor even the cutting. Because things were still manageable then—unmoored, maybe, a little out of control, but still endurable in some essential way. Lying on his back like that, with Stacy pressing the T-shirt to his wound, struggling to staunch the flow of blood, while the clouds built in the sky above them, Eric had felt an unexpected sense of serenity. Rain was coming; they weren't going to die of thirst. And if that was true, if they could so easily overcome this most pressing obstacle to their survival, why shouldn't they be able to overcome all obstacles? Why shouldn't they make it home alive?

There was the need for food, of course, hiding just behind the need for water—and what could rain possibly do for that? Eric peered up at the sky, puzzling over this dilemma, but without any success. All he managed to accomplish by focusing upon it was to rouse his lurking sense of hunger. "Why haven't we eaten again?" he said, his voice sounding far away even to himself—thick-tongued, weak-lunged. *The tequila,* he thought. And then: *I'm bleeding.*

"Are you hungry?" Amy asked.

It was a stupid question, of course—how could he not be hungry?— and he didn't bother to answer it. After a moment, Amy stood up, stepped to the tent, unzipped the flap, slipped inside.

Right there, Eric would decide the next morning. *When she went to get the food.* But he didn't note it at the time, just watched her vanish into the tent, then turned his attention back to the sky again, those clouds boiling upward above him. He wasn't going to move, he decided. He was going to stay right there, on his back, while the rain poured down upon him.

"It's not stopping," Stacy said.

She meant his wound, he knew. She sounded worried, but he wasn't. He didn't mind the bleeding, was too drunk to feel the pain. It was going to rain. He was going to lie here and let it wash him clean. Clean, he'd find the strength to reach inside himself, into that slit he'd cut below his rib cage, reach in with his hand and search out the vine, grasp it, yank it free. He was going to be okay.

Amy returned from the tent. She was carrying the plastic jug of water, the bag of grapes. She set the jug on the ground, opened the bag, held it out toward Stacy.

Stacy shook her head. "We have to wait."

"We've missed lunch," Amy said. "We were supposed to have lunch." She didn't lower the grapes, just kept holding them toward Stacy.

Once again, Stacy shook her head. "When Jeff gets back. We can—"

"I'll save some for him. I'll put them aside."

"What about Mathias?"

"Him, too."

"What's he doing?"

Amy nodded toward the tent. "Sleeping." She shook the bag. "Come on. Just a couple. They'll help with your thirst."

Stacy hesitated, visibly wavering, then reached in, plucked out two grapes.

Amy shook the bag again. "More," she said. "Give some to Eric."

Stacy took two more. She put one in her own mouth, then dropped one into Eric's. He cradled it on his tongue for a moment, wanting to savor the feel of it. He watched Stacy and Amy eat theirs; then he did the same. The sensation was almost too intense—the burst of juice, the sweetness, the joy of chewing, of swallowing—he felt light-headed with it. But there was no satisfaction, no diminishment, however modest, in his hunger. No, it seemed to leap up within him, to rouse itself from some deep slumber; his entire body started to ache with it. Stacy dropped another grape into his mouth, and he chewed more quickly this time, the swallowing more important than the savoring, his lips immediately opening for another one. The others appeared to feel a similar urgency. No one was talking; they were chewing, swallowing, reaching into the bag for more. Eric watched the clouds build as he ate. All he had to do was open his mouth, and Stacy would drop another grape into it. She was smiling; so was Amy. The juice helped his thirst, just as Amy had promised. He was beginning to feel a little more sober—in a good way—everything seeming to settle a bit, to coalesce around and within him. He could feel his pain, but even this was reassuring. It'd been a stupid thing to do, he knew, digging into himself with that knife; he couldn't quite grasp how he'd found the courage to attempt it. He was in trouble now. He needed stitches—antibiotics, too, probably—but he nonetheless felt strangely at peace. If he could just keep lying here, eating these grapes, watching the clouds darken above him, he believed that everything would be all right, that somehow, miraculously, he'd make it through.

It came as a bit of a shock to realize that—abruptly, without any apparent warning—the bag was almost empty. There were only four grapes left; they'd eaten all the rest. The three of them stared at the bag; no one spoke for a stretch. Pablo continued his ragged breathing, but Eric had reached the point where he barely even noticed it anymore. It was like any other sort of background noise—traffic beyond a window, waves on a beach. Someone had to say something, of course, to comment on what they'd done, and it was Amy who finally shouldered this responsibility.

"They can have the orange," she said.

Stacy and Eric remained silent. There'd been a lot of grapes in the bag; it ought to have been easy enough to set aside allotments for Mathias and Jeff.

"I have to pee," Stacy whispered. She was talking to him, Eric realized. "Can you hold your shirt?"

He nodded, taking the T-shirt from her, maintaining the pressure against his side. He could feel the vine again, shifting about inside him, just beneath the pain. It had gone away after he'd cut himself, but now it had come back.

"Do I have to use the bottle?" Stacy asked Amy.

Amy shook her head, and Stacy stood up, moved across the clearing. She didn't seem to want to venture into the vines. She crouched with her back to them, and Eric heard her begin to urinate. It didn't sound like very much, a brief spattering, and then she was rising again, pulling up her pants.

"They can have some of the raisins, too," Amy said, but quietly, almost as if she were speaking to herself.

Stacy returned, sat beside Eric. He thought she was going to resume holding the T-shirt against his wound, but she didn't. She picked up the plastic jug of water, uncapped it, poured a little on her right foot. Eric and Amy stared at her in astonishment.

"What the fuck're you doing?" Amy asked.

Stacy seemed startled by the sharpness in her voice. "I peed on myself," she said.

Amy reached, snatched the bottle from Stacy's hand, recapped it. "That's our *water*. You just poured it on your fucking foot."

Stacy sat for a moment, blinking in a theatrical way, as if not quite understanding what Amy was saying. "You don't have to swear," she said.

"We'll die without that—you know? And you're just—"

"I wasn't thinking, okay? I wanted to clean the pee off my foot and I saw the jug, and I—"

"Jesus fucking Christ, Stacy. How can you be so out of it?"

Stacy waved at the sky, the gathering clouds. "It's going to rain. We'll have plenty of water."

"So why didn't you wait?"

"Don't shout, Amy. I said I'm sorry, and—"

"Sorry doesn't bring the water back, does it?"

Eric wanted to say something, to stop or distract them, but the right words weren't coming to him. He recognized what was happening, what was starting here. This was how Amy and Stacy fought, in sudden, intense eruptions that seemed to arrive out of nowhere, little flash floods of rage that would come and go with a violence matched only by their brevity. A single inadvertent word could set them off—more often than not when they'd been drinking—and within seconds they'd be flailing at each other, sometimes literally. Eric had seen Stacy slash Amy's cheek with her nails, deep enough that she drew blood, and he knew that Amy had once slapped Stacy so hard that she'd knocked her to the floor. Then, inevitably, at the very peak of their ferocity, these encounters would collapse upon themselves. The girls would look at each other in mutual bewilderment, wondering how they'd managed to say all they'd said; they'd beg each other for forgiveness, would embrace, begin to cry.

And now here they were again, sprinting down that familiar path.

"Sometimes you can be so stupid," Amy said.

"Fuck off," Stacy muttered, barely audible.

"What?"

"Just drop it, okay?"

"You're not even sorry, are you?"

"How many times do I have to say it?"

Eric tried to sit up, felt a tearing sensation from his wound, and thought better of it. "Maybe you guys should—"

Amy gave him a look of pure disdain. He could see her drunkenness in her face, exaggerating her expressions. "Stay out of it, Eric. You've already caused enough problems."

"Leave him be," Stacy said. Both of their voices were too loud; it hurt his head to listen. He wanted to get up and leave them to this, but he was still bleeding, still in pain, still quite drunk; he didn't feel like he could move.

"If he fucking cuts himself again, I'm just gonna let him bleed."

"You're being a bitch, Amy. You realize that?"

"Slut."

Stacy looked astonished by this, as if Amy had spit on her. "What?"

"He's right—that's who you'd be."

Stacy waved this insult aside, struggling for an expression of detachment, aiming for the high ground, but Eric could see it wasn't working. They were approaching the scratching stage, he knew—the slapping, the kicking. "You're drunk," she said. "You're making a fool of yourself."

"Slut. That's who you *are.*"

"Can't you hear yourself slur?"

"Shut up, slut."

"*You* shut up, bitch."

"No. *You* shut up."

"Bitch."

"Slut."

"Bitch."

"Slut."

And then something odd happened. They both fell silent, staring off to Eric's right. Or not silent, because the two words continued, in their voices, going back and forth, back and forth—*Bitch . . . Slut . . . Bitch . . . Slut . . . Bitch . . . Slut*—only Amy and Stacy weren't speaking anymore; they were staring, first in surprise, then in something closer to horror, out across the hilltop, where their voices were rising now, shouting that harsh pair of words, beginning to blur together, one merging into the other.

BitchSlutBitchSlutBitchSlutBitchSlutBitchSlut . . .

It was the vine. It was mimicking them, as if mocking their fight, imitating the sound of their voices so perfectly that even as Eric realized what was happening, even as he stared at Stacy and Amy and saw that their mouths were no longer moving, that they'd fallen silent, that it couldn't possibly be the two of them he was hearing, he didn't quite accept it. Because it *was* their voices—stolen somehow, misappropriated, but their voices nonetheless.

BitchSlutBitchSlutBitchSlutBitchSlutBitchSlut. . . .

Mathias was standing over them suddenly, looking sleep-tousled, blinking, visibly waking up even as Eric watched him. "What is it?" he asked.

No one answered him. What, after all, was there to say? The voices grew softer, then louder again, branching out beyond those two words: *If he fucking cuts himself . . . You're not even sorry, are you?*

"It's the vines," Stacy said, as if this needed explanation.

Mathias was silent, his eyes moving about, taking things in—the plastic bag with its four remaining grapes, the bloody T-shirt pressed to Eric's abdomen, Pablo's motionless form, the nearly empty bottle of tequila. "Where's Jeff?" he asked.

I peed on my foot, the vine shouted. *They can have the orange.*

"Down the hill," Amy said.

"Shouldn't someone have relieved him?"

No one answered. They were all looking off into the distance, feeling shamed, wishing the voices would stop, that Mathias would leave them be. Eric's chest tightened—the first stirrings of anger. How could Mathias claim the right to judge them? He wasn't one of them, was he? They hardly even knew him; he was practically a stranger.

Sometimes you can be so stupid.

"Have you been drinking?" Mathias asked.

Again, they remained mute. And suddenly, there was Eric's voice, too, coming toward them from across the hilltop: *Mathias is the villain—definitely.* And then, almost like a record skipping: *Nazi . . . Boy Scout . . . Nazi . . . Boy Scout . . .*

Eric could feel Mathias turning to look at him, but he kept his gaze averted, peering off to the south, toward the clouds, which continued to darken and build. They were going to let loose soon, very soon; he wished it were now.

You shut up.

Leave him be.

Tell us something funny.

I'm the funny guy.

"How long has this been going on?" Mathias asked.

"It just started," Amy said.

They saved the knees.

Nazi.

Let him bleed.

You're drunk.

Nazi.

Fuck off.

Nazi. Nazi. Nazi.

Eric could see Mathias disengaging, making the decision, his face seeming to close somehow. "I'll go relieve him," he said.

Amy nodded. So did Stacy. Eric just lay there. He felt like he could hear the plant inside him, sense it vibrating against his rib cage, speaking, calling out. Couldn't anyone else hear it? *Slut,* it said in Amy's voice. And then, in Stacy's: *Bitch.* The balled-up T-shirt was completely soaked through now, like a sodden sponge; when he squeezed at it, blood cascaded warmly down his side.

Nazi.

Slut.

Nazi.

Bitch.

Nazi.

They watched Mathias turn, walk out of the clearing.

The voices continued for some time yet—Amy's and Stacy's and Eric's, coming from all different directions, talking one over the other, occasionally rising to a shout—and then, just as abruptly as they'd begun, they stopped. The silence wasn't as much of a relief as Eric would've expected, though; there was a tension to it, everything freighted with the knowledge that the vine could start again at any moment. And also the sense of being listened to, spied upon. It took awhile for them to gather the courage to speak, and when Stacy finally did, it was in a whisper.

"I'm sorry," she said.

Amy waved this aside.

"I wasn't thinking," Stacy persisted. "I just . . . I had pee on my foot."

"It doesn't matter." Amy gestured upward, toward the clouds. "We'll be fine."

"You're not a bitch."

"I know, honey. Let's just . . . let's forget it, okay? Let's pretend it didn't happen. We're both tired."

"Scared."

"That's right. Tired and scared."

Stacy shifted a little, edging toward her. She held out her hand, and Amy took it, clasped it.

Eric wanted to get up, follow Mathias down the hill, make everything clear to him. It had been his own voice shouting that word over and over again—*Nazi*—and he couldn't imagine what Mathias must be thinking now, didn't want to consider it, yet he kept probing at it, despite himself. *I should've explained,* he thought with a growing sense of panic. *I should've told him it was a joke.* He was in too much pain to pursue him, though, still bleeding heavily from his wound—at this rate, he didn't see how it would ever stop. But somebody had to go; somebody had to make it right. "Go tell him," he said to Stacy.

She gave him a blank look. "Tell who?"

"Mathias. That it was a joke."

"What was a joke?"

"Nazi—tell him we were just playing around."

Before Stacy could answer, Pablo startled them by speaking. It was in Greek, of course: a single word, surprisingly loud. They all turned to stare at him. His eyes were open, his head lifted off the backboard, the muscles in his neck standing taut, trembling slightly. He repeated the word—*potato,* absurdly, was what it sounded like to Eric. He lifted his right hand, made a beckoning motion. He seemed to be gesturing toward the plastic jug.

That rasping voice: "*Po-ta-to.*"

"I think he wants some water," Stacy said.

Amy picked up the jug, carried it to the backboard, crouched beside Pablo. "Water?" she asked.

Pablo nodded. He opened and closed his mouth, like someone mimicking a fish. "*Po-ta-to . . . po-ta-to . . . po-ta-to . . .*"

Amy uncapped the jug, poured some of the water into his mouth. Her hands were shaking, though, and it came out too quickly, nearly choking him. He coughed, sputtering, turned his head away.

"Maybe you should give him a grape," Stacy said. She picked up the plastic bag, held it toward Amy.

"You think so?"

"He hasn't eaten—not since yesterday."

"But can he—"

"Just try it."

Pablo had stopped coughing. Amy waited till he turned back toward her, then took out one of the grapes, held it up for him to see, raising her eyebrows. "Hungry?" she asked.

Pablo just stared at her. He seemed to be fading, sinking inward. For a moment, there'd been something like color in his face, but now it had gone gray again. His neck went slack; his head fell heavily against the backboard.

"Put it in his mouth and see what happens," Stacy said.

Amy slid the grape between Pablo's lips, pushing at it until it disappeared. Pablo shut his eyes; his jaw didn't move.

"Use your hand," Stacy said. "Help him chew it."

Amy grasped the Greek by his chin, pulling his mouth open, then pushing it shut. Eric heard the wet sound of the grape popping, and then Pablo was gagging again, turning his head to the side, retching. The squashed fruit spilled out, followed by a surprising amount of liquid. Black liquid, full of stringy clots. It was blood, Eric knew. *Oh Jesus,* he thought. *What the fuck are we doing?*

And then, making him jump, nearly the exact same words sounded in the air behind him: "What the fuck are you doing?"

Eric turned, astonished, and found Jeff standing above them, staring at Amy with a look of fury.

Sitting at the bottom of the hill, watching for the Greeks, Jeff had felt as if he were entering a slower, thicker version of time. The seconds had dragged themselves into minutes, the minutes had accumulated into hours, and nothing happened, nothing of note, nothing whatsoever—certainly not the thing he was there to stop from happening, the Greeks arriving, bumbling their way across the clearing, entering that forbidden zone into which Jeff and the others had fallen captive. He sat, the sun drawing precious moisture from his skin, adding its heat to the other discomforts of his body—his thirst and hunger, his fatigue, his growing sense of failure here, of doing and acting, only to inflict as much harm as he was attempting to prevent.

There was too much to think about, and none of it good.

There was Pablo, of course—how could Jeff help but think of Pablo? He could still feel the weight of the stone in his hand, the heat coming through that towel, could still hear the sound of bone shattering as he'd hammered at Pablo's tibia and fibula, could still smell the acrid stench of his burning flesh. *What choice did I have?* he kept asking himself, knowing even as he did so that this was a bad sign, this impulse to justify, to explain, as if he were fending off some accusation. *I was trying to save his life.* And these, too, were the wrong words to have echoing through his head—the *trying to* implying a failure, a thing hoped for, striven toward, but nonetheless unattained. Because it was true: Jeff was giving up on Pablo. Maybe, if rescue arrived in the coming hours, or even sometime tomorrow, he still might be saved. Was this going to happen, though? That was the question upon which everything hinged—the coming hours, the coming day—and Jeff was losing faith in it, relinquishing hope. He'd believed that by taking off the legs, or what remained of the legs, he might buy the Greek time—not much, but some—enough, maybe, just enough. But it wasn't going to end like that. He had to admit this to himself now. Pablo was going to linger for another day, or two, or three at best, and then die.

In great pain, no doubt.

There was always the chance that the Greeks might come, of course, but the more Jeff considered this possibility, the less likely it seemed. The Mayans knew exactly what they were doing here; they'd done it before, would almost certainly have to do it again. Jeff assumed that they must've stationed someone to guard the far end of the trail, someone to turn any potential rescuers aside, to divert and mislead them. Don Quixote and Juan would never be equal to this; even if they were coming, which Jeff doubted, they'd be easily deflected. No, if rescue were to arrive, it would be much later—too late, probably—weeks from now, after their parents realized that they'd failed to return and began to probe at this development, to worry and to act. Jeff didn't want to guess how long this might take—the calls that would have to be placed, the questions asked—before the necessary gears would start to turn. And, even then, would the search ever proceed beyond Cancún? Their bus tickets had been printed with their names on them, but were records kept of this? And, if that hurdle were somehow cleared, and the hunt shifted to Cobá, how would it ever proceed the extra thirteen miles into the jungle? Whoever it was who might be pursuing the case would be given photographs, Jeff assumed; he'd show these to the taxi drivers in Cobá, the street vendors, the waiters in the cafés. And perhaps the man with the yellow pickup would recognize them; perhaps he'd be willing to share what he knew. And then what? The policeman or detective would follow the trail, walk it to the Mayan village, bearing those four or five or six photographs—depending on whether he'd already managed to find out about Mathias and Pablo and connect them all together—and what would the Mayans offer him? Blank faces, certainly. A ruminative scratching of the chin, a slow shake of the head. And even if, by some miracle of persistence and shrewdness, this perhaps mythical policeman or detective managed to make his way past these assertions of ignorance, how long would it take? All those steps to labor his way through, with the potential for detours and dead ends at every stage—how long? Too long, Jeff guessed. Too long for Pablo. There was no question of this. And too long, he supposed, for the rest of them also.

They needed it to rain. That was the first thing, the most crucial. Without water, they weren't going to last much longer than Pablo.

And then there was the question of food. They had the small amount they'd brought with them—snacks, really—which might, through aggressive rationing, sustain them for two or three more days. But after that?

Nothing. Fasting. Starving.

Eric was in trouble, Jeff knew. The cutting, the pacing, the muttering—bad signs, all of them. And his wounds would become infected soon; there was no way Jeff could think of to prevent this. Time, once more, would come into play here. Gangrene, septicemia—they'd be slower than thirst, probably, but far faster than starving.

Jeff didn't think about the vines—didn't want to, wouldn't have known how to. They moved, made sounds; they thought and planned. And worse was to come, he suspected, though what this might entail, he couldn't begin to guess.

He sat. He watched the Mayans watching him. He waited for the Greeks to arrive, believing even as he did so that this wasn't going to happen. He thought about water and food and Pablo and Eric. When clouds began to build to the south, he peered toward them, willing them to grow, to darken, to drift ever northward. Rain. They would have to gather it. They hadn't spoken of this. He ought to have made some plan with the others, left directions for them to follow, but he was tired, had too much to think about; he'd forgotten. He rose to his feet now, stared back up the trail. Why wasn't someone coming to relieve him? This, too, they should've spoken of, should've planned, yet hadn't.

The clouds continued to build. There was that plastic toolbox from the blue tent. They could empty it, use it to collect some of the rain. There had to be other things they could adapt for this purpose, too, but he needed to be up on the hilltop to think of them, needed to see what was available.

He paced. He sat again. He watched the Mayans, the clouds, the trail behind him. The Mayans stared back, mute and impassive. The clouds continued to build. The trail behind him remained empty. Jeff stood and stretched, then paced some more. The sky had clouded over completely now; rain was imminent, he could tell, and he was just beginning to toy with the idea of turning, hurrying up the hill, balancing the risk of leaving the path unguarded against that of the rain coming while they were still unprepared for its arrival—brief and intense, as all such storms in this part of the world appeared to be—when he heard footsteps approaching down the trail.

It was Mathias.

Something was wrong; Jeff could see this just in the way Mathias moved. There was a taut quality to his walk; he was hurrying and holding himself back all at once. His face retained its usual expression of guardedness, but with a slight shift to it, almost indiscernible. It was the eyes, Jeff thought: a sense of wariness in them, even alarm. He stopped a few yards short of Jeff, out of breath.

"What is it?" Jeff asked.

Mathias waved behind him, up the hill. "You didn't hear?"

"Hear what?"

"They were talking."

"Who?"

"The vines."

Jeff stared at him—not disbelieving, exactly, but too startled to speak.

"Mimicking us," Mathias said. "Stacy and Amy and Eric—mimicking their voices."

Jeff considered this. He didn't believe it was enough to explain Mathias's agitation; there had to be something more. "Saying what?" he asked.

"I fell asleep, in the tent. And when I woke up . . ." Mathias trailed off, as if uncertain how to proceed. Then, finally: "They were fighting."

"Fighting?"

"The girls. Shouting things at each other."

"Oh Christ." Jeff sighed.

"They've been drinking. The tequila. Quite a bit, I think."

"All of them?"

Mathias nodded.

"They're drunk?"

Again, Mathias nodded. "They called me a Nazi."

"*What?*"

"The vines. Or Eric, I guess. It was his voice, but the vines were shouting it."

Jeff watched him. This was it, he realized; this was what had upset him. And why not? He had to feel alone here among them—he hardly knew them. He was an outsider, easily scapegoated. Jeff struggled to reassure him. "It was a joke, I'm sure. Eric, you know—that's what he's like."

Mathias remained silent, neither confirming nor denying this.

"I should get up there," Jeff said. "You'll watch for the Greeks?"

Mathias nodded.

Jeff started to leave, then caught himself. "What about Pablo?"

Mathias made a vague gesture, throwing out his hand. "The same," he said. "Not good."

With that, Jeff started quickly up the hill, running on the flatter stretches, slowing to a walk whenever it grew steep. He seemed to be losing his breath far more easily than he ought to have. It had only been a day since they'd arrived here, and already he could feel himself growing weaker. He had the sense that this physical decline somehow mirrored a more general deterioration: everything was slipping beyond his control. Stacy and Amy and Eric had spent the afternoon drinking tequila. How stupid could they be? Myopic, impulsive, irresponsible—three fools flirting with their own destruction. Then, of course, they'd turned on one another; they'd fought, shouting insults. And Eric, for some unknown reason, had called Mathias a Nazi. Jeff's disbelief in this tangle of events slowly surrendered to a building sense of rage. This was its own folly, he knew, and yet he couldn't resist its pull, couldn't quell the desire to punish the three of them in some way, to slap them back into a proper sense of gravity. He was still riding this wave of emotion when he finally reached the hilltop, stepped into the little clearing, and glimpsed Amy force-feeding a grape to the barely conscious Pablo.

"What the fuck are you doing?" he said, and they all turned to stare at him, startled by his presence there, the fury in his voice.

Pablo was vomiting, though that seemed the wrong word for it. Vomiting implied something dynamic and forceful; what Pablo was doing was much more passive. His head rolled to the side, his mouth opened, and a stream of black liquid spilled out. Blood, bile—it was hard to tell what it was. There was too much of it, though, more than Jeff would've thought possible. Black liquid with thicker skeins running through it, like clots. It formed a shallow pool alongside the backboard, too jelly-like, it seemed, for the dirt to absorb. Jeff was four yards away, but even at that distance he could smell it—putridly sweet.

"He was hungry," Amy said. Jeff could hear in her voice how drunk she was, the threat of a slur haunting each of her words. In her left hand, she was clenching the plastic bag that had once held their supply of grapes; there were three left now. The nearly empty tequila bottle was lying in the dirt beside Stacy. Eric was pressing a bloody T-shirt to his side.

Jeff felt his rage begin to expand inside his body, filling him, pressing outward against his skin, as if searching for an exit. "You're drunk. Aren't you?"

Amy looked away. Pablo had stopped vomiting; his eyes were shut now.

"All of you," Jeff persisted, surprising himself by how quiet he was managing to keep his voice. "Am I right?"

"I'm not," Eric said.

Jeff turned on him, almost lunging. *Stop,* he thought. *Don't.* But it was too late; he'd already begun to speak, his voice rising with each successive word, coming faster, harder, propelled by his anger. "You're not drunk?"

Eric shook his head, but it didn't matter, because Jeff hardly noticed the gesture. He hadn't paused for a response; no, he just kept talking, knowing he was handling this in the worst possible manner, but no longer able to stop himself, and not wanting to, either, because there was joy in it, too: the relief of speaking, of shouting. The release felt physical, almost sexual in its intensity.

"Because being drunk is really your only defense here, Eric—you understand? You fucking cut yourself again, didn't you? You cut your fucking chest. You have any idea what you're doing—how profoundly stupid you're being? You're sticking a dirty knife into your body every few hours, and we're trapped here, with a tiny fucking tube of Neosporin, whose shelf date has already expired. You think that's smart? You think that makes the slightest fucking sense? Keep it up and you're gonna die here. You're not gonna make it—"

"Jeff—" Amy began.

"Shut up, Amy. You're just as bad." He turned on her. It didn't matter whom he was yelling at; any of them would do. "I would've expected you, at least, to know better. Alcohol is a diuretic—it dehydrates you. You *know* that. So how the fuck could you—"

You think that's smart? It was his own voice, coming from somewhere to his left, jarring him into silence. *You think that makes the slightest fucking sense?* He turned, stared, knowing what it was but still half-expecting to see a person standing there, mimicking him. A wind had come up; it pulled at the vines, making their hand-shaped leaves sway and bob, as if in mockery.

Now it was Amy's voice: *Slut!*

And then Stacy's: *Bitch!*

"It's because you're yelling," Stacy said, her voice almost a whisper. "It does it when we yell."

Boy Scout, Eric's voice called. *Nazi!*

The clouds had thickened almost to the point of dusk; it was hard to tell what time it was. The storm was upon them, clearly, but night, too, seemed close at hand. And they weren't ready for it, not nearly, not any of it.

"Look," Amy said, gesturing skyward. She was trying very hard not to slur, he could tell, yet without much effect. "It doesn't matter—we'll get our water."

"But have you prepared for it?" Jeff asked. "It'll come and go, and you'll just be sitting here, watching it, won't you? Watching it run down into the soil, vanishing, wasted." Jeff could feel his anger dissipating, not in a satisfying way, either, not in a rush or a jolt, but in a slow, implacable seepage. He didn't want it to go, felt abandoned by its departure, as if it were a form of strength that was leaving him; his body seemed weaker for its withdrawal. "You're pathetic," he said, turning away from them. "All of you—fucking pathetic. You don't need the vine to kill you. You're gonna make that happen all on your own."

Stacy's voice called: *Then who's the villain?*

Sing for us, Amy, Eric's responded.

Bitch!

Slut!

Nazi!

And then his own voice again, sounding hateful in its anger: *You're drunk, aren't you?*

Jeff stepped to the orange tent, unzipped its flap, pushed his way inside. He scanned the supplies piled against the tent's back wall. The toolbox was waiting there, but nothing else of any relevance to his present needs. He crouched over the box, opened its lid, and found, oddly, not tools inside, but a sewing kit. A little pincushion cactused full of needles. Spools of thread on a double rack, covering the full spectrum of colors, like a box of crayons. Scraps of cloth, a small pair of scissors, even a tape measure. Jeff dumped everything onto the tent's floor, carried the empty box back out into the clearing.

Nothing had changed. Eric was still lying on his back, the bloody T-shirt pressed to his abdomen. Stacy was sitting at his side, with that same frightened expression on her face. Pablo's eyes remained shut, the ragged sound of his breathing rising and falling. Amy was beside him; she didn't look up when Jeff appeared. He set the box in the middle of the clearing, open to catch the rain. Then he started across the hilltop, toward the mouth of the shaft, where the supplies from the blue tent still lay tumbled together in a mound.

The plants continued their mimicry. Sometimes the voices came in a shout, other times very softly. There were long pauses, during which, it seemed, they might've stopped altogether, then sudden flurries of speech, the words and voices merging one into another. Jeff tried not to pay attention to them, but some of the things they said surprised him, gave him pause, made him wonder. He assumed that was the point, as hard as this was to believe, suspected that the vines had begun to speak now in an effort to drive the six of them apart, turn them one against another.

Stacy's voice said, *Well, Jeff isn't here, is he?* And then Eric's came: *Was Jeff a Boy Scout? I bet Jeff was a Boy Scout.* Laughter followed: Eric and Stacy's, mixing together, with an edge of mockery to it.

It was as if the vine had learned their names, knew who was who, and was tailoring its mimicry accordingly, the better to unsettle them. Jeff tried to think back over the past twenty-four hours, to remember the things he'd said, searching for possible difficulties. He was so tired, though, so benumbed, that his mind refused to help him. It didn't matter anyway, because the vine knew, and as Jeff started to pick through the pile of supplies beside the open shaft, he heard his voice begin to speak.

End it. Cut his throat. Smother him.

The longer we stay here, the better its chances.

It mimics things. It's not really laughter.

Then the whole hillside seemed to erupt at once—there were giggles and guffaws and chuckles and snickers—it went on and on and on. Interspersed with this was his own voice, shouting, as if trying to silence the noise, repeating the same phrase over and over again: *It's not really laughter. . . . It's not really laughter. . . . It's not really laughter. . . .*

Jeff retrieved the Frisbee from the tangle of supplies, the empty canteen, carried them back across the hilltop toward the orange tent. His idea was that as the Frisbee filled with rain, he could pour it into the canteen, the plastic jug, the bottle they'd been using to collect their urine. It wasn't the best plan, but it was all he could think of.

Amy and Stacy and Eric hadn't moved. The vine had sent forth another tendril; it was feasting on Pablo's vomit now, audibly sucking at it. The three of them were watching, slack-jawed: drunk. When the vine finished with the little puddle, it retreated back across the clearing. No one moved; no one said a thing. Jeff felt his anger stirring at the sight of this—their impassivity, their collective stupor—but he didn't speak. That was over now, the urge to yell. He set the Frisbee beside the open toolbox, then emptied Mathias's water bottle of their urine. The others watched him, silent, all of them listening to the vines as they quieted for a moment, only to jump again in volume, still laughing. The sound of strangers, Jeff assumed. Cees Steenkamp, maybe. The girl whom Henrich had met on the beach. All these piles of bones, their flesh stripped clean, their souls long ago unhoused, but their laughter preserved here, remembered by the vine, and called forth now, wielded like a weapon.

It's not really laughter. . . . It's not really laughter. . . . It's not really laughter. . . .

There were still some strips of nylon left over from the blue tent, and Jeff fiddled with them now, trying to think of a way to use them to catch the rain, or store the water once they'd collected it. He should've thought of this earlier, he knew; he could've used the sewing kit he'd found in the orange tent to stitch the lengths of nylon together into a giant pouch. But now he no longer had the time.

Tomorrow, he thought.

And then the rain began to fall.

It came in a rush, as if a trapdoor had swung open in the clouds above them, releasing it. There was no warning, no preparatory drizzle; one moment the sky was merely brooding, dark gray, with that held-breath quality the tropics often have before a storm's approach, a breeze lightly stirring the vines, and then, seemingly without transition, the air was full of falling water. Daylight faltered, took on a greenish hue one step short of darkness; the hard-packed earth beneath them turned instantly to mud. It felt difficult to breathe.

The plants fell silent.

The Frisbee filled in seconds. Jeff poured the water into the canteen, let the Frisbee fill once more, with equal rapidity, and poured again. Then he held the canteen out to Stacy. He had to shout to be heard over the rain, which sounded almost like a roar now. "Drink!" he yelled. His hat, his clothes, his shoes were all soaked completely through, clinging to him, growing heavy.

He poured the water from the Frisbee into the plastic jug, let it fill, poured again, let it fill, poured again. When he was finished with the jug, he started in on Mathias's empty bottle.

Stacy drank from the canteen, then passed it to Eric, who was still lying on his back, shirtless, the rain spattering mud across his body. He sat up awkwardly, clutching at his side, took the canteen.

"As much as you can!" Jeff shouted at him.

Soap, he was thinking. He should've checked the backpacks for a bar of soap. They would've at least had time to wash their faces and hands before the storm passed—a small thing, he knew, but he was certain it would've lifted everyone's spirits. *Tomorrow,* he thought. *It came today, so why shouldn't it come again tomorrow?*

He finished with Mathias's bottle, held out his hand for the canteen, refilled it, then passed it to Amy.

The rain kept pouring down on them. It was surprisingly cold. Jeff began to shiver; the others did, too. It was the lack of food, he assumed. Already, they didn't have the resources to fight the chill.

The Frisbee filled again, and he lifted it to his lips, drank directly from it. The rain had a sweetness that surprised him. *Sugar water,* he thought, his head seeming to clear as he drank, his body to take on an added solidity, a heft and gravity he hadn't realized he'd been lacking. He filled the Frisbee, drank, filled the Frisbee, drank, his stomach swelling, growing pleasantly, almost painfully taut. It was the best water he'd ever tasted.

Amy had stopped drinking. She and Stacy were standing there, hunched, hugging themselves, shivering. Eric had lain back down again. His eyes were shut, his mouth open to the rain. His legs and torso were growing muddier and muddier; it was in his hair, too, and on his face.

"Get him into the tent!" Jeff shouted.

He took the canteen from Amy, started to fill it once more as he watched her and Stacy pull Eric to his feet, guide him toward the tent.

The rain began to slacken. It was still falling steadily, but the downpour was over. Another five or ten minutes, Jeff knew, and it would stop altogether. He stepped across the clearing to check on Pablo. The lean-to hadn't done much to shelter him; he was just as wet as the rest of them. And, like Eric, he'd been back-spattered with mud—his shirt, his face, his arms, his stumps. His eyes remained shut; his breathing continued its irregular rasping course. Oddly, he wasn't shivering, and Jeff wondered if this were a bad sign, if a body could become so ravaged that even trembling might be beyond its strength. He crouched, rested his hand on Pablo's forehead, nearly flinched at the heat coming off him. Everything was a bad sign, of course; there were nothing but bad signs here. He thought of the vine, how it had echoed his own voice: *End it. Cut his throat. Smother him.* And he held the words in his mind, teetering on the edge of action. It would be easy enough, after all; he was alone here in the clearing. No one would ever know. He could simply lean forward, pinch shut Pablo's nostrils, cover his mouth, and count to— what? A hundred? *Mercy:* this was what he was thinking as he lifted his hand from Pablo's forehead, moved it down his face. He held it there, an inch or so above the Greek's nose, not touching him yet, just playing with the idea—*ninety-seven, ninety-eight, ninety-nine*—and then Amy was pushing her way out of the tent, carrying her drunkenness with her, stumbling slightly as she stepped into the clearing. Her hair was limp from the rain; there was a smear of mud on her left cheek.

"Is he okay?" she asked.

Jeff stood up quickly, hating the slur in her voice, feeling that urge to shout again, to sober her with his anger. He fought the temptation, though, not answering—*how could he answer?*—and moved back across the clearing toward the open toolbox.

Which, inexplicably, was nearly empty.

Jeff stared down at it, struggling to make sense of this development. "There's a hole," Amy said.

And it was true. When Jeff lifted the box, he revealed a thin stream of water pouring steadily from its bottom, which had a two-inch crack in it. He'd missed it somehow earlier, when he'd emptied the box of its sewing supplies. He'd been rushing; he hadn't taken the time to examine it. If he had, he might've been able to fix it before the rain came— *the duct tape,* he thought—but now it was too late. The rain had come; the rain was leaving. Even as he thought these words, it was falling more and more gently; in another minute or so, it would stop altogether. Disgusted with himself, he threw the toolbox, sent it tumbling away from him toward the tent.

Amy looked appalled. "What the fuck?" she said, almost shouting. "There was still water in it!"

She ran to the toolbox, set it upright again. It was a pointless gesture, Jeff knew. The storm had passed; the sky was beginning to lighten. There wasn't going to be any more rain—not today at least. "You're one to talk," he said.

Amy turned toward him, wiping at her face. "What?"

"About wasting water."

She shook her head. "Don't."

"Don't what?"

"Not now."

"Don't *what,* Amy?"

"Lecture me."

"But you're fucking up. You know that, don't you?"

She didn't respond, just stared at him with a sad, put-upon expression, as if he were the one at fault here. He felt his fury rising in response to it.

"Stealing water in the middle of the night. Getting drunk. What're you thinking? That we're playing at this?"

She shook her head again. "You're being too hard, Jeff."

"*Hard?* Look at all those fucking mounds." He pointed out across the hillside, at the vine-covered bones. "That's how we're going to end up, too. And you're helping it happen."

Amy kept shaking her head. "The Greeks—"

"Stop it. You're like a child. The Greeks, the Greeks, the Greeks— they aren't coming, Amy. You've got to face that."

She covered her ears with her hands. "Don't, Jeff. Please don't—"

Jeff stepped forward, grabbed her wrists, yanked them down. He was shouting now. "Look at Pablo. He's dying—can't you see that? And Eric's going to end up with gangrene or—"

"Shh." She tried to pull away, glancing anxiously at the tent.

"And the three of you are *drinking*. Do you have the slightest idea how fucking stupid that is? It's exactly what the vine would want you to—"

Amy screamed, a shriek of pure fury, startling him into silence. "I didn't want to come!" she yelled. She jerked her hands free, began to swing at him, hitting him in the chest, knocking him back a step. "I didn't want to come!" She kept repeating it, shouting, hitting him. "You're the one! *You* suggested it! I wanted to stay at the beach! It's your fault! Yours! Not mine!" She was hitting his chest, his shoulders; her face was contorted, shiny with dampness—Jeff couldn't tell if it was the rain or tears. "Yours!" she kept yelling. "Not mine!"

The vine started up again suddenly, also shouting: *It's my fault. I'm the one, aren't I? The one who stepped into the vines?* It was Amy's voice, coming at them from all sides. Amy stopped hitting him, stared wildly about them.

It's my fault.

"Stop it!" Amy shouted.

I'm the one, aren't I?

"Shut up!"

The one who stepped into the vines?

Amy spun on him, looking desperate, her hands held out before her, begging. "Make it stop."

It's my fault.

Amy pointed at him, her hand shaking. "You were the one! You know that's true! Not me. I didn't want to come."

I'm the one, aren't I?

"Make it stop. Will you please make it stop?"

Jeff didn't move, didn't speak; he just stood there staring at her.

The one who stepped into the vines?

The sky was darkening again, but it wasn't the storm. Behind the screen of clouds, the sun was reaching for the horizon. Night was coming, and they'd done nothing to prepare for it. They ought to eat, Jeff knew, and thinking this he remembered the bag of grapes. It wasn't only the drinking; she and the others had helped themselves to the food, too. "What else did you eat?" he asked.

"Eat?"

"Besides the grapes. Did you steal anything else?"

"We didn't *steal* the grapes. We were hungry. We—"

"Answer me."

"Fuck you, Jeff. You're acting like—"

"Just tell me."

She shook her head. "You're too hard. Everyone—we're all . . . We think you're too hard."

"What's that supposed to mean?"

It's my fault.

Amy spun, shouted out toward the vines again. "Shut up!"

"You've talked about it?" Jeff asked. "About me?"

"Please," Amy said. "Just stop." She was shaking her head once more, and now he was certain of it; she was crying. "Can't you stop, honey? Please?" She held out her hand.

Take it, he thought. But he made no move to do this. There was a history here, a well-trod path upon which conflict tended to unfold between them. When they argued, no matter what the topic, Amy would eventually grow upset—she'd weep; she'd retreat—and Jeff, however long he might resist the pull, would end up shuffling forward to soothe her, to pet her, to whisper endearments and assure her of his love. He was always, always, always the one to apologize; it was never Amy, no matter who might be at fault. And this was no different: it was "Can't you stop?" that she'd been saying, not *can't I,* or even *can't we.* Jeff was tired of it—tired at large, tired down into his bones—and he vowed to himself that he wasn't going to do it. Not here, not now. She was the one at fault; she was the one who needed to stop, who needed to step forward and apologize, not him.

At some point, without his noticing the exact moment, the vine had fallen silent.

It would be dark soon. Another five or ten minutes, Jeff guessed, and they'd be blind with it. They ought to have talked things through, ought to have set up a watch schedule, doled out another ration of food and water. Even now, in this final waning of light, they ought to have been up and doing. "Too hard," Amy had said. "We think you're too hard." He was working to save them, and behind his back they were gossiping, complaining.

Fuck her, Jeff thought. *Fuck them all.*

He turned away, left Amy standing with her hand held out before her. He stepped to the lean-to, sat down beside it, in the mud, facing Pablo. The Greek's eyes were shut, his mouth hanging partway open. The smell he was giving off was almost unbearable. They ought to move him, Jeff knew, lift him free from that disgusting sleeping bag—sodden and stinking with his body's effusions. They ought to wash him, too, ought to irrigate the seared stumps, flush them free of dirt. They had enough water now; they could afford to do this. But the light was failing even as Jeff thought these things, and he knew they could never do it in the dark. It was Amy's fault, this missed opportunity—Amy's and Stacy's and Eric's. They'd distracted him; they'd wasted his time. And now Pablo would have to wait until morning.

The stumps were still bleeding—not heavily, just a steady ooze—they needed to be washed and then bandaged. There was no gauze, of course, nothing sterile; Jeff would have to dig through the backpacks again, search for a clean shirt, hope that this might suffice. Maybe he could use the sewing kit, too, a needle and thread. He could search out the still-leaking blood vessels and tie them off one by one. And then there was Eric to think of also: Jeff could stitch up the wound in his side. He turned, glanced at Amy. She was still standing in the center of the clearing, motionless; she hadn't even lowered her hand. She was waiting for him to relent. But he wasn't going to do it.

"Tell me you're sorry," he said.

"Excuse me?" The light was fading enough that it was already difficult to see her expression. He was being a child, he knew. He was as bad as she was. But he couldn't stop.

"Say you're sorry."

She lowered her hand.

He persisted: "Say it."

"Sorry for what?"

"For stealing the water. For getting drunk."

Amy wiped at her face, a gesture of weariness. She sighed. "Fine."

"Fine what?"

"I'm sorry."

"For what?"

"Come on—"

"Say it, Amy."

There was a long pause; he could sense her wavering. Then, in something close to a monotone, she gave it to him: "I'm sorry for stealing the water. I'm sorry for getting drunk."

Enough, he said to himself. *Stop it here.* But he didn't. Even as he thought these words, he heard himself begin to speak. "You don't sound like you mean it."

"Jesus Christ, Jeff. You can't—"

"Say it like you mean it, or it doesn't count."

She sighed again, louder this time, almost a scoff. Then she shook her head, turned, walked off toward the far edge of the clearing, where she dropped heavily to the ground. She sat with her back to him, bent into herself, her head in her hands. The light was nearly gone; Jeff felt he could almost see it departing, draining from the air around them. He watched Amy's hunched form as it faded into the shadows, merging with the dark mass of vegetation beyond her. It seemed as if her shoulders were moving. Was she crying? He strained to hear, but the phlegmy rattle of Pablo's breathing obscured all other sounds within the clearing.

Go to her, he said to himself. *Do it now.* Yet he didn't move. He felt trapped, immobilized. He'd read once how to pick a lock, and he believed that he could do it if he ever needed to. He knew how to break free from the trunk of a car, how to climb out of a well, how to flee a burning building. But none of that helped him here. No, he couldn't think of a way to escape this present situation. He needed Amy to be the one, needed her to be the first to move.

He was certain of it now: she was crying. Rather than softening him, though, this had the opposite effect. She was playing on his sympathies, he decided, manipulating him. All he'd asked of her was that she say she was sorry, say it in a genuine way. Was that such an unreasonable thing? Maybe she wasn't crying; maybe she was shivering, because she must be wet, of course, and cold. As he watched, trying to decide between tears and the shivering, he saw her tilt to her side, lie down in the mud. This, too, ought to have elicited sympathy in him, he knew. But, once again, he felt only anger. If she was wet, if she was cold, why didn't she do something about it? Why didn't she get up and go into the tent, search through one of the backpacks, find herself some dry clothes? Did she need him to tell her to do this? Well, he wasn't going to. If she wanted to lie in the mud, shivering or crying, or both, that was her choice. She could do it all night, if that was what she desired, because he wasn't going to go to her.

Later, much later, after the sun had set, after Mathias had returned from the bottom of the hill and joined the others in the tent, after the sky had cleared and the moon had risen, its pale sliver shaved one step closer to nothingness, after Jeff's clothes had dried on him, stiffening slightly in the process, after Pablo's breathing had stopped at one point for a full thirty seconds before starting again with an abrupt gagging rattle, like a bedsheet being torn in half, after Jeff had thought a dozen times about going to Amy, rousing her, sending her into the tent, only to decide against it on each successive occasion, after he'd sat through his entire shift, and most of the shift to follow, not moving, wanting her to be the first to stir, to come and beg his forgiveness, or even, more simply, just wordlessly embrace him, Amy staggered to her feet. Or not quite: she rose, took a half step toward him, then fell to her knees and began to throw up. She was leaning forward on one hand; the other was pressed to her mouth, as if to hold back the vomit. It was too dark to see her properly. Jeff could make out her outline, the shadowy bulk of her body, but nothing more. It was his ears rather than his eyes that told him what was happening. He could hear her gagging, coughing, spitting. She tried to stand again, with the same result—another half step before she dropped back to her knees, her right hand still clutching at her mouth while her left seemed to reach toward him through the darkness. Was she calling for him? Beneath the gagging, coughing, spitting, did he hear her say his name? He wasn't certain—not certain enough at least—he didn't move. And now both her hands were pressing at her mouth, as if to dam that flow of vomit. But it wasn't possible, of course. The gagging continued, the choking and coughing. Jeff could smell it now, even over Pablo's stench—the tequila, the bile—and it kept coming.

Go to her, he thought yet again.

And then: *You're too hard. We all think you're too hard.*

He watched as she hunched low, her hands still pressed to her mouth. She hesitated like that, going silent finally: no more coughing or gagging or choking. For nearly a minute, she didn't move at all. Then, very slowly, she tilted over onto her side in the mud. She lay perfectly still, curled into a fetal position; Jeff assumed she'd fallen back asleep. He knew he was supposed to go help her now, wipe her clean like an infant, guide her back into the tent. But this was her own fault, wasn't it? So why should he be the one to pick up the pieces? He wasn't going to do it. He was going to let her lie there, let her wake at dawn with vomit caked to her face. He could still smell it, and he felt his own stomach turning in response to the stench—not just his stomach but his feelings, too. Anger and disgust and the deepest sort of impatience—they kept him by the little lean-to through the night, watching but not doing. *I should check on her,* he thought—how many times? A dozen, maybe more. *I should make sure she's okay.* He didn't do it, though; he sat watching her, thinking the words, recognizing their wisdom, their rightness, but not doing, all night not doing.

It was nearing dawn before he finally stirred. He'd nodded off some, his head bobbing in and out of consciousness as the moon climbed and climbed above him, then crested and began to sink. It had almost set before he managed to rouse himself, struggling to his feet, stretching, his blood feeling thick in his veins. Even then he didn't go to Amy, though; not that it would've mattered. He stared at her for a long moment—her still, shadowy mass in the center of the clearing—then shuffled to the tent, unzipped the flap, and slipped quietly inside.

Stacy had heard Jeff and Amy shouting at each other. It had been impossible to make out their words over the rain drumming against the tent, but she could tell that they were arguing. The vine had a part in it, too; she could hear it mimicking Amy's voice.

Yelling, *It's my fault.*

And then: *I'm the one, aren't I?*

It was just she and Eric in the tent. The storm made it too dark to see much. Stacy didn't know what time it was, but she could sense that the day was leaking away from them. Another night—she didn't know how they were going to manage it.

"If I sleep, will you watch over me?" Eric asked.

Stacy's thoughts felt muddy from too much alcohol. Everything seemed to be moving a little more slowly than it ought to. She stared at Eric through the dimness, struggling to process his question. The rain continued, the tent sagging beneath it. Jeff and Amy had stopped their yelling. "All night?" she asked.

Eric shook his head. "An hour—can you stay up for an hour? I just need an hour."

She was tired, she realized, as if simply talking about it was making it so. Tired and hungry and very, very drunk. "Why can't we both sleep?"

Eric gestured toward the supplies piled against the tent's rear wall. "It'll come back. It'll push its way in again. One of us has to stay awake."

He means the vine, Stacy thought, and for a moment she seemed to sense it there, hidden in the shadows, listening, watching, waiting for them to fall asleep. "Okay," she said. "An hour, then I'll wake you."

Eric lay down on his back. He was still pressing the balled-up shirt to his side. It was too dark in the tent to tell if the bleeding had stopped. Stacy sat beside him, took his free hand; it was clammy to the touch. They should dry off, she knew; they should change out of their wet clothes. She was cold, still shivering, but she didn't say anything, made no move toward the backpacks. The archaeologists were all dead, along with whoever might've come before or after them, and—stupidly—their belongings felt contagious to Stacy. She didn't want to wear their clothes.

Eric fell asleep, his hand going slack in hers. Stacy was startled by the rapidity with which he managed it. He began to snore, and it sounded oddly like Pablo's watery rasp—frighteningly so. Stacy almost woke him, wanting him to roll over and fall silent, but then, abruptly, he stopped of his own accord. That was scary, too, in a different way, and she leaned down, her ear right above his face, to make sure he was breathing.

He was, of course.

Bent low like that, her head nearly at a horizontal, only a foot or so above the tent's floor, it seemed easier to keep dropping than to struggle upward again. She lay beside him, pressing close. The rain was pass-ing—it was nothing but a drizzle now—and it felt almost peaceful in the tent. Stacy shut her eyes. She wasn't going to sleep—how could she have? It wasn't even night yet. Amy would be in soon, and they could sit up talking together, keeping their voices quiet, maybe even whis-pering, so that they wouldn't wake Eric. She was tired, it was true, but she'd given him her word, and she knew the vine was lurking all about them, just waiting for her to lower her guard. No, she wasn't going to sleep. All she was going to do was shut her eyes for a moment, so that she could listen to that soft pattering on the nylon above their heads, and perhaps daydream a little, imagining she was somewhere else.

When she opened her eyes again, it was very dark in the tent—pitch-dark, too dark to see. Someone was standing over her, shaking her shoulder. "Wake up, Stacy," this person kept saying. "It's your shift."

It was Jeff's voice, she realized. She didn't move, just lay on her back, peering up at him through the darkness. Things were returning to her, but too slowly to make much sense of them. The rain. Amy shouting

"Slut" at her. Jeff and Amy arguing. Eric asking her to watch over him. She felt hungover, but still drunk, too—a painful combination. Her head not only ached; it felt spillable in some strange way, as if, were she to move too quickly in one direction or another, she might pour out of herself. It wasn't something she could think clearly about; she simply knew that she didn't want to stir, that it would be perilous to do so. Her bladder was full to the point of discomfort, but even that wasn't sufficient to impel her into motion. "No," she said.

She couldn't see Jeff, but somehow she sensed his surprise, a stiffening in the shadows above her. "No?" he asked.

"I can't."

"Because?"

"I just can't."

"But it's your turn."

"I *can't,* Jeff."

He raised his voice, growing angry. "Cut the shit, Stacy. Get up."

He nudged her, and she almost screamed. Her entire body ached. She started to chant: "I can't, I can't, I can't, I can't—"

"I'll do it." It was Mathias's voice, coming from the far side of the tent.

She sensed Jeff lifting away from her, twisting to look. "It's her turn."

"It's okay. I'm awake."

Stacy could hear him getting up, rustling about, picking his way toward the tent's flap. He stopped just short of it, hesitating.

"Where's Amy?" he asked.

"Outside still," Jeff answered. "Sleeping it off."

"Should I—"

"Leave her be."

Stacy heard Mathias zipper open the flap, and something almost like light entered the tent. For a moment, she glimpsed all three of them: Eric lying motionless on his back, Jeff standing above her, Mathias stepping out into the clearing. *Thank you,* she thought, but she couldn't quite manage to push the words into speech. The flap closed, dropping them once more into darkness.

Without really meaning to, she was shutting her eyes again. Jeff was lying down a few feet to her left, mumbling to himself with an unmistakable air of complaint—about her, Stacy assumed. She didn't care. He was already mad at Amy, so why shouldn't he be angry with her, too?

Later, the two of them could laugh about it; Stacy would mimic him, the way he continued to mutter even now, murmuring and sighing.

I should check on Eric, she thought.

She tried to remember what had happened before she fell asleep. Had she awakened him first, as she'd promised? The more she considered this, the less likely it began to seem, and she was just starting to rouse herself, laboring to open her eyes again, maybe even sit up and prod at him, when Mathias began to shout Jeff's name.

It was the same thing all over again: waking with that musty smell surrounding him, the vine growing across his legs. *Inside me,* Eric thought as he reached to touch it. *My chest, too.*

Mathias was yelling from the clearing. There was movement in the tent, someone else stirring. It was too dark to see who. Eric was trying to sit up, but the vine was on top of him; it seemed to be holding him down.

Inside me.

"Jeff . . ." Mathias was yelling. "Jeff . . ."

Something had happened, something bad; Eric could hear it in Mathias's voice. *Pablo's died,* he thought.

"Jeff . . ."

Someone was standing up, moving toward the tent's flap.

"Oh God," Eric said. He'd pushed his hand down through the vine, was pressing at his chest, just above his wound. He could feel the vine beneath the skin there, a spongy mass covering his rib cage, spreading upward to his sternum. "The knife!" he called. "Get me the knife!"

"What is it? What's happening?" It was Stacy, right beside Eric, her voice sounding sleep-fuzzed, frightened. She clutched at him grabbing his shoulder.

"I need the knife," he said.

"The knife?"

"Hurry!"

From the clearing, Mathias continued to shout. "Jeff . . . Jeff . . ."

Eric's hand had moved down to his leg, where it found that same padded growth, just under the skin, climbing over his knee, up his thigh. He heard the flap being zippered open, turned to look. It was still night, but somehow not as dark outside as in. He glimpsed Jeff stepping out into the clearing.

"Wait," he called, "I need—"

But Jeff was already gone.

Jeff knew.

As soon as he heard Mathias begin to shout, he knew. He was up and out into the clearing, everything happening very quickly—too quickly—but not quickly enough to keep the knowledge at bay. It was in Mathias's voice, in the panic he heard there, the urgency. That was all Jeff needed.

Yes, he *knew.*

Up and out of the tent and across the clearing, all in darkness, with Mathias little more than a shadow, crouched above a second shadow, which was Amy. Jeff dropped to his knees beside them, reached for Amy's hand, her wrist, already cold to the touch. He couldn't make out either of their faces.

"I think it . . ." Mathias began, fumbling for the words, almost stuttering in his agitation. "I think it smothered her."

Jeff bent closer. The vine had grown across her mouth, her nose. He started to tug at it, the sap burning his hands. It had pushed its way inside her mouth, and he had to dig in with his fingers to pull it free, ignoring the rubbery feel of her lips, so cold—too cold.

From the tent, Eric had begun to shout again. "The knife! Get the knife!"

Not smothered, Jeff thought. *Choked.* Because he could smell the tequila, the bile, feel the dampness on the vine's leaves. He remembered Amy staggering to her feet, taking that half step toward him, her hand held to her mouth. He'd thought she'd been pressing it there to hold back her nausea, but he'd been wrong. She'd been pulling, he realized now, struggling to rip the plant from her face, to open a passage for her vomit, even as she suffocated upon it, falling to her knees, beckoning to him for help.

When he finished clearing her mouth, he tilted back her head, pinched shut her nostrils, bent his lips to hers—a tight seal, with no gaps. He could taste her vomit, feel the burn of the vine's sap on his tongue. He exhaled, filling her lungs, lifted his mouth free, moved to her chest, felt for her sternum, placed the heels of his hands against it, pressed downward with all his weight, counting in his head with each push—*one . . . two . . . three . . . four . . . five*—and then back to her mouth.

"Jeff," Mathias said.

There were stories Jeff could call upon here—false deaths—people pulled pulseless from deep water, blue-lipped, stiff-limbed. There were heart attacks and snakebites and lightning strikes. And choking victims, too—why not? People who ought never to have breathed again, and yet, through some miracle, some physiological quirk, were yanked back into life simply because someone who had no reason to believe, no reason to persist, did so nonetheless, breathing air into a corpse's lungs, pumping blood through a cadaver's heart, resurrecting them—somehow, some way—Lazarus-like, from the grip of their too-soon deaths.

"It's too late," Mathias said.

Jeff had learned CPR in a tenth-grade health class. Early spring in western Massachusetts, flies buzzing and bumping against the big windows, which looked out on the courtyard, with its flagpole, its tiny greenhouse. A short lecture, and then they practiced, the rubber dummy laid out on the linoleum, a female, oddly legless. She'd been given a name, Jeff remembered, but he couldn't recall what it was. Fifteen boys, taking turns with her—there'd been a few halfhearted sexual jokes, which Mr. Kocher frowned into silence. They were all embarrassed, anxious of failure, and trying not to show it. The dummy's lips had tasted of rubbing alcohol. Kneeling beside her head, Jeff had imagined the rescues that might lie in his future. He'd pictured his grandmother collapsed on the kitchen floor, his entire family—sister and parents and cousins and uncles and aunts—all of them frozen, helpless, watching her die; and then Jeff would calmly step forward, pushing his way through them, so that he could kneel beside her and breathe life back into her body, the simplest of gestures, yet God-like, too. A moment of grace—that was how he'd pictured it—full of serenity and self-assurance.

He exhaled, filling Amy's lungs.

Mathias reached, touched his shoulder. "She's not . . ."

Go to her, he'd thought—he remembered the words in his head. Sitting in the mud beside Pablo's lean-to, watching her stagger, drop to her knees, her hands at her mouth. *Do it now.* And why hadn't he?

There was movement from the tent, and Stacy appeared, came stumbling toward them. "It's inside him again," she said. "I—" She stopped, stood staring at them through the darkness. "What happened?"

Jeff shifted back to Amy's chest, felt for the sternum.

"Is she—"

My fault: There was no doubt of this, yet Jeff knew he couldn't afford to think on it now, had to resist its pull. Later, he'd have to confront those two words, bear their weight; later, there'd be no escape. But not now.

He began to push: *one . . . two . . . three . . . four . . . five.*

Then again, perhaps there wouldn't be a later. Because there was that possibility, too, wasn't there? No later, nothing beyond this place, Amy simply the first of them, with himself and the others soon to follow. And if that were the case, what did it matter, really? This way rather than another, now rather than in the coming days or weeks—couldn't it be a blessing, even, like any other abridgement of suffering?

"Jeff . . ." Mathias said.

He hadn't known. He hadn't been able to see. She'd been only fifteen feet away, but lost in darkness nonetheless. How could he have known?

Eric was yelling from the tent, calling for Stacy, for the knife, for help. *Not now,* Jeff thought, struggling to discipline himself. *Later.*

"Mathias?" Stacy said, sounding scared. "Is she . . ."

"Yes."

Babies pulled from trash cans, old women found slumped in their nightgowns, hikers dug out of snowbanks—the main thing was not to give up, not to make assumptions, to act without hesitation, and pray for that miracle, that quirk, that sudden gasp of air.

Stacy took a single step forward. "You mean—"

"Dead."

Jeff ignored them. Back to her mouth: the cold lips, the taste of vomit, the burn of the sap as he forced the air into her chest. Eric kept yelling from the tent. Stacy and Mathias were silent, not moving, watching Jeff work at the body—the lungs, the heart—straining for that moment of grace, which resisted him, fought him, wouldn't come. He gave up long before he stopped, kept at it for an extra handful of minutes out of simple inertia, a terror of what it meant to lift his lips from her mouth, his hands from her chest, with no intention of returning. It was fatigue that finally forced him to a halt, a cramp in his right thigh, a growing sense of light-headedness; he sat back on his heels, struggled to catch his breath.

No one spoke.

She called my name, Jeff thought. He wiped at his mouth; the sap made his lips feel abraded. *I heard her call it.* He picked up Amy's hand, clasped it in his own, as if trying to warm it.

"Stacy . . ." Eric shouted.

Jeff lifted his head, peered toward the tent. "What's wrong with him?"

he asked. The quietness of his voice astonished him; he'd expected something ragged, something desperate: a howl. He was waiting for tears—he could feel them, just beyond his reach—but they didn't come.

Wouldn't.

Later, he thought.

"It's inside him again," Stacy said, and she, too, spoke softly, almost inaudibly. It was the presence of death, Jeff knew, reducing them all to whispers.

He let go of Amy's hand, laid it carefully across her chest, thinking of that rubber dummy once more, those limp arms. He'd received a certificate for passing the test; his mother had framed it, hung it in his room. He could shut his eyes now and see all those certificates and ribbons and plaques hanging on the walls, the shelves full of trophies. "Someone should go help him," he said.

Mathias stood up without a word, started toward the tent. Jeff and Stacy watched him go, a shadow moving off across the clearing.

Ghostlike, Jeff thought, and then the tears arrived; he couldn't hold them back. No sobs, no gasps—no wailing or moaning or keening—just a half dozen drops of salty water rolling slowly down his cheeks, stinging where the vine's sap had burned his skin.

Stacy couldn't see Jeff's tears. She couldn't see much of anything, actually. She was in bad shape: tired, drunk, aching—in her muscles, in her bones—and thick-headed with fear. It was dark, too dark; it hurt her eyes, the straining to pull things into some semblance of themselves. Amy was lying on her back and Jeff was kneeling beside her—that was all she could see. But she *knew,* even so, had known as soon as she stepped out of the tent—not how, just the fact of it: *She's dead.*

She lowered herself into a crouch. She was two feet away from them; she could've touched Amy if she'd only reached out her hand. She knew she ought to do this, too, that it would be the right thing, exactly what Amy would've wanted of her. But she didn't move. She was too scared: Touching her would make it real.

"Are you sure?" she asked Jeff.

"Sure?"

"That she's . . . " Stacy couldn't bring herself to say it.

But Jeff understood; she sensed him nodding in the darkness.

"How?" she whispered

"How what?"

"How did she . . ."

"It grew over her mouth. It choked her."

Stacy took a deep breath, reflexively. *This can't be happening,* she thought. *How can this be happening?* That campfire smell was in the air again, and it reminded her that there were people at the bottom of the hill. "We have to tell them," she said.

"Who?"

"The Mayans."

She could feel Jeff watching, but he didn't speak. She wished she could make out his expression, because he was part of the unreality here, the not-happening quality—his calmness, his quiet voice, his hidden face. Amy was dead, and they were just sitting beside her, doing nothing.

"We have to tell them what's happened." Stacy's voice rose as she spoke. She could feel it more than hear it, her heart speeding up, burning through the tequila, the sleep, even the terror. "We have to get them to help."

"They're not gonna—"

"They have to."

"Stacy—"

"They have to!"

"*Stacy!*"

She stopped, blinking at him. She was having a hard time remaining in her crouch, her muscles jumping in her thighs. She wanted to leap up, run down the hill, bring this all to an end. It seemed so simple.

"Shut up," Jeff said, his voice very quiet. "All right?"

She didn't answer, was too startled. Briefly, she felt the urge to scream, to lash out at him, strike him, but then it passed. Everything seemed to collapse in its wake. Her fatigue was back suddenly, and her fear, too. She reached, took Amy's hand. It was cool to the touch, slightly damp. If it had squeezed back, Stacy would've shrieked, and it was this realization more than anything else that finally, unequivocally, brought the truth home.

Dead, Stacy thought *She's dead.*

"No more talking," Jeff said. "Can you do that? Just be here with me—with her—and not say another word?"

Stacy kept gripping Amy's hand. Somehow this made things easier. She nodded.

And so that was what they did. They remained there together, one on either side of Amy's body, waiting, not speaking, while the earth began its slow tilt toward dawn.

Eric kept begging Mathias to cut him open, but Mathias wouldn't do it, not in the dark.

"We've got to get it out," Eric insisted. "It's spreading everywhere."

"We don't know that."

"Can't you feel it?"

"I can feel that there's swelling."

"It's not swelling. It's the vine. It's—"

Mathias patted at his arm. "Shh," he said. "When it gets light."

It was hot in the tent, musty and humid, and Mathias's hand was slick with sweat. Eric didn't like the feel of it. He pulled away. "I can't wait that long."

"Dawn's almost here."

"Is it because I called you a Nazi?"

Mathias was silent.

"It was just a joke. We were talking about the movie they'll make. When we get back, how they'll turn you into the villain. Because you're German, right? So they'd make you a Nazi." He wasn't thinking straight, he knew, was talking too quickly. He was scared, and it seemed possible he wasn't making perfect sense. But he'd started down this road, and now he couldn't seem to stop himself. "Not that you are one. Just that they'll make you one. Because they'll need a bad guy. They always need one. Though I guess the vine could be the villain, too, couldn't it? So maybe you don't have to be a Nazi. You can be a hero, like Jeff. You'll both be heroes. Do they have Boy Scouts in Germany?"

He heard Mathias sigh. "Eric—"

"Just give me the fucking knife, okay? I'll do it myself."

"I don't have the knife."

"So go get it."

"When it starts to get light—"

"Call Jeff. Jeff'll do it."

"We can't call Jeff."

"Because?"

There was a pause, and Eric could feel Mathias hesitating. "Something bad's happened," he said.

Eric thought of the little lean-to, that stench of urine and shit and rot. He nodded. "I know."

"I don't think you do."

"It's Pablo, isn't it? He's died."

"No. It's not Pablo."

"Then what?"

"It's Amy."

"*Amy?*" Eric hadn't expected this. "What's wrong with Amy?"

There was that same pause again, that search for the right words. "She's gone."

"She *left?*"

He sensed Mathias shaking his head in the darkness. "She's dead, Eric. It killed her."

"What're you—"

"It smothered her. In her sleep."

Eric was silent, too shocked to speak. *Dead.* "Are you sure?" he asked, knowing even as he spoke that it was a stupid question.

"Yes."

Eric felt a spinning sensation in his head, an abrupt loss of traction. *Dead.* He wanted to get up and go see for himself, but he wasn't certain he had the strength. Someone needed to cut the vine out of his leg first, pull it from his chest. *Dead.* He knew it was true, yet at the same time he couldn't accept it. *Dead.* It was silly, but the movie they'd joked about had taken hold of his imagination: Amy was the good girl, the prissy one; she was supposed to survive, was supposed to float away with Jeff in their hot-air balloon.

Dead, dead, dead.

"Jesus," he said.

"I know."

"I mean—"

There was that pat of the hand again, that sweaty touch of skin. "Shh. Don't. There's nothing to say."

Eric let his head fall back onto the tent's floor. He shut his eyes for a while, then opened them, searching for the first hints of light coming through the orange nylon. But there was only darkness—all around him, only darkness.

He closed his eyes again and lay there, waiting for dawn, with that single word echoing through his head.

Dead, dead, dead, dead, dead . . .

Eric started to call from the tent again, as soon as the sun began to rise. He wanted the knife. Mathias stepped out through the little opening, stood in the clearing, staring at Jeff and Stacy. They were still sitting next to Amy's body, one on either side of it. Stacy was holding Amy's hand.

"What?" Jeff asked.

Mathias shrugged, tilted his head. The light hadn't yet gained much strength; it was tinged with pink. Off in the distance, in the jungle, Jeff could hear birds calling out, shrieking and cawing. He couldn't read Mathias's expression: worried, maybe. Or just uncertain. "I think you should come look."

Jeff got up, feeling stiff, heavy-limbed, his reserves running out on him. He followed Mathias back into the tent, leaving Stacy with Amy's body.

Inside, the light was still too dim to see much. Eric was lying on his back. His left leg and most of his abdomen were hidden beneath something, and it took Jeff a moment to realize that it was the vine.

He crouched beside him. "Why haven't you pulled it off?" he asked.

"He's afraid to tear them," Mathias said.

Eric nodded. "If they break off, they can go anywhere. Like worms."

Jeff prodded at the mass of leaves, bending close to see. The vines had pushed themselves into the wounds on Eric's leg and chest, but it was hard to tell how far they'd managed to get. Jeff needed better light. "Can you walk?" he asked.

Eric shook his head. "It'll crush them. They'll burn me."

Jeff considered this; it was probably true, he decided. "Then we'll carry you."

Eric seemed frightened by this. He tried to sit, but he only made it halfway, propping himself up on his elbow. "Where?"

"Outside. It's too dark in here."

There were five tendrils in all, coiling themselves around Eric's body. Three had attacked his leg, each of them entering a different wound. The other two had both pushed their way in through the cut on his chest. Jeff realized they'd need to snap them off from their roots if they wanted to carry him out of there, and he did it quickly, not saying anything, worried that Eric might protest. Then he gestured for Mathias to help him. Mathias took Eric's shoulders, Jeff his feet, and they picked him up. The five tendrils hung off his body, dangling toward the floor of the tent, writhing snakelike in the air, as they carried him out into the clearing.

They set him down in the dirt, midway between Pablo and Amy. Then Jeff stepped across the clearing, picked up the knife. It was a good thing, having a task like this; he could feel it helping him. Just holding the knife in his hand seemed to clear his mind, sharpen his perceptions. He hesitated for a second, staring about their little campsite. They were a desperate-looking bunch: dirty, their clothes falling off them. Mathias's and Eric's faces were thickly stubbled. Eric was covered in dried blood; the vines looked as if they were growing from his wounds rather than into them. Jeff had seen him glance toward Amy as they'd carried him out from the tent, just a quick exploratory peek, before he flinched away. No one had spoken; they all seemed to be waiting for someone else to do it first. They needed a plan, Jeff knew, a path to carry them beyond this present moment, something to occupy their thoughts, and he understood, too, that he would have to be the one to find it.

The light was growing stronger, bringing the first of the day's heat with it. Pablo's breathing—remarkably, unexpectedly—had become much quieter. For an instant, Jeff even thought the Greek might've died. He approached the lean-to, crouched beside it. No, he was still with them. But the phlegmy rattle had vanished; his breathing was steadier now, slower. Jeff touched Pablo's forehead, felt the heat coming off him, the fever still burning within his body. And yet something had changed. When Jeff pulled his hand away, the Greek's eyes eased open, stared up at him. They seemed surprisingly focused, too: alert.

"Hey," Jeff said.

Pablo licked his lips, swallowed dryly. "Potato?" he whispered.

Jeff stared at him, trying to make sense of this. "Potato?"

Pablo nodded, licking his lips again.

"He wants water," Stacy said from across the clearing. "That's Greek for water."

Jeff turned to look at her. "How do you know?"

"He was saying it before."

Eric was lying on his back, staring up at the sky. "The knife, Jeff," he said.

"In a moment."

Mathias was standing over Eric, his arms folded across his chest, as if he were cold. But Jeff could see the sweat on his face, making it seem to shine in the gathering light. Jeff caught his eye, pointed toward the water jug. It was sitting in the dirt beside the tent. Mathias picked it up, brought it to him.

Jeff uncapped the jug, held it in the air above Pablo, pointing. "Potato?" he asked.

Pablo nodded, opened his mouth, his tongue protruding slightly. There was something on his teeth, Jeff noticed, a brownish stain—blood, perhaps. Jeff lowered the jug, brought it to Pablo's lips, tilted a small amount of water onto his tongue. The Greek swallowed, coughing slightly, then opened his mouth for more. Three times, Jeff repeated this ritual. It was a good sign, he knew—this quieting of Pablo's breathing, this return to consciousness, this ability to stomach the water—but Jeff couldn't quite bring himself to accept it. In his mind, Pablo was already dead. He didn't believe that anyone could survive all that had happened to the Greek in the past thirty-six hours, not without elaborate medical intervention. The broken back, the amputated legs, the loss of blood, the almost certain infection—a few mouthfuls of water weren't going to compensate for any of that.

When Pablo shut his eyes again, Jeff moved back across the clearing, crouched beside Eric.

A plan—that was what they needed.

Clean the knife—wash the blood off its blade, build another fire to sterilize it. Maybe sterilize one of the needles from the sewing kit, too. Then cut the vine out of Eric, stitch him back up.

And someone should head down the hill before long to watch for the Greeks.

And they should sew the remains of the blue tent into a pouch, in case it rained again that afternoon.

And—what else? There was something he was neglecting, Jeff knew, something he was avoiding.

Amy's body.

He glanced toward it, then quickly away. *One step at a time,* he told himself. *Start with the knife.*

"It's going to take a few minutes to get ready," he said to Eric.

Eric started to sit up but then thought better of it. "What do you mean?"

"I have to sterilize the knife."

"It doesn't matter. I don't need—"

"I'm not cutting into you with a dirty knife."

Eric held out his hand. "I'll do it."

Jeff shook his head. "Three minutes, Eric. Okay?"

Eric hesitated, debating. Finally, he seemed to realize he didn't have a choice. He lowered his hand. "Please hurry," he said.

Clean the knife.

Jeff returned to the tent, started to dig through the archaeologists' backpacks, searching for a bar of soap. He found a toiletry kit zipped into a side pocket; there was a razor inside, a small can of shaving cream, a toothbrush and paste, a comb, a stick of deodorant, and—in a little red plastic box—a bar of soap. He carried the entire kit with him back out into the clearing, along with a small towel he'd also found in the backpack, a needle, and a tiny spool of thread.

The bar of soap, the towel, the knife, the needle, the thread, the plastic jug of water—what else was needed?

He turned to Mathias, who was sitting now, beside the little lean-to. "Can you build a fire?" he asked.

"How big?"

"Just a small one. To heat the knife."

Mathias stood up, began to move about the clearing, making his preparations. They'd left the remaining notebooks out in the rain yesterday; they were still too wet to burn. Mathias disappeared into the tent, searching for something else to use as fuel. Jeff poured a small amount of water from the jug onto the towel, then began to rub at the soap with it, working it into a lather. As he started to scrub at the dried blood on the knife's blade, Mathias reappeared, carrying a paperback book, a pair of men's underwear. He arranged these in the dirt beside Jeff, sprinkling some of the remaining tequila over them. The book was a Hemingway novel, *The Sun Also Rises.* Jeff had read it in high school, the same edition, the same cover. Looking down at it now, he realized he couldn't remember a single thing about it.

"Give him some of that," Jeff said, pointing at the tequila.

Mathias handed the bottle to Eric, who held it in both hands, looking up at Jeff uncertainly.

Jeff nodded, gesturing for him to drink. "For the pain."

Eric took a long swallow, paused to catch his breath, then drank again.

Mathias was holding the box of matches now. He'd opened it, taken one of them out. "Tell me when you're ready," he said.

Jeff poured some water onto the blade, rinsing it. When he was done, he took the tequila from Eric, set it on the ground. "After I cut it out, I'm going to sew you up, okay?"

Eric shook his head, looking scared. "I don't want to be sewn up."

"They won't close on their own."

"But it'll still be in there."

"I'm not going to leave any behind, Eric. I'll—"

"You won't be able to see it all. Some of it'll be too small. And if you sew it inside me—"

"Listen to me, all right?" Jeff was fighting to keep his voice low— reasonable and reassuring. "If we leave the wounds open, it'll just keep happening. Understand? You'll fall asleep, and it'll push its way in again. Is that what you want?"

Eric shut his eyes. His face began to twitch. Jeff could see he was struggling not to cry. "I want to go home," he said. "That's what I want." He inhaled deeply, something close to a sob, which he caught at the last moment. "If you sew it up, it'll—"

"Eric," Stacy said.

Eric opened his eyes, turned to look at her. She was still sitting beside Amy, clutching her hand.

"Let him do it, honey. Okay? Just let him do it."

Eric stared at her—at Amy, too. He took another deep breath, then a third one, and the trembling slowly left his face. He shut his eyes again, opened them. He nodded.

Jeff turned to Mathias, who'd been waiting through all this, the unlighted match pinched between finger and thumb. "Go ahead," Jeff said.

And then they all watched as Mathias coaxed the little fire into life.

Stacy was just a few yards away; she could see everything.

Jeff started on Eric's abdomen, enlarging the original wound, tugging gently at one of the tendrils as he sliced. He didn't have to go far—a couple of inches, no more—before the plant came free. Then he began to cut in the other direction, pulling on the second tendril. Again, it was only two or three inches before the vine slipped easily from Eric's body. It must've hurt, of course, but Eric just grimaced, his hands tightening into fists. He didn't make a sound.

Jeff handed the knife to Mathias, took the needle from him. Mathias had heated it in the tiny fire; he'd even threaded it for him. They didn't seem to have to talk, those two; somehow, they just knew what the other wanted, and did it. *Like Amy and me,* Stacy thought, and nearly broke into tears. She had to shut her eyes to stop herself, clenching them—clenching Amy's hand, too. The heat from her own body had warmed Amy's skin by now; if Stacy hadn't known better, she could've imagined that Amy was merely sleeping. But no, that wasn't really true. Already, an odd stiffness had begun to set in, the fingers curling slightly in her grasp.

She opened her eyes. Jeff was mopping away some of Eric's blood with the little towel, bending low, clasping the needle in his other hand, ready to begin his stitching.

Eric lifted his head slightly, stared. "What're you doing?"

Jeff hesitated, the needle poised an inch above Eric's abdomen. "I told you. We have to stitch it closed."

"But you didn't get it all."

"Sure I did. It came right out."

Eric gestured with his hand. "Can't you fucking see? It goes all the way up my chest."

Jeff examined where Eric was pointing—across the left side of his rib cage, then along his sternum. "That's just swelling, Eric."

"Bullshit."

"That's how the body reacts to physical trauma."

"Cut me there." He pointed at his sternum.

"I'm not gonna—"

"Do it and see."

Jeff glanced toward Mathias, then Stacy, as if hoping one of them would help.

Stacy tried, weakly. "Just let him stitch it up, honey."

Eric ignored her. He reached his hand toward Mathias. "Give me the knife."

Mathias looked at Jeff, who shook his head.

"Either cut me or give me the knife and let me do it."

"Eric—" Jeff began.

"It's inside me, damn it. I can feel it."

Jeff wavered for another moment, then handed the needle back to Mathias, took the knife from him. "Show me," he said.

Eric ran his finger along the left edge of his sternum. "Here. Where it's puffy."

Jeff bent over him, pressed the blade into his skin, then drew it downward, carving a line three inches long. Blood spilled out of the wound, ran down Eric's rib cage.

"You see?" Jeff asked. "No vine."

Eric was sweating, his hair clinging to his forehead. It was the pain, Stacy assumed. "Deeper," he said.

"No way." Jeff shook his head. "There's nothing there."

"It's hiding. You have to—"

"If I go deeper, I'll hit bone. Know what that'll feel like?"

"But it's *in* there. I can feel it."

Jeff was using the towel to blot at the blood. "It's just swelling, Eric."

"Maybe it's under the bone. Can you—"

"We're done. I'm stitching you up." Jeff handed the knife back to Mathias, took the needle from him.

"It'll start to eat me. Like Pablo."

Jeff ignored him. He kept swiping the blood away with his towel. Then he bent close, started to stitch.

Eric winced, shutting his eyes. "It hurts."

Jeff was hunched low over Eric's body, stitching and blotting, stitching and blotting, tugging at the thread to tighten it, drawing the wound closed. Very quietly, so softly that Stacy had to lean forward to hear him, he said, "You've gotta get ahold of yourself."

Eric was silent, his eyes still closed. He took a deep breath, held it, then let it out slowly. "I just . . . I don't want to die here."

"Of course not. None of us do."

"But I might—don't you think? All of us might."

Jeff didn't answer. He finished with the cut on Eric's sternum, knotted it off, then returned to the wound at the base of Eric's rib cage.

Eric opened his eyes. "Jeff?"

"What?"

"Do you think we'll die here?"

Jeff was starting to stitch, concentrating on the task, squinting. "I think we're in a hard place. I think we have to be really, really careful. And smart. And alert."

"You're not answering me."

Jeff considered this, then nodded. "I know." It seemed like he might add something further, but he didn't. He stitched and blotted, stitched and blotted, and when he finished with Eric's abdomen, he reached for the knife once more, shifting downward to the wounds on Eric's leg.

When it was over, Jeff let him drink some more tequila. Not much, not enough, but some. And he gave him aspirin, too, which seemed almost like a joke. Eric laughed when Jeff held out the bottle. Not Jeff, though, not the Eagle Scout—he didn't even smile. "Take three," he said. "It's better than nothing."

The stitches hurt; everything did. Eric's skin felt too tight for his body, as if it might begin to tear at any moment. It scared him to move, to try to sit up or stand, so he didn't attempt either. He lay on his back in the clearing, staring up at the sky, which was a startling blue, not a cloud in sight. *A perfect day for the beach,* he thought, then tried to imagine their hotel back in Cancún, the bustle going on there, how he and the others would've occupied themselves on a morning like this. An early swim, perhaps, before breakfast on the veranda. And then, in the afternoon, if it hadn't rained, maybe they'd have gone horseback riding: Stacy had said she'd wanted to try it before they left. Amy, too. Thinking this, Eric turned to look at them. Stacy kept pushing Amy's eyes shut, but each time she did it, they eased back open. Amy's mouth was hanging open, too. The vine's sap had burned the skin on her face; it looked like a birthmark. They'd have to bury her, Eric supposed, and he wondered how they'd manage to dig a hole big enough to accommodate her body.

It was his hunger he noticed first, not the smell that aroused it. He had a tight, crampy feeling in his stomach; his mouth was pooling with saliva. Reflexively, he inhaled. *Bread,* he thought.

At the same moment, Stacy said, "You smell that?"

"It's bread," Eric replied. "Someone's baking bread."

The others were lifting their heads, sniffing at the air. "The Mayans?" Stacy asked.

Jeff was on his feet, trying to track the scent, which was growing stronger and stronger, a bakery smell. He moved slowly along the periphery of the clearing, inhaling deeply.

"Maybe they've brought us bread," Stacy said. She was smiling, almost giddy with the idea; she actually seemed to believe it. "One of us should go down and—"

"It's not the Mayans." Jeff was crouching now at the very edge of the clearing, with his back to them.

"But—"

He turned toward Stacy, gestured for her to come and see for herself. "It's the vine," he said.

Mathias and Stacy both got up and went to sniff at the plants' tiny red flowers; Eric didn't need to. He could tell just from their expressions that Jeff was right, that, somehow, the vine had begun to give off the odor of freshly baked bread. Stacy returned to Amy's body, sat beside it. She pressed her hand over her mouth and nose, trying to block the smell. "I can't handle this, Jeff. I really can't."

"We'll eat some," Jeff said. "We'll split the orange."

Stacy was shaking her head. "It's not going to help."

Jeff didn't answer. He vanished into the tent.

"How can it *do* that?" Stacy asked. She glanced from Eric to Mathias and then back again, as if expecting one of them to have some explanation. Neither of them did, of course. She seemed like she was about to cry; she was pinching her nose shut, breathing through her mouth, panting slightly.

After a moment, Jeff reappeared.

"It's doing it on purpose, isn't it?" Stacy asked.

No one answered her. Jeff sat down, started to work on the orange. Eric and Mathias watched him, the fruit slowly emerging from beneath its peel.

"Why now?" Stacy persisted. "Why didn't it—"

"It wanted to wait until we were hungry," Jeff said. "Until our defenses were low." He sectioned the fruit, counting out the segments; there were ten of them. "If it had started earlier, it wouldn't have bothered us as much. We would've gotten used to it. But now . . ." He shrugged. "It's the same reason it waited to start mimicking our voices. It waits till we're weak before it reveals its strength."

"Why bread?" Stacy asked.

"It must've smelled it at some point. Someone must've baked bread here, or heated it at least. Because it imitates things—things it's heard, things it's smelled. Like a chameleon. A mockingbird."

"But it's a *plant.*"

Jeff glanced up at her. "How do you know that?"

"What do you mean?"

"How do you know it's a plant?"

"What else would it be? It's got leaves, and flowers, and—"

"But it moves. And it thinks. So maybe it just looks like a plant." He smiled at her, as if pleased, once again, with the vine's many accomplishments. "There's no way for us to know, is there?"

The smell changed, grew sharper, more intense. Eric was reaching for the word inside his head when Mathias said it: "Meat."

Stacy lifted her face skyward, sniffing. "Steak."

Mathias shook his head. "Hamburgers."

"Pork chops," Eric countered.

Jeff waved them into silence. "Don't."

"Don't what?" Stacy asked.

"Talk about it. It'll only make it worse."

They fell silent. *Not pork chops,* Eric thought. *Hot dogs.* The plant was still inside him; he was certain of this. Stitched inside him, biding its time. But maybe it didn't matter. It could mimic sounds and smells; it could think, and it could move. Inside his body or outside, the vine was going to triumph.

Jeff divided the orange into four equal piles, two and a half segments apiece. "We should eat the peel, too," he said. And then he portioned that out also. He gestured at Stacy. "You choose first."

Stacy stood up, approached the little mounds of fruit. She crouched over them, appraising each ration, measuring with her eyes. Finally, she reached down and scooped one up.

"Eric?" Jeff said.

Eric held out his hand. "I don't care. Just give me one."

Jeff shook his head. "Point."

Eric pointed at a pile, and Jeff picked it up, carried it to him. Two and a half slices of orange, a small handful of peels. If there'd been five of them still, there'd only be two segments apiece. That Amy's absence could be measured in such a paltry manner, half a slice of orange, seemed terribly sad to Eric. He put one of the sections into his mouth and shut his eyes, not chewing yet, just holding it on his tongue.

"Mathias?" Jeff said.

Eric heard the German stand up, go to claim his ration. Then everything was silent, each of them retreating to some inner place as they savored what would have to pass for their breakfast this morning.

The smell changed again. *Apple pie,* Eric thought, still not chewing, and struggling suddenly, inexplicably, against the threat of tears. *How does it know what apple pie smells like?* He could hear the others beginning to eat, the wet sound of their mouths working. He pulled his hat down over his eyes.

A hint of cinnamon, too.

Eric chewed, swallowed, then placed a piece of orange peel in his mouth. He wasn't crying; he'd fought off the impulse. But it was still there—he could feel it.

Whipped cream, even.

He chewed the tiny strip of peel, swallowed, slipped another one into his mouth. He could see the pie's crust in his mind—slightly burned on the bottom. And it wasn't whipped cream; it was ice cream. Vanilla ice cream, slowly melting across the plate—a small tin plate, with a mug of black coffee sitting beside it. Imagining this, Eric felt that urge to weep again. He had to squeeze his eyes shut, hold his breath, wait for it to recede, while the same four words kept running through his head.

How does it know? How does it know? How does it know?

There are some things we need to figure out," Jeff said.

The orange had been divided, then eaten, peel and all. Afterward, they'd passed the jug of water around their little circle, and he'd told the others to drink their fill. Water wasn't his chief concern anymore; after the previous night's downpour, he felt confident it would rain again—almost daily, he believed. And he knew it would help morale if they could manage to eliminate at least that one discomfort. So they ate their meager breakfast, then drank water until their stomachs swelled.

Later, they could try to sew a pouch out of the leftover blue nylon. Maybe they'd even manage to collect enough rain to wash themselves. That, too, would help lift their spirits.

They weren't sated, of course. How could they be? An orange, split between the four of them. Jeff tried to think of it as fasting, a hunger strike: how long could these last? In his head, he had a picture, a newspaper photograph, black and white, of three young men staring defiantly from their cots—weak, emaciated, but undeniably alive, their eyes ablaze with it. Jeff struggled to see the headline, to remember the story that went with the picture. Why couldn't he do this? He wanted a number, wanted to know how long. Weeks, certainly—weeks with nothing but water.

Fifty days?

Sixty?

Seventy?

But eventually, there had to come a moment past which fasting blurred into starving, and in Jeff's mind this was connected in some way to their meager store of provisions, to its continued existence, no matter how little they might actually be consuming. He'd convinced himself that as long as some small scrap of food remained for them to portion out, they'd be okay; they'd be in control. Because they were rationing, not starving.

Denial. A fairy tale.

And then there were the things he knew and couldn't hide from, the things he'd read about over the years, the details he'd absorbed. At some point, their hunger pangs would disappear. Their bodies would start to break down muscle tissue, start to digest the fatty acids in their livers, the machine consuming itself for fuel. Their metabolic rates would fall, their pulses slow, their blood pressures drop. They'd feel cold even in the sun, lethargic. And all this would happen relatively quickly, too. Two weeks, three at the most. Then things would rapidly get worse: arrhythmia, eye problems, anemia, mouth ulcers—on and on and on until there were no more *and*s for them to claim. It didn't matter if he couldn't remember whether it was fifty or sixty or seventy days; what mattered was that it was finite. There was a line drawn across their path—a wall, a chasm—and with each passing hour they edged one step closer to it.

After bread had come meat and after meat apple pie and after apple pie strawberries and after strawberries chocolate, and then it had stopped. "It's so we don't get used to it," Jeff had told the others. "So it catches us off guard each time it comes."

There was something they could do, of course, a resource at their disposal, but Jeff doubted the others would accept it. *Unpalatable* was the word that came to mind, actually—*They'll find the idea unpalatable*—and, even in his present extremity, he saw the humor in this.

Gallows humor.

There are some things we need to figure out. That was how he phrased it, the words sounding so misleading in their banality, so falsely benign. But how else was he to begin?

Eric was still lying on his back, his hat covering his face. He showed no sign of having heard.

"Eric?" Jeff said. "You awake?"

Eric lifted his hand, removed the hat, nodded. The skin was puckered around his wounds, drawn tight by the stitches, still oozing blood in places. Ugly-looking—raw and painful. Mathias was to Jeff's left, the water jug in his lap. Stacy was sitting beside Amy's body.

Amy's body.

"You need some sunblock on your feet, Stacy," Jeff said, pointing.

She peered down at her feet, as if not quite seeing them; they were bright pink, slightly swollen.

"And take Amy's hat. Her sunglasses."

Stacy shifted her gaze toward Amy. The sunglasses were hooked into the collar of Amy's T-shirt. Her hat had fallen off, was lying a few feet away—mud-stained and misshapen and still damp from the rain. Stacy didn't move; she just sat there staring, and finally Jeff rose to his feet. He stepped forward, picked up the hat, carefully plucked the sunglasses from Amy's shirt. He offered them to Stacy. She hesitated, seemed about to refuse, but then slowly reached to take them.

Jeff watched her put on the glasses, adjust the hat on her head. He was pleased; it seemed like a good sign, a first step. He returned to his spot, sat down again. "One of us ought to go and watch the trail soon. In case the Greeks—"

Mathias stood up. "I'll go."

Jeff shook his head, waved him back down. "In a minute. First we need to—"

"Shouldn't we, you know . . ." Stacy pointed at Amy's body.

Amy's body.

Jeff turned to her, startled. Despite himself, he felt a strange mix of hope and relief. *She's going to say it for me.* "What?" he asked.

"You know . . . " She pointed again.

Jeff waited her out, wanting her to be the one, not him. Why did it always have to be him? He sat watching her, willing her to speak, to say the words.

But she failed him. "I guess . . . I don't know. . . ." She shrugged. "Bury her or something?"

No, that wasn't it, was it? That missed the point entirely. It would have to be him; he'd been a fool to imagine any other possibility. He inclined his head, as if nodding, though it wasn't a nod at all. "Well, that's the thing," he said. "Sort of. The thing we need to talk about."

The others were silent. No one was going to help him here, he realized; no one but him had made the leap. *Like cows,* he thought, examining their faces. Perhaps the orange had been a bad idea—maybe he should've waited, should've spoken at the height of their hunger, with the smell of bread in the air, or meat.

Yes, *meat.*

"I think we're okay," he began. "Waterwise, I mean. I think we can count on the rain coming often enough to keep us alive. We can maybe sew a big pouch even, out of the nylon." He waved across the clearing, toward the scraps from the blue tent. The others followed his gesture, stared for a moment, then turned back to him.

Like sheep, he thought. He was waiting for the right words to arrive, but they weren't coming.

Stacy shifted, reached, picked up Amy's hand again, held it in her own, as if for reassurance.

There were no right words, of course.

"It's all about waiting, you know," he said. "That's what we're doing here. Waiting for someone to come and find us—the Greeks, maybe, or someone our parents might send." He was having trouble holding their eyes, and he felt ashamed of this. It would be better if he could look one of them in the face, he knew, but somehow it didn't seem possible. His gaze drifted from his lap to Stacy's sunburned feet to the puckered wounds on Eric's leg, then back again. "Waiting. And surviving through the waiting. If we can maintain a supply of water, that'll help, of course. But then it becomes a question of food, doesn't it? Because we don't have that much. And we don't know . . . I mean, if it's not the Greeks, if we have to wait for our parents, it could be weeks we're talking about, weeks before someone comes and rescues us from this place. And the food we have, even if we ration it, it's not going to last more than a couple days. If we could hunt, or snare things, or catch fish, or dig up roots, or search for berries . . ." He trailed off, shrugged. "The only thing besides us on this hill is the vine, and obviously we can't eat that. We've got our belts, I guess—and we could figure out a way to boil them, maybe. People have done that sort of thing, people lost in the desert, or adrift at sea. But it wouldn't really change much, would it? Not when we're talking weeks."

He girded himself for a quick scan of their faces. Blank, all of them. They were listening, he could see, but without any sense of where he was headed. He was trying not to startle them, trying to creep up to the thing that needed saying, and in this way give them the chance to anticipate it, to prepare themselves for it, but it wasn't working. He needed their help for it to work, and none of them was equal to the task.

"Fifty, sixty, seventy days," he said. "Somewhere in there, I can't remember—that's as long as anyone can last without food. And even before that, long before that, things start to go wrong, start to fail, break down. So let's say we're talking thirty days, okay? Which is what? Four weeks or so? And if it's not the Greeks, if it's our parents we're waiting for, how long will that take? Realistically, I mean. Another week before they expect us home, maybe a week beyond that before they really start to worry, then some calls to Cancún, the hotel, the American consulate—all that's easy enough. But then what? How long to trace us to the bus station, to Cobá, to the trail and the Mayan village, to this fucking hill in the middle of the jungle? Can we really depend on it being less than four weeks for all that to happen?"

He shook his head, answering his own question. Then he risked another glance at their faces—but no, they weren't understanding him. He was depressing them—that was all—frightening them. It was right in front of them, and they couldn't see it.

Or wouldn't, maybe.

He gestured toward Amy's body, kept his arm out in front of him, pointing, long enough so that they didn't have any choice. They had to look, had to stare, had to take in her graying skin, her eyes, which refused to stay shut, the burned, raw-looking flesh around her mouth and nose. "This—what's happened to Amy—it's terrible. A terrible thing. There's no way around it. But now that it's happened, we need to face it, I think, need to accept what it might mean for us. Because there's a question we have to answer for ourselves—a really, really diffi-cult question. And we have to use our imagination to do it, because it's something that'll only start to matter as the days go by here, but which we have to answer now, beforehand." He scanned their faces again. "Do you understand what I'm trying to say?"

Mathias was silent, his expression unchanged. Eric's eyes had drifted back shut. Stacy was still clasping Amy's hand; she shook her head.

Jeff knew it wasn't going to work, but he still felt he had to raise the issue, felt it was his duty to do so. He plunged forward: "I'm talking about Amy. About finding a way to preserve her."

The others took this in. Mathias shifted his body slightly, his face seeming to tighten. *He knows,* Jeff thought. But not the others. Eric just lay there; he might even have been asleep. Stacy cocked her head, gave Jeff a quizzical look.

"You mean, like, embalm her?"

Jeff decided to try another approach. "If you needed a kidney, if you were going to die without it, and then Amy died first, would you take hers?"

"Her kidney?" Stacy asked.

Jeff nodded.

"What does that—" And then, in mid-sentence, she got it. Jeff saw it happen, the knowledge take hold of her. She covered her mouth, as if sickened. "No, Jeff. No way."

"What?"

"You're saying—"

"Just answer the question, Stacy. If you needed a kidney, if you—"

"You know it's not the same."

"Because?"

"Because a kidney would mean an operation. It would be . . ." She shook her head, exasperated with him. Her voice had risen steadily as she spoke. "This . . . this is . . ." She threw up her hands in disgust.

Eric opened his eyes. He stared at Stacy with a puzzled expression. "What're we talking about?"

Stacy pointed toward Jeff. "He wants to . . . to . . ." She seemed incapable of saying it.

"We're talking about food, Eric." Jeff was struggling to keep his voice low, calm, to contrast it to Stacy's growing hysteria. "About whether or not we're going to starve here."

Eric absorbed this, no closer to comprehending. "What does that have to do with Amy's kidney?"

"Nothing!" Stacy said, almost shouting the word. "That's exactly the point."

"Would you take hers?" Jeff asked, and he waved toward Amy. "If you needed a kidney? If you were gonna die without it?"

"I guess." Eric shrugged. "Why not?"

"He's not talking about kidneys, Eric. He's talking about food. Understand? About eating her."

There was no more hiding from it now; the words had been spoken. There was a long silence as they all stared down at Amy's body. Stacy was the one who broke it finally, turning to Jeff. "You'd really do it?"

"People have. Castaways, and—"

"I'm asking if *you* would. If *you* could eat *her*."

Jeff thought for a moment. "I don't know." It was the truth: he didn't.

Stacy looked appalled. "You don't know?"

He shook his head.

"How can you say that?"

"Because I don't know what it feels like to starve. I don't know what choices I'd make in the face of it. All I know is that if it's a possibility, if it's something we can even agree to conceive of, then we have to take certain steps now, right now, before much time passes."

"Steps."

Jeff nodded.

"Such as?"

"We'd have to figure out a way to preserve it."

"*It?*"

Jeff sighed. This was going exactly as he'd anticipated, a disaster. "What do you want me to say?"

"How about *her?*"

Jeff felt a tug of anger at this, without warning, a righteous sort of fury, and he liked the sensation. It was reassuring; it made him feel he was doing the right thing after all. "You really think that's still her?" he asked. "You really think that has the slightest thing to do with Amy anymore? That's an *object* now, Stacy. An *it.* Something without movement, without life. Something we can either rationally choose to use to help us survive here, or—irrationally, sentimentally, stupidly—decide to let rot, let the vine eat into yet another pile of bones. That's a choice we have to make. Consciously—we have to decide what happens to this body. Because don't trick yourself: Flinching away from it, deciding not to think about it, that's a choice, too. You can see that, can't you?"

Stacy didn't answer. She wasn't looking at him.

"All I'm saying is, whatever our decision might be, let's make it with open eyes." Jeff knew that he should just let it go, that he'd already said too much, pushed too hard, but he'd come this far, and he couldn't stop himself. "In a purely physical sense, it's meat. That's what's lying there."

Stacy gave him a look of loathing. "What the fuck is the matter with you? Are you even upset? She's dead, Jeff. Understand? *Dead.*"

It took effort to keep his voice from rising to match her own, yet somehow he managed it. He wanted to reach forward, to touch her, but he knew that she'd recoil from him. He wanted both of them to calm down. "Do you honestly think Amy would care? Would you care if it were you?"

Stacy shook her head vehemently. Amy's mud-stained hat started to slide off, and she had to lift her hand to hold it in place. "That's not fair."

"Because?"

"You make it seem like it's a game. Like some sort of abstract thing we're talking about in a bar. But this is real. It's her *body*. And I'm not gonna—"

"How would you do it?" Eric asked.

Jeff turned toward him, relieved to have another voice involved. "'Do it'?"

Eric was still lying on his back, his wounds seeping those tiny threads of blood. He kept pressing at his abdomen, probing—a new spot now. "Preserve the, you know, the . . ." *Meat* was the right word—there wasn't any other—but it was clear Eric couldn't bring himself to say it.

Jeff shrugged. "Cure it, I guess. Dry it."

Stacy leaned forward, openmouthed, as if she might vomit. "I'm going to be sick."

Jeff ignored her. "I think there's a way to salt it. Using urine. You cut the meat into strips and soak it in—"

Stacy covered her ears, started shaking her head again. "No, no, no, no . . ."

"Stacy—"

She began to chant: "I won't let you. I won't let you. I won't let you. I won't let you. I won't let you. . . ."

Jeff fell silent. What choice did he have? Stacy kept chanting and shaking her head; her hat slid sideways, dropped to the dirt. Watching her, Jeff felt that weight again, that sense of resignation. It didn't matter, he supposed. Why shouldn't this be as good a place to die as any other? He lifted his hand, wiped at the sweat on his face. He could smell the orange peel on his fingers. He was hungry enough to feel the urge to lick them, but he resisted it.

Finally, Stacy stopped. There was a stretch of time then, where no one had anything to say. Eric kept probing at his chest. Mathias shifted his weight, the jug of water making a sloshing sound in his lap. Stacy was still holding Amy's hand. Jeff glanced toward Pablo. The Greek's eyes were open, and he was watching them, as if he'd somehow, despite everything, managed to sense that something important was being discussed. Looking at him, at his ravaged, motionless body, Jeff realized that the discussion didn't necessarily end here, that Amy's death almost certainly wasn't going to be the last. He pushed the thought aside.

They were all avoiding one another's gaze. Jeff knew no one else was going to speak, that he'd have to be the one, and he knew, too, that whatever he said would need to sound like a peace offering. He licked his lips; they were sun-cracked, swollen.

"Then I guess we should bury her," he said.

It didn't take long to realize that burying Amy wasn't a possibility. The day's rapidly growing heat alone would've ensured this. Even if it hadn't, there was still the problem of a shovel; all they had to dig with was a tent stake and a stone. So Jeff dragged one of the sleeping bags out of the tent, and they zipped Amy inside it. This involved a struggle of a different sort; Amy's corpse seemed intent upon resisting its enshrouding. Her limbs refused to cooperate—they kept snagging and tangling. Jeff and Mathias had to wrestle with her, both of them beginning to pant and sweat, before they finally managed to shove her into the bag.

Stacy made no attempt to help. She watched, feeling increasingly ill. She was hungover, of course; she was dizzy and bloated and achingly nauseous. And Amy was dead. Jeff had wanted to eat her body, so that the rest of them might, in turn, keep from dying, but Stacy had stopped him. She tried to feel some pleasure in her victory, yet it wouldn't come to her.

There was an odd moment of hesitation before the boys zipped shut the bag, as if they sensed the symbolic importance of this act, its finality—that first shovelful of soil thumping down onto the casket's lid. Stacy could see Amy's face through the opening; it had already taken on a noticeable puffiness, a faintly greenish tinge. Her eyes had drifted open once again. In the past, Stacy knew, they used to rest coins upon people's eyes. Or did they put coins in the mouth, to pay the ferryman? Stacy wasn't certain; she'd never bothered to pay attention to details like that, and was always regretting it, the half knowing, which felt worse than not knowing at all, the constant sense that she had things partly right, but not right enough to make a difference. Coins on the eyes seemed silly, though. Because wouldn't they fall off as the casket was carried to the graveyard, jostled and tilted, then lowered into its hole? The corpses would lie beneath that weight of dirt for all eternity, open-eyed, with a pair of coins resting uselessly on the wooden planks beside them.

No casket for Amy—no coins, either. Nothing to pay the ferryman.

We should have a ceremony, Stacy thought. She tried to imagine what this might entail, but all she could come up with was a vague image of someone standing over an open grave, reading something from the Bible. She could picture the mound of dirt beside the hole, the raw pine of the coffin bleeding little amber beads of sap. But of course they didn't have any of this, not Bible nor hole nor coffin. All they had was Amy's body and a musty-smelling sleeping bag, so Stacy remained silent, watching as Jeff leaned forward, finally, to drag the zipper slowly shut.

Eric pulled his hat back over his face. Mathias sat down, closed his eyes. Jeff vanished into the tent. Stacy wondered if he was fleeing them, if he wanted to be alone so that he could weep or keen or bang his head against the earth, but then, almost instantly, he reappeared, carrying a tiny plastic bottle. He crouched right in front of her, startling her; she almost backed away, only managed to stop herself at the last instant. "You need to put this on your feet," he said.

He held out the little bottle. Stacy squinted at it, struggling to decipher its label. *Sunscreen.* Jeff's khaki shirt was stained through with perspiration, salt-rimed around the collar. She could smell him, the stench of his sweat, and it gave strength to her nausea; she was conscious of the chewed fruit in her stomach, those scraps of peel, how tenuous their residence within her body was, how easily surrendered. She wanted Jeff to leave, wished he'd stand up again, walk off. But he didn't move; he just crouched there, watching as she hurriedly squirted some of the lotion onto her palm, then leaned forward to smear it across her right foot, careful to avoid the thin leather straps of her sandal.

"Come on," Jeff said. "Do it right."

"Right?" she asked. She had no idea what he was talking about; all her attention was focused on her effort not to vomit. If she vomited, the vine would slither forth and steal those slices of orange from her, those pieces of peel, and she knew there'd be nothing to replace them.

Jeff grabbed the bottle from her. "Take off your sandals."

She clumsily removed them, then watched as he began to massage a large glob of sunscreen into her skin. "Are you angry with me?" she asked.

"Angry?" He wasn't looking at her, just her feet, and it frightened Stacy, made her feel as if she weren't quite present. She wanted him to look at her.

"For, you know . . ." She waved toward the sleeping bag. "Stopping you."

Jeff didn't answer immediately. He started in on her second foot, and a drop of sweat fell from his nose onto her shin, making her shiver. Pablo's breathing was worsening again, that deep, watery rasp returning. It was the only sound in the clearing, and it took effort not to hear it. She could sense Jeff choosing his words. "I just want to save us," he said. "That's all. Keep us from dying here. And food. . . ." He trailed off, shrugged. "It'll come down to food in the end. I don't see any way around that."

He capped the bottle, tossed it aside, gestured for her to pull her sandals back on. Stacy stared at her feet. They were already burned a bright pink. *It'll hurt in the shower,* she thought, and had to fight back tears for a moment, so certain was she, abruptly, that there wasn't going to be a shower, not for her, not for any of them, because it wasn't only Amy; no one was going to make it home from here.

"What about you?" Jeff asked.

"Me?"

"Are you angry?"

A humming had risen in Stacy's skull—hunger or fatigue or fear. She couldn't have said which, knew only that one would account for it just as well as any other. She was far too worn out for anything as vigorous as anger to have much hold over her; she'd been here too long, gone through too much. She shook her head.

"Good," Jeff said. And then, as if he were announcing a prize she'd won for choosing the correct answer: "Why don't you take the first shift down the hill."

Stacy didn't want to do this. Yet even as she sat there searching for a reason to refuse him, she knew she had no choice. Amy was gone, and it seemed like this ought to change everything. But the world was carrying on, and Jeff was moving with it, worrying about sunscreen and the Greeks—planning, always planning—because that was what it meant to be alive.

Am I alive? she wondered.

Jeff picked up the water, held it out to her. "Hydrate first."

She took the jug from him, uncapped it, drank. It helped her nausea enough for her to stand.

Jeff handed her the sunshade. "Three hours," he said. "Okay? Then Mathias will relieve you."

Stacy nodded, and then he was turning away, already moving on to his next task. There was nothing left for her to do but leave. So that was what she did, the sunscreen making her feet feel slippery in her sandals, that humming sound rising and falling in her head. *I'm okay,* she said to herself. *I can do this. I'm alive.* And she kept repeating the words, mantra-like, as she made her way slowly down the trail. *I'm alive. I'm alive. I'm alive. . . .*

Eric was lying on his back in the center of the clearing. He could feel the sun against his body—his face, his arms, his legs—hot enough to carry a trace of pain. There was pleasure in it, too, though—pleasure not despite the pain but because of it. He was getting a sunburn, and what could be so terrible about that? It was normal; it could happen to anyone—lying beside a pool, napping on a beach—and Eric found a definite measure of reassurance in this. Yes, he *wanted* to be sunburned, wanted to be in the grip of that mundane discomfort, believing that it might somehow obscure the far more extraordinary stirrings of his body, the sense that his wounds would rip open if he were to move too suddenly, the suspicion—no, the certainty—that the vine was still lurking within his body, sewed up tight by Jeff's stitches, interred but not dead, merely dormant, seedlike, biding its time. With his eyes shut, his mind focused on the surface of his body, the burning tautness of his skin, Eric had stumbled upon a temporary refuge, all the more alluring for its tenuousness. But he knew he couldn't take it too far. There was an element of balance to the process, a tipping point he had to avoid. He was exhausted—he kept having to resist the urge to yawn—he was certain that if he relaxed even slightly, he'd drop into sleep. And sleep was his enemy here; sleep was when the vine laid claim to him.

He forced open his eyes, rose onto his elbow. Jeff and Mathias were tending to Pablo's stumps. They used water from the jug to flush the seared tissue; then Jeff threaded a needle, sterilized it with a match. Pablo still had half a dozen blood vessels leaking their tiny rivulets of red. Jeff was bending now to stitch them shut. Eric couldn't bear to watch; he lowered himself onto his back again. The smell of the match alone was too much for him, bringing back as it did the previous day's horror—Jeff pressing that heated pan against the Greek's flesh, the aroma of cooking spreading across the hilltop.

He should go into the tent, he knew; he should get out of the sun. But even as he thought this, he was shutting his eyes. He heard his own voice inside his head: *I'll be okay. Jeff is right there. He'll watch over me. He'll keep me safe.* The words just came; Eric wasn't conscious of forming them. It was as if he were overhearing someone else.

He could feel himself falling asleep, and he didn't fight it.

He awoke to find that the day had shifted forward—dramatically so. The sun was already beginning its long descent toward evening. There were clouds, too. They covered more than half the sky and were visibly advancing westward. These obviously weren't the usual afternoon thunderheads Eric and the others had witnessed here thus far, with their abrupt appearance and equally rapid dispersal. No, this seemed to be some sort of storm front sweeping down upon them. For the moment, the sun remained unobscured, but Eric could tell this wouldn't be true much longer. He could've sensed it even without glancing upward: the light had a feeling of foreboding to it.

He turned his head, stared about the clearing, still feeling sleep-dazed. Stacy had returned from the bottom of the hill; she was sitting beside Pablo, holding his hand. The Greek appeared to have lost consciousness again. His respiration had continued to deteriorate. Eric lay there listening to it—the watery inhalation, the wheezing discharge, that frightening, far too long pause between breaths. Amy's corpse was resting in the dirt to his left, enveloped in its dark blue sleeping bag. Jeff was on the far side of the clearing, bent over something, in obvious concentration. It took Eric a moment to grasp what it was. Jeff had sewn a large bucketlike pouch out of the scraps of blue nylon to collect the coming rain. Now he was using some of the leftover aluminum poles to build a frame for it, taping them together, so that the pouch's sides wouldn't collapse as it filled.

There was no sign of Mathias. He was guarding the trail, Eric assumed.

He sat up. His body felt stiff, hollowed out, strangely chilled. He was just bending to examine his wounds, probing at the surrounding skin, searching for signs of the vine's growth within him—bumps, puffiness, swelling—when Jeff rose to his feet, moved past him without a word, and disappeared inside the tent.

Why am I so cold?

Eric could tell that it wasn't a matter of the temperature having dropped. He could see the damp circles of sweat on Stacy's shirt; he could even sense the heat himself, but at an odd remove, as if he were in an air-conditioned room, staring through a window at a sunbaked landscape. No, that wasn't it; it was as if his *body* were the air-conditioned room, as if his skin were the windowpane, hot on the surface, cold underneath. This must be an effect of his hunger, he supposed, or his

fatigue or loss of blood, or even the plant inside him, parasitically sucking the warmth from his body. There was no way to say for certain. All
he knew was that it was a bad sign. He felt like lying down again, and
would've if Jeff hadn't reappeared then, carrying the two bananas.

Eric watched him retrieve the knife from the dirt, wipe it on his shirt
in a halfhearted effort to clean the blade, then crouch and cut each of
the bananas in half, with their peels still on. He waved for Eric and
Stacy to approach. "Choose," he said.

Stacy leaned forward to lay Pablo's hand gently across his chest, then
came and stooped beside Jeff, peering down at the proffered food. The
bananas' peels were almost completely black now; Eric could tell how
soft they must be just by looking at them. Stacy picked one up, cradling
it in her palm. "Do we eat the peel?" she asked.

Jeff shrugged. "It might be hard to chew. But you can try." He
turned toward Eric, who hadn't stirred. "Pick one," he said.

"What about Mathias?" Eric asked.

"I'm going to go relieve him now. I'll take it down."

Eric kept feeling as if he were about to shiver. He didn't trust himself
to stand up. It wasn't only his wounds, which felt so vulnerable, so easily reopened; he was worried his legs might not hold him. He held out
his hand. "Just toss it."

"Which?"

"There." He pointed to the one closest to him. Jeff threw it under-
hand; it landed in Eric's lap.

They ate in silence. The banana was far too ripe: it tasted as if it had
already begun to ferment, a mush of tangy sweetness that, even in his
hunger, Eric found difficult to swallow. He ate quickly, first the fruit,
then the skin. It was impossible to chew the skin more than partially; it
was too fibrous. Eric gnawed and gnawed, until his jaw began to ache,
then forced himself to swallow the clotted mass. Jeff had already finished, but Stacy was taking her time with her own ration, still nibbling
at the little nub of fruit, its skin resting on her knee.

Jeff lifted his eyes, examined the clouds darkening above them, the
sun in its diminishing quadrant of blue. "I put soap out for you in case
it starts to rain while I'm still down there." He gestured toward the blue
pouch. A bar of soap was lying in the dirt beside it. The plastic toolbox
was there, too; Jeff had used the duct tape to cover the crack along its
bottom. "Wash yourselves, then get inside the—" He stopped in mid-
sentence, turned toward the tent with a startled expression.

Eric and Stacy followed his gaze. There was a rustling sound: the sleeping bag was moving. No—*Amy* was moving, kicking at the bag, thrashing, struggling to rise. For a moment, they simply watched, not quite able to believe what they were seeing. Then they were rushing forward, all three of them, even Eric, his wounds forgotten, his weakness and fatigue, everything set aside, momentarily transcended by his shock, his astonishment, his hope. Part of himself already knew what they were about to find even as he watched Jeff and Stacy stoop beside the bag, but he resisted the knowledge, waited for the sound of the zipper, for Amy to come laboring toward them, gasping and bewildered. *A mistake, it was all a mistake.*

He could hear Amy's voice, calling from inside the bag. Muffled, panic-filled: "Jeff . . . Jeff . . ."

"We're right here, sweetie," Stacy shouted. "We're right here."

She was scrambling for the zipper. Jeff found it first, yanked on it, and an immense tangle of vine erupted out off the bag, cascading onto the dirt. Its flowers were a pale pink. Eric watched them open and close, still calling, *Jeff . . . Jeff . . . Jeff . . .* The thick clot of tendrils was writhing spasmodically, coiling and uncoiling. Entwined within it were Amy's bones, already stripped clean of flesh. Eric glimpsed her skull, her pelvis, what he assumed must be a femur, everything tumbled confusedly together; then Stacy was screaming, backing away, shaking her head. He stepped toward her, and she clutched at him, tightly enough for him to remember his wounds again, how easy it would be to begin to bleed.

The vine stopped calling Jeff's name. Perhaps three seconds of silence followed, and then it started to laugh: a low, mocking chuckle.

Jeff stood over the bag, staring at it. Stacy pressed her face into Eric's chest. She was crying now.

"Shh," Eric said. "Shh." He stroked her hair, feeling oddly distant. He thought of how people sometimes described accidents they'd suffered, that floating-above-the-scene quality that so often seemed to accompany disaster, and he struggled to find his way back to himself. Stacy's hair was greasy beneath his hand; he tried to concentrate on this, hoping the sensation might ground him, but even as he did so, his gaze was slipping back toward the sleeping bag, toward the skein of vines—still writhing, still laughing—and the bones tangled within it.

Amy.

Stacy was sobbing now, uncontrollably, tightly embracing him. Her nails were digging into his back. "Shh," he kept saying. "Shh."

Jeff hadn't moved.

Eric could feel it inside his chest—the vine—could feel it shifting deeper, but even this seemed strangely far away to him, not really his concern at all. It was shock, he decided; he must be in shock. And maybe that was a good thing, too; maybe that was his psyche protecting him, shutting down when it knew events had gone too far.

"I wanna go home," Stacy moaned. "I wanna go home."

He patted at her, stroked her. "Shh . . . shh."

The vine had eaten Amy's flesh in half a day. So why shouldn't it inflict something similar upon him? All it would have to do was make its way to his heart, he supposed, and then—what? Slowly squeeze it, still its beating? Thinking this, Eric became conscious of his pulse, of the fact—both banal and profound all at once—that it would stop someday, whether here or somewhere else, and that when it did, he'd stop, too. These beats sounding faintly in his head—they were finite, there was a limit to them, and each contraction of his heart brought him that much closer to the end. He was thinking, irrationally, that if he could only slow his pulse, he might manage to live longer, to stretch out his allotted heartbeats—add a day, maybe two, or even a week—was probing at the illogic of this, when the vine fell silent. For a moment, there was only the rasp of Pablo's breathing in the clearing—stopping and starting, stopping and starting. Then, quietly at first, but rapidly growing in volume, there came the sound of someone gagging.

It was Amy, Eric knew. She was vomiting.

Jeff turned from the bag, the tangle of vine, the loosened bones. There was a clenched immobility to his face. Eric could see how hard he was working not to cry. He wanted to say something, wanted to comfort him, but Jeff was moving too quickly, and Eric's mind wasn't supple enough; he couldn't find the proper words. He watched Jeff stoop to retrieve the remaining piece of fruit, then rise, start toward the trail. He was just exiting the clearing when Amy's voice emerged, very faintly, through the gagging: *Help me.*

Jeff stopped, turned back toward Eric.

Help me, Jeff.

Jeff shook his head. He looked helpless suddenly, startlingly young, a boy fighting tears. "I didn't know," he said. "I swear. It was too dark. I couldn't see her." He didn't wait for Eric's response; he spun away and strode quickly off.

Eric stood there, staring after him—Stacy still pressed tightly against his body, weeping—while Amy's voice grew fainter and fainter, pursuing Jeff down the hill.

Help me, Jeff. . . . Help me. . . . Help me. . . .

Jeff hadn't gone more than a hundred feet before the vine fell silent. He would've thought he'd find some relief in this, but it wasn't true. The quiet was even worse, the way the voice stopped so abruptly, the inexplicable feeling of aloneness that followed in its wake. It was the sound of Amy dying, of course—that was what Jeff was hearing—her voice cut off in mid-cry. He felt the tears coming and knew they were too strong for him this time, that he had no choice but to submit. He crouched in the center of the trail, folded his arms across his knees, buried his face within them.

It was absurd, but he didn't want the vine to know he was crying. He had the instinct to hide himself, as if he feared the plant might find some pleasure in his suffering. He wept but didn't sob, restricting himself to a furtive sort of gasping. He kept his head bowed the entire time. When he finally managed to quiet, he rose back to his feet, using his shirtsleeve to wipe clean the dampness, the snot. His legs felt shaky, his chest strangely hollow, but he could sense that he was stronger for the purging, and calmer, too. Still grief-stricken—how could he not be?—still guilt-ridden and bereft, but steadier nonetheless.

He started down the hill again.

Above him, to the west, clouds were continuing to build, darkening ominously. A storm was coming—a big one, it appeared. Jeff guessed they had another hour, maybe two, before it reached them. They'd have to huddle together in the tent, he supposed, and it made him anxious, the thought of all four of them in that confined space, time stretching slowly out. There was also the question of Pablo. They couldn't just leave him in the rain, could they? Jeff searched vainly for an answer to this dilemma; he imagined the backboard dragged inside with them, the wind whipping at the nylon walls, water dripping from the fabric above, while that terrible stench rose off the Greek's body, and he realized immediately that it wasn't possible. Yet no other solution came. *Perhaps it won't rain,* he thought, knowing even as he did so that he was acting like a child, no better than the rest of them, passively hoping that whatever he found too horrible to contemplate might simply go away if he could only avert his eyes for a sufficient stretch of time.

Mathias was sitting cross-legged at the bottom of the hill, facing the tree line. He didn't hear Jeff approach, or, hearing him, didn't bother to turn. Jeff sat beside him, held out the halved banana. "Lunch," he said.

Mathias took the fruit without a word. Jeff watched him begin to eat. It was Friday; Mathias and Henrich were supposed to have flown back to Germany today. Jeff and the others would've given them their E-mail addresses, their phone numbers; they would've made vague but heartfelt promises to visit. There would've been hugs in the lobby; Amy would've taken their picture. Then the four of them would've stood together at the big window, waving, as the van pulled away, bearing the two brothers toward the airport.

Jeff wiped his face on his sleeve again, worried that there might be some residue of his weeping still visible there, tear tracks down his dirt-smeared cheeks. It seemed clear that Mathias hadn't heard the vine, and Jeff was surprised by the degree of relief he felt in this. He didn't want the German to know, he realized, was frightened of his judgment.

She called me. She called my name.

The Mayans were stringing up a plastic tarp just inside the tree line— to provide some shelter from the coming storm, Jeff assumed. There were four of them working at it—three men and a woman. Two other men sat near the smoldering campfire, facing Jeff and Mathias, their bows in their laps. One of them kept blowing his nose in a dirty-looking bandanna, then holding the cloth up to examine whatever he'd expelled. Jeff leaned forward, peered left and right along the corridor of cleared ground, but he could see no sign of their leader, the bald man with the pistol on his belt. They were probably working in shifts, he supposed, some of them guarding the hill, while the others remained back at the village, tending to their fields.

"You'd think they'd just kill us," he said.

Mathias paused in his eating, turned to look at him.

"It takes so much effort, sitting here like this. Why not just slaughter us from the start and be done with it?"

"Maybe they feel it would be a sin," Mathias said.

"But they're killing us by keeping us here, aren't they? And if we tried to leave, they wouldn't hesitate to shoot us."

"That's self-defense, though, isn't it? From their perspective? Not murder."

Murder, Jeff thought. Was that what was happening here? Had Amy been murdered? And if so, by whom? The Mayans? The vine? Himself? "How long do you think it's been going on?" he asked.

"It?"

Jeff waved about them, at the hillside, the cleared ground. "The vine. Where do you think it came from?"

Mathias started in on the banana's skin, frowning slightly, thinking. Jeff waited while he chewed. There was a trio of large black birds shifting about in the trees above the Mayans' tarp. Crows, Jeff guessed. Carrion birds, drawn by the smell of Pablo or Amy, but too wise to venture any nearer. Mathias swallowed, wiped his mouth with his hand. "The mine, I guess," he said. "Don't you think? Someone must've dug it up."

"But how did they contain it? How did they have time to seal off the hill? Because they would've had to hack down all this jungle, plow the dirt with salt. Think how long that must've taken." He shook his head— it didn't seem possible.

"Maybe you're wrong about them," Mathias said. "Maybe it isn't about quarantining the vine. Maybe they know how to kill it but choose not to."

"Because?"

"Maybe it would just keep coming back. And this is a way of holding it at bay, confining it. A sort of truce they've stumbled upon."

"But if it's not about quarantining it, why won't they let us leave?"

"Maybe it's just a taboo they have among themselves, passed down through the generations, a way of ensuring that the vine never escapes its bounds. If you step into it, you can't come back. And then, when outsiders started to arrive, they simply applied the taboo to them, too." He thought about this for a moment, staring off toward the Mayans. "Or it could even be religious, right? They see the hill as sacred. And once you step on it, you can't leave. Maybe we're some sort of sacrifice."

"But if—"

"This is just us guessing, Jeff," Mathias said, sounding fatigued, a little impatient. "Just talk. It's not worth arguing about."

They sat together for a stretch, watching the crows flap from branch to branch. The wind was picking up, the storm almost upon them. The Mayans were moving their belongings back into the tree line, beneath the shelter of the tarp. Mathias was right, of course. Theorizing was pointless. The vine was here, and so were they, while the Mayans were over there. And beyond the Mayans, far out of reach, lay the rest of the world. That was all that mattered.

"What about the archaeologists?" Jeff asked.

"What about them?"

"All those people. Why hasn't someone come searching for them?"

"Maybe it's still too early. We don't know how long they've been missing. If they were supposed to be here for the summer, say, would anyone even be worried yet?"

"But you think someone will come? Eventually, if we can just hold out long enough?"

Mathias shrugged. "How many of those mounds do you guess there are? Thirty? Forty? Too many people have died here for us all simply to vanish. Sooner or later, someone's bound to find this place. I don't know when. But sooner or later."

"And you think we can last that long?"

Mathias wiped his hands on his jeans, stared down at them. His palms were burned a deep red from the vine's sap; his fingertips were cracked and bleeding. He shook his head. "Not without food."

Reflexively, Jeff began to catalog their remaining rations. The pretzels, the nuts. The two protein bars, the raisins, the handful of saltines. A can of Coke, two bottles of iced tea. All of it divided among four people—five, if Pablo ever revived enough to eat—and meant to last for . . . how long? Six weeks?

One of the crows dropped into the clearing, began to edge its way hesitantly toward the two men sitting by the campfire. The man with the bandanna flapped it at the bird, and the crow flew back up into the trees, cawing. Jeff stared after it.

"Maybe we could spear one of those birds," he said. "We could take a tent pole, tape the knife to it, then use some of the rope from the shaft, tie it to the bottom of the pole, like a harpoon. That way, we could throw it into the trees, then drag it back to us. All we'd have to do is figure out a way to barb the knife, so that—"

"They won't let us get close enough."

It was true, of course; Jeff could see this immediately, but he felt a brief flicker of anger nonetheless, as if Mathias were purposely thwarting him. "What if we tried to clear the hill? Just started chopping at the vine. Pulling it up. If we all—"

"There's so much of it, Jeff. And it grows so fast. How could we—"

"I'm just trying to find a way through this," Jeff said. He could hear how peevish he sounded, and he disliked himself for it.

Mathias didn't seem to notice, though. "Maybe there isn't a way," he said. "Maybe all we can do is wait and hope and endure for as long as we're able. The food will run out. Our bodies will fail. And the vine will do whatever it's going to do."

Jeff sat for a moment, examining Mathias's face. Like the rest of them, he looked shockingly depleted. The skin on his nose and forehead was beginning to peel; there was a gummy paste clinging to the corners of his mouth. His eyes were shadowed. But within this deterioration there nonetheless appeared to be some remaining reservoir of strength, which no one else, including Jeff, seemed to possess. He looked calmer than the rest of them, oddly composed, and it suddenly struck Jeff how little he actually knew about the German. He'd grown up in Munich; he'd gotten his tattoo during a brief service in the army; he was studying to become an engineer. And that was all. Mathias was generally so silent, so retiring; it was easy to convince yourself that you knew what he was thinking. But now, talking with him at such length for the first time, Jeff felt as if the German were changing moment by moment before his eyes—revealing himself—and he was proving to be far more forceful than Jeff ever would've guessed: steadier, more mature. Jeff felt small beside him, vaguely childish.

"You have this phrase in English, don't you? A chicken whose head has been chopped off?" Mathias used two fingers to mime running about in circles.

Jeff nodded.

"We're all becoming weaker, and that's only going to get worse. So don't waste yourself on unessentials. Don't walk when you can sit. And don't sit when you can lie down. Understand?"

The Mayan boy had reappeared while they were talking, the tiny one. He was sitting beside the campfire now, practicing his juggling. The Mayan men were laughing at his efforts, offering what seemed to be advice and commentary.

Mathias nodded toward them. "What did your guidebook say about these people?"

Jeff pictured the glossy pages; he could almost smell them, feel their cool, clean smoothness. The book had been full of the Mayans' past—their pyramids and highways and astrological calendars—but seemingly indifferent to their present. "Not much," he said. "It had a myth of theirs, a creation myth. That's all I remember."

"Of the world?"

Jeff shook his head. "Of people."

"Tell me."

Jeff spent a few seconds thinking back, pulling the story into order. "There were some false starts. The gods tried to use mud first, and the people they fashioned out of it talked but made no sense—they couldn't turn their heads, and they dissolved in the rain. So the gods tried to use wood. But the wooden people were bad—their minds were empty; they ignored the gods. So the whole world attacked them. The stones from their hearths shot out at their faces, their cooking pots beat them, and their knives stabbed them. Some of the wooden people fled off to the trees and became monkeys, but the others were all killed."

"And then?"

"The gods used corn—white corn and yellow corn. And water. And they made four men out of this who were perfect. Too perfect, actually, because the gods became frightened. They were worried that these creatures knew too much, that they'd have no need for gods, so they blew on them and clouded their minds. And these things of corn and water and blurred thoughts—they were the first men."

There was a roll of thunder, sounding surprisingly close. Jeff and Mathias both glanced skyward. The clouds were about to obscure the sun; any moment now it would happen. "We didn't see any monkeys," Mathias said. "Coming here through the jungle." This seemed to sadden him. "I would've liked that, wouldn't you? To have seen some monkeys?"

There was such an air of resignation to this statement, of looking back at something now forever unattainable, that it made Jeff nervous. He spoke without thinking, startling himself. "I don't want to die here."

Mathias gave him half a smile. "I don't want to die anywhere."

One of the Mayan men began to applaud by the campfire. The boy was juggling, the rocks arcing fluidly above his head, a look of amazement on his face, as if he weren't quite certain how he was accomplishing this feat. When he finally dropped one of the stones, the men cheered, slapping him on the back. The boy grinned, showing his teeth.

"But I guess I will, even so, won't I?" Mathias said.

There was a question in Jeff's head, a single word—*Here?*—but he didn't speak it. He was afraid of what Mathias might answer, he knew, frightened of the German's potential indifference to the possibility, his dismissive shrug. Pablo would go first, Jeff supposed. And then Eric. Stacy would likely be next, though maybe not; these things were probably hard to guess. But in the end, if Mathias was right, they'd all be reduced to vine-covered mounds. Jeff tried to imagine what would be left of himself—the zipper and rivets on his jeans, the rubber soles of his tennis shoes, his watch. And this shirt he'd pilfered from the backpacks, too, this fake khaki that he assumed must be some sort of polyester—it would be left draped across his empty rib cage. For some reason, this last image was the most unsettling detail of all, the idea of dying here in a stranger's clothes, so that when someone finally discovered them—and Mathias said it would have to happen, sooner or later—they'd assume the shirt had belonged to him.

"Are you a Christian?" he asked.

Mathias appeared amused by the question. He offered him that same half smile. "I was baptized one."

"But do you believe?"

The German shook his head, without hesitation.

"So what does dying mean to you?"

"Nothing. The end." Mathias cocked his head, looked at Jeff. "And you?"

"I don't know," Jeff said. "It sounds stupid, but I've never really thought about it. Not in a real way." It was true. Jeff had been raised an Episcopalian, yet in an absentminded manner; it had simply been one more duty of his childhood, no different than mowing the lawn, or taking piano lessons. Safely off at college, he'd stopped going to services. He was young, healthy, sheltered; death had held no sway over his thoughts.

Mathias gave a soft laugh, shook his head. "Poor Jeff."

"What?"

"Always so desperate to be prepared." He reached out, gave Jeff's knee a pat. "It will be whatever it is, no? Nothing, something—our believing one thing or another will matter not at all in the end."

Saying this, Mathias rose to his feet, stretching his arms over his head. He was getting ready to leave, Jeff could tell, and he felt a thrum of panic at the prospect. He couldn't have said why exactly, but he was afraid of being alone here. It was a premonition, of course, though Jeff never would've believed in the possibility. For some reason, what surfaced in his head was the memory of pulling the vine free from Amy's mouth, the slimy dampness of it, the smell of bile and tequila, the way the tendrils had clung to her face, resisting him, twisting and coiling as he tore them away. He shivered.

"What sort of place do you live in?" he asked.

Mathias stared down at him, not understanding.

"In Germany," Jeff said. "A house?

Mathias shook his head. "A flat."

"What's it like?"

"Nothing special. It's tiny. A bedroom, a sitting room, a kitchen—on the second floor, overlooking the street. There's a bakery downstairs. In the summer, the ovens make everything too hot."

"Can you smell the bread?"

"Of course. I wake to it every morning." It seemed like that might be all he was going to say, but then he continued. "I have a cat. His name is Katschen; it means kitten. The baker's daughter is watching him while I'm away. Feeding him, cleaning out his box. And watering my plants. I have a big window in my bedroom—how do you say it in English? A bay window?"

Jeff nodded.

"It's full of plants. Which is funny, I suppose. Every night, I went to sleep in a room full of plants. I found them calming." He laughed at this; so did Jeff. And then the clouds swept across the sun. Instantly, the light changed, became somber, autumnal. The wind gusted, and they both reached up, pressing their hats to their heads. When it passed, Mathias said, "I guess I'll go now."

Jeff nodded, and that was it; there was nothing more to say. He watched Mathias walk off up the trail.

There was the smell of cooking in the air. At first, Jeff thought it must be the vine again, fashioning some new torment for him. But when he turned back toward the clearing, he saw that the Mayan woman had set the big iron pot on its tripod over the fire; she was stirring something within it. Goat, Jeff thought, sniffing at the air. They were eating earlier than on the previous evenings, perhaps in the hope of finishing their meal before the storm's arrival.

Beneath the aroma of the food and campfire, Jeff could smell his own body. Stale sweat, with something worse lurking within it, some hint of Pablo's stench clinging to him, his urine and shit, his rotting flesh. Jeff thought about that bar of soap in the clearing outside the tent, readied for the rain's arrival. He tried to imagine what it would feel like to lather and scrub and rinse, but he couldn't bring himself to believe that it would have any impact, couldn't imagine that he would ever be cleansed of this foulness. Because it didn't feel merely like a physical sensation. No, the corruption seemed to run far deeper, as if what he reeked of was not simply sweat and urine and shit but also failure. He'd actually thought that he could keep them alive here; he'd believed that he was smarter and more disciplined than the others, and that these traits alone might save them. He was a fool, though; he could see that now. He'd been a fool to cut off Pablo's legs. All he'd managed to do was prolong the Greek's suffering. And he'd been a fool—worse than a fool, so much worse—to sit there pouting while, fifteen feet away from him, Amy had choked to death. Even if, through some miracle, he managed to leave this place alive, he couldn't see how he'd ever be able to survive that memory.

Time was passing. The Mayans finished their meal; the woman used a handful of leaves to wipe clean the pot. The men sat with their bows in their laps, watching Jeff. The boy had given up on his juggling; he'd retreated into the tree line, was lying down beneath the tarp. The crows continued to flap restlessly from branch to branch, cawing at one another. The sky grew darker and darker; the trees began to sway in the wind. Every time it gusted, the plastic tarp made a sharp snapping sound, like a rifle shot.

And then, finally, just as the day was edging its way into an early dusk, the rain arrived.

Stacy was in the tent with Eric.

She'd lost herself for a stretch, out there in the clearing, standing over that sleeping bag, while the vine writhed about at her feet, laughing. She'd started to cry, clutching Eric, and the tears had just kept coming. Long after Jeff had departed for the bottom of the hill, after the vine had fallen silent, even after Mathias had reappeared, she'd continued to sob. It had frightened her; she'd started to wonder if she'd ever be able to stop. But Eric kept hugging her, stroking her, saying, "Shh . . . shh," and eventually, through fatigue, if nothing else, she'd felt herself begin to quiet.

"I have to lie down," she'd whispered.

That was how they'd ended up inside the tent again. Eric had unzipped the flap for her, followed her through it. When she'd collapsed onto the remaining sleeping bag, he had, too, snuggling up behind her. After the tears, there came a heaviness, a sense of not being able to go on. *This, too, will pass,* Stacy told herself, and tried to believe it. She remembered sitting at the bottom of the hill that morning, all alone, how interminable those three hours had felt, how impossible to survive. And yet she'd managed: She'd sat there in the sun, struggling not to think of Amy—struggling and failing—and one moment had led to the next, until suddenly she'd turned and found Mathias standing behind her, telling her it was time, that she was done, that she could hike back up the hill.

Her throat ached from crying; her eyes felt swollen. She was so tired, so desperately tired, yet the idea of sleep filled her with fear. She could feel Eric's breath against the back of her neck. He was hugging her, and at first it had seemed nice—soothing, quieting—but now, without warning, it began to shift, began to feel as if he were clutching her a little too tightly, making her conscious of her heart, still beating so quickly in her chest.

She tried to shift away, only to have him pull her closer. "I'm so cold," he said. "Are you cold?"

Stacy shook her head. His body didn't feel cold to her; it felt hot, in fact, almost feverish. She was sweating where they touched.

"And tired," he said. "So fucking tired."

Stacy had returned from the bottom of the hill and found him lying in the clearing, on his back, his mouth hanging open: asleep. Jeff had been sewing his pouch; he'd called out to her as she'd emerged from the trail, told her to get herself some water. Even then, Eric hadn't stirred. He must've napped for two hours, she guessed, maybe three, yet his fatigue still hadn't left him. She could hear it in his voice, how close he was to sleep, and for some reason this, too, made her want to pull away. She shifted again, more forcefully, and he let her go, his arms falling limply off her. She sat up, turning to stare at him.

"Will you watch me?" he asked.

"Watch you?"

"Sleep," he said. "Just for a bit?"

Stacy nodded. She could see the wounds on his leg, the ugly ridges of Jeff's stitching, shiny with Neosporin. His skin was smeared with blood. He was cold and tired, and he had no obvious cause to be either of these things. Stacy consciously chose not to pursue this observation, not to follow it to some conclusion. She closed her eyes, thinking, *This, too, will pass.*

His touch startled her, making her jump. He'd reached out, taken her hand, was lying there, smiling sleepily up at her. Stacy didn't retreat, but there was effort in this; she could feel herself wanting to flee from him, from the heat his flesh was giving off, the damp slickness of his grip. *It's inside him:* that was what she was thinking. She attempted a smile, which she managed, but just barely. It didn't matter, because Eric's eyes were already drifting shut.

Stacy waited till she was certain he'd fallen asleep, then slipped free of his grasp, edging backward, leaving his hand lying open on the tent's floor, palm up, slightly cupped, like a beggar's. She imagined dropping a coin into it, late at night on some dark city street; she pictured herself hurrying off, never to see him again.

This, too, will pass.

Mathias was out in the clearing, sitting beside Pablo. Stacy could hear the Greek's breathing, even above the wind, which had begun to rise, gradually but implacably, buffeting the nylon walls. It had grown dim inside the tent, almost dark. Eric was a snorer, and he was starting up now. Stacy used to imitate the sound for Amy, honking and snorting, the two of them giggling over it late at night in their dorm room, sharing secrets. The pain of this memory felt startlingly physical: a throbbing sort of ache, high up in her chest. She touched the spot, massaged it, willing herself not to cry.

This, too.

Somehow, she sensed the rain's approach. *Here it comes,* she thought, and she was right: an instant later, the storm arrived. The water fell in sheets, windblown, as if a giant wet hand were rhythmically slapping at the tent.

Stacy leaned forward, prodded Eric's shoulder. "Eric," she said.

His eyes opened—he peered up at her—but somehow it didn't seem as if he were awake.

"It's raining," she said.

"Raining?"

Stacy could see him touching his wounds with his hands, one after another, as if to check if they were still there. She nodded. "I have to help Mathias. All right?"

He just stared at her. His face looked haggard, strikingly pale. She thought of all the blood he'd lost in the last forty-eight hours, thought of Jeff pulling those tendrils from his body. She shuddered; she couldn't help it.

"Will you be okay?" she asked.

Eric nodded, reaching to drag the sleeping bag over his body. And that was enough for Stacy; she darted off, ducking past the flap, into the rain.

Within seconds, she was drenched. Mathias was standing in the center of the clearing, letting the Frisbee fill, pouring its contents into the plastic jug. His clothes were clinging to him, his hat drooping shape-lessly on his head. He held out the Frisbee, the plastic jug, gesturing for her to take them; when she did, he moved quickly toward Pablo, who was lying motionless on the backboard, eyes shut, the rain blowing in on him. Stacy waited for the Frisbee to fill, then poured the water into the jug, repeating this process again and again while Mathias struggled with the lean-to, trying to adjust it so that it might give the Greek more shelter. It seemed like a hopeless task; the wind kept gusting, knocking the rain almost horizontally through the air. Short of bringing Pablo into the tent, there was no way to protect him.

Stacy capped the jug. The pouch was filling; it seemed like it was working. The rain fell and fell and fell, turning the clearing into mud. Stacy could feel it deepening, her sandals slowly sinking. She noticed the bar of soap, which was lying half-immersed beside the pouch, and picked it up, began to scrub at her hands and face. Then she tilted her head back, let the rain rinse her clean. It wasn't enough, though. She wanted more, and without really thinking, she stripped off her shirt, her pants, even her underwear. She stood in the center of the clearing, naked, lath-ering her breasts, her belly, her groin, her hair, washing the dirt—the sweat and grease and stink—from her body.

Mathias was bent low over the lean-to, taping the lengths of nylon more tightly to the aluminum poles, the wind tugging at him. He turned, as if to ask for Stacy's help, but then just stared, his gaze passing over her nakedness, moving slowly upward. He couldn't seem to meet her eyes; he flinched from them, turned back to the lean-to without a word.

The light, already faint to begin with, was rapidly draining from the clearing. Stacy had long ago lost track of time, so it was difficult to de-cide if this were some effect of the storm, growing ever darker above them, or if, behind the mass of clouds, the sun had finally begun to set, bringing the day to its abrupt close. There was thunder—growling, low and guttural—and the rain was falling forcefully enough to sting her skin. It kept getting colder and colder, too. She had to clench her jaw to keep her teeth from chattering; she was shivering, the chill sinking into her bones.

Bones.

Stacy turned toward the sleeping bag, the knot of vines spilling from its mouth, the glints of white shining wetly in the fading light. She had the odd sense that someone was watching her, felt suddenly exposed in her nakedness, and hugged herself, hiding her breasts beneath her folded arms. She glanced toward Mathias—who remained with his back to her, absorbed in his struggle with the lean-to—then toward the trail, thinking Jeff might've returned from the bottom of the hill. But there was no one there, and no sign of Eric, either, peering out at her from the tent. The sensation remained, however, growing stronger, uncomfortably so. It was only when she turned to stare off across the hillside, at the rain falling steadily upon all those green leaves, making them duck and nod, that she realized what the source was.

It was the vine: she could feel it watching.

She sprinted for the tent, leaving her wet clothes abandoned in a muddy heap behind her.

It was even darker inside than outside; Stacy could barely make Eric out, had to strain to discern him lying on the tent's floor, the sleeping bag pulled tightly around his body. She thought his eyes were open, thought she could see him peering toward her as she entered, but wasn't certain.

"I washed myself," she said. "You should, too."

Eric didn't respond, didn't speak or move.

She stepped toward him, bending. "Eric?"

He grunted, shifted slightly.

"You okay?" she asked.

Again, he grunted.

Stacy hesitated, watching him through the dimness. The wind kept shaking the tent's walls. The nylon above her was leaking in a handful of different places, water *plop-plop-plopping* to the floor, forming slowly expanding puddles. She couldn't seem to stop shivering. "I have to get dressed," she said.

Eric just lay there.

Stacy stepped to the rear of the tent, crouched over the backpacks, dug through them until she found a skirt, a yellow blouse. She quickly rubbed herself dry with a T-shirt, then pulled the skirt and blouse on, naked underneath—she couldn't bear the thought of wearing a stranger's panties. The skirt was short, riding up her thighs; the blouse was tight. Whomever they'd once belonged to must've been even tinier than she was.

Stacy was feeling somewhat better—not good, exactly, but not quite as wretched as before. The humming in her head had nearly vanished. Her hunger, too, seemed to have diminished; she felt empty, husklike, but strangely serene within this. She was still shivering, and she thought briefly of climbing in under the sleeping bag with Eric, cuddling up against him, that heat radiating off his flesh. But then she remembered Mathias, out in the clearing, fighting to create some small measure of shelter for Pablo, and she crept back to the flap, peered into the gathering dark. The light was almost completely gone now. Mathias, only ten feet away from her, was little more than a shadow. He was sitting beside Pablo, in the mud, hunched beneath her sunshade. He'd managed to lower the lean-to, but it was hard to tell how much good it was doing the Greek.

"Mathias?" Stacy called.

He stared toward her through the downpour.

"Where's Jeff?" she asked.

Mathias glanced over his shoulder, as if he expected to find Jeff lurking somewhere in the clearing. Then he turned back to her, shook his head. He said something, but it was hard to decipher above the sound of the rain.

Stacy cupped her hands, called out, "Shouldn't he be back?"

Mathias rose to his feet, stepped toward her. The sunshade seemed more symbolic than practical: it wasn't really doing anything to block the rain. "What?" he said.

"Shouldn't Jeff be back?"

Mathias shifted his weight from foot to foot, thinking, the tops of his tennis shoes vanishing into the puddled earth, then reappearing, then vanishing again. "I guess I should go down and see."

"See?"

"What's keeping him."

Stacy's head started to hum again. She didn't want to be left alone up here with Eric and Pablo. She tried to think of something to say, a way to keep Mathias near the tent, but nothing came.

"Can you watch Pablo?" he asked.

She hesitated. She was clean and dry, and the idea of relinquishing these two tenuous comforts filled her with dread. "Maybe if we wait, he'll—"

"It's just going to get darker. I won't be able to see if I wait much longer." He held the sunshade toward her, and she reached to take it, extending her arm into the rain, goose bumps forming on her skin. Mathias dragged his hat off his head, wrung it out, put it back on. "I'll try to be quick," he said. "All right?"

Stacy nodded. She gathered her courage, ducked out though the tent flap. It was like stepping into a waterfall. She moved toward Pablo's lean-too, crouched beside it, trying not to see the Greek—his gaunt, mud-spattered face, his wet hair—too frightened to confront his misery, his suffering, knowing that there was nothing she could do to ease it. She held the sunshade above her head, pointlessly—it was just something for the wind to yank at. Mathias remained there for another moment, watching her, the rain pouring down upon them. Then he turned and strode off across the clearing, vanishing into the darkness.

Eric had curled into a ball, burrowing beneath the sleeping bag, trying to find some warmth. The rain was falling, and Stacy and Mathias were outside in it. The wind kept gusting, shaking the tent. Eric was exhausted, but he wasn't going to let himself sleep, not without someone watching over him. He was just going to shut his eyes, only for an instant, a handful of seconds, shut his eyes and breathe, resting, not sleeping. Then Stacy was back, quite suddenly, stooping over him, asking if he was okay. She was wet, she was naked, and she was dripping on him; the roof was also dripping. And Eric thought, *I'm asleep, I'm dreaming.* But he wasn't, or only half so. He was conscious of her in the tent with him, could hear her rummaging through the backpacks, patting herself dry, pulling on new clothes. He felt with his hand, searching out his wounds, worried that the vine might've attacked him while he'd lain there drowsing, but he discovered no sign of this. He ached—his entire body seemed to be throbbing. Even his fingertips felt bruised, the soles of his feet, his kneecaps—everything.

He heard voices and lifted his head. Stacy was standing by the tent flap, silhouetted there, talking to Mathias. Eric's eyes drifted shut once more, only for a moment it seemed, yet when he reopened them, he was alone. He checked his wounds again, thought about sitting up, but he couldn't find the strength for it. The rain was loud enough to make it hard for him to think; it sounded like applause.

He could feel himself sinking back into sleep, and he fought against it, struggling to surface. He was teaching, his first morning at his new job, but every time he tried to speak, the boys would start to clap, drowning out his voice. It was a game—somehow he understood this—yet he wasn't certain of the rules, knew only that he was losing, and that if this kept up, he'd be fired before the day was through. Oddly, he felt comforted by the prospect. Part of himself was still awake—he knew he was dreaming. And from this still-sentient sliver of consciousness, Eric could even manage to analyze the dream. He didn't want to be a teacher—this was what it was saying, that he hadn't ever wanted to be one, but could only admit it to himself now, trapped here, never to return. *What, then?* he thought, and the answer came in a way that made him understand this, too, was part of the dream—this self-appraisal—because what he realized he'd always wanted to be was a bartender in an old-fashioned saloon, not a real saloon, either, but a movie saloon, from a black-and-white Western, with swinging doors, a drunken poker game in the corner, gunslingers dueling in the street. He'd fill mugs with beer, slide them down the countertop. He'd have an Irish accent, would be John Wayne's best friend, Gary Cooper's—

"It's making it up. Okay? Eric? You know that, don't you?"

The tent was dark. Stacy was crouched above him again—wet, dripping—prodding at his arm. She seemed frightened, jittery with it. She kept glancing over her shoulder, toward the flap.

"It's not real," she said. "It didn't happen."

He had no idea what she was talking about, was still half-immersed in his dream, the boys clapping, the creak of the saloon doors swinging open. "What didn't?" he asked.

And then he heard, faintly, beneath the rain's downpour the words *Kiss me, Mathias. Will you kiss me?* It was a woman's voice, coming from the clearing. *It's okay. I want to.* It sounded like Stacy, but the voice was blurred slightly; it was her and not her all at once.

Stacy seemed to sense what he was thinking. "It's trying to pretend it's me. That I said that. But I didn't."

Hold me. Just hold me.

And then, what sounded like Mathias's voice: *We shouldn't. What if he—*

Shh. No one will hear.

"It's not me," Stacy said. "I swear. Nothing happened."

Eric pushed himself up off the floor, sat cross-legged, the sleeping bag wrapped around his shoulders. From outside, in the rainswept dark, came the sound of panting, softly at first, but then growing in volume.

There was Mathias's voice again, almost a sigh: *God, that feels good.*

The panting became moaning.

So good.

Harder, Stacy's voice whispered.

The moans built slowly, inexorably, toward a mutual climax, with something like a scream coming from Stacy. Then there was silence, just the rain splattering down, and the start-stop rasp of Pablo's breathing. Eric watched Stacy through the darkness. She was wearing someone else's clothes. They were a size too small for her, clinging wetly to her body.

It shouldn't matter, of course. Maybe it had happened, and maybe it hadn't—either way, he'd be a fool to worry over it at a time like this. Eric could see the logic in such an argument, and he spent a few moments struggling to find a way to achieve the proper distance for so rational an approach. He toyed with the idea of laughing. Would that be the right strategy? Should he shake his head, chuckle? Or should he hug her? But she was so wet, and dressed in those strange clothes, like a whore, actually. The thought came unbidden. Eric even tried to suppress it, but it wouldn't let him be, not with her nipples standing so erect beneath her blouse, not with that skirt riding up her thighs, not with—

"You know it's not real," she said. "Don't you?"

Just laugh, he thought. *It's so easy.* But then, without really meaning to, he started talking, his voice spilling out of him, propelling him down a different path altogether. "It doesn't make things up."

Stacy was silent, watching him. She folded her arms across her chest. "Eric—"

"It mimics things. Things it's heard. It doesn't create them."

"Then it's heard someone having sex at some point, and it mixed our voices in."

"So that's your voice? You said those things?"

"Of course not."

"But you said it mixed your voices in."

"I mean it took our voices, things we've said, and it put them together to say new things. You know? It took one word from one conversation, and another word from—"

"When did you say 'harder'? Or 'kiss me'?"

"I don't know. Maybe it—"

"Come on, Stacy. Tell me the truth."

"This is stupid, Eric." He could sense how frustrated she was becoming, could feel her working to control it.

"I just want the truth," he said.

"I've told you the truth. It's not real. It's—"

"I promise I won't be angry."

But he was already angry, of course; even he could hear it in his voice.

This wasn't the first time Eric had asked Stacy to confess to some infidelity, and he felt the weight of all those other conversations now, pressing down upon him, prodding him forward. There was a pattern these confrontations inevitably followed, a script for them to honor: he'd badger her, reason with her, methodically eliminate her evasions and diversions, slowly cornering her until the only choice remaining was honesty. She'd start to cry; she'd beg his forgiveness, promise never to betray him again. And somehow, despite himself, Eric would always find a way to believe her. The idea of having to pursue this course now, of having to plod through each of its many steps, filled him with exhaustion. He wanted to be at the end already. He wanted her weeping, begging, promising, and it enraged him that even here, even in their current extremity, she was going to make him work for it.

"Look at me," Stacy said. "Do you really think I'd have any interest in fucking *anyone* at this point. I can't even—"

"Would you fuck him at another point?"

"Eric—"

"Would you have fucked him in Cancún?"

She gave a loud sigh, as if the question were too demeaning to answer. And it was, too. On some level, Eric understood this. *Calm thoughts,* he said to himself. *A calm voice.* He was fighting hard to summon them, but they wouldn't come.

"*Did* you fuck him in Cancún?" he asked.

Before Stacy could answer, her voice started up again: *Hold me. Just hold me.*

We shouldn't. What if he—

Shh. No one will hear.

Then, once more, the panting began, gradually rising in volume. Eric and Stacy were both silent, listening. What else could they do?

God, that feels good.

The panting deepened into moans. Eric was concentrating on the voices, which maintained that same slightly smudged quality. Sometimes it seemed as though they definitely belonged to Stacy and Mathias; other times, he could almost bring himself to believe her, that they weren't real, that it hadn't happened.

So good, he heard, and he thought, *No, of course not, it can't be him.*

Harder, he heard—that urgent whisper, so full of hunger—and he thought, *Yes, definitely, it has to be her.*

The climax came, finally, and then there was just the rain again, and

Pablo's breathing, and the wet flapping of the tent each time the wind gusted. Stacy edged toward him. She reached and rested her hand on his knee, squeezing it through the sleeping bag. "It's trying to drive us apart, sweetie. It wants us to fight."

"Say 'Hold me. Just hold me.'"

Stacy lifted her hand from his knee, stared at him. "What?"

"I want to hear you. I'll be able to tell if I hear you say it."

"Tell what?'

"If it's your voice."

"You're being an asshole, Eric."

"Say 'No one will hear.'"

She shook her head. "I'm not gonna do this."

"Or 'harder.' Whisper 'harder.'"

Stacy stood up. "I have to check on Pablo."

"He's fine. Can't you hear him?" And it was true: the sound of Pablo's breathing seemed to fill the tent.

Stacy had her hands on her hips. He couldn't make out her face in the darkness, but he could tell somehow that she was frowning at him. "Why are you doing this? Huh? We have so much else to deal with here, and you're acting like—"

"Amy was right. You're a slut."

This seemed to hit home; it slapped her into momentary silence. Then, very quietly, she whispered, "What the fuck, Eric? How can you say that?"

He heard a trembling in her voice, and it nearly gave him pause. But then he was speaking again; he couldn't stop himself. "When did you do it? Tonight?"

It was hard to tell, but it seemed like she might be crying.

"You were naked when you came in," he said. "I saw you naked."

She was wiping her face with her hand. The rain increased suddenly, jumping in volume; it felt as if the tent might collapse beneath it. Instinctively, they both ducked. It lasted only a few seconds, though, and in its passing, the world seemed oddly quiet.

"Were there other times, too?"

Stacy made a sniffling sound. "Please stop."

Eric hesitated. For some reason, that peculiar sense of heightened silence was beginning to unsettle him—it seemed ominous, threatening. He glanced out toward the clearing, as if expecting an intruder there. "Tell me how many times, Stacy."

She shook her head again. "You're being a bastard."

"I'm not angry. Do I seem angry?"

"I hate you sometimes. I really do."

"I just want the truth. I just want—"

Stacy started to scream, making him jump. Her fists were clenched; she was yanking at her hair. She yelled, "Shut up! Can you do that? Can you please just shut the fuck up?" She stepped forward, as if to strike him—her right arm raised over her head—but then stopped in mid-stride and turned toward the tent flap.

Eric followed her gaze. Mathias was standing there, stooping, one foot in the tent, one foot still outside. He was completely drenched. It was hard to discern much more than that in the darkness, but Eric had a sense of the German's confusion. He seemed as if he were about to retreat back into the night, deferring to their privacy.

"Maybe you can tell me," Eric said to him. "Did you fuck her?"

Mathias was silent, too startled by the question to offer an answer.

"The vine was making sounds," Stacy explained. "Like we'd had sex."

Eric was leaning forward, peering at Mathias's face, trying to read his expression. "Say 'God, that feels good.'"

Mathias still had one foot out in the rain. He shook his head. "I don't understand."

"Or 'We shouldn't. What if he—' Can you say that?"

"Stop it, Eric," Stacy said.

Eric spun on her. "I'm not talking to you. All right?" He turned back toward Mathias. "Just say it. I want to hear your voice."

"Where do you think you are?" Mathias asked.

Eric couldn't think of a response to this. *Hell* was the word that came to him. *I'm in hell.* But he didn't say it.

"Why would you even care—at this point, I mean—if Stacy and I had fucked? Why would it matter? We're trapped here. We don't have any food. Henrich and Amy have both been killed. I can't find Jeff. And Pablo—"

He stopped, cocked his head, listening. They all did.

The silence, Eric thought.

Mathias vanished back out into the rain.

"Oh God," Stacy moaned, hurrying after him. "Oh please no."

Eric stood up, the sleeping bag still wrapped around his shoulders. He stepped to the flap, peered toward the lean-to. Mathias was kneeling beside the backboard; Stacy was standing behind him. The rain poured down on both of them.

"I'm so sorry," Stacy kept saying. "I'm so sorry."

Mathias rose to his feet. He didn't say anything; he didn't need to. His expression of disgust as he shoved his way past Eric into the tent was far more eloquent than any words he might've uttered.

Stacy lowered herself into a crouch, the rain spattering her with mud. She hugged her legs, began to rock back and forth. "I'm so sorry. . . . I'm so sorry. . . . I'm so sorry. . . ."

Eric could barely make out Pablo on his backboard, beyond her, just visible in the darkness. Motionless. Silent. While they'd argued in the tent, while the storm had beaten down on them from above, the vine had sent forth an emissary. A single thin tendril had wound itself around the Greek's face, covering his mouth, his nose, smothering him into death.

Even after the rain had begun to fall, Jeff had maintained his post at the bottom of the hill. If the Greeks had set out that morning, then it seemed possible the storm could've surprised them on the walk in from the road. Jeff spent some time attempting to guess how Juan and Don Quixote would react to its arrival, whether they'd turn around and try to flee back to Cobá, or duck their heads and hurry onward. He had to admit that the latter of these two options seemed least probable. Only if they were nearly there, if they'd already left the main trail and were making their way along that final, gradually uphill stretch, could he envision them persisting through this downpour.

He decided he'd give them twenty minutes.

Which was a long time, sitting out in the open, unsheltered, with that rain beating down upon him. The Mayans had retreated into the tree line, were crowded together beneath their tarp. Only one of them remained in the clearing, watching Jeff. He'd fashioned a sort of poncho for himself, using a large plastic garbage bag, from which he'd torn holes for his head and arms. Jeff could remember making a similar garment once, on a camping trip, when he and his fellow Boy Scouts had been caught unexpectedly in a two-day rainstorm. As they'd made their way home, they'd been forced to ford a river. It was the same one they'd crossed on their hike into the woods, a week earlier, but it had risen dramatically since they'd last glimpsed it. The current was fast, chest-deep, very cold. Jeff had stripped to his underwear, floundered across with a rope slung over his shoulder. He'd tied it to a tree so that the others could follow, holding on to it for support. He could remember how daring he'd believed himself to be for attempting this feat—a hero of sorts—and he felt slightly embarrassed by the recollection. It came to him now that he'd spent his entire life playing at one thing or another, always pretending that it was more than a game. But that was all it had ever been, of course.

The rain fell in a steady torrent. There was thunder but no lightning. It was nearly dark when Jeff finally checked his watch, stood up, turned to go.

The trail had grown muddy, slippery with it; climbing was hard work. Jeff kept having to stop and catch his breath. It was during one of these pauses, as he glanced back down toward the bottom of the hill, struggling to judge how far he'd come, that the idea of fleeing occurred to him once more. The light had faded enough that he could no longer see the tree line. A mist was rising from the cleared ground, further obscuring his view. The downpour had doused the Mayans' campfires; unless they were prepared to spend the night standing guard almost shoulder-to-shoulder along the jungle's margin, it seemed perfectly possible that Jeff might find a passage through them.

The rain maintained its onslaught, but for the moment Jeff was hardly conscious of it. He was famished; he was completely used up. He wanted to go back to the tent, wanted to open the tiny can of nuts they'd brought and parcel it out among them. He wanted to drink from their jug of water until his stomach began to hurt; he wanted to close his eyes and sleep. He fought against these temptations, though—and that sense of failure, too, which continued to cling to him, promising him yet another disappointment—and struggled for something like hope, a sentiment that was already beginning to feel oddly unfamiliar. He asked himself: *Why shouldn't it work?* Why shouldn't he be able to creep down the hill and find the clearing deserted, the Mayans huddling together beneath their plastic tarps, hiding from the deluge? Why shouldn't he be able to slip past them, undetected, vanishing into the jungle beyond? He could hide there till dawn, start for Cobá at first light. He could save them all.

But no—he was doing it again, wasn't he? More foolishness, more pretending. Because wouldn't the Mayans have anticipated something like this? Wouldn't there be sentries waiting for him, arrows nocked?

And then Jeff would just have to retrace his footsteps back up the hill, all the more tired and cold and hungry for the wasted effort.

Round and round he went like this, tilting first in one direction, then the other, while the rain fell upon him and the darkness continued to deepen. In the end—despite his hunger, his fatigue, his anticipatory sense of failure—it was Jeff's upbringing that finally triumphed, his New England roots asserting themselves in all their asceticism, that deep Puritan reflex always to choose the more arduous of any two fates.

He made his way slowly back down the trail to the bottom of the hill.

And it was exactly as he'd anticipated—the mist, the rain, the gathering dark—he couldn't see more than fifteen feet in any direction. If the Mayan with the makeshift poncho was still on duty in the center of the clearing, he was hidden from sight now. Which meant, of course, that Jeff, in turn, was equally invisible. All he had to do was edge to his left, twenty yards, thirty at the most; this would put him midway between the Mayans sheltering beneath their tarp here and the ones at the next encampment. And then, if he crept forward, cloaked in the darkness, the mist, the rain, he might very well manage to reach the jungle unobserved.

He turned to his left, started walking, counting his strides in his head. *One . . . two . . . three . . . four . . .* The rain had already saturated the clearing, transforming its soil into a deep, viscous mud that clung heavily to his feet. Jeff thought of his earlier attempt to flee, that first night, when he'd tried to sneak down through the vines, how the tendrils had cried out, alerting the Mayans of his approach, and he wondered why the plant was remaining so quiet now, so motionless. Surely it must've sensed what he was intending. It was possible, of course, that this silence betrayed how negligible Jeff's chances were, that the vine could perceive the Mayans standing guard even through the darkness, the mist, the rain, that it knew he'd never make it—he'd either be turned back or killed. At some remove within himself, Jeff could even grasp what this portended, could recognize that the logical course, the sensible one, would be to surrender now, to retreat up the hill to safety.

Yet he kept walking.

Thirty strides, and then he stopped. He stood there peering toward the jungle. All he could hear was the rain slapping down into the mud. The wind tugged at the mist, stirring it deceptively. Jeff kept pulling shapes from the darkness, first to his left, then his right. Every cell in his body seemed to be warning him to turn back while he still could, and it baffled him why this should be so. Here, after all, was the moment he'd been yearning for, was it not? This was escape; this was salvation. How could he possibly renounce it? He tried to gird himself, tried to imagine what it would feel like to be lying in that tent five days from now as the hunger started to take hold, his body failing beneath it, how he'd think back to this moment and remember his hesitation here—the fury he'd feel with his cowardice, the disgust.

He took a single step out into the clearing, then went still as another shape materialized from the mist, quickly vanished. This would be the way to do it, Jeff was certain—one cautious step at a time—but he knew, too, that he wasn't equal to such a path, that if he was going to venture this, he'd have to do it at a run. He was too worn-out for any other method; his nerves weren't equal to the challenge of the wiser, more wary approach. The risk, of course, was that he'd end up charging straight at one of the Mayans, stumbling directly into him. But perhaps it wouldn't matter. Perhaps, if he were moving quickly enough, he'd be past the man, vanishing once more into the darkness, before a weapon could even be raised. All he had to do was make it to the jungle and they'd never find him, not in this weather—he was certain of it.

Jeff understood that if he kept thinking, kept debating, he wouldn't do it. He either had to make the leap now, immediately, or turn back. Perhaps this alone ought to have given him pause, but he didn't let it. To turn back would be to accept yet another failure here, and Jeff couldn't bring himself to do that. He thought back to that long-ago riverbank, the rope slung across his shoulder, the aplomb with which he'd plunged into the current—the utter self-confidence—and he struggled to reclaim that feeling, or some shadow of it.

Then he took a deep breath.

And started to run.

He hadn't gone five steps before he sensed motion to his left, one of the Mayans rising to his feet, his bow before him. Even then, Jeff might've still had a chance. He could've stopped, could've turned back, smiling ruefully at the man, hands high over his head. The bow had to be raised, remember—it had to be drawn and aimed—so there ought to have been plenty of time for Jeff to demonstrate how harmless he was, how acquiescent. But it was too much to ask of him. He was in motion now, and he wasn't going to stop.

He heard the man shout.

He'll miss, Jeff thought. *He'll—*

The arrow hit him just below his chin, piercing his throat, entering on the left side, exiting on the right, passing completely through his body. Jeff fell to his knees, but he was instantly back up on his feet, thinking, *I'm okay; I'm not hurt,* while his mouth rapidly filled with blood. He managed three more steps before the next arrow struck him. This one entered his chest, a few inches beneath his armpit, burying itself almost to its fletches. Jeff felt as if he'd been hit with a hammer. His breath left him, and he could sense that he wasn't going to get it back. He fell again, harder this time. He opened his mouth, and blood poured forth from it, a great surging gush splattering down into the mud beneath him. He tried to rise, but he didn't have the strength. His legs wouldn't move; they felt cold and far away, somewhere behind him in the darkness. Everything was becoming increasingly blurry—not just his vision but his thoughts, too. It took him a moment to understand what was grabbing at him. He thought it was one of the Mayans.

But of course that wasn't it at all.

The tendrils had reached out into the clearing and were wrapping themselves around his limbs now, dragging him backward through the mud. He tried to rise once more, managed an awkward sort of push-up before the vine jerked his left arm out from under him. He fell onto the arrow still protruding from his chest, the weight of his body pushing it deeper into himself. The tendrils kept tugging him toward the hillside. The mud beneath him felt oddly warm. It was his blood, Jeff knew. He could hear the vine sucking noisily at it, siphoning it up with its leaves. There were figures looming on the far periphery of his vision, a handful of Mayans, staring down at him, bows still drawn. "Help me," he begged, his voice making a gurgling sound as it passed through the blood, which continued to fill his mouth. His words were inaudible, he knew, yet he kept struggling to speak. "Please . . . help . . . me."

That was all he could manage. Then a tendril covered his lips. Another slipped wetly across his eyes, his ears, and the world seemed to shift back a step—the Mayans peering down at him, the rain, the warmth of his blood—one step and then another, everything retreating, everything but the agony of his wounds, until finally, in the last long moment before the end, all that remained was darkness: darkness and silence and pain.

The rain continued into the night, unabated. The tent's walls became saturated with it; the dripping leaks steadily multiplied. A puddle of water soon covered the entire floor, nearly an inch deep. The three of them sat in it together, in the dark. It was impossible to sleep, of course, so Stacy and Eric passed the time talking.

Eric begged her forgiveness, and she gave it to him. They leaned against each other, embracing. Stacy slid her hand down to his groin, but he couldn't seem to get an erection, and after awhile she gave up. It was warmth she wanted anyway—figurative and literal—not sex. His skin seemed colder than hers, though, markedly so, and the longer they embraced, the more it began to feel as if he were draining the heat from her own flesh, chilling her. When he coughed suddenly, hunching forward, she used it as an excuse to pull away from him.

She tried not to think about Pablo, but she couldn't stop herself. It felt strange to sit there, knowing that the vine was stripping the flesh from his bones, that he'd be a skeleton before morning. Off and on, as the night progressed, Stacy started to weep over this—over her part in it, her failure to protect him. Eric comforted her as best he could, assuring her that it wasn't her fault, that the Greek's death had been a given from the moment he fell down the shaft, that it was a mercy for it finally to be over.

They spoke of Jeff, too, of course, pondering his absence, probing at the various possibilities it presented, returning obsessively to the prospect of his having found a way to flee. And the more they discussed it, the more obvious it began to seem to Stacy. Where else could he possibly be? He was making his way back to Cobá even now; before the sun set tomorrow, they'd be rescued. Yes. They weren't going to die here after all.

Mathias remained quiet through all of this. Stacy could sense him in the darkness, four feet away from them; she could tell he was awake. She wanted him to speak, wanted him to join in the construction of their fantasy. His silence seemed to imply doubt, and Stacy felt threatened by this, as if his skepticism might somehow have the power to alter what was happening. She needed him to believe in Jeff's flight, too, needed his help to make it true. It was absurd, she knew, childish and superstitious, but she couldn't shake the feeling, was growing slightly panicky in the face of it.

"Mathias?" she whispered. "Are you asleep?"

"No," he replied.

"What do you think? Could he have escaped?"

There was the sound of the rain falling upon the tent, the steady dripping from the nylon above them. Eric kept shifting restlessly about, creating ripples in their little puddle. Stacy wished he would stop. The seconds were ticking past, one after another, and Mathias wasn't answering.

"Mathias?"

"All I know is that he's not here," he said.

"So he might've run, then. Right? He might've—"

"Don't, Stacy."

This caught her by surprise. She peered toward him. "Don't what?"

"If you let yourself hope, and then you're wrong, think how terrible you'll feel. We can't afford that."

"But if—"

"We'll see in the morning."

"See what?"

"Whatever there is to see."

"You mean, you think he might be—"

"Shh. Just wait. It'll be light in a few more hours."

It was shortly after this that they heard Pablo's breathing start up again. There was that ragged intake of air, that whistling exhalation, then the pause before it all recommenced. Despite herself, knowing better even as she did so, Stacy sprang to her feet. Mathias had also risen; they brushed against each other as they both made their way toward the tent flap. He grabbed at her, holding her wrist, stopping her.

"It's the vine," he whispered.

"I know," she said. "But I want to make sure."

"I'll do it. You wait here."

"Why?"

"It wants us to see something, don't you think? Something it's done to him. It's hoping to upset us."

Outside, there was another rasping inhalation. It sounded exactly like Pablo; even after all she'd witnessed here, it was hard to believe that it wasn't him. But she knew Mathias was right, and knew, too, that she didn't want to glimpse whatever it was the vine had prepared for them out there beneath the lean-to. "Are you sure?" she asked.

She sensed him nod. He let go of her wrist, moved to the flap, bent to zip it open.

Almost instantly, as soon as he stooped out into the rain, the breathing stopped. Then a man's voice began to shout. He was speaking in a foreign language; it sounded like German to Stacy. *Wo ist dein Bruder? Wo ist dein Bruder?*

Stacy sat back down. She reached for Eric's hand, found it in the dark, clasped it tightly. "It's talking about his brother," she said.

"How can you tell?" Eric asked.

"Listen."

Dein Bruder ist da. Dein Bruder ist da.

Mathias reappeared, the rain running off him, audibly dripping to the tent's puddled floor. He zipped the flap shut, returned to his spot beside them.

"What happened?" Stacy asked.

He didn't answer.

"Tell me," she said.

"It's eating him. His face—all the flesh is gone."

Stacy could sense him hesitating. *There's something else,* she thought, and she waited for it.

Finally, very softly, Mathias said, "This was on his head. On his skull."

He held something up in the darkness, extended it toward her. Stacy reached out, warily took it from him. She moved her hands over it, tracing its shape. "A hat?" she asked.

"It's Jeff's, I think."

Stacy knew he was right—immediately—yet didn't want to believe him. She searched for another possibility, but nothing came. The hat was saturated with water; it felt heavy. She had to resist the temptation to throw it aside. She leaned forward, handed it back to Mathias. "How did it get there?" she asked.

"The vine must've, you know . . ."

"What?"

"It must've taken it and passed it up the hill from tendril to tendril, then set it there, and called us out to find it."

"But how did it get it? In the first place, I mean. How did it—" She stopped, the answer coming to her even as she asked the question—so obvious, actually. She didn't want to hear Mathias say the words, though, so she veered in a new direction, straining to assert a different possibility. "Maybe he dropped it. Maybe as he was running across toward the trees, he—"

The voice from the clearing interrupted her, calling out again: *Dein Bruder ist gestorben. Dein Bruder ist gestorben.*

"What's it saying?" Eric asked.

"First, it asked where Henrich is," Mathias replied. "Then it said he's here. Now it's saying he's dead."

Wo ist Jeff? Wo ist Jeff?

"And that?"

Mathias was silent.

Jeff ist da. Jeff ist da.

Stacy knew what it was saying—it was easy enough to guess—but Eric hadn't made the leap. "It's something about Jeff?" he asked.

Jeff ist gestorben. Jeff ist gestorben.

Eric squeezed her hand, tugging at it. "Why won't he tell me?"

"It's the same thing, Eric," Stacy whispered.

"The same thing?"

"It's asking where Jeff is. Then saying that he's here. Saying that he's dead."

Outside, the voice multiplied suddenly, surrounding them, spreading itself across the hilltop. It became a chorus, which steadily rose in volume, chanting: *Jeff ist gestorben. . . . Jeff ist gestorben. . . . Jeff ist gestorben. . . .*

The rain stopped just before dawn. By the time the sun began to rise, the clouds had already started to thin and part. Eric and Stacy and Mathias emerged from the tent at the first hint of light—hesitantly, stiffly—surveying the night's damage.

The vine had spread over the backboard, covering it, completely burying Pablo's remains. Half a dozen tendrils had pushed their way into the blue pouch, draining whatever water it had managed to capture during the storm. And Amy's bones had been dragged free of the sleeping bag, scattered haphazardly across the clearing. Eric watched Stacy move about with a dazed expression, stooping to collect them. She laid them in a small pile beside the tent.

Eric had developed a cough during the night, a deep-chested, hacking sort of bark. His head ached; his clothes were wet, his skin chapped from sitting in the puddle. He was hungry, exhausted, cold, and found it hard to believe that any of this would ever change.

Mathias crouched beside the backboard, started to pull the vines from Pablo's corpse. Eric was tired enough that he didn't feel quite awake; everything had once again taken on that faraway quality, both comforting and frightening. So when he idly scratched at his chest and felt the bulge there, lurking just beneath his skin, he reacted with a remarkable air of calm. "Where's the knife?" he asked.

Mathias turned to glance at him. "Why?"

Eric lifted his shirt. It looked much worse than it had felt, as if a large starfish had somehow surfaced between his rib cage and his skin. And it was moving, too, inching slowly but visibly downward, toward his stomach.

"Oh my God," Stacy said. She turned away, covering her mouth with her hand.

Mathias rose to his feet, stepped toward him. "Does it hurt?"

Eric shook his head. "It's numb. I can't feel it." He showed him, pushing at the bulge with his finger.

Mathias scanned the clearing, searching for the knife. He found it lying near the tent, half-buried in the mud. He picked it up, tried to wipe some of the dirt off its blade, rubbing it against his jeans. They were still wet, and the knife left a long brown streak across them.

"It's down there, too," Stacy said. She was pointing at his right leg, but with her gaze squeamishly averted.

Eric bent to look. And it was true: there was a snakelike lump winding its way upward from the top of his shin to his inner thigh. He touched it hesitantly; it also felt numb. The swelling coiled almost completely around his leg, starting in front, then angling up behind his knee, before stopping just short of his groin. *I should be screaming,* Eric thought, but for some reason he maintained that lofty sense of distance. Stacy was the one who appeared most upset; she couldn't seem to meet his eyes.

Eric held out his hand for the knife. "Give it to me."

Mathias didn't move. "We have to sterilize it," he said.

Eric shook his head. "No way. I'm not waiting for you to—"

"It's dirty, Eric."

"I don't care."

"You can't cut into yourself with something this—"

"Jesus Christ, Mathias. Would you fucking look at me? Do you really think it's an infection I have to worry about? Or gangrene? Either somebody comes and rescues us within the next day or two or this shit's gonna kill me. Can't you see that?"

Mathias was silent.

Eric held out his hand again. "Now give me the fucking knife."

Jeff wouldn't have done it, Eric knew. Jeff would've gone by the book, would've gotten out the soap and water, would've built the fire, heated the blade. But Jeff wasn't there any longer, and it was Mathias's decision now. The German hesitated, staring at the starfish in Eric's chest, the snake coiled around his leg. Eric could see him making his choice, and he knew what it would be.

"All right," Mathias said. "But let me do it."

Eric took off his shirt.

Mathias glanced about, appraising the muddy clearing. "Do you want to lie down?"

Eric shook his head. "I'll stand."

"It's going to hurt. It might be easier if you—"

"I'm okay. Just do it."

Mathias started with his chest. He made five quick incisions, in the shape of an asterisk, directly above the starfish-shaped bulge, then reached inside and slowly pulled the vine from Eric's body. There was an astonishing amount of it; Mathias had to tuck the knife in his back pocket, then use both hands to drag the slimy mass free. It emerged thrashing, covered in half-clotted blood. The pain was intense—not the cutting, but the drawing forth—it felt as if Mathias were ripping out some essential part of Eric's body, a vital organ. Eric thought of those images from Jeff's guidebook, the Aztecs with their long knives, yanking the still-beating hearts from their captives' bodies, and his legs almost buckled. He had to grab Mathias's shoulder to keep from falling.

Mathias tossed the writhing mass aside; it landed with a wet sound in the mud, coiling and uncoiling. "Are you okay?" he asked.

Eric nodded, let go of Mathias's shoulder. Blood was streaming down his torso, running into the waistband of his shorts. He balled up his T-shirt, pressed it to his wound. "Keep going," he said.

Mathias lowered himself into a crouch, drew the knife in one smooth movement up and around Eric's leg. Again, it wasn't the incision that hurt; it was when Mathias reached in and pried the vine from his flesh. Eric cried out: a moan, a howl. It felt as if he were being flayed. He dropped heavily to the ground, landing on his rear end. Blood was pumping thickly from his leg.

Mathias held the tendril up for him to see. This one was much longer, its leaves and flowers more developed, almost full-sized. It twisted in the air, seemed to lift toward Eric, reaching for him. Mathias threw it into the mud, stepped on it, crushing it—the first one, too.

"I'll get the needle and thread," he said, and he started for the tent.

"Wait!" Eric called. "There's more." His voice emerged shaky and thin; it frightened him how weak he sounded. "It's all up and down my leg. It's in my shoulder, my back. I can feel it moving." It was true, too: he could feel it everywhere now, lying just beneath his skin, like a muscle, flexing.

Mathias turned to stare at him, one step short of the tent. "No, Eric," he said. "Don't start." He sounded tired; he looked it, too—slumped and sunken-eyed. "We have to sew you up."

Eric was silent—dizzy suddenly. He knew he didn't have the strength to argue.

"You're losing too much blood," Mathias said.

For a moment, it seemed to Eric as if he might faint. He lowered himself carefully onto his back. The pain wasn't diminishing. He shut his eyes, and the darkness waiting for him there was full of color: a bright, flickering orange deepening toward red at the margins. He could feel the voids the tendrils had left behind in his chest and leg—somehow this seemed central to his pain, as if his body were experiencing the vine's removal as a sort of theft, as if it wanted it back.

He heard Mathias entering the tent, then returning, but he didn't open his eyes. He watched the colors pulsate in the darkness, saw how they jumped in brightness when the German bent over him and began to stitch shut the wound on his leg. There was no talk of sterilizing the needle; Mathias simply set to work. The incision was a long one; it took him some time to finish. Then he gently pushed Eric's hands aside, lifted the blood-soaked T-shirt away, and started in on his chest.

Eric grew slowly calmer. The pain didn't lessen, but that familiar sense of distance was returning, so that it almost began to feel as if he were observing his body's distress rather than inhabiting it. The sun had climbed free of the horizon now—it was becoming hot—and this helped, too. He finally stopped shivering.

Stacy was on the far side of the clearing; Eric could hear her moving about there. It seemed to him that she was avoiding him, that she was afraid to come near. He lifted his head to see what she was doing, and found her crouched over Pablo's pack. She pulled the remaining bottle of tequila from it. "Does anyone want any?" she called, holding it up.

Eric shook his head, then watched as she bent to peer into the pack again. Apparently, there was an inner pocket. He heard her unzip it. She rummaged about inside, lifted something out. "His name was Demetris," she said.

"Whose?" Mathias asked. He didn't glance up from his stitching.

Stacy turned toward them, holding a passport. "Pablo's. His real name. Demetris Lambrakis."

She rose, brought the passport across the clearing. Mathias set down the needle, wiped his hands on his jeans, took it from her. He stared at it for a long moment without speaking, then handed it to Eric.

The photo inside showed a slightly younger Pablo—a bit plumper, too—with much shorter hair and, absurdly, a mustache. He was wearing a jacket and tie; he looked as if he were trying not to smile. Eric noticed—again, as though from some great distance—that his hands were shaking. He gave the passport back to Stacy, then lowered his head. *Demetris Lambrakis.* He kept repeating the name in his mind, as if trying to memorize it. *Demetris Lambrakis . . . Demetris Lambrakis . . . Demetris Lambrakis . . .*

Mathias finished with the stitching. Eric heard him move off toward the tent again. When he returned, he was carrying the can of nuts. He opened it and divided its contents into three equal piles, counting them out nut by nut, using the Frisbee as a platter. Mathias was in charge now, Eric realized. All three of them seemed to have agreed upon this, without anyone needing to discuss it.

Eric had to sit up to eat, and it hurt to do so. He spent a moment examining his body. He looked like a rag doll, handed down through generations of careless children, sewn and resewn, its stuffing leaking between the seams. He couldn't see how he was ever going to make it home from here, and this reflection settled, siltlike, inside him. He felt himself growing heavy with it, resigned. But his body didn't appear to care; it continued to assert its needs. The mere sight of the nuts filled him with a fierce hunger, and he ate them quickly, shoving them into his mouth, chewing, swallowing. When he was finished, he licked the salt from his fingers. Mathias offered him the plastic jug, and he drank from it, conscious of the vine once more, shifting about within him.

The sun kept climbing higher, growing stronger. The mud was beginning to dry in the clearing, their footprints solidifying into small shadow-filled hollows. All three of them had finished their rations, and now they sat in silence, watching one another.

"I guess I should go look for Jeff," Mathias said. "Before it gets much hotter." The idea seemed to cause him great fatigue.

Stacy was still holding the bottle of tequila; it was resting in her lap.

She kept twisting its cap on and off. "You think he's dead, don't you?" she asked.

Mathias turned to peer at her, squinting slightly. "I want it not to be true just as much as you do. But wanting and believing—" He shrugged. "They're not the same, are they?"

Stacy didn't answer. She brought the bottle to her lips, tilted her head back, swallowed. Eric could sense Mathias's desire to take the bottle from her, could see him almost doing it but then deciding not to. He wasn't like Jeff; he was too reserved to be a leader, too aloof. If Stacy wanted to drink herself into some sort of peril here, then that would be her choice. There was no one left to stop her.

Mathias climbed to his feet. "I shouldn't be long," he said.

Instantly, Stacy set the bottle aside, jumped up to join him. "I'll come, too." Once again, Eric had the sense that she was frightened of him, terrified of what was happening inside his body. He could tell she didn't want to be left here with him.

Mathias peered down at Eric, at his shirtless, bloodied, mud-smeared torso. "Will you be okay?" he asked.

No, Eric thought. *Of course not.* But he didn't say it. He was thinking of the knife, of being alone in the clearing with it, free to act as he chose. He nodded. Then he lay there in the sun, feeling strangely at peace, and watched as they walked off together, disappearing down the trail.

Stacy and Mathias stood for a while at the bottom of the hill, staring out at the cleared swath of ground and the wall of trees beyond it. The sun had already baked a thin, brittle skin across the dirt, but beneath this the mud was still ankle-deep. The Mayans were moving laboriously about in it, the muck sticking in clumps to their feet. Stacy watched two of the women spreading things out to dry. They had a big pile: blankets, clothes.

There were three Mayans standing beside the campfire. One of them was the bald man from that first day, with the pistol on his hip. The other two were much younger, barely more than boys. They both had bows. The bald man's white trousers were rolled to his knees, in what Stacy guessed must've been an effort to keep them clean. His shins looked very thin, almost withered.

Mathias stepped out into the clearing, his shoes vanishing beneath the mud. He glanced to the left, stared. His face didn't change, but Stacy knew what he was looking at, although she couldn't have said how. The tequila had settled into her stomach with a sour sensation, making her light-headed; sweat was running down her back. There was only one thing for her to do now—she had no choice—but she took her time with it, not wanting to join Mathias quite yet, wanting to find some buffer between his seeing and hers. She carefully removed her sandals, one after the other, set them in the center of the trail, side by side. Then she stepped forward, out into the mud. It was colder than she would've guessed possible—it made her think of snow—and she concentrated on that (*white like the bald man's trousers, white like bone*) while she peered off toward the little mound twenty-five yards away from them, a tiny peninsula of green protruding into the cleared soil, like a finger. The day's growing heat threw a shimmer across it; Stacy could've easily convinced herself that it was nothing but a mirage. She knew better, though, knew it was Jeff, knew that he'd abandoned them, just as Amy had, and Pablo, that it was only the three of them now. She reached for Mathias's hand, half-worried he might not let her take it, but he did, and they started forward like that, in silence.

They moved along the base of the hill, keeping close to the vines, trudging through the mud. They didn't talk. The bald Mayan followed them, accompanied by the two young bowmen. It wasn't very far; it didn't take long to get there.

Mathias crouched beside the little mound, started to pull the tendrils from it, slowly revealing Jeff's body. He was still recognizable, only partially eaten, as if the vine had curbed its hunger, wanting them to know, without any doubt, that Jeff was dead. He was lying on his stomach, stretched out, his arms above his head; it looked like he'd been dragged there by his feet. Mathias rolled him over. There were wounds on his throat, one on either side, and his shirt was completely saturated with blood. The flesh had been stripped from the bottom half of his face, revealing his teeth and jawbone, but his eyes were untouched. They were open, staring cloudily up at them. Stacy had to look away.

She was startled by how calm she was acting; it frightened her. *Who am I?* she thought. *Am I still me?*

Mathias unbuckled Jeff's watch from his wrist. Then he reached into his pocket, removed his wallet. There was a silver ring on Jeff's right hand, and Mathias retrieved this, too. He had to work at it—tugging—before it finally slipped free.

Stacy could remember going with Amy to buy the ring. They'd found it in a pawnshop in Boston. Amy had presented it to Jeff on the anniversary of their first date. Over the years that followed, Stacy and she had spent many hours trying to imagine its original owner—what he'd been like, how he'd ever managed to reach the point where he'd needed to pawn such a beautiful object. They'd created a whole character out of this fantasy, a failed musician, a sometimes junkie, sometimes pusher, whose great, perhaps apocryphal claim to fame was that he'd once sold Miles Davis an ounce of heroin. They'd given him a name, Thaddeus Fremont, and whenever they glimpsed an older, downtrodden man shuffling through the world, they'd nudge each other and whisper, "Look—there's Thaddeus. He's searching for his ring."

Mathias held out Jeff's things to her, and she took them from him.

"I should've gotten Henrich's, too," he said. "He wore a pendant—a good-luck charm." He touched his chest, showing her where it had hung. Then he spent a moment staring along the clearing, as if he were thinking of going to fetch it now. But when he stood up, it was to turn back toward the trail.

They set off together, walking side by side—once more, in silence. Stacy's feet were caked in mud; it felt as if she were wearing a pair of heavy boots.

"Not that it worked," Mathias said.

She turned, glanced at him. "Not that what worked?"

"His good-luck charm."

Stacy couldn't think how to react to this. She knew it was a joke, or an attempt at one, but the idea of laughing, or even smiling, in response to it seemed abominable. The humming had returned inside her skull; she was having trouble suddenly keeping her eyes open. For some reason, talking made them ache. She kept walking, her arms folded across her chest, hugging herself, Jeff's watch gripped in one hand, his wallet and ring in the other. She waited for enough time to pass so that it could seem as if Mathias hadn't spoken—until they were nearly at the trail again—and then she said, "What do we do now?"

"Go back to the tent, I guess. Try to rest."

"Shouldn't one of us watch for the Greeks?"

Mathias shook his head. "Not for another hour or so."

Stacy's mind shifted toward the tent, the little clearing. She thought of Pablo on his backboard, the agony he'd suffered there. She thought of herself, how she'd bent to collect Amy's scattered bones that morning, so casually, as if she were tidying up after a party.

Those words were inside her head again: *Am I still me?*

Without any warning, she started to cry. It was like a coughing fit—two dozen full-bodied sobs—they came and went in less than a minute. Mathias waited beside her till they passed. Then he rested his hand on her shoulder.

"Do you want to sit for a moment?" he asked.

Stacy lifted her eyes, looked about them. They were standing in four inches of mud. To their right, the hillside climbed steeply upward, swathed in its vine. To their left, midway across the clearing, stood the three Mayans, watching them. She shook her head, wiped at her face. "Eric's dying, isn't he?" she said. "It's inside him, and he's going to die."

Her hands had opened as she'd sobbed; she'd dropped Jeff's watch, his wallet and ring. Mathias crouched to retrieve them. They were muddy now, and he tried to wipe them clean on his pants.

"I don't know if I can handle it, Mathias. Watching him die."

Mathias slid Jeff's ring into the wallet. His hands were bleeding, she noticed, the skin cracked and scored from the vine's sap. His clothes were hanging off him in shreds. His stubble was thickening into a beard, and it made him seem older. He nodded. "No," he said. "Of course not."

Stacy turned, stared toward the three Mayans. They had a way of watching her without ever meeting her gaze. She assumed this was something they'd consciously learned to do, a trick to make their duty here less arduous on themselves. It seemed to her that it would have to be much harder to kill someone once you'd looked them in the eyes. "What do you think they'd do if we stepped forward now?" she asked. "If we just kept walking, right at them?"

Mathias shrugged. The answer was obvious, of course. "Shoot us."

"Maybe we should do it. Maybe we should just get it over with."

Mathias watched her; he seemed to be giving the idea serious consideration. But then he shook his head. "Someone's going to come, Stacy. Eventually. How can we say for certain that it won't be today?"

"But it might not be. Right? It might not be for weeks. Or months. Or ever."

Mathias didn't answer; he just stared at her. From the first moment they'd met, she'd found his gaze—so somber, so unflinching—a little frightening. After a few seconds, she had to look away. He reached and took her hand then, and, still not speaking, led her back along the clearing to the trail.

Eric could feel the vine moving about inside his body. It was in the small of his back, his left armpit, his right shoulder. The knife lay ten feet away from him—mud-stained, still damp with his own blood. He'd assumed that he'd immediately begin to cut himself, as soon as Stacy and Mathias left the clearing, but then the moment arrived and he'd discovered he was too scared to do it. He'd already spilled a terrifying amount of blood—he could just look at his body and see this—and he wasn't certain how much more he could afford to lose.

He sat up, took a deep breath, then folded into himself, coughing dryly. There was no phlegm, just the sense of something residing in his chest that shouldn't be there, something his body was trying, unsuccessfully, to expel. Eric had been battling this cough all night; it seemed strange to him that he shouldn't have realized earlier what its source was. It was the vine, of course—he was certain of this. Yes, there was a tendril growing inside his lungs.

I should go into the tent, he thought. *I should lie down. It doesn't matter if it's wet.* But he didn't move.

He coughed again.

It would've been easier, he believed, if Stacy had stayed with him. She could've talked to him, argued. He might've listened—who could say? And if he hadn't, she could've always grabbed at his arm, held him back. But she wasn't there—she'd abandoned him—so there was no one to stop him now when he stood up and retrieved the knife.

He sat back down, holding it in his lap.

He tried his word games again, his imaginary vocabulary test, but he couldn't remember what letter he'd reached last. The shiftings inside his body made it hard to concentrate. It seemed important that he keep track of them. *The top of my right foot . . . the nape of my neck . . .*

Eric leaned forward, scratched at his left calf, felt a lump there. He stared down at it, watching it flatten itself out, then bunch together again slightly lower on his leg. It was nearly the size of a golf ball. When he probed at it with his finger, there was that familiar sense of numbness.

The incision wouldn't hurt, he knew; it was the pulling forth that would make him cry out. As he sat thinking this, he noticed another bulge. This one was on his left forearm, much smaller than the others, about three inches long and thin as a worm. He touched it, and it vanished, burrowing down into his flesh.

All this was too much for Eric, of course: he couldn't just sit quietly, watching these things appear and disappear across his body. Something needed to be done, and there was really only one solution, wasn't there?

He lifted the knife from his lap, leaned forward, began to cut.

Somehow, the trail up the hill seemed to have grown much steeper since Stacy'd last climbed it. As they made their way ever higher, she started to pant, her clothes clinging to her sweaty body. She had a cramp in her side. Mathias appeared to sense her distress, and—even though they were nearly to the top—he stopped so she could rest. He stood beside her, staring off across the hillside while Stacy struggled to catch her breath.

Her heart had just begun to slow, when the voices started.

Wo ist Eric? Wo ist Eric?

They turned, looked at each other.

Eric ist da. Eric ist da.

"Oh Jesus," Stacy said. "No."

Eric ist gestorben. Eric ist gestorben.

They both began to run, but Mathias was faster. He was already in the clearing by the time she reached it. She found him there, gesturing, speaking the same word over and over again with great sternness. In his fatigue and distress, he'd fallen back upon his native language. *"Genug,"* he kept saying. *"Genug."*

It took Stacy a moment to understand that he was addressing Eric. There was a ghoul in the clearing—that was what she first thought—some new horror spawned from the mine's mouth: blood-streaked, naked, wild-eyed, with a knife in its hand. But no, it was Eric. He appeared to have stripped much of his skin off his body. It was hanging from him in shreds; Stacy could see his leg muscles, his abdominals, a glint of bone at his left elbow. His hair was matted along the right side of his head, and she realized he'd cut off his ear.

Mathias's voice rose toward a yell: *"Genug,* Eric! *Genug!"* He was gesturing for Eric to set down the knife, yet it seemed clear to Stacy that Eric wasn't going to do this. He looked terrified, savage with it, as if it were some stranger who'd been attacking him.

"Eric," Stacy called. "Please, sweetie. Just—"

Then Mathias was stepping forward, reaching to yank the knife from Eric's hand.

Stacy knew what was going to happen next. "No!" she shouted.

But it was already too late.

Once Eric started, it had been impossible to stop.

First there'd been that bulge in his calf, and that was easy: he'd made a single short cut with the knife, and there it was, right beneath his skin, a tightly coiled ball of vine, no bigger than a walnut. He'd pulled it from his body, tossed it aside. Then he'd started in on his forearm. This was when things became a bit more complicated. He made a small incision where he'd glimpsed the wormlike bulge, and found . . . nothing. He probed with the tip of the knife, then enlarged the bloody slit, drawing the blade in a smooth line from wrist to elbow. The pain was intense—he was having a hard time maintaining his grip on the knife—but his fear was worse. He knew the vine was in there, and he had to find it. He kept cutting, digging deeper, then moving laterally, pushing the knife beneath the skin on either side of the incision, prying it upward, peeling it back, until he'd managed to expose his entire forearm. There was more and more blood—too much of it—he could no longer see what he was doing. He tried to wipe it away with his hand, but it just kept coming. His skin was hanging from his elbow like a torn sleeve.

There was an abrupt clenching in his right buttock, as if a hand had grabbed him there, and he pushed himself to his feet, dropping his shorts and underwear, twisting to stare. He couldn't discern anything, though, and was about to begin probing with the blade, when he felt movement in his torso, just above his belly button, something shifting slowly upward. He quickly switched his attention to this spot, slashing at it with the knife. The vine was right beneath the surface here; a long tendril tumbled forth, more than a foot of it, dangling from his wound, twisting and turning in the air, blood running down it, spattering into the dirt. The tendril was still attached to him, rooted somewhere higher in his body. He had to draw the knife nearly to his right nipple before the thing slipped free of him.

Then it was his left thigh.

His right elbow.

The back of his neck.

There was blood everywhere. He could smell it—a metallic, coppery odor—and knew that he was getting weaker, moment by moment, with its loss. Part of him understood this was a disaster, that he needed to stop, needed never to have begun. But another part was aware only that the vine was inside his body, that he had to get it out, no matter what the cost. They could sew him up when they returned; they could wrap him in bandages, tie tourniquets around his limbs. The important thing was not to stop before he was through, because then all this pain would be for nothing. He had to keep cutting and slicing and probing until he was certain he'd gotten every last tendril.

The vine was in his right ear. This seemed impossible, but when he reached up and touched the lumpy mass of cartilage, he could feel it there, just beneath the skin. He wasn't thinking anymore; he was simply acting. He began to saw at the ear, keeping the knife flat against the side of his head. He'd started to moan, to cry. It wasn't the pain—though that was nearly unbearable—it was how loud it sounded, the blade tearing its way through his flesh.

Next came his left shin.

His right knee.

He was peeling the skin back from his lower rib cage when Mathias reappeared in the clearing. Time had started to move in a strange manner, both very slow and very fast at once. Mathias was yelling, but Eric couldn't grasp what he was saying. He wanted to explain what he was doing to the German, wanted to show him the logic of his actions, yet he knew that it was impossible, that it would take too long, that Mathias would never understand. He had to hurry—that was the thing—he had to get it out of him before he lost consciousness, and he could sense that this terminus was fast approaching.

Then Stacy was in the clearing, too. She said something, called his name, but he hardly heard. He had to keep cutting—that was what mattered—and it was as he was bending to do this that Mathias rushed toward him, reaching for the knife.

Eric heard Stacy shout, "No!"

He was shaky—he didn't feel entirely in control of his body—he was reacting by reflex. All he intended to do was fend Mathias off, push him away, clear enough space to finish what he'd begun. But when he threw out his hands to do this, one of them was still holding the knife. It came as a shock, how easily the blade punched into the German's chest, slipping between two of his ribs, just to the right of his sternum, sticking there.

Mathias's legs gave out on him. He fell backward, away from Eric, and the knife went with him.

Stacy started to scream.

"*Warum?*" Mathias said, staring up at Eric. "*Warum?*"

Eric could hear blood in Mathias's voice, could see it spreading across his shirt. The knife's handle was moving back and forth, jerking, metronomelike. This was from Mathias's heart, Eric knew. He'd shoved the knife straight into it.

Mathias tried to rise. He managed to sit up, leaning back on one hand, but it was obvious that this was as far as he was ever going to get. *"Warum?"* he said again.

Then the vines were in motion once more, snaking quickly into the clearing, grabbing at the German, coiling around his body. Stacy jumped forward. She struggled to free him—she did her best—but there were far too many of them.

Eric could feel himself fading. He had to sit, and he did so clumsily, half-falling, dropping into a large puddle of blood—his own and Mathias's. It was absurd, but he still wanted the knife, would've crawled forward and pulled it from the German's chest if only he'd had the strength. He watched it jerk back and forth, back and forth, back and forth.

More and more tendrils kept coming. Stacy was yanking at them, sobbing now.

Soon they'd be reaching for him, too, Eric knew.

He shut his eyes, only for an instant, but it was long enough. By the time he opened them again, the knife had ceased its fretful twitching.

Stacy sat with Eric, his head resting on her lap. The vine had claimed Mathias's corpse, dragging it away. She could still see his right shoe protruding from the mass of green, but otherwise he lay completely covered. The tendrils were quiet, motionless, just the occasional soft rustling as they worked to consume his body.

Stacy couldn't understand why the vine wasn't slithering forth to capture Eric, too. She wouldn't be able to defend him—just as she hadn't been able to defend Mathias—and she was certain the plant must know this. But all it sent out was a single long tendril, which sucked noisily at the immense puddle of blood that surrounded them, slowly draining it.

It left Eric be.

Not that there was any doubt as to where this would end: Stacy could see he was dying. At first, it seemed as if it might be over in a matter of minutes. Blood was seeping and dripping and running in thin strings off him, pooling in the hollows around his clavicles, welling upward from his deeper wounds. There was a strong smell coming off him, vaguely metallic, which, for some reason, reminded Stacy of collecting coins as a child, polishing pennies, sorting them by date.

She stroked his head, and he moaned. "I'm right here," she said. "I'm right here."

He startled her by opening his eyes: he peered up at her, looking scared. When he tried to speak, it came out as a whisper, very hoarse, too soft to hear.

She leaned close. "What?"

Once more, there was that faint whisper. It sounded as if he were saying someone's name.

"Billy?" she asked.

He closed his eyes, dragged them open again.

"Who's Billy, Eric?"

She saw him swallow, and it looked painful. Breathing looked painful, too. Everything did.

"I don't know a Billy."

He gave a slow shake of his head. He was concentrating, she could tell, working to articulate the words. "Kill . . . me," he said.

Stacy stared down at him. *No,* she was thinking. *No, no, no.* She was willing his eyes to drift shut again, willing him to slip back into unconsciousness.

"It . . . hurts. . . ."

She nodded. "I know. But—"

"Please . . ."

"Eric—"

"Please . . ."

Stacy was starting to cry now. This was why the vine had left him untouched, she realized: it was to torment her with his passing. "You'll be okay. I promise. You just have to rest."

Somehow, Eric managed a crooked smile. He reached, found her hand, squeezed. "Beg . . . ging . . . you."

That was too much for Stacy; it knocked her into silence.

"The . . . knife . . ."

She shook her head. "No, sweetie. Shh."

"Beg . . . ging . . ." he said. "Beg . . . ging . . ."

He wasn't going to stop, she could tell. He was going to lie there with his head in her lap, bleeding, suffering, beseeching her assistance, while the sun continued its slow climb above them. If she wanted this to end—his bleeding, his suffering, his beseeching—she would have to be the one to do it.

"Beg . . . ging . . ."

Stacy carefully shifted his head aside, stood up. *I'll get it for him,* she was thinking. *I'll let him do it.* She moved to the edge of the clearing, stepped into the vine; she crouched beside Mathias's body, parted the tendrils. The plant had already stripped the flesh from his right arm, all the way to his shoulder. His face was untouched, though, his eyes open, staring at her. Stacy had to resist the urge to push them shut. The knife was still protruding from his chest. She grasped it, tugged, and it slipped free. She carried it back to Eric.

"Here," she said. She put it in his right hand, closed his fingers over it.

He gave her that lopsided smile again, that slow shake of his head. "Too . . . weak," he whispered.

"Why don't you rest, then? Just shut your eyes and—"

"You . . ." He was shoving the knife back toward her. "You . . ."

"I can't, Eric."

"Please . . ." He had her hand, the knife; he was pressing them together. "Please . . ."

It was over, Stacy knew—Eric's life. All he had left here was torment. He wanted her help, was desperate for it. And to ignore his pleading, to sit back and let him suffer his way slowly into death, simply because she was too squeamish, too terrified to do what so clearly needed to be done, couldn't this be seen as a sort of sin? She had it in her power to ease his distress, yet she was choosing not to. So, in some way, wasn't she responsible for his agony?

Who am I? she was thinking once again. *Am I still me?*

"Where?" she asked.

He took her hand, the one with the knife in it, brought it to his chest. "Here . . ." He set the tip of the blade so that it was resting next to his sternum. "Just . . . push . . ."

It would've been so easy to pull the knife away, toss it aside, and Stacy was telling her body to do this, ordering it into motion. But it wasn't listening; it wasn't moving.

"Please . . ." Eric whispered.

She closed her eyes. *Am I still me?*

"Please . . ."

And then she did it: she leaned forward, shoving down upon the knife with all her weight.

Pain.

For an instant, that was all Eric was conscious of, as if something had exploded inside his chest. He could see Stacy above him, looking so frightened, so tearful. He was trying to speak, trying to say *Thank you* and *I'm sorry* and *I love you*, but the words weren't coming.

They'd gone to a roadside zoo in Cancún one afternoon, as a lark. It had held no more than a dozen animals, one of which was labeled a zebra, though it was clearly a donkey, with black stripes painted on its hide. Some of the stripes had drip marks. While the four of them stood staring at it, the animal had suddenly braced its legs and peed, a tremendous torrent. Amy and Stacy had both collapsed into giggles. For some reason, this was what came to Eric now—the donkey relieving itself, the girls grabbing at each other, the sound of their laughter.

Thank you, he was still struggling to say. *I'm sorry. I love you.*

And the pain was slowly easing . . . everything was . . . moving further away . . . further away . . . further away . . .

The vine claimed his body. Stacy didn't try to fight it; she knew there was no point.

The sun was directly overhead; she guessed she had six more hours or so before it would begin to set. She remembered Mathias's words— "How can we say for certain that it won't be today?"—and tried to draw some hope from them. She'd be okay as long as it was light. It was the dark that frightened her, the prospect of lying alone in that tent, too terrified to sleep.

She shouldn't have been the one to survive, she knew; it should've been Jeff. He wouldn't have been scared to watch the sun start its long journey westward. Food and water and shelter—he would've had a plan for all of these, different from hers, which wasn't really a plan at all.

She sat just outside the tent and ate the remaining supplies—the pretzels, the two protein bars, the raisins, the tiny packets of saltines— washing them down with the can of Coke, the bottles of iced tea.

Everything—she finished everything.

She stared out across the clearing and thought of the many others who'd died in this place, these strangers whose mounds of bones dotted the hillside. Each of them had gone through his or her own ordeal here. So much pain, so much desperation, so much death.

Fleeing headlong from a burning building—could that be called a plan?

Stacy could remember how they'd talked about suicide late one night, all four of them, more drunk than not, choosing prospective methods for themselves. She'd been slouched on her bed, leaning against Eric. Amy and Jeff had been on the floor, playing a halfhearted game of backgammon. Jeff, ever efficient, had told them about pills and a plastic bag—it was both painless and reliable, he claimed. Eric proposed a shotgun, its barrel in his mouth, a toe on the trigger. Amy had been drawn to the idea of falling from a great height, but rather than jumping, she wanted someone to push her, and they argued back and forth over whether this could count as suicide. Finally, she surrendered, choosing carbon monoxide instead, a car idling in an empty garage. Stacy's fantasy was more elaborate: a rowboat, far out to sea, weights to bear her body down. It was the idea of vanishing she found so attractive, the mystery she'd leave behind.

They'd been joking, of course. Playing.

Stacy could feel the caffeine from the Coke, the iced tea; she was becoming jittery with it. She held her hands up before her face, and they were shaking.

There was no rowboat here, of course, no idling car or shotgun or bottle of pills. She had the drop into the shaft. She had the rope hanging from the windlass. She had the Mayans waiting at the bottom of the hill with their arrows and their bullets.

And then there was the knife, too.

How can we say for certain that it won't be today?

She found her sunshade, used the roll of duct tape to repair the damage the storm had wrought upon it. She retrieved the bottle of tequila from the center of the clearing. Then she set off down the trail.

Carrying the knife.

The Mayans turned to appraise her as she approached: her bloodstained clothes, her trembling hands. She sat at the edge of the clearing, the knife in her lap, the sunshade propped against her shoulder. She uncapped the bottle of tequila, took a long swallow.

It would've been nice if she could've figured out a way to fashion some sort of warning for those who were yet to come. She would've liked that, to be the one whose cleverness and foresight was responsible for saving a stranger's life. But she'd seen that pan with its single word of caution scraped across its bottom; she knew others had tried and failed at this, and she saw no reason why she should be any different. All she could hope was that the mute fact of her presence here, the low mound of her bones sitting at the path's mouth, would signal the proper note of peril.

She drank. She waited. Above her, the sun eased steadily westward.

No, you couldn't really call it a plan at all.

Stacy spilled some of the tequila onto the knife's blade, scrubbed at it with her shirt. It was silly, she knew—both pointless and hopeless— but she wanted it to be clean.

She grew calmer as the day drew toward dusk. Her hands stopped shaking. She was scared of many things—of what might come after-ward, most of all—but not of the pain. The pain didn't frighten her.

When the sun finally touched the western horizon, the sky abruptly changed, taking on a reddish hue, and Stacy knew that she'd waited long enough. The Greeks weren't coming, not today. She thought about the approaching darkness, pictured herself once more alone in the tent, lis-tening to whatever noises the night might offer, and she knew she didn't have a choice.

She thought briefly about praying—*for what, forgiveness?*—only to realize she had no one to pray to. She didn't believe in God. All her life she'd been saying that, instinctively, unthinkingly, but now, for the first time—about to do what she was about to do—she could look inside and claim the words with total assurance. She didn't believe.

She started with her left arm.

The first cut was tentative, exploratory. Even here, at the very end, Stacy persisted in being herself, never leaping when she could wade. It hurt more than she'd anticipated. That was okay, though—that was fine—she knew she could bear it. And the pain made it real in a way that it hadn't been before, gave these last moments an appropriate heft. She cut deeper the second time, starting at the base of her wrist and drawing the blade firmly toward her elbow.

The blood came in a rush.

She switched the knife to her left hand. It was hard to get a good grip—her fingers didn't seem to want to close, and they were slick with blood now—but she managed it finally, pressed the blade to her right wrist, slashed downward.

Perhaps it was just the fading light, but her blood seemed darker than she'd expected—not nearly as bright as Eric's or Mathias's—inky, almost black. She rested her wrists in her lap, and it flowed down over her legs, feeling hot at first, then gradually cooler as it began to pool around her. It was odd to think that this liquid was part of her, that she was becoming less and less for its steady loss.

Who am I? she thought.

The Mayans were watching. Somehow they must've sensed that she was the last, because the women were already beginning to break camp, gathering things up, rolling them into bundles.

Stacy had assumed her heart would be racing, pumping faster and faster with each passing second, but it turned out to be just the opposite. Everything—inside and out—seemed to be steadily slowing. She was astonished by how serene she felt.

Am I still me?

The vines came snaking toward her. She heard them start to suck at the puddled blood.

She should've cut the rope off the windlass, she realized. Why hadn't she thought to do this? She tried to reassure herself that it didn't matter, that her corpse was going to remain here as a sentinel, warning any future visitors away, but she knew it wasn't true, could sense it even before the tendrils began to grab at her, dragging her off the trail. She fought as best she could, right up to the very end, struggling to rise, but it was too late. It had gone too far; she no longer had the strength. The vine held her down—covered her, buried her. She died with a sensation of drowning, with the memory of that rowboat, far out to sea, those weights pulling her ever deeper, the green waves closing above her head.

The Greeks arrived three days later.

They'd taken the bus to Cobá, then hired the yellow pickup truck to ferry them out to the trail. They'd made three new friends in Cancún—Brazilians—whom they'd brought along for the adventure. The Brazilians' names were Antonio, Ricardo, and Sofia. Juan and Don Quixote had both become deeply smitten with Sofia, though it appeared that she might be engaged to Ricardo. This was hard to tell for certain, however, since the Greeks couldn't speak Portuguese, and the Brazilians, of course, didn't know Greek.

They were having fun together, even so. They were chattering and laughing as they made their way into the jungle. Ricardo was carrying a cooler full of beer and sandwiches. Antonio had brought along a boom box, and he played the same CD over and over again on it—he was trying to teach the Greeks how to salsa. Juan and Don Quixote cooperated in this for Sofia's sake, for the joy of hearing her laughter at their clumsiness.

It was impossible to miss the turnoff toward the ruins. There'd been too many comings and goings of late to disguise the narrow path. The dirt was well trodden, the brush beaten back.

Just as they were about to start down it, Ricardo noticed a little girl watching them from the far side of the field. She was tiny, perhaps ten years old; she was wearing a dirty-looking dress, had a goat on a rope. She seemed upset—she was jumping up and down, waving at them— and they stopped to stare. They gestured for her to approach—Ricardo even held out one of their sandwiches as an enticement—but she wouldn't come any closer, and finally they gave up. It was hot in the sun. They knew they were nearly at their destination and were impatient to get there.

They started down the path.

Behind them, Juan and Antonio saw the girl drop the goat's rope, sprint off into the jungle. They shrugged at each other, smiled: *Who knows?*

Through the trees, across the little stream, and then suddenly they found themselves in bright sunlight again.

A clearing.

And beyond the clearing . . . a hill covered in flowers.

They paused here, stunned by the beauty of the place. Ricardo took a bottle of beer from the cooler and they shared it among themselves. They pointed at the flowers, commenting upon them in their dual languages, saying how lovely they were, how stunning. Sofia took a photograph.

Then, all in a line, they started forward again.

They didn't hear the first horseman arrive. They were already too far up the hill, calling Pablo's name.

A NOTE ON THE TYPE

The text of this book was set in Garamond No. 3. It is not a true copy of any
of the designs of Claude Garamond (ca. 1480–1561), but an adaptation of his
types, which set the European standard for two centuries. It probably owes as
much to the designs of Jean Jannon, a Protestant printer working in Sedan in
the early seventeenth century, who had worked with Garamond's romans
earlier, in Paris, but who was denied their use because of Catholic censorship.
Jannon's matrices came into the possession of the Imprimerie nationale, where
they were thought to be by Garamond himself, and were so described when
the Imprimerie revived the type in 1900. This particular version
is based on an adaptation by Morris Fuller Benton.

COMPOSED BY
Stratford Publishing Services, Inc.,
Brattleboro, Vermont

PRINTED AND BOUND BY
Berryville Graphics,
Berryville, Virginia

DESIGNED BY
Iris Weinstein